CILLA
The adventures of a
WELSH MOUNTAIN PONY

Pauline Braddock

The Author asserts the moral right to be
identified as the author of this work

Cover by JB

ISBN 978-1-291-80254-2

Authors note

Cilla is the thread around which this story is woven.

She was born near the Brecon Beacons in Wales and sold as a youngster into England.

At the age of 30 years she found herself back in Wales a few miles from where she was born.

This much of the story is true, but the remainder is fiction.

I knew her when we lived in Kent where she was owned for the last years of her life by my friend Angela to whom this book is dedicated with love.

Pauline Braddock

Cilla circa 1978

PRELUDE

A wild cold wind raced across the valley swirling around Eppynt Mountain, blowing a light covering of snow into drifts and filling the gulleys. The far distant Brecon Beacons were white, standing out against the dark grey sky.

Although it was early spring, the snow was reluctant to thaw and let the new green shoots of grass push through. The mountains were a cold inhospitable place at this time of year.

The old stallion, tough and hardy from spending most of his life out on these hills, watched as the sky cleared. Soon his herd would be able to search for something to eat. All his mares were in foal, they had been turned on to the common heath when last year's foals were weaned. There was mile upon mile of empty heathland, and over the months they had wandered far from home, onto the MOD land. They had all been terrified by loud explosions and bright flashes, men shouting and running all over the place. The stallion had been disorientated, and taken his mares in the wrong direction, away from home. He went west instead of east, going higher to get away from danger.

There were lots of boulders that gave a degree of shelter. They stood, hunched up, tails to the wind and heads down waiting Patiently for the wind to ease so they could leave the shelter of the rocks to wander off searching for anything green and edible. They longed for the warm spring weather when the sun would bring on the lush grass they needed to produce rich milk for their foals.

One of the mares wandered away from the herd to find a quiet sheltered spot, her time to foal was near. The stallion called to her, watching her slow progress, she wouldn't go far, and by morning there would be his first foal. Many more would soon be added to his little herd.

She found a place out of the wind and deep in dead bracken. With a sigh she lay down grateful for the soft bed. Very soon the foal would be born. It was a filly, as black as the crows that circled above, with a white star and white socks!

The mare licked her baby dry and waited while it struggled to its feet and found a teat for that first important feed.

Soon they would go back to the herd, but for a day or two she must stay in the shelter of the rocks to allow her baby to gain strength, so it could run with the herd.

The snow vanished quickly as the sun warmed the land.

The mare had produced a lovely foal, strong, and full of promise for the future.

ONE

The wind drummed on the window and rain swept across the yard forming little rivulets swirling down the slope and into the lower fields.,

Anwyn stood looking out of the kitchen window searching for a break in the clouds. It had to stop raining soon; everything was soaking, water lying in great puddles all over the fields. The ground was saturated, mud everywhere. Please let it stop she sighed. Enough is enough!

On the Aga a big saucepan of soup was bubbling away and some newly baked bread was cooling on the table. It was time to feed the gang, if she could find them all.

"Boys...get down here" she shouted from the bottom of the stairs, "Foods on the table!" Then she opened the back door, flinching as the rain hit her face. A bell hung beside the door, she gave it a good hammering.

"OK mother were coming", came a voice from the barn across the yard.

"Hold you're horses ma, won't be a minute" shouted Dai, her oldest son.

The two men crouched down against the weather and dashed for the open door and the smell of newly baked bread.

"Get those boots off and hang your coats up, your dripping all over my clean floor!" Before they could answer her the kitchen door crashed open and the youngest boys burst in. Rhys and Tomas were twins, almost eleven, always hungry and never still or quiet. They seemed to have endless energy from the moment they got out of bed until they get back there!

"Sit down...*SIT*", said mother labelling out steaming soup. "Wash your hands Dai, I can smell sheep on your clothes from here."

The twins were already scoffing their soup and soaking large chunks of bread in it. Father sat opposite them glad to be in the warm kitchen and out of the rain. "I think the sky's clearing a bit", he said reaching for the bread. "Maybe the worst of the weather has gone through."

"Someone's at the door" said Dai sitting down and reaching for the bread

"Always at meal times", sighed his father getting up to see who it was knocking. The kitchen was suddenly quiet as they strained to hear who it was at the door.

"Hello Morgan....is that so duwduw.....on Eppynt.........well thanks.....but ...I'm sure it can't be...well thanks anyway........thanks for your trouble" The front door closed.

Four anxious faces turned to face him as he came back to the kitchen.

"Who's dead?" Rhys asked quite sure it was the worst news. Father sat down, picked up his spoon and started to drink his soup.

"Who was it Dave?" Anwyn was becoming worried.

"Oh nothing to be worried about mother. It was Morgan from across the hill, he's been shooting up on Bryn Du. He reckons he saw our stallion, but I told him it couldn't be as our herd were on the common. Pass me the bread Tomas, you've had plenty."

"How sure are you Dave, have you been up to the common recently?" asked Anwyn.

"Not since we started lambing ...been too busy....have you been up there Dai?"

"No   I went up on the quad bike just before lambing, they certainly were there then."

"Surely they would never go that far from the common" said father "That's beyond the MOD land...I can't believe they would ever go that far! Dai....I think maybe it would be as well just to check up on the common. Would you go and have a look....take the bike....quicker than riding Glory. Do that.....there's a good lad. Put all our minds at ease."

"Is it possible, could Magnus take his girls that far?" Anwyn asked quietly.

"Well... old Morgan was quiet sure it was him...we'll know soon enough when Dai gets back."

Dai was back. "No sign of them Dad."

Father said nothing for a while. "OK. We'd better go up to Eppynt tomorrow....find them, and drive them back!"

"So Morgan was right. Good of him to tell us" said Rhys

8

"Certainly was. It'll be a nice ride so long as the rain holds off. A long one mind you….it'll take all day…Dai..you come with me."

The twins looked up expectantly. "Can we come Dad?...*PLEEEEASE.*"

"What about school….you can't just take a day off when you feel like it…..your grades weren't that good on your last report *were* they? Rhys and Tomas usually got A's or A+, but last term they had slipped down to B's. They had a new teacher, Mr Evans, he was very strict. He couldn't tell which twin was which. So he wrote their names on a piece of card and pinned them on their jumpers…a silly mistake…in no time at all the badges were swapped and Rhys became Tomas and Tomas Rhys!

Understandably the boys were not his favourite pupils, and their marks were not as good as they should have been. But a day's ride across to Eppynt with their Dad and Dai would be some treat and so exciting.

"Please Mum, Dad…can we go just this once….Mr Evans won't mind us not being there."

"He'll be very glad I should think" said Dai, "Let the blighters come…we'll need some extra help if we have to drive them all home."

So the boys won, on the condition they did what they were told and didn't go hooting and hollering like Red Indians as soon as they got on the hill.

Having settled that, father began planning tomorrow's expedition. "Now we'd best put them in the top Paddock where we can see them from the house, the mares should be close to foaling I think. You three lads take the quad bike and a couple of bales of straw and litter up the old barn. Check the water and make sure the fencing is OK…..oh, and leave the gate open so we can drive them straight into the Paddock."

"Put your boots on", called mother as the twins pushed and jostled each other to the door.

"I'll drive", said Tomas trying to get out first.

"Not on your life", said Dai, grabbing has young brother, "I'm the oldest, so *I'll* drive. You two can throw me some bales down from the stack in the barn." They went arguing and pushing each

9

other across the yard. Their mother smiled as she collected up the dinner plates.

"You shouldn't tease them Dave, you knew you were going to take them all along!"

"I know...one day from old Evans won't make any difference...besides it'll be a nice ride for them, and their ponies could do with some work...it's a hell of a long way mother."

It was almost dark by the time the three boys got back to the house. They had managed to keep most of the straw in the barn in spite of a furious game trying to bury each other. The fences were checked and plenty of water in the trough thanks mainly to Dai. They had done a good job.

In the kitchen tea was ready, they were famished, nothing like a bit of hard work and fresh air to give you an appetite Dad always says.

The twins were still very excited about the long ride tomorrow and didn't object when they were sent up to bed a bit earlier than usual. We'll be away a bit sharpish, Dad had said as they disappeared up stairs. That meant *very* early.

Hard work had really tired them out so before long they were both snoring gently. Dai looked in on them later when he decided to go to bed. He smiled, they looked quite angelic when they were asleep butter wouldn't melt in their mouths! He closed the door and tiptoed to his room at the far end of the house. He could hear his Parents talking in the kitchen below. They would soon stoke up the Aga, turn the cats out then lock up for the night.

Another day tomorrow...a great day.

Feed buckets started rattling, ponies whinnied and Dave's big cob started kicking at his stable door as the first light of dawn touched the horizon. He always demanded to be fed first, everyone else had to wait!

This morning Dai was busy measuring out pony nuts and corn, not too much for the twins Section A ponies, they were pretty fit and could be quiet a handful if they had too much corn.

His own cob he spoiled dreadfully, she got a full bucket with carrots on top. A cob, but smaller than his father's big beast. He

10

had been given her when he was just twelve; she was the love of his life. Glory was five, he had broken her to ride, and a lovely mare she had grown into. Dai had shown her a lot as a youngster and they had many wins to their credit.

The ponies all fed and eating well, Dai rushed back to the kitchen where his mother had lovely rashers of bacon and freshly laid eggs all sizzling in the pan. The twins were already stuffing their mouths full and washing it down with steaming hot tea

"Call Dad Tomas, trust him to be last one down!" But before he could get to his feet his father's heavy boots could be heard clumping down the stairs.

"He's coming!. Said Dai grabbing his plateful of food and mug of tea. "We'll be away soon."

"Come on Dave, I thought you wanted to be away early", said mother playing him up. "These boys have been waiting for you for hours!...Eat up now while it's still hot."

"Ponies fed?" asked Dad

"Yep...all fed and ready to go!"

"Well then chaps, what are we waiting for....tack up and let's get started."

A mad rush for the door by the twins, jackets pulled off the back door and boots pulled out of the boot box.

"Tomas..get those spy glasses you bought at the car boot sale."

"You mean my *BINOCULARS* Dad?" He replied sounding important putting one over on his Dad!

"Yes yes, go and get them." Binoculars indeed, that's what spyglasses are he said to himself.

Tomas was very proud of his binoculars and kept them beside his bed, he polished them every time he used them, and always put them back in the leather case when he had finished.

"Go quick and get them Tom" said mother. "I'll get your pony tacked up for you."

"Thanks mum." He was off like a shot and soon came running back through the kitchen with the strap round his neck and tucking the glasses inside his jacket.

Suddenly the yard was full of noise and action. The ponies came alive whinnying at each other sensing the excitement in the air and wanted to be part of it. Father's cob was snorting and stamping his feet.

"Be still you silly bugger, how can I get your girth on *stand still*!" Dave was getting impatient.

"Language!" shouted someone; it sounded like Dai in the next stable.

Mother laughed quietly. "He'll get his foot trodden on in a minute, and then we'll hear some ripe language."

Finally they were all ready and mounted up. The boys had wax jackets on and hard hats properly done up with chin straps fastened. They were ready for anything the day might bring! As they rod up the drive the sun was just peeping above the hills. Spring looked as if it had at last arrived. It was going to be a fine dry day.

Storm, the big cob, stamped his feet on the tarmac wanting to go faster, but father had a firm hold on the reins. He'll settle down soon he thought, it would be an energy sapping day if he didn't.

Half way up the drive Dai shut the gate to stop the herd they hoped to find, from running down into the yard and causing mayhem. They needed to turn them straight into the Paddock. With luck, and father on his cob behind them, hopefully they would. "Mother's going to curse us if she wants to go shopping, she'll have to get out of the Disco to open and shut the gate."

"No, I think she would understand why we shut it." Said father to general agreement. "I'll ride ahead for a bit. Maybe this old fool will settle. Look after the boys Dai…don't let them go galloping off as soon as we get on the grass, or they might set Storm going and then you might not see me for the rest of the day, just a trail of dust as I disappear over the hill!" They all laughed but gave the big cob plenty of space.

Dai pulled Glory back a Pace or two and dropped back behind the twins. "I don't know why Dad likes that old cob so much, it's as mad as a hatter." He joked with his brothers, but all three knew their father could manage his cob. He was a wonderful rider; soon Storm would give up and settle to a steady walk.

The twins ponies now decided to join in the fun skittering sideways at every opportunity, shying at anything that caught

12

their eye, only Dai's cob was walking quietly and sensibly, he stroked her arched neck, he was so proud of her, she was almost ready to enter ridden cob classes at shows this summer. Just a little more schooling and Dai's continued patience with her and results would come.

She was a bright chestnut with a small white blaze and four white socks, very flashy, truly living up to her name, she really was glorious. The twins secretly admired her even though she belonged to their brother. Father had promised they would have a cob foal each when they got to twelve, he said they would have to break the cobs in when they got to three or four years old. They would be big boys by then. No problem.

The problem they had at the moment was staying with their ponies that were being very stupid and playing up more than usual.

"I hope you calm down in a minute" Rhys said to his pony Merlin. "Or my arms will be longer by the time we get home."

Tomas was being bumped around just as much by his pony Star, flighty at the best of times, but a real 'star' at gymkhana games. In fact she was *the* star in the pony club junior team. He was hoping they would be chosen for the Prince Philip cup team this year if he didn't grow too big. It was an advantage to be tall if you had a smallish pony in gymkhana games, easier to vault on and grab flags out of the buckets. Today he had other things to think about, not least of all staying behind his Dad.

Gradually all four horses started to walk sensibly. Always walk the first mile out and the last mile back, was a rule drummed into them since they were very small and just about off the lead rein, it gave the ponies a chance to settle down if they were a bit fresh and playful and cool down on the way home if they had had a hard ride and were a bit hot. Trouble is that on the hills with miles and miles of heather and soft turf in front of them, the three of them found it an impossible rule to keep!

"I think we'll head over towards Merthyr Cynog and come up to the ranges by the road there, if the red flag is down and the gate open we can ride across the ranges, it'll save several miles", father turned round in his saddle. "Got your eye glasses Tom, you might be able to see if the flag is flying." He smiled to himself, Tomas was so proud of his binoculars. This would be the first time he had used them seriously, Dave imagined his son's chest swelling and a big grin on his face.

"Yep, I've got them ready Dad, just got to polish the lenses."

"You won't see the flag from here", Dai pointed out, "It's miles away yet."

"They're very powerful glasses." Tomas said not to be outdone. He stood up in his stirrups and scanned the horizon. Dai was right, he couldn't see any red flag. "I can't see any flags Dad...does that mean we can cross the range?"

"I think we had better go on for another mile or so, and then you can have another look" said father.

Tomas tucked the glasses back in his jacket. Soon, he thought, soon we'll see the red flag and then they'll be glad I've got my binoculars.

The big cob had at last decided that they weren't going hunting or rounding up stray cattle so relaxed and was walking quietly. Dai rode up beside his father again. "We'll have to cross two streams if we go this way Dad, they might well be quiet full after all the rain yesterday. What about Rhys and Tomas, do you think their ponies will be able to wade through?"

They rode on in silence, certainly the streams would be very full, father hasn't thought of that. "We'll worry about that when we get there son, but thanks for reminding me...it's nice and flat here...let's have a pipe opener...it'll wake those two scamps up!" Without warning he gave Storm his head and he shot away.

Dai swore quietly, he wasn't ready either, and Glory leaped forward after the big cob. Very soon the four of them were galloping along on the soft turf, the little ponies straining to keep up with father out in front, hair flying, showering the three behind with earth thrown up by the speeding cob!

"Woe up Storm boy...steady now" Dave whispered to his cob. Ahead was the gentle drop down to the first of the streams. It was certainly full, more than normal anyway. He could see one or two places where the ponies could splash through if they brought the herd back this way.

Dai caught up with his Dad who had stopped, "Phew... that was good fun, Glory needed that!" A few minutes later, with a lot of excited shouting the twins arrived, red faced and blowing almost as hard as their ponies.

14

"You should have seen Merlin go! WOW! I'm going to train him for pony racing" Rhys was beaming

Tomas was close behind. "That wasn't fair…you pushed past me and I had to swerve…*I* could have won!

"Maybe next time, eh lad", father smiled down at him. "Now. Who's going to jump that stream?" They all looked down the hill; there was a lot of water and moving quite fast. "What..no volunteers?....Better follow me then boys….I'll show you the way." He turned Storm round to get a good run at it. Dai and the twins got behind looking a bit doubtful.

"Storm doesn't like water, never has and never will…likes jumping even less!" said Dai.

"He'll never jump it", whispered Rhys.

"READY THEN" called Dad. Then dug his heels in, and with lots of encouragement from the boys, he sent Storm at the stream.

The twin's couldn't resist it. They set off after Dad's cob at a gallop, straight for the stream.

Storm came to a slithering halt, almost unseating Dave. Glory was very close behind, and had no chance of making it. Both stopped a few inches from the water. With shouts of excitement the boys came galloping past, the little ponies leapt, stretched and flew across the stream!

The boys turned to face the two on the opposite bank, still looking at the fast flowing brown torrent. "It's not too wide Dad…your two cobs might just about make it." They laughed. "Shall we come back to give you a lead?"

"Cheeky little buggers" whispered Dai

"You stay where you are, we'll find a way across further up stream. Don't move." Shouted their father,

The twins were beside themselves with laughter, the ponies also seemed to be enjoying the moment and wanted to do it again.

"Steady now Star" said Tomas stuffing his binoculars back in his jacket; they nearly came up and hit him when they were jumping the stream. They were pushing and shoving each other, the argument about the race long forgotten, when they saw father and Dai cantering towards them. They must have found a shallow place and splashed across, both cobs were soaking wet.

15

"Come on now, let's waste no more time. Keep up lads", the three boys dropped in behind Storm. On towards Merthyr Cynog.

After walking at a steady pace to calm the ponies down, not to mention the twins, they came to the second stream that Dai had reminded his father about. The twins looked at each other and started to giggle, would they dare give a repeat performance and jump across past their Dad? Yes, they probably would. This time however the stream was nothing like as deep, so with a lot of persuasion Storm huffed and snorted his way across the little shallow stream!

Now they were on the road that took them through Merthyr Cynog and up onto Eppynt Mountain.

"Tomos my boy, out with your spy glasses and have a look for any red flags, they should be seen from here", father said shielding his eyes looking up the hill. Tomos stood up in his stirrups again and made a great fuss of cleaning the lenses. "Get on with it boy."

"OK OK, be patient Dad, the focus is wrong."

"Oh my", muttered Rhys.

"Actually Dad, I checked up on the list in your office", Dai said. "The ranges are open all this week."

"So did I, but look at the lads face!"

They both turned away so that Tomas couldn't see them laughing.

"No red flag on the mast Dad...I can see the gate too...its open."

"Thanks Tom...well we better keep moving. We'll cut across the ranges instead of following the road it'll save us some miles. Watch where you're going now, it gets pretty rough up here." They jogged on following the tracks the army lorries had made.

The sun was high in the sky now and it was getting quiet hot, a wonderful day for a ride.

"Look Tom look, a Red Kite", Rhys's sharp eyes had caught site of the bird high above them, circling round and round, wings outstretched riding on thermals, getting ever higher.

The binoculars came out again, this time Tomas didn't bother to polish the lenses. He stopped his pony to get a good look at the bird. This was why he had spent all his money at the car boot

16

sale, to get a good close look at birds like this Red Kite. He spent hours laying on his back in the garden watching birds. "No…it's only a Buzzard", he said as he replaced the glasses.

"Sorry, it looked just like a Kite to me."

"They're quiet similar, different plumage though." Tomas explained.

Dai and his father looked at each other smiling. "He'll be famous one day", said Dai

"If I don't wring his neck first." Father said with admiration in his voice.

The track they were following gradually disappeared as they started climbing again. They came to a river, the sort man and pony could not jump or splash through, and followed it higher and higher. The hillside was very open. Not a tree insight, hardly a breeze, clear blue sky and warm sunshine.

These ponies should be close to this water on a day like this, thought Dave; they can't be far away now surely. Why on earth did that old fool of a stallion bring them all up here? Maybe the guns were firing and he panicked, lost his bearings. Funny though, they usually stay no more than a mile or so from home. He rode on in silence, even the boys were quiet, riding along half asleep.

Time to stop for a rest beside the river, thought Dave. Here was a nice grassy patch, the ponies need a drink and we could have a bite to eat!

Father rummaged in his saddle bag which was fuller than usual, he always carried spare halters and a length of rope, also a first aid kit for both horse and rider! You can never tell what might happen when you're out riding in these hills, he would always say. Today there were thick chicken sandwiches, four large slices of fruit cake *and* a flask of tea.

"My word, mother's done us proud. She doesn't want us to starve", he laughed. "Jump down boys…give the ponies a rest…we'll have our lunch." The boys slid to the ground and led the ponies to the river for a drink before tucking into the food.

Dai wandered a little way up river looking for fish, suddenly he shouted. "Dad, there's fresh hoof prints here….pony

17

size....they must be close, these are tracks made today.....and fresh droppings...*must* be them!!

Father walked up to have a look, the twins came running after him. "I'll have a look with the binoculars", shouted Tomas.

"Yes...do that son, you might well see them. Better still...ride up to that ridge, you might be able to see for miles from there."

Tomas climbed back on Star and trotted to the ridge. He immediately saw fresh hoof prints and more droppings, the ponies had been here for sure.

He hurriedly took out his binoculars and scanned the miles of open country before him....not a pony insight! They must be near he thought..but where?

Star pricked her ears and gave a little mumble of a whinny. "Where are they Star", he said to her. "Where are they?" She was looking up the hill at an outcrop of boulders, further away too his left.

Tomas   refocused   the   glasses   and   sat   very still......there..something moved, a tail swishing he was sure. Still he sat concentrating on the rocks, not daring to hope. It was so quiet up there, not a breath of wind, just the hum of insects and the mournful cry of a Buzzard circling way above.......then he nearly dropped the glasses when a tiny foal appeared at the edge of one of the boulders. *I've found them it's got to be them* he thought.

Star gave another mumble of a whinny, tossed her head, and suddenly the lost ponies were all standing there looking across the plain at the young rider and his pony.

He still couldn't move...he wanted to shout, but his mouth was too dry with the excitement. He turned Star and raced back down the hill even forgetting to put the glasses away that swung dangerously round his neck. **"I've found them...I've found them"**, he shouted as loud as he could. **"Up on top of the hill...close to some rocks."**

Father jumped to his feet as Star slid to a stop nearly bumping into Storm.

"I'm sure it's them...I saw them up there." He was breathless and flushed with excitement.

"Where boy where…calm down now", Father grabbed Star's bridle and steadied the pony. "Where did you see them? Tell me!"

He vaulted up onto Storm. "Take it quietly now, we don't want to scatter them all over the place…Dai, you and Rhys wait here, clean up our mess, we won't be long. Steady now Tom, there's no rush, let's just have a look; we don't want to be rounding up someone else's stock! Let me have your spyglasses so I can check them over…I'll soon know if their ours."

"There's a foal with them, looks black from here."

"A foal eh, that'll be an early one then", Dad muttered. "Now then Tom, show me how to work these spyglasses." They rode up to the ridge and Tomas pointed to the boulders. They were still there, heads up, looking at them. Six ponies. "Where's that old fool of a stallion, I don't see him."

"There", whispered Tomas. "Just to the right of the big rock and a bit further back. He's watching us!"

Sure enough, the stallion was there, watching the two riders, ready to turn and drive his mares away.

"That's him…that's him, whispered his father. "That's Magnus…yes that's him all right….he's older than both of you..and Dai even. Old enough to know better. Come on then, back to the others to plan our manoeuvres. I'll be back Magnus", shouted Dad.

The old stallion heard that familiar voice and lifted his head. "I'll be waiting", he seemed to say!

A plan was hatched. The twins were to ride round the hill below the ridge and come up behind the herd.

When father waves they must shout and holler as loud as they can to get the ponies moving down the hill. Then follow them at a safe distance, keeping them going towards Father and Dai, who would position themselves either side of the herd keeping them bunched together. Once they were moving in a tight group, then the pace could relax to a steady trot. That was the plan. It had to work first time, they wouldn't get a second chance.

Tomas and Rhys came up well behind the herd, keeping well clear so as not to frighten them.

"We'd better get this right Tom", said Rhys seriously. "Or those pregnant mares might pop before we get them home." They rode on watching Magnus who was watching them. "Here Tom...I've just had a nasty thought. Your riding a mare!...I hope Mags doesn't take a fancy to her...that *would* be a laugh."

Tomas didn't think that was at all funny. He looked at the stallion. He wouldn't...would he?

"There's Dad waving. Come on Rhys we can get them moving now." He must forget about Magnus, Dad would look after him; Rhys was just winding him up. Now the fun would begin!

They did as they were told. Shouting and waving their arms making the sort of noise they frequently were ticked off for! Their ponies were so startled by the racket that they leaped in the air and set the herd scampering down the hill. Tomas saw the foal briefly dashing along beside its mother, and then it was lost in the melee of galloping ponies.

Magnus charged around them all, shaking his head close to the ground getting his mares together in a tight bunch, making Father and Rhys's job that much easier! He led them at a good pace down the track beside the river where the four of them had stopped for their meal.

Dai and father hadn't expected them to come quiet so fast, but thanks to Magnus things couldn't have turned out better!

"Let 'em run for a bit Dai, they won't keep this pace up for long." He turned to shout at the twins. "Keep back you two, not so close...get back Rhys...let them slow.... *SLOW UP MAGNUS YOU OLD FOOL....SLOW NOW!*

It was all excitement for the twins, just like westerns on the tele. Tomas wished he had a cowboy hat he could wave at the herd...Oh well they could still shout like the cowboys...and shout they did!

Dave was beginning to wish he hadn't asked them to make so much noise. They were in danger of starting a stampede, what fun this ride was turning out for them.

"I think Dad wants us to slow down a bit." Shouted Rhys

"What...I can't hear you."

"Stop shouting...slow up...we're too close to them!"

"OK….Steady lass.. steady now..we're too close", Tomas realised they had got the herd running too fast. "Phew, that was fun..wish we could do this more often! He shouted to his brother.

Rhys was fighting to hold Merlin back; his pony was wild eyed and didn't want to stop. They were pulling at their ponies, trying to slow them down and laughing. What fun that had been.

Ahead of them the herd was at last slowing, puffing and snorting. Magnus and his pregnant mares only to eager to stop this mad gallop. He was an old stallion, all this dashing about was not good for him. The herd relaxed, moving at a more leisurely pace.

Dai and his father were keeping a careful eye on the mares, especially the foal. It was very pretty, probably only a few days old. It was keeping up so far and if there was a problem and it couldn't keep going. Dave would carry it across his saddle!

They had a job turning the stallion and mares through the gate onto the MOD land. Magnus became very agitated.

"Dai…were there manoeuvres up here recently?"

"I'm not sure, there is often something going on. The army have war games, and then there are hundreds of troops rushing around firing all sorts of weapons, bright flashes and loud explosions going off all the time. Often at night. That would scare me, never mind the ponies!"

"Yea…I bet that's what happened. He must have been disoriented and took his mares high up on the hill to safety instead of back to the common."

Today he was being asked to cross this piece of hell and for a moment tried to turn back, but that voice he knew and trusted was telling him it was safe. "Go on Magnus…good lad, get on." Yes he knew.

The twins had gone very quiet, it had been a long day, all the fun and excitement seemed to be over, and they still had miles to go. Their hands were sore from holding their ponies back and after riding behind the herd for mile after mile they were hot and dusty. The ponies certainly were tired, walking along with heads almost touching the ground, looking forward to soft bedding and a full hay rack.

21

Merthyr Cynon came and went. Now the ponies knew where they were, this was their hill, the common land where Magnus and his mares *should* have been. The ponies were suddenly more alert, even Magnus, he recognised where they were and picked up the pace, breaking into a trot.

Father gave a big 'well done' thumbs up to the three boys, and told them to relax, the herd knew where they were going, no need to keep driving them. It wasn't that far, over the hill then down the valley and home.

Magnus felt young again and wanted to canter. Of course, now he remembered the man beside him. He was home again, bringing his mares off the mountain.

Anwyn watched the weary riders come down off the hill. Dave, Dai, Rhys and Tomas, all present and correct. She smiled remembering a saying heard once before, something to-do with a war. 'I counted them all out and counted them all back'. Her family were all home, tired and dirty, but all in one piece. What a relief.

Dave rode ahead to block the lane so that the herd had to turn into the paddock. He needn't have worried, Magnus knew exactly where he was going, he had walked this way countless times, and all his mares followed him. As soon as they were in the paddock and the gate was closed, all heads dropped to graze, just glad to rest.

The foal was exhausted and collapsed just inside the gate, no amount of licking and nudging from its mother would induce it to stand and feed. Eventually after a big stretch as it rubbed its head in the long grass, it was asleep in no time. At last the mother was able to leave her foal and start to graze herself.

Anwyn and Dave stood leaning on the gate watching the herd while the twins had gone with strict instructions to look after their ponies. Not dash into the house first leaving the ponies tacked up in the yard. They were both tired and stiff, every bone in their bodies seemed to ache, but they knew fathers hand would hurt their sore back sides if they didn't see to the ponies first.

22

Luck was on their side! Mother had already been there. Stables mucked out and fresh straw put down, water buckets were checked and hay nets full, ready for hungry ponies!

The twins looked at each other with relief. Good old mum, all they had to do now was hang up the saddles and bridles, put the ponies in stables, close the doors and walk stiffly back to the house.

"Hi...how about some help in here", shouted Dai. He had father's cob to see too as well as his own horse. The two boys were suddenly and conveniently deaf! "Lazy little devils", he muttered, forgetting what it was like to be just ten years old and out all day driving a herd of ponies home. "Never mind...*I'll* do it all. As usual!"

Dave and Anwyn were still checking the mares; all seemed to be close to foaling and would have to be looked at again before Dave went to bed.

"*Anwyn*..look here....that foal is a filly!...I've just noticed!! Looks just about done in. I think I'd best take her to the barn don't you think?" He scooped her up in his arms, and walked across the paddock with the mare trotting along following closely.

The boys had done a good job laying a deep bed of straw early that morning, so Dave laid the foal gently in the corner. "I'll look at her before bed love."

"She's so pretty, such a sweet head"" Anwyn said. "Come on Dave", putting an arm round his waist. "Suppers ready, and I'm sure you are all hungry...spicy chicken and then apple tart and cream to follow. How does that sound old man?"

"Bloody good *Old Girl*...lead me too it."

It had been a good day...a great day.

TWO

The little black foal was none the worse for her long trek down from Eppynt Mountain, a bit stiff but looking quite chirpy.

Not long after the herd had settled back at the farm there were more foals frolicking around their mothers.

Anwyn and Dave checked them every day. They were a healthy lot, the warm sun on their backs and good grass for their mum's milk spurred them on.

"I rather like that black filly Dave, that one that came down from the hill." They were watching the foals at play. "Good shoulders and she moves a treat!"

"Yea..I have been thinking of running her on, pity the mother's not much to look at or we could have had a crack at the Royal Welsh with that pair."

Anwyn laughed. "You never give up do you Dave, always got your eye on the next show! There were fifty or so mares and foals entered last year."

"I know", said her husband refilling his pipe. "But just fancy winning in a class like that."

"Come on father, let's go and check the lambs, you're more likely to have a winner over there." Dave struck a match and started puffing away.

"Here walk with me woman...I'll blow smoke over you, keep these damned midges away...their vicious tonight."

The pair, arm in arm, walked away from the ponies Paddock, across the yard and into the sheep shed. Dave flicked the light switch and lit up the interior. A vast shed full of Beulah Speckle Faced sheep, his pride and joy.

The flock was started many generations ago by John Griffiths when he was given some Beulah Speckle Face by his father-in-law as a wedding gift. Since those days the flock had grown to over two hundred prize sheep, recognised by many as the best flock for miles around.

Dave's sheep were treated like royalty; they repaid him by winning time after time at the Royal Welsh. The walls in the office were covered with prize cards and rosettes, going back many many years to Dave's father and *generations* before that.

There were old photos of some of the old man's winning animals, brown with age and curling at the edges. All Dave's ewes and lambs could be traced back to those original ewes. Mansel, Dave's father, thought that one of the old photos was taken at Sibertswold farm in the Welsh borders where old John Griffiths's wife came from. He had always assumed that *this* farm was called Sibertwold after his wife's farm all those years ago.

In years gone by the ewes lived most of their lives out on the common, coming down to the farm briefly to lamb if the weather was really bad, but most of the time they lambed out on the hill, then it was a case of trudging across the hill with a lamp to check the flock over and over again!

Those days were hard on the hill farmers, but Dave's father had persisted and his flock had improved. Eventually things improved and he was able to bring the best of his ewes into the shelter of the farm for lambing. Nothing compared to the huge shed Dave managed today. Mansel had had a dream and today his son could look with pride at his flock started all those generations ago by his ancestors. He often wondered if one of *his* sons would take over the farm, maybe Dai? He had a good eye for sheep.

"Come on my love; stop dreaming…we've still got the cattle to check." Anwyn brought him back to earth again.

Thank goodness he had a good wife at his side. She never complained, just got on with it all.

There was a good fire in the living room, the three boys were in bed, father slumped in his favourite chair eyes closed, he would just sit there and think about tomorrow. Ten minutes later when Anwyn brought him his night cap he was gone, sleeping like a baby, spectacles in one hand and his pipe in the other.

Tomorrow there would be more lambs, more calves and maybe another foal, but for now he could do no more, bed was calling and he was quick to answer.

The next day started at the *usual* early hour. The twins had to be fed and made ready for school. At quarter to eight the school bus would be at the gate, they were usually late and the driver

25

complained because he had to wait, which made him late getting to the school. Mornings never got off to a good start for the boys.

Dave had a better start. Mitzie had whelped during the night, there were five strong puppies squirming about in her bed. She was a cross between a Kelpie and a Border collie.

Kelpie's are an Australian sheep dog, very fast with tremendous stamina, crossed with the Border collie for their intelligence and you had a very sharp working dog. Mitzie was no exception. She was bright alert and very good with sheep, not too fast or flighty, but steady with a strong eye.

Today she was busy with her pups, so the other dogs would have to do without her for a few weeks. These pups were important. Dave stroked her head gently, she was a good bitch, he would miss her company today, she was usually always at his heel, rain or snow, summer or winter, she was always there at his side.

Later in the morning he would move her basket into the kitchen, her pups were worth a great deal of money and had been booked before they had been born by keen trialling men.

Anwyn would object to start with, a dogs place was out in the yard, but who could resist Mitzie and her puppies…especially as they were worth at least £500 each! No she wouldn't mind.

The rain was back again tattling against the kitchen windows and bouncing off the yard. Dave pulled his water proof coat tighter and hurried across to the sheep shed; it was much warmer in there.

A hundred ewes called to him, he was late this morning feeding up because of Mitzie. He filled his trolley with sheep nuts and set off down the long line of pens. In days gone by he fed them inside the pens, but a full grown Bealah was quiet a size and Dave got knocked off his feet many times in the rush to get at the feed troughs. Now he had all the troughs outside the pens, the sheep poked their heads through the hurdles for the nuts leaving Dave safe! Water was fed to the ewes automatically; no carrying buckets as he remembered when he was a lad. Things had certainly improved; he now had the quad bike to check the animals on the common instead of riding Storm. Improved? Well he always enjoyed riding Storm up on the hill….

26

The bell by the back door clanged noisily, a summons to the house for coffee and a slice of walnut cake that Anwyn had made yesterday, his favourite. He took a last look at the sheep all with heads down eating, closed the barn doors and hurried back to the kitchen.

"I thought I'd pop down to the town and do a spot of shopping...Take your wet coat off Dave..." She said while pouring out a big mug of coffee and adding cream. "I can call in on mum and Dad, make sure they are OK. This weather will play havoc with your Dad's arthritis wont it."

"Yeah... sure thing, take them some eggs or something. Tell them I'll get down to see them as soon as I can, it's so wet everywhere, takes me twice as long to get anything done."

"I know love; your Dad knows what it's like in this weather."

The Grandparents had moved into a little house in the town when they gave over the farm to Dave and his family. There had been plenty of room for all of them in the old rambling farm house, but they had insisted there could only be one boss on the farm and it was time for them to move out and give the youngsters a free hand.

"Ask them to come to dinner on Sunday love, they'll like that. If the weather is not too bad I could take Dad for a ride round the farm on the quad bike."

Anwyn smiled, she wasn't at all sure Mansel would be up for that, but they would enjoy seeing the boys.

Sunday dinner was always special; it would be lovely to have the whole family sitting round the old oak table. No one could remember how old the table was; Granny said it had stood there when she came to the farm as a young bride. She told the boys how she had tied their father to one of the legs with a long rope when he was a toddler, to stop him escaping across the yard while she was cooking.

Various puppies had also left marks on the stout table legs, until eventually she had banned dogs from the kitchen altogether and sent them to live in the kennels.

Fourteen people could sit down to dinner if they kept their elbows tucked in! What tales the old table could tell, how many tears had been shed, what laughter at the many Christmas's and so many giant turkeys sitting in pride of place in the centre of this

27

table with many hungry people sat round it. Yes, Anwyn thought, as she brushed some cake crumbs of the table, she would ask them to come on Sunday for dinner, and cook up a feast!

Well this Sunday would only see seven sitting down for the meal, but she would make sure there was plenty to eat.

Anwyn drove too town later in the morning calling in to see Granny and Grandpa before going on to shop for the Sunday dinner. She had some large joints of home grown beef in the freezer, and would make plenty of Yorkshire puddings, that was a good start to her plans!

As soon as Anwyn had driven away, Dave picked up Mitzies basket of puppies and carried them into the house. Where could he put them? They didn't want to be in the way, the kitchen was the hub of the busy farm, every one congregated in there; even visitors came too the back door and straight into the long low kitchen. He stood just inside, where *could* he put these pups? He needed to find a safe place, somewhere they wouldn't get trodden on, not to close to the Aga, that threw out too much heat and would be too warm.

Mitzie didn't like being in the kitchen she would prefer the outdoor kennels and fresh air, but all Dave could think about was the two thousand five hundred pounds squeaking in his arms! The little bitch ran and hid under the old welsh dresser that had stood in the kitchen as long as the oak table. That's it! He remembered Grandpa used to call it 'The Dog House', and if he had been very naughty he would be sent to sit under there and not come out until he was called. Well what better place, Mitzie was already sitting under there, so Dave pushed her basket with the precious pups in after her. He covered the floor with newspaper in case of accidents and left Mitzie and her family to settle down.

He had to get on outside, there was always so much work to do. Mitzie watched him go out and slam the door. Usually she would have been at his side the moment he stepped into the yard, but today the pups needed her more, she licked them affectionately and squeezed into the box with them. The kitchen was lovely and warm; perhaps when they were all asleep she could leave them for a minute or two and have a sniff around the kitchen. For now she must have a little sleep!

28

Anwyn was back! Loaded with shopping bags, she dumped one load on the table and went out to the car for another lot, a box full of groceries from Tesco.

Mitzie woke up with a start when the door burst open, by the time Anwyn came back she was standing beside the welsh dresser, wagging her tail slowly. She wasn't sure what sort of reception she was going to get, she put on her saddest face and waited.

Anwyn didn't notice her at first; it wasn't until the hungry pups started squeaking. She looked round. Puppies...she could hear puppies, in her lovely clean kitchen!

Mitzie plucked up courage and took a step away from the dresser, licked her lips and swallowed trying to look very apologetic.

"How did you get in here?"Anwyn cried. "Where are the puppies...show me."

Mitzie was worried, this didn't look too promising. She fled back to her pups.

"Under my dresser of all places." She opened the back door and shouted. "David Griffiths get yourself in here...NOW!" Giving the bell a mighty swipe. "DAVE, I want you...get back in here at once"......Anwyn turned and smiled at Mitzie. "Show me your puppies then Mitzie, good girl, let me have a peep." Mitzie relaxed, her tail thumped on the floor, things were looking better...she hoped.

Dave came rushing across the yard; he thought there had been an accident or something worse. Before he could say anything Anwyn gave him a slap with the newspaper she'd just bought.

"What's this then?!..What are the puppies doing here under my dresser? You put them in here as soon as my back was turned...didn't you...you crafty old devil!" Then she laughed..."Nice pups though, good girl Mitzie...good girl."

Dave tried to speak but Anwyn hadn't finished with him yet. "You'll have to close them in somehow Dave or someone could tread on them once they start moving."

He moved the kettle on to the Aga hot plate to make some tea while his wife unpacked the shopping. "I've been thinking about that, there may be something I can use."

"Mum and Dad are coming for the day on Sunday, they're looking forward to it..the boys will be pleased. I'll get that big joint of beef out of the freezer." Anwyn's mind was already occupied by the Sunday dinner, pups forgotten.

Dave made the tea, relieved that Mitzie could stay in the kitchen while the pups were small.

The attic at the far end of the house was like Aladdin's cave. Over very many years previous families of Griffiths had stored things up there, things that might come in useful one day. Dave climbed the rickety stairs and opened the attic door. He hadn't been up there for years; he thought somewhere amongst the clutter was just the thing he wanted to keep the pups safe. He looked at the dust covered array of long forgotten objects. Right at the far end under the window and behind an old iron bedstead, was a Penny Farthing bicycle! How old that must be, at least a hundred years he thought. I must ask Dad when he comes on Sunday; *he* would never have ridden it surely. Prams, old and broken chairs, a chest of drawers all covered in dust and cobwebs, and there! Just what he was looking for, tucked away in a corner, the play pen his children had used not that many years ago. With a bit of tinkering he was sure he could make it fit around the Welsh Dresser.

Anwyn got up early, it was Sunday and she had plenty to do before the Grandparents arrived for coffee. A big trifle she made yesterday was in the old larder, with its slate floor and shelves going back more than a hundred years. The trifle needed a top layer of whipped cream, but that would only take a few minutes to finish, next to it was a large apple tart, Dave's favourite. There were still cheese scones to make, deliciously warm to have with the coffee.

Dai usually got up early to help his father feeding up the animals and this morning the twins were early as well. They knew from experience to keep out of the kitchen when their mum was baking. They ate their breakfast and disappeared!

Grandparents arrived in their old Land Rover. It was a bit battered and suffering serious problems with rust underneath, but it was still reliable. Mansel bought it many years ago and said he would pass away before it was sent to the scrap yard! It was only because Dave was such a good mechanic; he had spent many hours welding bits of the chasse to get it through the MOT. He was forever under the bonnet keeping it on the road. 'Old Land Rovers never die, they just rust away!' This one didn't have much longer to go, thought Dave as it came coughing and rattling down the drive. It was perhaps Grandpa's last reminder of his farming days so Dave was determined to keep it going for as long as possible.

After a gigantic lunch Dave took his father to look at the sheep. "What have you got to show this year son?" He asked as they walked along the rows of pens.

At the far end of the shed were a few ewes, aristocratic sheep you could tell, not quiet in show condition, but well on the way. Dave climbed into the pen followed by his Dad so that they could look over them critically.

Dave waited in silence as Mansel inspected them with hand and eye. "They're not a bad bunch son...I've seen better...but not *much* better. Now where's that ram you spent a fortune on at Buelth sales last autumn?" They turned to the other side of the shed where stood three powerful rams with good heads and strong limbs. "Well you got that right son; they'll take some beating, 'specially this one!." He said with his hand on its back. Dave sighed with relief, his Dad was very hard to please when it came to this particular flock, he had after all been responsible for keeping the standard so high before his son had taken over the farm. This flock had the reputation of being the best Beulah's in Wales.

Elonwy too was out and about looking at the stock with Anwyn. They made their way up to the top paddock to look at the ponies. Gran had a good eye for a pony and was eager to see old Magnus again "You old fool Mags, fancy going all that way when you know not to go on the ranges." She scratched his ears and pulled a few bits of bracken out of his mane. "I don't know how he keeps his mane so long, it's almost down to his knees, you'd think he would have rubbed it on something out on those hills wouldn't you?"

Anwyn nodded in agreement, but she was anxiously waiting to see what Gran thought of the foals. The little black filly stood out amongst the others, taller and appeared so self assured; she was the leader of the little gang of foals. The first to start a new game dashing across the paddock and the first to the gate if they had visitors!

They walked amongst the ponies, stroking and petting old familiar friends, a quiet word here a gentle pat there, closely followed by the inquisitive foals. Then they turned to look at this year's foals. The black filly had got bored with this game of follow my leader, and trotted off dancing across the turf, tail erect and head in the air!

"Oh you little show off" said Anwyn laughing at her antics.

"I like that one dear." Elonwy muttered. "A filly too! Just look at that action...and what a lovely head. Oh Anwyn dear, you'll keep her on won't you?" She gazed longingly at the foal. "I don't remember seeing such a beauty!"

It was just what Anwyn wanted to hear, if Gran thought she was lovely it had to be right. So the black filly's future began to take shape on that Sunday afternoon in early spring.

"I did think about the Royal Welsh for that one, but the Section A pony classes have so many entries, and the mare's not that good, I think she'd let the foal down. That's its mother, the grey over by the hedge." She waited for Grans opinion.

"It's old Merrylegs isn't it!" She never forgot a pony. "She used to do well I remember, lead rein pony for the boys wasn't she...seems such a long time ago" Gran sauntered slowly towards the mare. "Hello there Merry old girl, how you doin; then?" Merrylegs pricked her ears and turned to look at Gran as her foal dashed up to her for a feed. The two women stood looking at the pony. "I don't know love, if you spent some time on her, trimmed her up a bit she wouldn't look too bad. She's lost her top line and she needs to muscle up a bit....but damn it all Anwyn, she's a brood mare now, not a show pony. Come on girl, where's that competitive streak you always used to have? Get her in and get to work on her."

32

Gran didn't often have that much to say, so a very surprised and amused Anwyn walked with her back to the gate....followed by the black foal!

It was decided then that the black foal would go to the Royal Welsh Show. First however she would have to be registered, given a name and carry the stud prefix. There were ten weeks to the show, could Anwyn get mare and foal ready by then?.....she would have a damn good try!

Ten weeks! Anwyn hurried over her usual Monday morning chores. Sheets to change, dirty clothes to collect.

The washing machine droned away in the utility room until the first load was ready to hang out on the line. Thankfully it was a windy day so the clean sheets were soon flapping away in the early morning sun. Second load in the machine and mother was off, halter in hand, up to the ponies paddock.

Merrylegs was easy to catch, her foal just followed into the yard where Anwyn put them into a stable, threw some hay in and dashed back indoors to get the second load of washing pegged out on the line, make Dave his coffee and get some meat from the freezer for supper. Then she could start on Merry!!

The rest of the morning was spent just getting the rubbish out of Merrylegs mane and tail. How she had collected so much was a mystery, it needed every hair to be combed out separately...and she had an awful lot of hair!

She worked her way gradually down the mane, time flew by. Dave needed his lunch; she looked at her watch, midday already....help!

Back indoors again; something hot for Dave, perhaps he would make do with a sandwich today...no, that wouldn't be fair, he'd been out on the farm since seven o'clock; she would *have* to cook something. In the end she settled for some cold meat left over from the Sunday roast, fried potatoes and pickle. He could fill up with some of the apple pie also from yesterday's lunch. Dave was very easy to please with food and ate whatever was put in front of him. So that was Dave's lunch settled.

If she could just get Merry's mane and tail sorted today it would be a good start. Elonwy was right as usual. Under all that dirt and long tangled hair was appearing a nice pony, not the best in the world, but a pony that was worth showing.

The pony that walked back to the paddock latter in the afternoon was certainly an improvement. Her main and tail hung down silky smooth, Anwyn was happy with her days work, perhaps, maybe, she could get the pony looking really good by mid July. Still, she had made a start and day by day with patience Merry would again be a pony worth showing!

The foal would be no problem; she would show herself off with her pretty head and that lovely floating action you *had* to look at her!

April, May and now it was June. The months had just flown by and the Royal Welsh show was looming!

All Mitzie's puppies had had their eyes and ears tested at eight weeks. They all passed but still had to be vaccinated, another trip to the Vets. Finally they were all passed one hundred percent fit, and were sold to their new owners. Mitzie had done them well and now she would be back with Dave and the sheep!

Everyone was busy; entries for shows had to be made early and in great detail. A horse entry had to have the names of its sire, dam, Grandsire etc. All sheep entered had to be vaccinated and their paperwork all up to date.

Dave's sheep were all clipped to a certain style, exact to an inch, feet trimmed and polished, the work in the sheep shed never ended, Dai was always there to help despite wanting to be out schooling Glory.

The twins were forever having to be taken to the pony club to practice for the team games, it was chaos!

Anwyn tried desperately to keep calm organising her day so that Merrylegs and her foal got their fair share of attention.

Above all farm work had to take priority when hay was ready to be cut. For five or six days tractors trundled in and out of the yard, day and night carting bales to the barns. Dave needed a lot for the farm; the surplus would be sold privately or to contractors.

34

Mansell and Elonwy usually took over the running of the house, keeping the kettle on the hob and food ready, while Anwyn drove one of the tractors; the whole family helped to get the hay in before rain could spoil it.

Merry and her foal were entered for the Royal Welsh. There had been endless arguments about a name for the foal. Nobody could agree; Rhys thought Beauty was a nice name, but Dai scoffed at that. "Every other black pony you meet is called 'Black Beauty'"

Time was fast running out. Entries had to be in and no late entries were accepted it stated in the entry form.

It was Tomas who thought of the winning name; the family were all enjoying a rare evening together watching an old variety show on the tele. He was dozing sitting at the end of the couch; a lovely lady was singing the latest pop song, dancing around and pointing her toes. Father laughing said "She moves just like our little foal, jumping about like that...who is she boys? I quiet fancy her!"

"Her name's Cilla Dad, Cilla Black" mumbled Tomas half asleep. Suddenly he sat up, wide awake. "That's it...Cilla...for the foal. Cilla Black!!"

Silence..no one spoke...."I think that's a lovely name" said mother. "Cilla she shall be! I shall go and fill in that entry form right now.

So the little black foal had a name at last. Cilla; or her full stud name Sibertswold Cilla.

THREE

The winter had been awful; snow hanging about for weeks and weeks followed by a very wet spring. At last the weather had turned for the better and now in July the sun shone all day in a clear blue sky.

Suddenly the Royal Welsh was only a few days away; the sheep were all but ready to go, they were entered in several classes during the four days of the show which meant that Dave and his right hand man Dai would have to stay there and sleep in the little caravan since neither of them fancied sleeping in a pen with the sheep! So the caravan had to be cleaned out and stocked with provisions.

Grandpa would tow the van to Llanelwedd while Dave would take the livestock double deck trailer, to carry all the sheep. Mother, Granny, and the twins would all drive up on Monday with Merrylegs and Cilla in the horse box.

The sheep must be there early on Sunday, find the right pens before the rush of late comers started. Dave's pens had to be decorated with the stud name and other bits and pieces; clean straw put handy, water buckets etc etc. A lot to do in preparation for their four day stay at the show.

Anwyn had pinned a list up in the kitchen of things they had to take and day by day the list grew longer. The new white halters the sheep had to be shown in hand with, they weren't in the show trunk yet! Dai's white coat needed a button sewn on. The handlers had to wear whitestock men's coats; fortunately the pony classes weren't so fussy, so long as the handlers were smartly dressed.

Mansel and Elonwy arrived on Saturday morning to help with the final preparations; they would stay until the show was over looking after the farm.

Early Sunday morning the sheep must be loaded, any final touching up Grandpa was there to do; he was an expert with sheep and would help to get them loaded up in the double decker.

36

Ponies could wait until Sunday to be washed, once the men had gone and things had quietened down a bit! Was it worth it? Anwyn asked herself…yes ..of course it was!

Sunday promised to be a fine day at five in the morning when the alarm went off. A grey mist shrouded the Beacons and the sky was just turning pink as the sun began to climb above the hill; already the air was warm, it would be hot by midday, especially at the show ground that was situated in a bowl and seemed to concentrate the sun's heat!

The household began to wake up and stumble bleary eyed down to breakfast where Elonwy was already busy in the kitchen. "Eat a good breakfast all of you, it may be a long time before you men get another bite to eat!" She had prepared plenty of food and a large teapot full for a good many mugs.

After breakfast things started to unravel. 'Have you seen this?'…'Have you seen that?'..'Where's this?'…'Where's that?' etc. Grandma sat calmly in the kitchen suggesting places they might look, whilst all around was chaos.

Mother was busy getting the caravan ready for Dave and Dai. She filled every available cupboard with food, clean clothes hung in the minute wardrobe; they would use sleeping bags, but it would probably be too hot for them. Gas cylinders checked, water tank, both full.

The caravan was hitched up to Grandpa's Land Rover, so it was just the sheep to load. They weren't going to oblige!

"STUPID BUGGERS!!...GET UP!" Shouted Dave waving his arms, cursing his lovely sheep and getting hot. Dai ran backwards and forwards trying to help but just getting in the way! In the end Mansell came rattling a bucket of food.

"Come up my lovelies..come up." He quietly called, and the sheep being sheep followed him without a backward look, into the trailer. Soon both decks were full and ready to go. 'Good old Grandpa' thought Dai.

Dai ran into the kitchen to get the 'Don't forget list' "Just checking" He called to Granny as he dashed out again. They seemed to have got everything so off they went waving to the others left behind.

With smoke and a clashing of gears the two old Land Rovers pulled out of the yard and up the drive. It wasn't a long drive to Builth Welles, about forty-five minutes, but it seemed to take longer, the stock trailer with its precious cargo of sheep was heavy and there were steep hills to negotiate.

Grandpa was in the lead, he never *ever* drove at more than forty miles per hour, really frustrating Dave! Better safe than sorry he would say; his old Land Rover kept chugging along as if it agreed with him.

"I can see it!" shouted Dai. "I can see the flags and marquees in the showground, we're nearly there!"

Dave drove slowly through the town following his father, over the river bridge and there it was just ahead. They had arrived.

Cilla and Merrylegs needed a bath! Unfortunately for Merry having gone almost white in her old age, every smudge of mud showed, she would have to go through the whole show treatment. On the other hand Cilla's stubby mane only needed a wash; her tail was growing nicely and would have a shampoo with conditioner.

It was decided to do Merry first; she had to have a complete makeover and would take a long time to dry.

The twins collected several buckets and filled them with warm water. Mother rolled up her sleeves and trouser legs! Poor Merrylegs, she hadn't been treated like this in years, not since she was a lead rein pony for the boys. In those far off days she had been a dapple grey, like a rocking horse. Time had turned her hair snowy white, only her lovely silky mane and tail still showed signs of her former colour.

Anwyn scrubbed and scrubbed, shampoo bubbled flew everywhere gradually the water running off the pony turned from muddy brown to soapy brown and eventually clear of mud and soap suds! Only when she could see Merries skin bright pink did she stop scrubbing and sat back. "Oooh…that's better…..OK boys, take her for a walk…Don't let her roll whatever you do, keep on the drive."

Cilla was next. She didn't like having her tail stuffed in a bucket of warm soapy water and just hated it being rinsed with

38

cold water from the hose pipe, but fortunately the torture didn't last long; having her lovely white socks washed wasn't too painful, tomorrow they would get a good handful of chalk to make them really sparkle!

When the boys came back Merry was ready to be tied up in the sun to finish off drying. Cilla was tied up next to her; she was just learning to be led around by one of the twins, it was an important part of her education as tomorrow she would have to do it properly, no fooling about, it must be perfect!

Rhys would be helping his mother in the ring tomorrow; he was to show Merry while she would lead Cilla. The boys had tossed a coin for the honour of helping her show the ponies. Rhys had won, Tomas was disappointed but he could help at the next show. There was sure to be a 'next show' now that mother had got the showing bug again!

"Tea's ready." Shouted Gran. They had been so busy all afternoon they had forgotten all about her, but tea sounded a good idea.

There were mugs of tea waiting on the kitchen table and plates of scones covered in jam and cream. Gran had been busy as well, she liked cooking for all the family, especially hungry boys!

There was a big fruit cake still in the oven. That was for tomorrow, they could smell it baking as soon as they raced into the kitchen. On the sideboard were trays of pasties cooling, also for tomorrow, well perhaps they could have one or two for supper Gran agreed.

Tomorrow would be a long exciting day and Elonwy wanted to be sure the family had enough food with them; the prices the stall holders at the show charged were criminal, so she baked some more pies and fruit tarts just to be on the safe side!

The ponies were fed, rugged up and bedded down for the night; boys sent to bed early without complaining for a change and at last mother and Gran were able to sit down, put their feet up and relax.

The alarm clock suddenly came to life; it was five o'clock. Anwyn opened one eye. '*I don't want to get up*' she thought. '*Why was that clock still ringing...it's still dark*'. She turned over

39

stretching out for Dave. He wasn't there!....'*Where was he'?* Suddenly she jumped out of bed; duwduw it's the show!!

Off she raced to wake the twins, get them out of bed; knock on Gran's door, she was already up; get herself dressed, downstairs, kettle on, toast in the machine. Someone had set the table for breakfast; must have been Elonwy before she went to bed.

Out to the ponies, they must be fed before the journey to the show; she switched the light on in their stable, they stared at her blinking in the sudden light. She checked them for stains picked up during the night. They had either been good or careful where they had lain, both were spotless. *'Phew thank goodness'* she thought glad she wouldn't have to start scrubbing again at five thirty in the morning; they must be on their way in about an hour, that would get them to the show ground in time for the pony classes. Not a lot of spare time to get them ready for the ring.

Gran had caught the twins before the dashed out and sat them down at the table making sure they ate their breakfast. "Plenty of time to eat boys, don't rush your food Rhys, mother won't go without you"

Mother came in from the yard, relieved to see the boys up, dressed and eating their breakfast.

"Ponies OK...still clean?" asked Tomos"

"Yep..they're eating and they look great!!"

Elonwy went on packing her shopping basket full of food to take with them. *'What would we do without Gran'* thought mother; she could never be as calm and organised as her.

Finally it was time to go; just the ponies to load, Anwyn hoped they would go up the ramp without a fight, and they did. The boys tied them up; they did look good in their blue show rugs and with matching tail bandages. "Well boys..you never know, today might be our lucky day. Help Gran with the baskets and we'll be off!"

Anwyn knew how crowded the show ground would be when they got there. Parking was always a nightmare, all the horse transport had to park on 'Horse Box Hill', it meant a stiff climb up the A483 to where the entrance was and then to find a space to park was almost impossible, Mother had been dreading this since they left the farm this morning.

Parking the trailer was always a problem for her, she could never reverse a trailer, it never went where she wanted it to go despite Dave's attempts to teach her.

At the entrance gate the various passes were sorted out and one entrance fee paid for a passenger without one, when the young man was about to ask her to park just inside the gate on the left, which was at least a quarter of a mile walk down to the main ring and the same back each time the ponies were called, it was a steep hill.

"Excuse me young man."

"Yes madam?"

"My mother is disabled and has difficulty walking, is there any where nearer the ring we can park?" The boys had to cover their mouths to stop laughing. Gran could walk all day and never get tired.

"Oh yes….just follow me!" He jumped into a golf buggy and shot away. They went down and down the hill turning right at the bottom into a little parking area next to the entrance to the ring!

"Just put the chain up when you go out…we keep this space for the oldies…..have a good day."

"Well what a nice man…sorry Gran, but it worked. It was much too far to walk the ponies every time and we would never have found such a lovely place as this."

Gran and Tomas were sent off, still chuckling, to collect the competitor's numbers while mother and Rhys checked the ponies. It was going to be a long day for them. Particularly Cilla, who had already endured a long ride in the old trailer that rattled and banged and was quiet bumpy at times.

Anwyn opened the little passenger door. "How you doing girls?" she asked as she climbed in with them. a stroke for Cilla and a pat for Merry. Their smart rugs came off and brushes and sponges came out. Anwyn kept all the grooming kit in her show box, everything but the kitchen sink, Dave would chide her! She unscrewed the top on the plastic water container and poured some into a bucket.

Mother took care of Cilla, she didn't need a lot of brushing, her coat was like velvet and had a lovely natural shine; she

41

wouldn't need 'Showshine' or 'Glowcoat' to make her shine, hours of patient grooming had seen to that. The chalk block would only be used just before they went into the ring.

Rhys had started work on Merrylegs; he loved this little pony, she had been their first, so gentle and kind. She never let them fall off, she would stop if she felt her rider wobbling or losing their balance. The boys were sorry when they grew too big to ride her but glad that she was still part of the family! Mum said she was too kind to sell and would run out on the hill with the other mares.

Now here she was again, being prepared for the show ring; a good many years had elapsed since her last show, Rhys was sure all the buzz and excitement around her would make her remember everything, she was certainly keen to get started despite her age!

Gran and Tomas were back with the numbers and a catalogue of entries as the first class was being called into the collecting ring; Cilla and Merry were in the second class. A quick look at the catalogue showed over thirty ponies entered so plenty of time before they would be called.

The chalk block came out now and Cilla had to stand very still so that none of the chalk got onto her black bits, it certainly made her socks sparkle. Mother rubbed it in well with her hands and cursed silently when she forgot, and wiped her hands on her clean trousers. As ever Gran came to the rescue with a clothes brush.

"Right now Rhys my boy..get your show clothes on...and don't forget your hard hat." Anwyn reminded him.

"Do I ha.."

"Yes you do....rules, if you went in without a riding hat you would be thrown out!"

Now they were ready to go; both ponies had show bridles on, buckles polished to perfection, glinting in the sun. Anwyn could not have done more, she was satisfied they all looked their best, ponies and handlers.

They were quite close to the collecting ring thanks to the helpful lad at the gate, so they just had to follow the sign 'HORSES ONLY', through the stable yard. The walkway for

42

horses took them straight into the collecting ring which you could only enter if you had the right competitor Pass.

Mother was closely watching the other mares and foals making their way down to the collecting ring. None of the foals were as tall or mature as Cilla, some quiet small and looked very young, their coats looking blotchy still changing colour. Cilla could hold her own in this company Anwyn thought; she was behaving perfectly so far.

Merrylegs was very excited and kept spinning around. "Stand still Merry...calm down there's a good girl." It was getting quiet hot and Rhys had his best tweed jacket on.

The first class was just finishing; rosettes handed out to proud owners and unhappy people leaving with nothing to show for all their hard work, some of whom had travelled many miles to take part.

"Right now" said the collecting ring steward. "Tell me your numbers and then walk round the ring." Anwyn told Rhys to let two or three go before he led Merry in, it gave Cilla something to follow and look at. She pranced a bit and took time to settle down and walk properly; all the foals were excited, some would settle , others would not, the judge would understand, they were only babies, most at their first show. There were many more foals than Anwyn at first thought.

The mares were to be judged first and then the foals; two separate classes. All walked round the ring while the judge looked at each pair as they passed him. Mother had told Rhys to stay awake and show Merry properly as quite often judges would have spotted the likely winner in the first parade!

Rhys was trying to remember everything his mother had told him, there seemed to be so much he had to learn.

Once they had all walked past the judge, the ring steward stopped them and sent them off one at a time without the foals to trot up past the Grandstand and straight towards the judge.

Rhys waited patiently; there were a lot of mares in front of him. Merry was still playing up a bit, stamping her feet and throwing her head about. "Steady Merry" he said stroking her neck. It was nearly their time to go.

43

"Right.. You ready young man? The steward looked down at Rhys who suddenly felt very small. A quick look to make sure the judge was ready. "Off you go sonny…good luck!"

Rhys tried to remember everything mother had said; *'start slowly and then give her her head and run with her, she will go fairly fast, just let her run"* Well, Merry knew what to do even if Rhys didn't! She set off at a spanking trot, throwing her feet forwards and pointing her toes.

As they flew past the Grandstand a great roar broke out, it seemed that everyone was clapping and cheering. Rhys ran as fast as he could; Merry tucked her head in, she seemed to love every minute of it. Round the top of the ring they flew only checking their pace when a large steward appeared in front of them!

"Steady lad…did you enjoy that?" he was laughing.

Rhys remembered just in time to make Merry stand while he made a quick bow to the judge. Was the judge laughing as well, he couldn't be sure. It was with some trepidation that he made his way back to the line of other ponies. *Had he gone too fast? Had he messed it up? What was mother going to say?* Mother was smiling, it must have been OK!

Cilla had been playing up when Merry was trotting round the ring with Rhys, but as soon as her mother was back she relaxed and demanded a quick suckle.

"I thought you were never going to stop; whatever got into the old girl, she really looked good; didn't you hear the crowd cheering; well done darling, you showed her well, thanks a lot love!" Anwyn was so pleased with her son who was gasping, trying to get his breath back! He hadn't heard the cheering, he'd been to busy trying to keep up with Merry!

All the ponies had been passed the judge and had been inspected one by one; it took ages. Now they all lined up for his final inspection. Some ponies only got a quick glance, others he studied for some time before going on to the next.

Rhys knew what to do, so did Merrylegs. She stood like a statue, sparkling in the sunshine. He stood a little in front of her, he'd got her head just at the right height and her neck arched….perfect.

The judge stopped beside them for what Rhys thought was ages. He didn't dare move...*'concentrate on your pony'*....he could almost hear his mother's voice.

"Well done young man" said the judge and walked on to the next pony. He relaxed a little and stood beside Merry giving his mother a nervous smile while he pretended to be busy straightening her mane.

"Walk round please" called the judges steward.

This is it thought Rhys, now we will know! *'Concentrate on your pony...never stop showing her'*. Mother's words still drumming in his head!

He walked at Merry's shoulder holding a loose rein, she tucked her head in and pointed her toes almost like a ballet dancer! *'You didn't walk like that when we brought you down from the mountain'* he thought still concentrating and didn't notice the steward signalling with his bowler hat.

"Come in lad....stand next to the grey pony." They were second!

Mother was laughing when she brought Cilla to stand with Merrylegs again. "Wow Rhys!" was all she could say. "Good old Merry."

The judge was handing a big red rosette to the man with the grey pony and then came to Rhys standing second.

"It was a very hard job separating you two" he said. "But the grey had youth on her side...I must say your pony moves beautifully. You showed her very well young man; I didn't think you would stay with her at times. Well done lad...well done!" He said as he gave Rhys a big blue rosette and shook his hand.

The day was getting better and better for Rhys, he felt as if he was going to explode!

The steward was smiling too. "I want you back for the championship, so don't go far away." He walked on following the judge who was handing out all the other rosettes.

"Foals forward please" called the steward

"Good luck mum" Rhys whispered as Cilla took her place in front of Merry. She was quite happy to go without her mother, they had practiced and practiced until she was confident enough

45

to walk and trot on her own, so long as there was a reward by way of a carrot at the end of it…and today there was.

All the foals were trotted past the judge, and then lined up in front of their mums for a final inspection. He hardly looked at Cilla!! Anwyn was so disappointed, all that hard work. She looked wonderful, her coat was as black as night, the sun shone on it and it gleamed; her white socks were still brilliant and had caught every ones eye as she had floated round the ring. She was standing now, head up ears pricked looking full of confidence, surely the judge must have noticed her?

At last he was walking back up the line still looking at the foals; he seemed to have made up his mind. He stopped and looked long and hard at Cilla; he walked forward and handed the first rosette and card to Anwyn!

"I've not seen such a lovely foal for a long time…congratulations, she's a stunner!"

Rhys was jumping up and down with excitement "Well done Cilla, well done mum." The steward had to calm him down so that the mare and foal could do their lap of honour past the big Grandstand. The cheering and shouting was just the same, but this time Rhys was ready for it. This time they both ran even faster. Cilla couldn't keep up as she floated over the grass never breaking her stride; Anwyn ran as fast as she could keeping pace with her and glowing with pride.

What a day; first and second at the Royal Welsh Show, things couldn't get any better.

But they did! Merrylegs took the Reserve Champion prize; the judge said he had never had such lovely mares in the same class and they deserved to be Champion and Reserve.

The Grand Parade was held towards the end of the day. All prize winners, horses, sheep and cattle had to Parade round the main ring one after the other; the announcer read out the classes and details of the animals as they went Past the Grandstand.

It was three o'clock and Anwyn, Rhys, Merry and Cilla were waiting in the collecting ring to parade. Bothe ponies were very tired by now; it had been a long very hot day, especially for the foal.

Suddenly mother stumbled twisting her ankle badly. "I can't walk ...I'd never be able to get round the ring like this!"

"You must, we're nearly ready to go." Rhys said sounding worried.

"I can't walk on it dear..I'm sorry." And limped to the fence at the side of the collecting ring. "Here Tom...you take Cilla for me....just follow Rhys, Cilla's too tired to play up."

Tomas came to life very quickly; he had felt left out of it all day since his brother was having so much fun. Mother tied her number round his waist, fixed the red rosette on his belt. Tidied his hair and gave him Cilla.

"Just don't let go of her, no matter what happens...DON'T LET GO!"

The ring steward came dashing up to them. "Come on you boys...we're waiting for you!" He was getting flustered; there were so many animals to get into the ring in the correct order.

"Good luck boys." Gran called out to them as Tomas took Cilla with a big grin on his face; he was in the Grand Parade.

Mother watched them go, proud of her ponies and even more proud of her twins! She walked over to Gran and Grandpa; they had come to the collecting ring in case they were needed to help get the ponies ready.

"Your ankle got better very quickly" said Gran.

"Yes didn't it" Anwyn said laughing.

The Parade wound its way slowly round the enormous main ring. The Champion and Reserve of each class was brought forward to stand in front of the presidents box as the Parade was halted for a few moments while the announcer read out the details, breeding etc.

Rhys and Tomas were approaching the well decorated president's box with Welsh flags hanging from the fence.

"Now two fine examples of Welsh Section A Mountain Ponies. Merrylegs of Gwyddil and her foal Sibertwold Cilla. Owned and bred by Mr and Mrs David Griffiths and shown by their twin boys Rhys and Tomas. Well done boys! The mare is thirteen years old her foal showing for the first time. I'm told that David has some fine Beaulah Speckle Faced sheep we shall see soon.

47

As soon as the horses had all paraded, the sheep and cattle were sent in. Sheep, not being very good at being led were transported on flatbed trailers in pens; it was safer than having sheep running all over the show ground and allowed the enormous crowd to see them.

David and Dai were on one of the flatbeds with their exhibits, rosettes decorating the animals. They also heard the commentator praising their flock and telling the crowd that the Griffiths family had started this herd four generations ago and had shown here many times with great success.

There were thousands of people in the Grandstand and all round the ring all clapping and cheering. They certainly had had a very successful day!

FOUR

The rest of the summer flew past with lots of shows to enter and the pony club camp was sure to be great fun. The twins hadn't been old enough to attend camp before, but now they had turned eleven and supposedly responsible they could both go to camp.

The ponies went with them together with all the equipment and clothes they would need for a week under canvas. The ponies would be kept in temporary stables on a nearby farm, while the club members slept and ate in tents in an adjoining field. It promised to be great fun so long as the weather stayed fine; sleeping in a tent in the pouring rain didn't seem quite so appealing to Rhys,

Tomas knew the pony club games team would all be there practising like mad and he desperately wanted to be part of it.

Star wasn't as big as most of the ponies selected, but she was fast and very quick on her feet. If he didn't drop the flag, or the spuds, they stood a good chance of being spotted by the team trainer.

Rhys wasn't so keen on galloping up and down a field, although Merlin was very fast, he wasn't going to miss out, so mother suggested he tried for the dressage team.

Dressage! That was for girls so he wasn't exactly enthusiastic....but on thinking about it.....dressage could lead to three day eventing. Sooo..perhaps.....yes, he really would like to have a go at that. After all, some of the best three day eventers were men; even Mr Fox-Pit started off in his local pony club.

So it was decided; they put their names down on the appropriate list, sent the application forms off and waited for the letter back from the organiser.

Meanwhile mother had called a friend who was well thought of in the dressage world, would she please give Rhys and his pony a few lessons?

Although he had been riding forever it seemed, this dressage riding was something quite different and his horse didn't find all this collection stuff to his liking! A walk was a walk and a canter a canter; he was more of a problem pupil than Rhys.

Gradually, with a lot of practice and even more patience progress was made. Kate, their teacher, began to get quite hopeful, they still had a long long was to go, but the basic movements were coming.

The first time Rhys and Merlin managed to walk collectedly in a straight line down the centre of the school raised a cheer from Kate! It was so difficult to do, even such a simple thing correctly, but at last when they looked at the tracks Merlin had left in the sand arena, there was the evidence; a dead straight line, not a hoof print to left or right, just a lovely straight line!

After that progress was quicker and before the pony club started they had mastered all the movements necessary for the elementary test.

Kate was satisfied, they wouldn't let themselves down they had worked very hard to get this far in such a short time in spite of continual sarcasm from his brother. *'It's such a girly thing..you'll be the only boy in the group!'* he chided.

Rhys just smiled and as Kate said even that great event rider Fox-Pitt had started in the pony club. Rhys could be patient if it meant he might ride like that man when he grew up.

Mother had got more shows lined up once the pony club was over. One at Cardigan and a big show at Haverford West, but for the next few weeks the boys and their ponies had priority.

The mares and foals still lived in the top paddock, but soon they would be separated, the mares to the hill with Magnus again and the foals to the big barn where they would live together until it was time for the sales, then Dave and Dai drove Magnus and the mares out of the farm and up onto the hill, far away from the calling foals.

Anwyn tried not to hear the upset foals, she knew from experience they would soon settle down and forget all about their mothers, but that first day was always hard. The foals had to learn to eat pony nuts and drink water from a trough, up to now they had lived on grass and their mother's milk and weaning was difficult for them.

Cilla had been eating hard food for some time; Merry had pony nuts and corn when they were in a stable together and at the show, so she had learnt early on to poke her nose in the feed bin

50

and scrounge a mouthful of tasty food! Now it was up to her to show the other foals how to eat hard food. Within a day or so they had all forgotten about their mothers and were eating properly.

The sales were still some weeks away and by then the foals had to learn to walk quietly on a lead rein. Cilla again would show them how to do that and Anwyn was sure her foals would look good and behave sensibly; such an advantage if a well behaved foal was shown to possible buyers, they would always fetch a bit more money than a wild scruffy terrified foal, but which of her foals could she possibly keep? Dave said quite emphatically NONE!

Cilla was so lovely and already a winner at the Royal Welsh surely she could stay? NO!

Anwyn sulked for days...she *would* keep her no matter what Dave said, so when the entries for the sale went to the post, Cilla's name wasn't on it! Neither was another little foal called Gemini; she was the last of the foals born in the top paddock, smaller than the others so wouldn't make much money, she was very sweet and given time would grow into a lovely lead rein pony.

Dave was furious. It was bad enough to keep Cilla, the one foal he was hoping would make top price, but to keep TWO!

Anwyn wouldn't be beaten on this matter, Cilla was the best foal they had ever bred and she could show again and again and still be a winner and in any case you couldn't keep one foal on its own, it needed a companion to play with and Gemini was the one.

"You'll never make a business woman...never!" Shouted Dave. Mother smiled to herself, she had won that battle. The two foals were lucky, they would stay at Siberswold.

Pony club camp, the long awaited week had arrived.

Mother took the boys and their ponies to the farm near Brecon where the children were divided into four groups, or rides, and would wear the appropriate colour band on their riding hats.

There were various team competitions held during the week; best kept stable...cleanest tack...smartest ride etc. all the points

51

were added up at the end of the week and the winning ride won a prize.

The tents were alright, but for boys who had never camped before it was all very exciting.

The Discovery and trailer were unpacked, ponies settled with water and hay in their blue ride stables and boys disappearing in the distance, so Anwyn was free to set off for home and a nice quiet week.

Dave was still in a bad mood; he slammed doors and stalked round the house like a caged bear. Would he ever get over this Anwyn wondered, Cilla was staying with Gemini and that was that!

Later she learnt from Dai that he had met the auctioneer for the pony sales in the market that week and had asked about the foals going to the sale. It seems they have buyers coming from Germany and Holland and prices were expected to be sky high! No wonder Dave was cross, now she could understand, but it was too late now. She would have to tread very carefully for the next few days; the atmosphere in the farm was not good!

The happy campers came to the rescue. They had forgotten something or other so it meant a quick dash to the camp at Brecon where mother spent a lovely day watching the children and forgot about Dave and the foal problem.

Rhys was doing quite well in the dressage group although Merlin would have sooner been with the group practicing gymkhana games in the next field; every time the trainer shouted 'GO' Merlin jumped in the air. A collected canter was out of the question; Rhys's patience was wearing a bit thin, he so wanted to be good at this dressage, but his pony was making it *very* difficult.

Someone suggested the trainer should start the games with a flag instead shouting which was causing havoc in the adjoining field! As a result Merlin settled down and remembered his collected walk and canter; he even managed to stand still while Rhys mounted and dismounted instead of galloping off as soon as he put a foot in the stirrup; a good ploy for gymkhana races, but frowned upon in the dressage ring.

Tomas was having a marvellous time; one of the boys in the club team was unable to come to the camp, which meant they were one short for the senior team. Star had been spotted flying up and down a line of bending poles and plucking flags out of a bucket at full gallop! Would he like to practice with the senior team as reserve rider?

You bet he would; in Tom's mind he was already at the Horse of the Year Show and in the final of the Prince Philip pony club games!! He was too excited for words.

Although Star was smaller than the other ponies in the team, she was so fast and quick on her feet, they were soon competing on equal terms with them.

Anwyn went home happy, smiling as she thought about the twins and the fun they were having. She would cook Dave a lovely supper and just maybe apologise for upsetting him earlier.

During the week while the boys were at camp, things at home were very quiet; Dai was aware of the tension between his parents and tried to keep out of their way as much as possible.

Gradually the atmosphere improved as they were beginning to speak to each other again, and by the end of the week things were almost back to normal!

On the last day of the Pony Club Camp an open day was arranged; parents and friends to come and watch the games and competitions, followed by the prize giving.

Anwyn wanted Dave to come with her, but he said he was too busy; his prize sheep were due for a worming and foot bath that couldn't wait for a day or so. She was disappointed, but Dai and Elonwy would go anyway, while Mansel would help Dave with the sheep. Nothing unusual there then, things were back to normal.

Pony club camp was a hive of activity when they arrived; the stables were open for parent's inspection, they had been judged earlier that morning. Everything looked very clean and tidy; mother said she was sure that the stables at home would in future be just as good. The happy campers said 'no such luck'. Dai agreed with them for a change!

The children had to wear their best riding clothes for open day, which impressed Gran who was a stickler for turnout, she had to agree, everyone looked smart. All the girls, there were more girls than boys, had to wear hair nets under their hats or plait their hair; any boy with long hair had to go to a barber and have a trim. Rhys and Tomas were lucky, they escaped that outing.

The games and competitions were great fun; something for everyone, even the young and less experienced had their own classes. The biggest surprise of the day for Gran and Daiwas Rhys; he *won* in the mini three day event and his dressage score was very good, not the best but not too far off the leaders!

Merlin made up for it in the show jumping and the fastest time ever in cross country jumping; Rhys said he just flew over the jumps and didn't hesitate at anything, look out Mr Fox-Pitt!

Tomas was happy to be part of the Pony Club Games team even as the reserve rider; both Tom and his pony galloped their hearts out, impressing the trainer with the progress they had made during the week; he had a quiet word with mother and promised that Tomas would have a place in next year's team, so long as he didn't grow too tall for his pony!

After the games were over and prizes presented. The twins had done quite well; Rhys had been judged the most improved rider, the District Commissioner said his progress from cowboy to three day eventer was quite remarkable and she hoped he would go on improving his dressage score as obviously jumping was no problem for Merlin.

Mother wasn't too happy for her son to be called a cowboy while Tomas, on the other hand, had ridden like a wild Red Indian all day, to the delight of his trainer!!

It was nice to see her two boys going in different ways for a change; they were growing up at last, not doing the same things all the time. They wore identical cloths; read the same books had much the same interests, but now, for the first time they were striking out in different directions.

Parents were asked to collect the children and ponies early the following morning. Tonight there was a party; parents not invited!

On the way home Anwyn was thinking out loud about what to get for tea. She suggested that Gran and Grandpa stay; she would make something special for Dave since he had been a bit neglected this week.

Suddenly Gran said she had a good idea; as the boys were away why didn't they *go out* for a meal, it would make a lovely end to the day.

Did Elonwy sense things hadn't been too good recently, or was it really a spur of the moment idea? Anyway, it was a good one.

"Yes Gran, let's do that, it will be lovely." So that evening they all went to a little pub out in the hills where they knew the food to be very good.

They ate drank and were merry; the happy loving relationship restored. Life would return to its steady comfortable pace at Sibertswold Farm.

The twins were back from camp full of jokes and tales about other children and their ponies; they still had another two weeks until they started at their new schools. The twins were moving up to the high school while Rhys was going to the sixth form college to study for A Levels.

New school uniforms, books, pens, satchels etc had to be bought out of whatever profit the farm had made over the past year; but with luck the hay should sell well and there were some nice lambs growing fat on the hill; meat prices were quiet high at present, then there were some of Dave's special flock to sell, they were sure to make good money. If everything went as planned they should manage.

The holidays were practically over and still the sun shone in a cloudless sky. It was hot...very hot; the bracken on the mountain was already turning a rusty colour as the ground dried up and the grass stopped growing.

There were a few holiday makers about parking their caravans and camping up on the mountain on the tinder dry land.

Dave had pulled off the road on his way back from the market to talk to a family who had just arrived and were pitching a tent; he pointed out to them the danger of camping there surrounded by gorse and bracken; he was politely told to 'fuck off' and mind his own business!

"You just can't talk to some people, they think they can set up their tents anywhere with disregard for the countryside or the people and their stock who farm here!" he said angrily to Anwyn when he got home. "I'm going to phone the police...praps they can do something about them." He knew however it was inevitable that in a day or so others would be camping up there.

Sure enough. Just a couple of days after Dave's confrontation with the campers, Dai was riding Glory up on the hill when he could smell smoke! He rode higher up the hill and there in the distance... fire!! For a moment he sat and watched the flames spreading, a long way from him, but the wind was fanning the flames; the fire was moving towards him and the farm!

He set Glory down the hill at a gallop. He had to warn his father; the sheep were grazing the hill and would probably move away quickly, but sheep could be incredibly stupid at times and were just as likely to stand and watch the flames!

Glory stumbled a few times on the hard baked ground and she began to panic, smoke becoming quite thick and Dai was pushing her so fast. "Come on Glory...we must get home fast!" She flicked her ears; she understood the desperation in her young rider's voice. They stumbled and slipped but managed to stay upright.

The smoke was getting thicker as they reached the lane leading to the farm, he dared not gallop down the drive, the tarmac was to slippery at the best of times, so he tried to keep to the narrow strip of grass at the side close under the hedge.

"DAD....DAD...THE HILLS ON FIRE!!" Dai shouted as Glory slid to a stop in the yard. Dave heard him and rushed out of the barn.

"ON THE HILL..THE SHEEP!!" He choked and coughed as Dave grabbed the cobs bridle and mother caught Dai as he almost fell off Glory.

"Steady on son...get your breath back....take a deep breath"
Father looked anxiously at Dai, the smoke was beginning to
reach the farm. "Now where's the fire?"

Dai gulped, coughed and swallowed hard. "On the
hill...where the sheep are; it's coming this way..the
wind...blowing the fire towards us. What shall we do Dad?"

"First son, you go and see to Glory." Dave said trying to
sound calm. "Put her in her stable, check her for any cuts and
give her a drink, You have both done well!"

"I'll phone the fire brigade" said mother. "And Morgan! I'd
better let him know..he probably does already, also the Evan
boys. We will need them all."

"Tell them to bring something to beat with..we might be able
to hold it back until the firemen get here" shouted Dave. "I'll get
up there on the quad; keep the boys with you."

Mitzie saw Dave running for the quad bike and jumped up
onto the carrier, her usual seat. "Not this time Mitzie...boys hold
her; I'll come back for her if need be." He shot off scattering
gravel as he accelerated away; the twins watched open mouthed
as he disappeared.

"Wow...let's get the bikes and have a look! Tomas suggested.

"Dad said we must stay here until he comes back."

"But he might be ages and we'd miss the fun."

"Best we wait a bit" Rhys said thinking it could be dangerous
on the mountain.

"Chicken!!"

The twins went on arguing until mother came out and grabbed
them. "You stay here or I'll box your ears, you heard what your
father said!"

Up on the hill Dave was bouncing along a sheep track as fast
as he could looking left and right for his sheep. Hopefully they
would be further over or moving away from the flames, you
could never predict with sheep...stupid creatures.

He drove on gradually getting higher, perhaps he would be
able to see better. But the higher he got the thicker was the
smoke, it was stinging his eyes and down his throat, he stood up
on the foot rests and drove as fast as dared; suddenly he was out
of the smoke.

Now he could see where the flames were heading; he was clear of the fire, it seemed to him that the flames were spreading along parallel but not crossing the road. He desperately hoped the heat and sparks wouldn't blow across, on the other side was his top field and stored under tarpaulin sheets were several tons of best hay!

Blast and damnation...where were the bloody sheep...a hundred or more couldn't just disappear!!

The fire was coming up behind him, already the path he was on had vanished under the spitting flames; he would have to go higher up the hill and ride across the heather and try to get round the fire.

He set off again bouncing across the parched terrain. *'I wish I had Toms spy glasses...I should have brought them'.* the quad bike was making hard work of cross country driving, it wasn't designed for this sort thing, but it gamely grunted and rattled its way up the hill.

Suddenly he saw movement further up, he rubbed his stinging eyes, did he imagine it....no...it was sheep....a hundred or so lovely, fat sensible sheep running away from the fire, up to the top of the mountain where the ground was rocky, no fire hazard up there, they would be safe for now!

With a sigh of relief he turned for home, all he had to worry about at the moment was getting down off the hill and back to the farm.

By taking a wide sweep behind the fire Dave managed to get back onto the lane about half a mile from the farm drive. Speeding home he could see the fire was almost opposite his top field where several hundred pounds worth of hay was stacked, fortunately covered with tarpaulin sheets, but at the mercy of windblown sparks setting it alight.

Anwyn and the three boys had already spotted the danger, thanks to Tomas and his binoculars, and were now loading the discovery with brooms, shovels and hessian sacks, anything that could be used as beaters to keep sparks from reaching the hay.

"Get some buckets boys." Shouted Dave as he parked the quad bike. "There's water in the trough up there." They rushed around and found only five buckets. "There are some in the

58

stables..hurry boys." There was one in the foals stable. "Sorry Cilla, we need your bucket." Said Tomas as he grabbed it and went running out to the Land Rover.

"Get in…get in, let's go" said mother anxious to get to the top field as quickly as possible. The sooner they got to the top field the better chance they had of keeping the fire back from the hay. If they could stop the fire from crossing the road there was a good chance the hay would be saved.

The Discovery revved up and they raced away up the drive, leaving the yard silent and empty, except for Mitzie who walked towards the barn and lay down in the shade of the stables where Cilla and Gemini were watching her through the open stable door!

Forgotten in the panic, and being inquisitive by nature, they went to investigate the empty yard, ambled up the empty drive onto the lane….. and disappeared.

Three fire engines were up on the mountain spraying the flames and getting it under control; as things settled down, the chief fire officer spoke to the farmers who had been fighting the fire for most of the day, thanking them for the hard work and assuring them that it would be watched to make sure it wouldn't flare up again.

Anwyn and the boys had worn themselves out damping down sparks, rushing from place to place to beat and stamp on anything smoking. Dai had been on top of the hay stack doing a great job keeping the tarpaulin wet to discourage any sparks the wind might blow in his direction. Tomas kept him supplied with water buckets he regularly filled from the water trough nearby. Now, at last, the family could rest their weary arms and look at the damage the fire had caused.

The hillside was burnt black, the fir trees stood like black statues reaching hopelessly for the sky, while the red fire engines stood out defiantly on the hill side. Little pockets of fire still smouldered where heather roots burst into life when a breeze caught them.

Acres of hill grazing would be lost for a year at least; the bracken the local farmers baled up for winter bedding had all gone; now they would have to buy in straw, a very unwelcome expense, all because some camper had dropped a cigarette end onto tinder dry grass.

Slowly Auwyn collected her family, although Dave was reluctant to leave the hill which was still smouldering in places, but he was too exhausted to go on, and in any case the firemen were staying for at least the next twenty four hours. So he got into the Disco and she drove them back to the farm.

It was growing dark by the time the family had recovered sufficiently to think about feeding the animals.

The twins were too tired to go out again and were sent upstairs for a bath and hair wash. Dai offered to see to the horses; Glory first, he had almost forgotten their mad gallop down the hill and felt guilty for leaving her so long unattended. Carefully he felt over her body, searching for any cuts or splinters picked up on the hectic dash for the farm. Her legs felt a little warm and puffy, not surprising the way he had made her gallop down the hill; he would get Dad to look at her, maybe he should hose them down, he remembered Dad hosing Storms legs after a day out hunting; father was probably asleep by now so he decided to do it anyway.

Dai put her back in the stable, spending a lot of time brushing her. "Good night my darling..sorry about today!" He said as he shut the stable door; now the foals.

He had already retrieved the buckets from the back of the Disco, so he filled two and went into the barn.....it was empty....all the gates were open.......not a pony anywhere!! "Oh SHIT" he shouted very loud "Shit shit shit!!" As if we haven't had enough trouble today...now mother's pride and joy have gone; but where?

He suddenly remembered the gates on the drive were all open as they drove home; they could be anywhere by now. *'Oh lor...tonight of all nights'* he thought. *'No good just standing here looking at the empty barn...mother has to be told'* He went into the kitchen not knowing what to say. Father was asleep in his arm chair; mother was washing up the dishes, she turned as she heard him come in.

"You were a long time Dai, was Glory OK?"

"Mum…..Cilla and Gemini, the barns empty they've gone."

"What do you mean **gone**….they can't have gone they **must** be in there, have you looked carefully?"

"Yes, I looked everywhere."

"In the yard?"

"Yes…the gates are all open from this morning. They've gone." Mother rushed to the door, it was dark outside.

"We'll not find them tonight mum." He sat at the table utterly dejected, head in his hands trying not to cry.

FIVE

Dave woke up surprised to find he was in the kitchen with his wife asleep at the table with her head on her arms; it was past midnight, something must be wrong. The half empty box of tissues was a clue. "What's wrong love...why aren't you in bed?

"Oh Dave....the ponies have gone....Dai looked everywhere. Someone left the gates open when we rushed to get to the fire...now they've gone and I don't know where to start looking for them." Tears came again.

"Don't cry love, we'll find them, they can't be far away. Soon it'll be light and I'll go out on the quad and find the little blighters! Come on, let's get to bed for a few hours, we can't do anything yet...come on love, I'll find them don't you worry. Tom will go out with his spy glasses, they won't have gone far. Anwyn managed a smile, please let them be found.

Anwyn slept very little and was down in the kitchen at daybreak; she made coffee and toast, set the table for the family while trying to plan her day. Where did you start looking for two straying foals?

Taking the coffee with her she walked down to the big field by the river; all the young ponies were kept there, foals yearlings and two year olds; maybe Cilla and Gemini would be with them, that would be marvellous. It would have been easy enough for them to have wandered down there without being noticed in all the excitement yesterday.

There was no sign of them; disappointed she made her way back to the house taking the longest possible route, looking in every field and building. Dai was right, they had gone.

Back in the yard she looked up at the hill, blackened by yesterdays fire; such an expanse of open country, unfenced, they could be anywhere! She searched the hill side shading her eyes against the rising sun, but nothing was moving; a few buzzards circled the blackened earth looking for an easy meal; she thought there were sheep moving slowly down the hill.

That would be Dave's first job today; checking that flock. A lot of lambs were almost ready for market, just waiting for the

62

best prices. Dai would come with him to count heads, and then they would concentrate on the missing ponies.

Mitzie came out of her kennel, stretched, her tail wagging as she recognised Anwyn. "You'll have plenty of work today Mitzie, you can be sure of that." She scratched the bitch's back. Mitzie loved that and wound herself round mother's legs.

Working dogs didn't get much petting, spoilt them for work Dave said, but she had always been special, very loyal and always ready for work, rain or shine it didn't matter to her, a whistle from Dave and she would come rushing to his heal.

"Can you help me today Mitzie, can you find ponies as easily as sheep?" She put her head on one side and wagged her tail again; Dave has always said she understands everything that's said to her. "Come on then, I'll find you some scraps for breakfast."

As soon as Dave got back from checking his sheep and after a cup of coffee, he set off on the quad, He said he would check with the firemen still on duty if they had seen the two foals, and would then go up in the hills, maybe call in to see Morgan.

When Dave had gone she asked Dai to saddle Storm for her; she had to do something and had decided to ride up on the hill to look for them; better than moping around the house she thought. He was a bit strong for her, but they would cover so much ground, a few blisters on her hands were a small price to pay for his willingness to go anywhere she asked.

Dave got back mid afternoon to find Dai in the kitchen. "Where's mother? I hope she hasn't gone looking."

"'Fraid so Dad; she's taken Storm and gone up the hill"

"Oh my God...why didn't you go with her Dai?"

"She told me to look after the farm and that she wouldn't be long"

"When did she go?"

"About an hour after you went."

"I think we'd better see if we can find her Dai...anything might happen...Storm's too strong for her."

"I told her that and she....wait I think that's her!...yep...she's back Dad. I'll help her down and put Storm away."

Dave gave a great sigh and collapsed in the arm chair, wishing he had some good news for her when she appeared in the kitchen.

Anwyn was very glad to be home, she had been a long way over the hill wondering around, before she turned back; she was tired! "Oh Dave, I just *had* to get out and look!"

"I know love; I was worried sick when I got back and Dai told me you had taken Storm! You managed OK it seems, where did you go?"

"Over the hill...no sign of them, have you any news?"

"No good news....I spoke to the firemen, they told me that one of the engines on its way nearly ran over a couple of ponies...that *must* have been them. They jumped a hedge, scared out of their wits by the noise of the siren and galloped off up the hill. At least we know in which direction they went." Dave got up and poured them a cup of tea.

"Well they've moved on from there." Anwyn was close to tears.

"I got as far as Taigwynion farm, do you remember Arwyn? It must be at least ten years; I started the Quad to come home and it ran out of petrol. But luckily he had a can; I must remember to return the favour. Anyway, we were chatting about the ponies and he told me that a few days ago all the foals from that wild herd way up in the hills were rounded up and taken somewhere to be sold. It's just occurred to me that maybe the mares heard our two calling and took them for their own.

"Well that's a long shot Dave, is it possible?"

"I suppose it is, we'll just have to keep looking when we go hunting on the mountain"

Anwyn wouldn't give up, she drove to any horse sale advertised no matter how far; Leominster, Brecon, Llanybudder. She had posters printed with Cillas photo on them; LOST or STOLEN in big black letters. They were put in every tack shop, feed shop, Vets practices and market places; anywhere where horsey people might see them.

The boys were back at school and for the next few months ponies had to take second place.

Mother insisted that homework had to be done carefully and night after night lights burned brightly in the boys bedrooms!

Tomos and Rhys had separate rooms now, they had shared the same room since they were born; Anwyn said it was time they had their own space. Tomos was delighted, he had the small room up under the roof, a small widow looked out over the lower fields, and almost level with the birds. He sat for hours at that window with his binoculars, home work forgotten; until Dave caught him staring at the Red Kites, books not even opened! The binoculars were confiscated until he could prove the homework was completed.

It was sometime later when Anwyn had almost given up hope of finding Cilla that she made one more trip to Llanybudder market. A miserable damp day with lots of horses of all sizes penned up, two or three to a pen, all looking wet and dejected.

Some gypsy children were dragging a black and white cob around outside, hoping to catch someone's eye, with two small ones sitting on its back their legs pumping away at its sides!

Poor thing, it was a mare and looked half starved, her mane and tail were filthy, a tangled mass of thistles and gorse; no one had thought to take a brush to her, yet she was so kind to the noisy children, just followed wherever they led her. Stopped when they did or walked on when the one holding the rope said *'get on'*.

Anwyn went up to the older and nosiest boy. "Can I look at your cob sonny?"

"Yea, course....she's free year old, broke ta ride'n drive." He stood the cob up straight and yanked the children off her back. "Bugger off" he shouted....and they ran!

Anwyn ran a hand down the cobs legs.

"Sound as a bell she is lady." The young lad had been well drilled in what to say. "Sound as a bell, never been lame in 'er life."

How could this ragged boy, not as old as the twins, have such a good sales pitch she wondered? "Thank you young man" Anwyn muttered.

"OK lady...do you want to 'ave a ride on 'er...I gota saddle."

"No thank you." What *was* she thinking of? Dave would be furious, the boys would fall about laughing; mother on a gypsy pony. A filthy dejected gypsy pony...all black and white patches.....well!

Maybe she was missing Cilla? She had fought so hard to keep her; perhaps she just needed a pony for herself? Dave would understand; maybe.

Too late now!! The auctioneers hammer came down with a bang; Anwyn had just bought her gypsy pony.

Morgan was at the sale and had been watching Anwyn; he edged over to stand beside her. "What's your man going to say to that my dear...due due....not his sort I think"!

Fortunately he had his empty trailer so mother's new purchase was soon on her way to a much better home, followed by Anwyn in the Disco.

"I'll drop her off in the yard my dear. I won't stop for a chat, lots to do before it gets dark...good luck!"

"Thanks so much Morgan, are you sure you won't come in for a cuppa, I know Dave would love to see you."

"No thanks Anwyn. I'll just drop the pony and get on."

The boys had just been dropped off the school bus; they were surprised to see Morgan coming up the drive with his trailer.

"Have you brought the ponies back?" Rhys shouted.

"Oh no no not today boys; been to the sale that's all...can you close the gate for me?...bye."

Dai closed the gate, it was never left open these days. "Why was he here do you think? He asked. Perhaps mum went to the sale as well"

"Yeah...could be" Tomos said as he kicked a stone down the drive, they weren't in any hurry to have to start homework!

"Do you think she bought something?" Tomos said at last.

"Could be" Dai replied, and with a rush all three set off down the drive, round the corner into the yard.

They stopped dead in their tracks. It must be a joke!!! She wouldn't buy *that!* No...it must belong to someone else, she doesn't know any gypsies.

Rhys was the first to laugh, soon followed by his brothers. The cob looked at them with sad eyes. It was black and white and very dirty *and* very thin; it belonged to someone else surely.

"Come in you three and take your uniforms off. Tea in the pot and cake in the tin" Mother seemed quite her usual self, not mad at all.

They were still laughing and jostling each other as they trapped into the kitchen.

"I'll get supper started in a minute, just got something to-do."

"See to your pony first" said a cheeky voice. That set them all laughing again. She wasn't sure which one it was so she flicked her tea towel at the nearest.

It was a golden rule in the family never to be broken; no matter how tired you were always see to your pony first. She had to smile, cheeky little devils!

Dave was back; they all heard the quad bike drive into the yard followed by a long silence! The tension in the kitchen was unbearable, no one spoke, four nervous faces watched the door.

"Bloody hell fire!!" They all heard that.

Tomos could see out of the window. "He's looking at the pony. No, he's coming in."

The boys scrambled to be out of the kitchen while mother gently put down the kettle she was clutching.

BANG the door slammed back.

"What the devil is that thing out there?"

"I bought it."

"I can see that woman...what on earth for?"

"She looked so sad."

"WHAT!"

She looked sad...I felt sorry for her."

Dave slammed the door shut. "Haven't we got enough ponies without buying a thing like that."

"I wanted to help her; I wanted a cob for me! I liked riding your Storm, but he is too big and the boy's are too small.....She's mine and I know she'll be fine. Just needs a bit of loving...So there you have it!"

Dave stood open mouthed. Anwyn never spoke like that to him! He was speechless.

67

"I'll just go and put her in the old stable and settle her down....Teas in the pot..cake in the tin.

Supper was a very quiet affair. The boys kept their heads down and hurried through the meal, excusing themselves early...lots of homework to finish.

Anwyn cleared the dishes in silence. Water splashed into the sink and she attacked the washing up with unusual energy.

Dave lit his pipe and pushed his chair back. "Alright love...you win, but why a piebald?? They'll all laugh if you go hunting on that."

"No Dave...no one will laugh. Under all that hair and dirt is a lovely pony...you'll see; give her six months and you won't recognise her."

"I hope not"

"Don't you see? I didn't realise how much I missed riding 'till I went out on your cob looking for Cilla, but he's too big and strong for me. I saw her in the sale and knew I had to bring her home and give her a chance."

Dave got up and went to his wife slipping an arm round her waist and gave her a hug. "It's OK love, I'm sure your right....she'll make a nice ride for you......just right for an old lady!"

A fistful of soap suds whistled past his ear followed by the washing up mop. She chased him round the kitchen table until he was caught.

"I give in" he said laughing. "I give in." Then with a quick twist mother was in his arms just like a couple of teenagers!

"OK" she said red faced and smiling. "But don't you ever call her a gypsy pony again...promise?"

"Promise" he said with his fingers crossed.

In the morning after the boys had gone to school and all the usual chores had been done, Anwyn set about the new pony. She was certain there was a nice animal under all that muck; the framework all looked good, plenty of bone; she was desperately thin, but good food and a warm stable out of the worst of the weather would soon remedy that. She just needed a lot of TLC.

It took all that day to get her mane and tail restored to something like presentable; each hair was lovingly parted from the tangled mess and brushed down. Anwyn decided her mane was far too long, so several inches had to come off.

That's better she thought, now there was a nice neck line coming, just needs a bit of muscle now, and only time would put that on.

When her tail was washed it was pure white but much too long, so like her main several inches disappeared.

Anwyn eventually stood back with her hands on her hips and surveyed her pony. Not bad she thought, not bad at all.

She gave the pony a hug. "You and I are going to be good friends" she whispered "I can feel it in my bones."

The pony whickered softly and licked her hand. She suddenly noticed the pony's feet had been trimmed. They had been so long and split it caused her to walk badly. It was Dave! He'd said nothing, just went out first thing that morning and did the job. Anwyn would cook him something special for supper this evening and the family could think of a name for her pony. "And if anyone suggests 'Gipsy' they'll feel my hand on their bottom!"

Several names were offered. Patch, Painted Lady, too long, Ugly Duckling, Rhys sat down quickly! And a few other names equally unsuitable.

It was Tomos, quiet, sensible Tom who came up with the winner. "Why not call her 'Magpie? She's black and white just like the bird."

Everyone agreed, it would no doubt be shortened to Maggie or Pie in a few days, but for now she was Magpie.

Mother decided to do nothing with Magpie for at least six months She was so thin and in such poor condition it would take quiet a time for her to pick up; in the mean time she was groomed, and stabled at night. As winter crept in the pony had improved considerably.

Dave stopped calling her a pony; she began to look more like a cob and gradually they all referred to her as Mother's Cob!

Magpie had one more trick that none of the family had expected. She could jump!

69

In early spring Anwyn turned her out in a little paddock on her own. The grass was coming on well in there; she could see the other ponies in the adjoining field so she had company.

Just before it got dark Anwyn went to catch her, the paddock was empty! "Damn...don't say I've lost another!" but just as she started to panic Magpie whinnied to her; she was with the youngsters in the next field. Anwyn clipped the lead rein to her head collar and thankfully walked her down to her stable for the night.

Dave thought the fence must be down somewhere. He would take her down there tomorrow morning and mend it.

True to his word he led Maggie down to her field, closed the gate and started to walk along the hedge, checking the fence as he went.

He was half way round when the youngsters in the other field noticed Magpie was back and started calling her. Maggie pricked her ears, tossed her head, did a mighty buck and cantered across towards the gate between the two fields; she didn't slow down. "Oh bloody hell" exclaimed Dave as she rose up in the air like the bird she was named after, clearing the gate with inches to spare! "Oh my God; Mother was right, she bought a good'en there!"

There was no point in checking further. He stood beside the gate, a good four feet or more of solid oak, and she had cleared it so easily.

He walked slowly back to the house, Anwyn must be told, this was no quiet hack she had bought, Maggie was something special, *very* special. The boys would want her, no doubt about that.

Mother just smiled. "I told you she was special and you all laughed.

SIX

Two years had passed since the awful fire up on the mountain and the disappearance of Cilla and Gemini. Now the family seldom spoke of them, mother sometimes wondered out loud where they had got to, but life had moved on and today Dave and Tomos were having a rare days hunting together.

The meet was miles away at Beulah; it promised to be a good day up in the hills where neither of them had been before. Wild open country where the hounds could run freely; no roads or fences to slow them down.

Tomos had Maggie, he had grown so much in the last two years, and was much too big for Star, so mother reluctantly agreed to let him ride her cob, so long as he stayed with his Dad.

As predicted by Anwyn, her little black and white cob had surprised them all and had matured into a very smart cob. A joy to ride, very light in your hands, responsive and never pulled your arms out, no matter how excited she got and, of course, she could jump!

Tomos, sitting at the window in his tower like bedroom one morning, had seen her leap the gate and canter off to join the other ponies. 'Phew, she made *that* look so easy' he thought. How tall was she now, must be full grown; had she gone over fourteen two hands? If not she was still legally a pony.

He was fourteen now and still had two more years to go in pony classes, and a cob like Maggie could easily carry his weight with no problem; show jumping beckoned Tomos, never mind Pony Club games, that was for little children. No, he had his mind set on winning the jumping classes on his mum's cob! He would suggest it to her when she was in a good mood.

Rhys was also after a ride on Magpie! She might be black and white, that couldn't be helped, but he thought she might be good at dressage. She was very responsive with a lovely action and quick to learn; he could train her with Kate's help. Yes, he would talk to mother about his ideas for Magpie; perhaps she would agree, he really needed a bigger pony.

So mother was quite amused, how their little minds had changed since they first saw *her* cob tied up in the yard, a wet bedraggled pony, half starved and sad.

Now they both wanted to ride her little cob, well, she would think about it, make no promises, just have a think quietly by herself.

So it was with great excitement for one boy and a touch of jealousy for the other that Tom got to go hunting on a glorious autumn morning with his Dad.

There were a great many riders at the meet, Tom was so excited, it promised to be a lot of fun. Some hard riding up on the hills, but fantastic scenery and loads of wild life.

He had tucked his binoculars inside his jacket so if the Red Kites were flying he could have a good look at them and any other wild life that may be visible, even a Golden Eagle! Some had been released up here, near the reservoir last summer.

The field moved off and headed into the woods; hounds were sent ahead followed by the Master. They soon picked up a scent and streamed out of the trees.

"Only ten minutes and they've put up a fox" Dave shouted to his son. "Hold on Tom....here we go!"

Storm leapt forward with Maggie right on his heels. They galloped across the land close to the track, the Field Master trying to keep some sort of order not letting anyone pass him. To catch up with the hounds was a mortal sin; you would be told politely to clear off and go home!

The twins had been hunting since they were small boys and knew the rules.

The hounds were working well and had several good runs of a mile or so, always heading higher and higher up into the hills. After an hour or so the hunt paused for a blow to allow the hounds to rest.

Tomos pulled out his binoculars and scoured the sky; just a few Buzzards and the odd Red Kite wheeling on thermals gradually getting higher. He was watching the Kite, it suddenly dived close to a stand of trees on the horizon. He lost sight of the

Red Kite in the background of gorse bushes, but there were some ponies amongst the trees.

At this distance they all looked really scruffy; they were obviously wild hill ponies. As Tomos watched more came out of the trees, and then another that he hadn't noticed at first, black, practically invisible against the trees.

Tomos watched; it seemed taller than the other ponies and a much finer build. All the ponies stood watching the activity down below.

He was so far away he couldn't see clearly, but he thought it had white socks.

"Dad....have a look at those ponies!" he said grabbing Dave's arm. "Look at the black pony just left of the trees way up there."

Dave wanted to move on; the hounds were on the move trying to pick up a scent. He snatched the glasses from Tom's out stretched hand and looked where Tomos was pointing.

He suddenly became very quiet, fiddled with the focus and looked again.

One of the hounds had picked up a scent and with a roar and a lot of horn blowing the pack streamed after him. The sudden uproar spooked the ponies; as Dave watched the black pony as it trotted away. Four white socks brilliant in the sunshine.

"My God Tom....you've found Cilla!!! And look...that dark grey one following her.....that's Gemini, it's got to be. Well damn me, after all this time. Where are we boy? I've no idea where we are. We'll never catch them, not out here." Dave's mind was racing.

Tomos wanted to laugh, he'd never seen his father so flustered, but it was so good to know the ponies had survived; they must be full grown now, but completely wild.

Dave was still watching Cilla and Gemini. "They'll take a bit of catching after all this time running free; we'll need a lot of help, that's for sure!......Come on son, I've had enough hunting for today, let's go home and tell mother we've found her babies!"

The two cobs were loaded and they set off for home chatting amicably. They couldn't understand how two small foals found their way so far from the farm.

"I reckon I was right, the wild mares took them for their own" Dave said remembering his conversation with Arwyn. "Their foals had been taken from them and they probably heard ours calling!"

Dave called in to tell Morgan the news before driving home. "Run in and tell your mother; I'll unload the cobs."

Tomos was about to run in when he remembered. 'Always see to your pony first'. "No it's alright Dad, after two years another ten minutes won't make any difference."

"You're a good lad Tom; come on then, let's get them unloaded and fed."

Anwyn just didn't believe it. She laughed, cried, wiped her eyes and cried again. She danced Tomos around the kitchen table, then Dave.

"We're hungry mother! What's for tea?" Dave asked as he relaxed into his favourite chair. Life was back to normal.

It took a lot of organising; pens had to be made and as many neighbours as possible had to be persuaded to join the round up before the two ponies were caught.

No one seemed to know who owned the 'wild herd', so Dave released them back into the hills.

SEVEN

Cilla and Gemini had grown as wild as a pair of rabbits. Anwyn was so dismayed, she thought Cilla would remember her and be glad she was home again; the pair of them just wouldn't settle down.

One morning, determined to get close to Cilla, mother went into their stable. Gemini panicked and shot across the pen followed by Cilla; both ponies were dashing round and round. Anwyn found herself pressed up against the gate.

"You'd better come out mother" said a quiet voice behind her. Dai opened the gate just enough for her to squeeze out. "You OK? You shouldn't have gone in there yet, they're still pretty wild."

"I know Dai, but I do so want to catch Cilla again, she used to be so friendly; I don't understand how she's got *so* wild. They certainly both looked wild, ears flat and eyes showing white with fear.

"She'll come back to you mum, just give her a bit of time; they've had a rough couple of days being rounded up and losing their friends up there. She'll come to you soon, you see."

Dai was good with animals, quiet and gentle but strong if he needed to be. Dave said he would miss him if he went away to college; 'my right hand man' he called him. He could do the work of any grown man, quicker and more efficiently than most.

College was a threat lurking at the back of Dave's mind, the boy had brains and it would be a pity to waste that gift. Farming was changing so fast these days; two years away from home and he would learn so much about other aspects of farming. On the other hand he had spoken about being a vet. A five year course if he manages to get *exemplary* exam results. A lot to think about for the young lad.

Dai decided to do something about the wild ponies in the barn! He had a theory that had worked with Glory when she was young and frisky; he managed to calm her down so tomorrow he would start to educate Cilla. Gemini would follow Cilla, so she wasn't going to be a problem.

75

He half filled a bucket with pony nuts and a chopped up apple, pushed a bale of straw just inside their stable and sat on it with the bucket between his knees. Cilla and Gemini panicked, and stuck their heads in the corner as far from Dai as possible.

He sat there quietly, occasionally stirring the nuts; their ears working overtime, listening.

Cilla was the first to break the spell and move; she turned her head and had a quick look at Dai. Then just as quickly turned back. He smiled "Come on then" he said quietly, "Come on Cilla my girl...come on then." No movement from either of them. "You must come to me" he shook the bucket. "I'm not coming to you"

He sat there for most of the morning. Once or twice Gemini or Cilla turned to look at Dai, but neither could summon up enough courage to come for the nuts.

After supper he told Anwyn he would take the feed to the two ponies. They were still scared but were soon at the feed troughs. He was sure they would come to him tomorrow.

Dai was back with the bucket after breakfast. This time, although the ponies dashed to the corner, they turned to look at him. That's better, a little step forward he thought. They raised their heads and sniffed the air...pony nuts and apples, but what else?

Curiosity was getting the better of Cilla; she stamped the ground, the boy didn't move, just sat quietly on the straw bale.

She stamped again and pawed the ground, tossing her head; still he didn't move.

Any minute now thought Dai. Any minute now and she'll come to me....... And she did!

Carefully, step by step and with a lot of head tossing she gradually got closer to the bucket. Dai didn't dare move; he sat there waiting for Cilla to have the courage to start eating the nuts.

Gemini stood close behind her watching with her enormous black eyes. She really was very pretty and almost brave enough to walk up to Dai and sniff his boots; maybe tomorrow!

Cilla emptied the bucket, licked up the last crumbs and gently sniffed the hands holding the bucket.

76

Dai wanted to move, to leap up and shout for joy, instead he had to hold his breath and keep so still, any sudden movement now would undo all the hours sitting on this bale waiting for the ponies to relax and come to him.

Finally, after what seemed a lifetime, Cilla turned away and walked back to the corner. Dai could breathe again! He got to his feet and stretched; Cilla watched from the safety of the corner. They watched each other, the boy looked harmless. He smiled "You're not *so* wild Cilla are you."

Gradually over the next few weeks she responded quickly and would walk up to Dai, stand still while he put her headcaller on.

Gemma was easy, she simply followed Cilla's lead and did whatever she did; two educated for the price of one!

Dai had asked his mother not to go into the stable until he was ready. She agreed, he was up to something that was for sure.

Anwyn found out on Christmas morning when Dai proudly gave his mother her lovely Cilla back; quiet, well balanced and groomed to perfection! She hugged him and then Cilla. What a wonderful surprise. What a wonderful Christmas present.

The Grandparents arrived in the morning to a kitchen full of delicious smells. The turkey had been in the oven since seven and looked scrumptious.

Dave made coffee, but before they could sit down to enjoy it they were dragged out to the barn to see the 'renovated' Cilla!

No one could believe it was the same pony that had arrived terrified just a few weeks ago. Dai was congratulated over and over again.

He got quite embarrassed, said it was nothing but patience really; but inside he was so proud, as pleased as punch. A job well done.

Christmas day was wonderful, everyone was in high spirits; the turkey was delicious and Grans Christmas pudding, brought to the table flaming in the old tradition, cream poured on each portion went down a treat.

After lunch and having consumed two bottles of wine, everyone retired to the front room and flopped down into armchairs or the sofa.

Dave had cleared the inglenook earlier and today a huge log fire burned in the hearth; no ordinary log fire, each log was about three feet long and would burn all-day and night.

Grandpa was the first to fall asleep, too much wine and Christmas pudding, together with the smell of apple logs burning in the hearth! Perhaps he was dreaming when he was a young lad playing in this self same room, under the Christmas tree that reached from floor to ceiling, laden with sweets and presents, just as it was today. Some things never changed and a family get together at Christmas was something they all looked forward to.

The local hunt was meeting on Boxing Day in the town square. All the family, mum Dad and the three boys, all wore their best riding clothes. With the hunt in their red coats it was a lovely sight, every one well mounted.

Mother was as excited as the boys. Maggie looked a picture now that she had stopped growing and filled out, Anwyn was rightly proud of her.

Elonwy would have joined them given half a chance, she used to love hunting in her younger days, but thankfully there were no more cobs available, so Mansel drove her to the meet in the Land Rover to cheer the riders on their way, then back to the farm to prepare a meal ready for the family who were sure to be starving after a day riding up on Eppynt mountain.

The winter had been cold with a lot of snow, but early in the New Year prospects looked good. The twins were doing well at school Tomos had won a prize for his art work and Rhys was a member of the junior rugby team, they enjoyed school and worked hard.

Dai, now in the sixth form and a school prefect, had a great deal of homework to contend with every night and was often still at it when he should have been in bed. However he always insisted on helping his Dad in the yard when he got home from college, mother felt sorry for him, he looked so tired, but he was young and as strong as a bull, so she assumed he could cope.

EIGHT

At the end of January Dave decided to sell the store cattle, there were only a few young bullocks, fat enough for market, but costing more to feed than they were worth. The price wasn't good at the moment, but the farm had to make money, so he made up his mind, they had to go.

As soon as there was a decent weather forecast Dave wanted to bring his hill sheep down into the big sheep shed. They were due to start lambing in a few weeks. The boys would ride their ponies up on the hill to find them, then he would take the dogs and bring them quietly in. That was the plan, every year it was the same, it rarely worked, but the boys were older now and a bit more sensible!

This weekend looked promising, a sharp frost clearing early then clear skies all day.

The boys were up early and out on their ponies as soon as it was light enough to see. They knew roughly where the sheep would be, they had been fed in the same area every day since the weather closed in and with luck they would be grazing in the same place.

It was a lovely morning for a ride up into the hills, there was a fair amount of frost but the heather made the going soft. The ponies were skittish having been in stables for most of the week and were enjoying the outing.

It wasn't long before Dave came chugging along on the Quad bike shouting at his dogs, Mitzie sitting in the carrier, the two collies running beside them.

The boys soon found the sheep and gradually they got them in a group and heading down the hill,

Dave saw them coming and waited with the dogs until they were a reasonable way down the hill. The dogs could also see the sheep and were anxious to get to work.

"Away" said Dave, and they flew up the hill, Mitzie outrunning the other two easily, and got behind the sheep. They knew exactly what to do, they didn't really need Dave.

79

Quickly the two collies took up positions one on either side of the sheep and without any fuss the hundred or so sheep trotted down the hill. Sometimes an awkward ewe would dash off in the opposite direction taking half the flock with her. The dogs would have to work hard to get them all together again, but today it looked as if things were going well.

The boys followed the flock keeping a good distance behind and keeping a sharp lookout for any strays. Most of the ewes looked heavy in lamb.

Dai loved watching the collies work, they were so quick. If a sheep strayed, they would have the runaway back with the flock in no time! Mitzie moved like lightning, back and forth, back and forth keeping, the flock moving, not hurrying them but not allowing any to stop and graze. It was days like this that he knew he would miss if he went away to college next year.

Dave went on ahead to open gates safe in the knowledge that the sheep were in safe hands and would arrive down at the farm quite soon.

Sunday was not going to be a day of rest! The team sorted through the ewes, pregnant ones in one pen, barren ewes in another and the 'don't knows' in another. It took all day and they all smelt like sheep in the end!

Monday was market day in Brecon. Dave had sorted out some fat lambs which he loaded into the trailer early, the market would be busy and if he wanted to get the best price he would have to get there early while the dealers still had fat wallets and hadn't already bought their quota for the day.

The lambs sold well so he was happy! He celebrated with a cup of coffee and a bacon roll in the market cafe. He sat down with some old farmer friends and learnt some *very* disturbing news, something that made his blood run cold and put him off his bacon roll.

Somewhere in the midlands one of the lorry drivers had heard there was an outbreak of foot and mouth!

So far there was no confirmation by the ministry, but it would only be a day or two before the whole of England Wales and Scotland would be on the alert. The chatter and good humour usually found in the market was subdued. Everyone there a farmer and most *livestock* farmers whose very future depended on their stock. Their entire stock could be wiped out; a signature on a sheet of paper by a ministry vet was all that was needed to destroy a farmer's livelyhood!

Every animal, cloven hooved, sick or not on the affected farm *and* farms within a certain distance would have to be slaughtered, the carcasses burnt.

Was it just a malicious rumour started by an idiot? His mind was in turmoil as he drove home. If it wasn't!.....Well.....he couldn't think what might happen. The disease spreads like wildfire and there was no cure that he was aware of.

He was driving slower and slower the more he thought about it. Suddenly he was startled by someone blowing their horn right behind him. '*What now*' he thought. It was Morgan climbing out of his Land Rover.

"You all right Dave, you were wandering all over the road, thought maybe you were not well."

"No...not really Morgan. Just heard a nasty rumour at the market and it got me thinking. Didn't see you there."

"Yea, I was for a bit, just having a nosey round. So what's the rumour?"

"Foot and mouth in England!"

"Dieu dieu"

"One of the lorry drivers said it was two or three days ago that it was found somewhere."

"Not confirmed yet?" now Morgan was sounding worried.

"If it's true we'll hear soon enough....trouble is that lorry could well bring it down here on its wheels!"

"Best I get my sheep down off the hill then, they'll have to go in the barn."

"I'll be over and give you a hand, let me get my dogs first."

"Thanks Dave...bring Mitzie, my Badger is too old to be of much use these days." He went back to his vehicle muttering and shaking his head.

Poor old boy, thought Dave, he didn't have many sheep and only a few acres of grass, how he managed to survive up there nobody knew. His farm was really remote only a track leading to it a good four miles passed Sibertswold.

81

The twins just loved the old man. They would often ride over to see him. Anwyn usually sent a cake and vegetables with them. Morgan would light his pipe and tell them tales about his life up there on the hill when he was their age.

Dave drove into the yard and called out to Anwyn that he was going over to see Morgan, "He needs a bit of help" was all he said; no point in worrying her yet.

"Mitzie come." She came rushing up and jumped up onto the quad bike. "Rob...Moss." The two collies ran alongside as he set off to Morgans.

What on earth would he do if foot and mouth got into Wales. It might be here already. I should be checking my flock not going to get Morgan's mixed bunch of ewes down he thought, but you had to help each other in times like this. Help Morgan and then go back for his own sheep and hope to God it was only a rumour; if not he dare not think about the future.

That night Dave an Anwyn watched the late news on the BBC. It was confirmed.

Foot and mouth at a farm in the Midlands confirmed, Ministry of Agriculture regulations are enforced. Any movement of sheep, cattle, pigs and goats strictly forbidden!

"Too bloody late" said Dave. "They've had at least three days to do that. The disease could have spread anywhere by now."

It was lucky they had managed to sell all the store cattle and a few fat lambs that morning. It might well be the last sale he would ever make.

Sure enough, as each day passed, more outbreaks were reported; it was spreading so fast countrywide no one could relax. A farm near Wrexham was quarantined and soon followed with outbreaks along the Welsh border; any day now it would be in Wales.

Farmers received mail from the Ministry Of Agriculture to place something in their gateways that they could soak in disinfectant so that vehicles entering and leaving must drive through it, and all vehicles must have wheels thoroughly washed, before leaving the property.

When these instructions were pushed through Dave's letter box he thought the end of his farming life was near. All he could do was keep checking his flock every day and pray!

He had well over two hundred ewes in two barns and seven prize winning rams in a separate building. Anwyn helped push them through the crush; it took all day scanning each sheep for the telltale signs.

Now the area around Brecon was affected. Farmers were taking every possible precaution as instructed, but nothing stopped the spread of its tentacles into every valley and up every hill.

The ministry vets were everywhere in their white coats, but the outbreak was so invasive that local practices were asked to help. Any farm found with just one infected animal was quickly quarantined and all live stock on that farm slaughtered, taken away and incinerated.

Anwyn and Dave were going frantic. The boys were unable to get to school because the bus wasn't running. They couldn't go by car; the police were stopping unessential movement of vehicles. It was a total shut down, yet still the disease clawed its way over the neighbourhood, catching up with Dave in the last week of February. Morgan was hit within a day of Sibertswold being quarantined.

Dave reported one ewe with the signs and by mid day two more. The vets arrived that afternoon in their white coats and yellow boots.

All his commercial flock, the sheep that lived out on the hill would have to be shot, only four were showing signs of foot and mouth.

The vets wanted to inspect his prize flock of Beaulas in the shed at the other end of the yard, but Dave, almost insane with worry locked the doors and threatened them with his shot gun. "You'll not shoot my Beaulas....we've bred this flock for a hundred year or more....you'll not come in here and shoot perfectly healthy sheep!"

The ministry men backed off. "We'll have to contact our superior officer."

"Clear off, the lot of you...you've done enough damage for one day...clear off!" He knew they would be back the next morning but he wasn't giving up his prize flock without a damned good fight.

Elonwy and Mansel tried to get up to them to help in any way they could, but the police turned them back at the end of the lane. "There's a mad man with a twelve bore at the farm sir."
"Rubbish...he's my son" Elonwy was getting angry.
"Sorry....he may be, but I still can't let you through."

The white coats and yellow boots arrived early. Dave was waiting.
Anwyn and the boys hid in the house.
The leader of the white coat brigade came to speak to Dave who was standing, gun in hand outside the Beaula shed.
"Good morning Mr Griffith. We don't want any trouble sir, but we have to do our job. An officer from the ministry will be here to speak with you later about your other sheep; he'll be here soon. We'll get on and deal with the infected flock. So sorry sir." He walked away and very soon Dave heard the pop pop of the humane killers doing their work in his barns.
Mother closed the old wooden shutters on the kitchen windows to stop the boys looking out and the noise of the killing coming in. The volume of the tele was turned up. Homework for the boys had been arranged by phone, so they had plenty to occupy their minds. Half term started next week so the school would be closed anyway.

Dave sat waiting outside the shed that held his future for the *important* man to arrive. He couldn't make himself go anywhere near the sheep sheds where carcases were being stacked up to be loaded into lorries and taken to Eppynt mountain.
Contractors had dug massive pits many yards long. Old wooden railway sleepers placed in the bottom and set alight. Thousands upon thousands of carcases were incinerated up there, just a very small fraction were Dave's sheep.
He got up and went to talk to the ponies to try and relax. Storm always wanted attention, nothing like a good brushing. The others were much the same and he found it was relaxing, just being near them.

84

Anwyn brought him a cup of coffee and a bun, he put the twelve bore down. "You OK love?"

"Yeah...Just been talking to the ponies...calmed me down a bit. Where's this bloody ministry man?"

As if on cue a shiny, very new, Range Rover drove down into the yard!

"Stop there!" He shouted as he stood up grabbing the gun.

Anwyn dashed back to the kitchen as an elderly man climbed out of the Range Rover; he wore the white coat and yellow boots of everyone who came visiting these days, however this ministry man put on a bowler hat!

Dave had to smile. Some years ago when he was just starting in `farming, it was the latest idea to get cows in calf quickly using 'artificial insemination'. A ministry vet would call to do the job usually wearing a spotless white coat and a bowler hat. 'The bull with a bowler hat' farmers called them!

"Mr Griffith...good to meet you." He came forward hand outstretched.

Dave caught off guard quickly pointed the gun at the ground and shook his hand. "Mornin" he muttered not knowing what to expect next.

The ministry man had a brief case full of forms he started to thumb through. "I hear you had a spot of bother yesterday?" He eyed the twelve bore. "Let's see if we can sort something out in a sensible way shall we?"

Dave grunted.

"Now David...may I call you David? Good. Now David, I see from my list you have over a hundred pedigree Beulah Speckled Face sheep here?" He eyed the closed doors behind Dave.

"I have...and you're not getting anywhere near them. They're all one hundred percent fit and well."

"Yes yes I understand that....but I have to be sure. Don't you see, before I can go into the case further."

Dave reluctantly unlocked the door and slid it open. One hundred and thirty ewes looked up expectantly. Beautiful, fat, healthy pampered sheep in prime condition.

The ministry man was visibly impressed.

"You'll not go in 'till I'm sure you're not carrying anything nasty on your lovely yellow boots." He was just beginning to

85

enjoy this conversation. "Now sir, do we wash the boots or have you seen enough?"

"I'm sorry Mr Griffith....sorry David....please try to understand. I *have* to look at them. I can't help you unless I am certain, completely and *absolutely* certain, they are *all* fit."

"Wash your boots in the bin then and we'll go in."

Boots washed to Dave's satisfaction he led 'Ministry' in.

"On this side I have the barren ewes" they were all munching quietly on the hay. "In the middle pens are the pregnant ewes; singles in the first row, twin lambers in the second. Against the far wall are the yearlings, they should be ready to show soon, or go to the sheep sales in the autumn. Would you like to see the rams....they're at the far end."

Dave marched him down the spotless aisle between the pens; he was at a loss for words. Six magnificent rams stood up as they approached. "These six are the finest Beulah rams you will find anywhere in England or Wales!" He stood back, his tour complete, he had done his best.

Ministry man was busy writing on his clip board. "Have you any records of their breeding I can look at David?" He wasn't so sure of himself now, just groping for a loophole.

"I have records going back best part of a hundred years. You will have to come to my office." Off marched Dave a bit more confident now. "Wash your boots if you don't mind." He said as they approached the back door.

He led Ministry man through the kitchen. "Take those boots off, I've just swept up in the hallway." Anwyn said in her sternest voice!

Ministry pulled his lovely yellow boots off as quickly as he could, he'd heard about these Welsh farmers' wives, tough as old boots, and he wasn't going to upset this one.

The boys were still sitting round the table studying their school work started yesterday. They looked at each other and tried not to giggle!

"Here Dai, take the gun, don't let anyone near the Beulhas."

"No Dave you shouldn't ask him." Said Anwyn "Sit down Dai."

"Sorry mum." He snatched up the gun and ran out. He knew it wasn't loaded, Dad had run out of cartridges last time they went shooting; he'd been fooling these people all day! Good old Dad.

Dave took Ministry man into the farm office, a lovely bright room looking out over the garden. The walls were lined with shelves holding all Dave's books about the breeding of his flock going back many, many years.

Old photos of his Grandfather showing sheep eighty years ago or so, more recently of his father showing at the Royal Welsh. Photos of Dai taken last summer with a champion ewe and one of three generations, Dave, Grandpa and Dai with a winning progeny group.

Cilla was up there on the wall as well, the best Welsh Section A foal; she had also earned her place on the wall of honour!

Dave was in his element, this was his office, neat and tidy, everything in its place. "Now....stock records....how far would you like to go back, ten, fifty or more years?" He tapped each folder as he asked.

Mr Ministry was overwhelmed, he'd been in countless farm offices since this foot and mouth had started and had never seen one so well organised as this.

"I'm very impressed David." He waved at the shelves of records. "And your wonderful sheep housing, spotless. I can't find fault with anything, congratulations. Let's get this dreadful business over and done with." He pulled out masses of forms from his brief case. "I can't promise anything, but in truly special cases, where the very best stock are under threat not yet infected, *and* you can prove that you have always bred to improve the breed...only then in exceptional cases, can I waive slaughter of the herd......you can keep your Beulah's provided they remain healthy. The farm will remain under quarantine for at least eight weeks. Stay clear for that long....I think you'll be safe."

"Thank you Mr....I don't think I caught your name?"

"Roberts."

"Thanks Mr Roberts, would you like a cup of tea after all that?"

"Please, that would be appreciated."

"Anwyn" Dave shouted. "Cup of tea for us please; to *almost* celebrate!"

87

"This is an awful business David. I have to see so many farmers to try and explain what has to happen and why. Your close neighbour Mr Morgan, he was beside himself. There was nothing I could do for him. Between you and me David, I increased the number of sheep he had killed to give him a bit more compensation He's so old, I really felt for him!"

"That was very good of you. He must be in his eighties you know. We keep a look out for him; our boys ride over to see him often. I'll pop over when all this is done with."

Dave walked Mr Roberts back to his brand new Range Rover. "Goodbye and thank you, it's a very big relief. Dai bring me the gun please." He opened the breach...two empty barrels. "It was never loaded!"

"I'll not let on." He said as he drove off.

Dave was about to go back indoors when the dead meat lorry arrived. He showed the driver where to go, signed the necessary forms and he drove to the barns to load his slaughtered commercial flock. All going because four sheep were showing signs of this dreadful disease. They would get compensation, but that didn't sugar the pill.

They would have a family discussion tonight to discuss the future. It would concern all of them in one way or another, they weren't out of danger yet, after all they hadn't lost everything like poor old Morgan, he had nothing left but his cottage and his old dog.

After supper mother cleared the table and Dave brought the farm accounts in from his office. He called the boys down from their various rooms, put clean sheets of paper and pencils on the table.

He tried to make sense of what their assets would be now the main income had disappeared. The Beaula sheep were, with luck safe, and could bring in an income if he sold more than he had planned, keeping the very best reducing the size of the flock by about a half.

With fewer sheep grazing they could make a lot more hay; weather permitting good hay always sold well if made with the sun on it.

So far things weren't looking too bad on paper, but in reality things might be quite different. It depended on the Beulahs staying healthy and a long dry summer for haymaking!

Saving the farm was the top priority it had been in the family for several generations and with three boys one of them would surely take it on eventually.

He asked mother if she had any bright ideas? "We could keep a lot more chickens; sell more eggs."

"Good idea...but the initial outlay for houses and wire for their runs might cost too much don't you think?.....We'll look into that."

Then there were the ponies. Rhys and Tomos had outgrown their ponies and had for some time realised that their little friends would have to go to new homes.

Star would fetch a good price being well known in the pony club world. Anwyn smiled, she was remembering the first time she had watched Tom and Star at the county show. Now he was captain of their team and short listed to ride for Wales, but as he said, he was too big and heavy for Star and without his ever willing partner he was nothing, just another boy rider. Yes, they could sell Star.

She went down on Dave's list of assets.

Rhys felt guilty now about Merlin. They'd been partners for eight years, but, like his brother, he too was too big and heavy for the pony. So Merlin went on the list next to Star.

As promised, the boys had been bought a cob foal each. Not old enough to ride yet, but in a year or so they would be ready to break in. Mother would let them ride Magpie for the time being, and Dai, feeling guilty, said they could borrow Glory if and when he went away to college in the autumn.

The twins were very grateful, the two cobs would suit them very well and they promised to be careful.

Now the kitchen was silent waiting for mother to add to Dave's list of assets. She had some lovely section A ponies in the bottom paddock. Quite a few youngsters that could go to Fayre Oak sale in September and make good money. One in particular that would make heaps.... Cilla! Could she...would she part with the lovely Cilla?

Dave sucked the end of his pencil waiting.

89

"Mother.....what about your ponies? There are twenty or so out there."

"I know Dave, I know.....we can't keep all of them......the only sensible thing to do is sell them, they should make good money. Most would make lovely kids ponies."

"And Cilla?"

She hesitated, wiped her eyes, blew her nose, got up from the table. "And Cilla" She said and hurried out of the kitchen.

After the family meeting and a check on the assets, it seemed they could just scrape through this awful year. Everyone would have to keep spending to an absolute minimum. There was just enough left in the kitty for mother to buy some hens. The boys got busy building fox proof runs for them.

The ministry vet came every week to check the Beulah's; they all remained stubbornly fit.

After two anxious months the area was declared free of the virus and life began to return to near normality.

Most of their local farming friends had suffered badly but had survived. Some had to diversify doing farm holidays or B&B, others rented their land for grazing until they could afford to restock.

Anwyn and Dave worried about Morgan; he lost all his sheep, everything he got up for every day was gone. He never went out even though the restrictions had been lifted.

Dave or Anwyn would drive over to see him once or twice a week now. He seemed to grow older and feebler at each visit. Usually he would be sitting in the sun with Badger by his side, both asleep or just gazing out at his empty fields.

The year that had started so badly ground on with only the slightest glimmer of hope. Would Anwyn be able to sell her young ponies well at the Fayre Oak sales in September?

Cilla was taken to as many of the biggest shows as they could get to without driving long distances, keeping cost down. She was a three year old, fully mature and in first class condition, winning Junior Champion at five shows in South Wales, including the Royal Welsh for the second time.

A Fayre Oak auctioneer came to see them soon after Anwyn had posted the entry forms for all her ponies, including Cilla, off to them. He suggested, as there were so many ponies she had entered, they should be entered as a group at the end of the first day's sale. A 'Reduction of Sibertswold Stud' he thought would be an attractive title.

The overseas buyers would still be there for the second day, and with Cilla highlighted on the front cover of the catalogue, prices for Sibertswold ponies would soar, he thought!

Anwyn was delighted the auctioneer had taken such an interest in her ponies, and soon sorted out some photos of her best for him to take back to Hereford.

The foals and yearlings had to be taught good manners, which kept Anwyn and the boys very busy over the next few months. The better they behaved in the sale ring the better price they would make, so every day the ponies were led around the little paddock, walking and trotting, learning!

Early one morning, Dave and Anwyn were feeding the sheep and hens. The boys had just left for school, when a gun shot rang out followed a few minutes later by another. Who could be shooting on the hill this time of day thought Dave? 'Oh God'.........

"Stay here Anwyn!!" He shouted as he dashed for the quad bike and raced off up the hill. He had an awful premonition, but couldn't accept it, surely not, he prayed, surely not.

He raced down the track to Morgans cottage.....he was too late! He had shot Badger and then himself.

Dave rushed to his old friend and sat him upright on his favourite bench. He was barely conscious.

"So quiet Dave.....Nothing left"

"Oh Morgan" Dave whispered.

"You're a good man Dave" he croaked......then he was gone.

Dave put his hat back on his head and straightened his grubby jacket.

He looked so peaceful sitting in the sun, his old dog lying beside him.

"Damn! Damn! Damn!" Dave shouted and wept at the passing of his old friend. Foot and mouth had claimed yet another victim.

A few weeks later Dave received a mysterious letter from a solicitor in Brecon asking him to call in at his earliest convenience. No one had any idea what it could be about.

He hadn't been in any trouble, no parking fines outstanding, income tax not paid, so he made an appointment and went, somewhat nervously, to see the solicitor.

It turned out that his old friend Morgan who had committed suicide after losing everything as a result of the foot and mouth epidemic, had left everything to Dave and Anwyn.

They decided they would keep the cottage and modernise it.

Finally Anwyn agreed the ponies were all ready for sale,,,and good luck to them.

About this time across the border in England, there was a lot of interest in the forth coming Fayre Oak sale, especially about a Sibertswold pony. Events were taking a turn which would affect Cilla's future

NINE

The day started early in Lambourn. This was racing country and the village was bursting with small men and large horses, in fact the horses outnumbered the humans by about five to one! Pampered and cosseted, these were the aristocrats of the horse world; nothing was thought to be too good for them. They lived a life of luxury, more so than the army of youngsters and bandy old men who cared for them so lovingly.

On the outskirts of this village was a trainer called Pat O'Rourke. He had a small yard of thirty race horses. Nothing compared with some of the more famous yards who could boast of over one hundred horses in training.

Pat was good at his job and ran a happy yard, all his lads worked well and everything ran smoothly.

His daughter Sue ran the house and took care of her Dad, she also had a few stables away from the racing yard where she broke in youngsters, yearlings and two year olds before they took their place in the racing game.

At six in the morning Sue was already in the kitchen a mug of steaming tea in her hand. She could see the lights were on in the yard and some lads scurrying about.

It was Sunday and only half the usual staff would be on duty.

The horses also had a days' rest, no training gallops, just a quiet day in their stables. They were all fed, groomed and the stables cleaned out before the head lad would let the lads go, to be back again for evening stables. Same routine, groom, feed, clean out stables, put down clean straw, fill hay nets, check rugs were on straight, and wait for the Gov' to do his evening rounds. Then, all being well, off they would go, either to the pub or back to the hostel for supper.

The routine never changes, race days or not. Except on Sundays when owners often chose to come and admire their horses and have a chat with Pat or the lad looking after their horse.

Today Sue's least favourite owner was calling to see Silver Serpent, his useless chaser. The horse was well bred and had at one time been good at the game. Since then he had fallen a few times and lost interest in racing. The owner had bought the horse

93

at Ascot sales, someone had seen him coming with his big fat wallet and pushed the price up far beyond it's real value!

Now Sue's father must try to get Serpent back on the race track, fit and willing to run, a hard job.

The owner was besotted with the grey horse, sure a miracle would happen and he would soon be leading in a winner at Cheltenham. Unfortunately that was unlikely to happen, but as her Dad said the man pays his bills promptly at the end of each month and so he must try to make his dreams come true.

Sue disliked the man, he was rude and arrogant, treating everyone like idiots. He drove a brand new Range Rover and was always dripping with gold, two or three gold chains of various thickness round his neck, gold bracelets on both wrists and rings on nearly every finger.

The lads all thought he must have come into a lot of money fairly recently. The general feeling was that he was as crooked as a bent pin and had come by his wealth illegally!

However he paid his bills and was generous to the lad who looked after Serpent, always a twenty pound note pressed into his hand after a visit. The lad wouldn't hear anything against his owner and looked forward to the next visit.

In the morning another owner just dropped in to see his horse, it had run at Newton Abbot yesterday and had come a creditable second, he was thrilled and just called in to see the horse and leave Pa a bottle of Glenfiddich. He was gone in half an hour, the sort of owner Sue liked!

At two o'clock Mr 'money bag' Briggs arrived, complete with wife and two children. Oh dear, thought Sue, small children running riot around the yard was not a good idea, race horses were highly strung and one or two of them were likely to bite given half a chance, it could end in disaster.

Mrs Briggs carefully got out of the Rover, the first time Sue had seen her. A small stout woman, very high heels, pointed toes, a red mini-skirt showing fat thighs and a black fur jacket, probably mink. Lots of makeup, dyed blond hair and of course lots of gold jewellery.

Just what you'd expect thought Sue. *'Be polite, they're customers and they pay their bill on time'*. "Hello...how nice to see you all".

The children looked down their noses at Sue. "Where's me Dad's 'orse then?" asked the little boy. "Which one o' these old nags is ours?" They ran off round the yard jumping up at the doors and tapping the startled horses on the nose. "'Ere 'e is" shouted the boy catching sight of the grey horse. "Get 'im out girl..I wanna ride!"

Thankfully Mr Briggs caught hold of the boy before he came to any harm. "Dead keen 'e is 'aint ya William?"

William was looking furious and poked his tongue out at Sue.

"Dad won't be long Mr Briggs, he's just on the phone". Said Sue.

"OK darlin' we don' mind waiting". The children were off again. "I wanna word wiv you luv when the kids arn' around", he led Sue by the elbow into an empty stable.

She was about to scream when Briggs pushed the Fayre Oaks catalogue into her hands. "Ere look at this, be quick while they're not about. I wan'you to buy me that pony on the cover!"

Sue gasped. "Mr Briggs I don't buy ponies". She looked at the cover again....a really striking pony...**'Sibertswold Cilla. Five times Junior Champion this summer'**. It said in bold letters. "I wan' that pony for me lit'le girl, for Christmas. So you go to that sale an' buy it for me".

"It will be very expensive".

"Money don' ma'er...I wan' that pony, supposed to be the best in Wales, well, only the bests good enough for me li'le girl. You go an' buy it!"

Fortunately Pat arrived with the head lad, he looked surprised to find Mr Briggs in the empty stable with Sue.

"Just a bit o' private business Pat...now, where's me lovely Serpent, 'ows 'e doin' then?" Calm as you like he switched on the charm and walked away with Pat. "I'll be in touch" he called over his shoulder.

"Yes,,,OK". What *had* she let herself in for?

Mrs Briggs having lost interest in the horses was making her way back to the Range Rover. She was having trouble walking over the cobbled yard in four inch heels towing her reluctant daughter.

Sue went to her rescue. "Here let me help" and she put her arm round her flabby waist.

"Thanks luv...I shouldn't 'ave wor' these shoes, not for this job, but we've gota go to Marlborough to look at a school for William".

"Do you mean Marlborough College?"

"Yea, do ya know it luv...is it any good, he needs a good school...got'a learn to talk proper has our Will".

Sue swallowed hard. "I believe it's very expensive".

"Yea , well that don't mean nothin' these days. Where's me old man. We gota get goin".

Sue helped Mrs Briggs into the car. "Come on Lizzie ..get in".

"I 'aint seen Dad's 'orse", pouted a little edition of her mother. "I wanna see the 'orse".

There was no sign of Mr Briggs or her Dad, so she wasn't about to be rescued. "Come on then!" she grabbed Lizzie's hand. "I'll show you your Dad's horse".

The small girl trotted happily beside Sue. "You got'a 'orse then?"

"Yes...I've got a horse, her name's Flicker".

"Is she as big as me Dads 'orse?"

"Yes just about".

"I like 'orses!"

Sue looked down at the child; maybe she wasn't so bad after all. "Here we are , this is your Dad's horse, what do you think of him?" She ushered the small girl into the stable.

"Blimey! Ee aint 'alf big" surprise written all over the little girl's face.

With one swift movement she swung Lizzie up onto the horses back. "How's that then Lizzie?"

The child giggled with delight. "I 'aint ever sat on a 'orse 'afore...ees lovely", she patted Serpents neck. "'Ees really lovely 'aint ee?"

Sue smiled; the little girl was in heaven. "'Ees lovely", she kept repeating.

Serpent standing at seventeen hands was the tallest horse in the yard, yet little Lizzie was quite happy sitting on his back!

"Lizzie where you gone?...we gota go" a shriek from her mother.

Sue helped Lizzie down. "I gota go" she said reluctantly. She hugged Serpents leg, the only part of him she could reach. "I love you big 'orse, I love you" she whispered and was gone.

"Thank you" she shouted back at Sue. "Thank you big 'orse".

The Range Rover sped out of the yard, a little girl waving furiously. "Bye" she shouted but she wasn't waving at Sue but at her 'big 'orse.

"You've made a friend there Sue!" laughed her Dad.

"Yes haven't I!" she smiled. Maybe she would go to Wales to buy that lovely pony after all.

True to his word Mr Briggs was on the phone a few days later. He would send a cheque already signed by him with a covering letter from his bank to the auctioneers, so that the cheque would be accepted , all Sue had to do was fill in the amount.

"You do know it will be very expensive Mr Briggs, probably over a thousand pounds?"

"Just buy it girl...don' ma'er what it costs, I want that pony!"

Sue agreed she would go to the Fayre Oak Sale and come back with the pony, no matter what it cost.

"Eer, before I go, what ya done to me little girl, she 'ant stopped talking about my Serpent since we got 'ome...did she really sit on 'im?"

"Yes Mr Briggs, she really did sit on your horse. She's a lovely kid. Bye now".

By the end of the week she had got a stable ready for the pony. She managed to bribe one of the lads to give it a coat of white paint and mend the broken door. Some clean straw and all would be ready.

The stable was in her own little yard where she had two yearlings she was working on for her Dad. These were the old stables that originally went with the house but had been replaced by the racing yard with its lovely wooden stable blocks and plans for another thirty when funds permitted.

Sue loved the old stables; the walls were made of stone and were at least two feet thick. She also had a stone barn and a food shed set high up on straddle stones to make sure it stayed free of vermin. Her Jack Russell. Patch, lived in the food store just in case a clever rat worked out a way of getting in!

The following Saturday she would take the small two-horse box lorry to Builth Wells and enjoy a day at the Fayre Oak Sales. Her Dad said she must take the head lad with her, he didn't like the idea of her walking about all day with a blank cheque in her pocket, not everyone at the sales were as honest as they might be!

Briggs had offered to send one of his 'boys' to look after her for the day, an offer she had firmly refused. Steve, the head lad, was quite capable of looking after her and the cheque that was pinned inside her jacket!

Sue was looking forward to bidding for the pony especially as there was no limit on the amount she could spend. She had after all been to Tattersall Sales at Newmarket with her Dad to buy a youngster, but there was always a limit to what they could spend. Her Dad never went over the agreed limit.

To have a free hand to pay whatever it cost was almost like a dream come true...except the lovely pony would never be hers.

It was going to be a Christmas present for Lizzie.

TEN

Transporting twenty ponies was a headache. But by hiring an enormous horse transporter and using their three trailers they could all go together in a convoy.

Dave decided to take them all on the Friday evening, the day before the sale, to get them all there and settled in before the mass of ponies arrived early on Saturday morning.

It would be busy when they arrived, but not nearly as frantic as it would be on Saturday when all the buyers arrived.

Most of the morning was taken loading the Disco with enough food to keep the ponies well fed until they went off to their new homes.

Feed buckets, a fork and broom to keep the pens neat and tidy. How many bales of hay? They certainly didn't have enough hay nets, so it would have to go down loose on the floor. All problems Dave had to sort out by lunch time.

At last the big transporter arrived and the mass exodus began. The youngest ponies were loaded in the lorry, older ones in their three trailers.

Cilla was the last to load. Anwyn led her up into the trailer for the last time. Her spirits were low, it had taken years to breed these lovely ponies, and each one was special to her.

Tomorrow was going to be a difficult day.

The ponies had spent the night in the permanent stables belonging to the show ground, a short walk from the sale ring and pens.

Dave stayed with them after sending Anwyn and the boys back home. They would be back early Saturday morning.

He was up, having had a shower in the stockmen's accommodation block by six am. Several people were in the restaurant and he joined them at breakfast.

Eventually the conversation got round to the picture on the front cover of the catalogue. There were five of them sitting round the table. One of them knew of Sibertswold stud, and claimed to have been beaten by Cilla here at the Royal Welsh!

All agreed she was a lovely looking pony. Dave kept his head down and said nothing.

"Depends how she moves." Someone suggested. "Don't mean a thing if she don't move good!"

Dave kept quiet, he couldn't help smiling. Wait and see he thought, just you wait and see.

The family were back, plus Grandparents, all eager to help.

Tomos had painted a large banner to hang on the wall behind their ponies. SIBERTSWOLD PONIES it read, and along the bottom were painted ponies galloping along, each one a portrait of their ponies in the sale.

Dai and Rhys hung the banner and climbed down to admire their work. No one could miss their ponies now.

At the entrance to the sale pens each pony had to have its registration paper checked and a lot number stuck on its quarters. It took quite some time but eventually they were all led into the pens allocated to Anwyn.

The sale would start at ten prompt, but already at eight thirty people were beginning to show interest in the ponies, especially Cilla and Gemini who were sharing a pen.

By nine the crowed had grown significantly, a group of Dutch buyers seemed to be very interested in Cilla.

Could they go into the pen to have a closer inspection? Yes of course they could.

Could they see her move please? Yes of course they could.

Anwyn called Rhys who was sent out with Cilla, followed by a crowed of interested people that included Sue and Steve!

Rhys led her quietly round the grass arena, letting her take it all in, the white railings, banks of flowers, loud speakers and the crowd come to see this pony advertised on the front of the catalogue.

He shortened the lead rein. "Let's go Cilla." He whispered.

An audible gasp from the spectators as she floated over the grass, her feet hardly seeming to touch the ground!

Sue looked at Steve. "Wowee, no wonder moneybags' wants this one! What a lead rein pony she'll make."

100

Gemini was next to be inspected by an interested couple, the same routine for Rhys. He picked up her feet one at a time, then got her to walk backwards. Rhys had taught her a few tricks, one was a bit risky. There were masses of people watching as he unclipped the lead rein and put it in his pocket! "Walk on Gem, walk on." She remembered the trick and followed him around the arena like an old dog! People laughed and clapped. Mother hadn't dared to look.

A bell clanged loudly. It was ten o'clock, the sale was about to begin.

The crowd started drifting into the sale ring, thoughtful people had got there early and reserved their seats, there were nothing like enough, and those unlucky ones crowded into every vantage point available, a noisy jostling mass of buyers and people just there to see horses being auctioned.

The sale ring was huge, masses of flowers banked up everywhere and spot lights shining down onto the centre where the horses would be exhibited.

Two auctioneers shared the day between them. The first climbed up to his rostrum, checked that the microphone was working, and the sale began.

If Sue had wanted to pick up a bargain, this was the time to do it, no one was anxious to bid and ponies were selling for very little money. By about lot five prices began to rise, she watched for a while, then wandered outside to look at the ponies again.

There was no one looking at Cilla's pen, so she went straight up to have a really close look at this wonder pony!

A young lad was sitting outside her pen reading a book. After a few minutes he looked up. "Hello... a couple of beauties aren't they?"

"Certainly are, I hope to buy Cilla, but they both are lovely ponies, do you own them?"

"Well, not *me* exactly. My mother bred them."

"Can I go in?"

"Certainly" said Rhys, opening the gate and holding Gemini. "She's rising four, unbroken for riding, but she's done a hell of a lot of shows!" He nodded towards all the rosettes hanging on the front of the pen.

101

"Are they all hers?"

"Yep. Every one, all won this summer!" Sue was really impressed. "As I say, we haven't broken her in yet, I think it's better to break your own ponies, get a better result, no bad habits you have to correct!"

What an intelligent lad, she thought. "I agree. I break my father's race horses; you get a much better result if no one butts in as you say. The horses bond with you and trust you. It makes life so much easier." She would have liked to have stayed talking, he seemed so sensible and obviously thought along the same lines as she did. Pity the lads in her father's yard weren't as savvy as him.

Dave saw the potential buyer, and sauntered up. "Hello, I'm his Dad."

"Oh Dad, this lady says she's going to buy Cilla! I'm sorry I don't know your name?"

"Sue."

"Shall I take her outside; you really should see her move."

"That's OK. I saw her earlier, showing off! You've been most helpful." Then half laughing "If you want a job with race horses give me a call."

"That's kind of you, but I'm hoping to go to university to study law."

Law! University! Dave was astonished, Rhys had not *ever* mentioned this to any of them. Well good luck to the boy, Anwyn will be pleased when I tell her, a lawyer, well well.

During the afternoon several potential buyers came back to look again at the Sibertswold ponies. The Dutch spent time looking at all their ponies, particularly Cilla. Then a woman from Carmarthen who produced show ponies, she fell in love with Gemini.

The boys were kept busy trotting them up and down, and then all too soon it was time to get them ready for the sale ring. Best bridles on the older ponies and neat leather head collars on the young ones. A quick brush over and then two by two they were led quietly down to the sale ring.

102

Sue had been to the sales office during the day to get a purchasers card and leave her address, also to check the bankers letter had been received by the auctioneer and that there was no problem with Mr Briggs cheque. She could spend up to five thousand pounds; the auctioneer wished her good luck! No wonder she felt weak at the knees.

Steve had been looking for her; the Sibertswold ponies were beginning to come in. They didn't want to miss Cilla after coming all this way, and they managed to find a space at the ring side.

The ponies were making good money; they were beautifully presented and turned out. The yearlings and two year olds all behaved perfectly.

Sue was getting a bit stressed, she felt hot and her hands were sticky, would they never get round to the black pony!

Gemini pranced into the ring. *"Now then"* the second auctioneer had just taken his place and was in good voice. *"What a lovely pony we have here. Take a good look at her; you won't see a prettier pony than this.....what will you start me at. Five hundred?....Oh I see you all want her, Six hundred....Seven hundred.....and fifty."* The auctioneer was doing a good job. *"Eight."* Only three hands went up. *"And fifty."* Two hands shot up, the lady from Carmarthen and a man from Devon.

The man standing next to Sue knew them both. They owned two of the top showing yards in the country. He thought they probably had clients already in mind, he told her.

"Nine hundred then." The sale room was silent watching the duel going on at the ring side. Both hands went up. *"And fifty."* Sue couldn't breathe.

"One Thousand! Any more?" A long wait. The highest price so far today. There was a murmur of excitement from the crowd.

The man shook his head and turned away defeated. The gavel went down with a bang.

"SOLD for one thousand pounds. Thank you."

The lady from Carmarthen held her card high and jumped in the air with relief. The crowd were clapping and cheering as Cilla danced into the ring, they suddenly became quiet!

Anwyn was leading her; everyone was entranced by this lovely pony.

"Come on girl, let's see her move!" Someone shouted. So Anwyn obliged.

Cilla appeared to float round the ring, her feet barely touching the ground.

"Well now ladies and gentlemen. What can I say? We always save the best till last! Just feast your eyes on this fantastic filly. She was born on Eppynt Mountain. A *proper* Welsh Mountain Pony! won in hand at all the major shows in Wales this summer. You won't see the likes of her in many a year." He paused for a drink of water, and for effect! "Where shall we start?"

Sue licked her lips and got her buyers card ready.

"You going to bid?" asked the man next to her.

"Yes"

"Hold on a bit, let them get started, what's your limit?"

"No limit" she replied with a nervous tremor.

"Blimey!"

The auctioneer got to his feet. "Five hundred to start." A forest of hands went up.

"Six hundred." Still many cards were waved.

"Seven....Eight....Nine hundred." Still Sue hadn't bid. Only a few cards were raised now.

"One thousand." A cheer from the crowd. Sue's neighbour gave her a nudge. "OK love, join in now! I reckon it'll be between you and those German buyers very soon".

The auctioneer spotted her immediately.

"A new bidder! Eleven hundred. The lady to my right."

"Twelve.....Thirteen."

"Keep your hand up, let 'em see you're determined." Her friendly neighbour was getting excited!

"Fourteen hundred." Her hand was rock steady now. The Germans were talking amongst themselves. Their bidder nodded.

"You've got em, one more and they'll give in!" A whisper in her ear.

"One thousand five hundred." Sue's hand held high.

The auctioneer held his gavel up. "Any advance?" He called. "Seventeen fifty if it helps?" looking at the German bidder.

The Germans had more discussions, then bowed to her and turned away. She had won!

"SOLD. Fifteen hundred pounds. You have her madam, thank you." And the gavel fell.

The crowed went mad, cheering and shouting their approval and slapping her on the back.

"How long will it be before I see that one at the end of your Dad's string trotting up through Lambourn I wander?" said her neighbour.

She turned to look at him, stunned.

"See you Steve...bye."

"Who *was* that?"

Steve laughed. "He owns the Cart and Horses. Funny the people you bump into at a sale. We'll have a drink there when we get back."

"I had better go and pay for that gold plated pony! Then we can get on our way."

In the sales office there were crowds of people waiting to pay for their purchases. The young man she had spoken to earlier saw her waiting and beckoned to her. "You bought your pony then. I'll get you a receipt and pass to get out. Just fill in the cheque and she's all yours."

Sue, still a little shocked at having paid so much, took off her jacket and fumbled for the cheque which she had sewn into the inside pocket!

"I'm sorry, have you got some scissors, my stitching is better than I thought. I can't get the damned cheque out!" Everyone within ear shot laughed.

Sue blushed. "Sorry to be a nuisance."

"For you madam nothing is too much trouble!" He fiddled around under the table. "Here we are, now let me help you."

Now she was very embarrassed, people were watching and laughing, some even clapping

"There you are. All you have to do now is fill in the amount!." Why did he make such a thing about it she thought as she filled in the amount neatly, carefully spelling out *one thousand five hundred pounds* and then in numbers.

105

The cheque was whisked away. "Won't keep you a minute madam."

Sue, still feeling embarrassed fidgeted, standing on one foot, then the other. She was sure everyone was watching and waiting for the wretched man to reappear.

"Here we are then, a receipt for Mr Briggs and a pass to get you on your way." A long pause. Then, just as Sue was about to turn away, he produced, with a flourish from under the table, a huge bouquet! Perhaps he wasn't so bad after all.

Now everyone there *did* clap and cheer, including Steve who was there beside her. "Come on Sue, let's get the pony and get out of here. I've had enough shocks for one day." They squeezed their way out of the office, "Here give me the flowers, I'll get the lorry and meet you out there in about ten minutes?"

"OK, I'll be as quick as I can; might have to have a chat with the owner!" She hurried back to Cilla's pen, but as she approached she saw Anwyn there saying a last good buy. The pony's head was down licking her hand.

Sue wasn't going to interrupt, but Anwyn saw her coming. "Just saying good bye. I've had such a lot of fun with her, she's very special."

"I know. I'll take great care of her."

Anwyn wiped her eyes. "I'm going now Cill" she kissed her lovely soft nose. "I'm going now and I won't be back. I love you." She dashed out of the pen and was quickly lost in the crowd.

Sue watched her go knowing exactly how she felt. She was so sorry for her. "Well I guess it's just you and me now Cilla. Let's go home".

Dave and the boys waited until all their ponies had gone with their new owners and then started collecting up all the brushes and equipment used to keep the ponies looking in show condition, it was a sad moment for them all.

Tomos climbed up and took down the big banner.

"Did you design the banner?" A man asked him.

"Yes."

"And the painting, I'm very impressed?"

106

"I did it to make people look at our ponies, seemed to work!" He folded up the banner.

"Keep painting young man, you have talent!"

"Thank you sir thanks very much." He certainly enjoyed painting; at school the art teacher had entered his Red Kite painting in a national competition for the under sixteen's class, it had won. Perhaps he should think more seriously about art.

Anwyn watched Cilla being loaded into the race horse lorry and wished she hadn't. It was so difficult seeing her disappear, she loved that pony, tears trickled down her cheeks as the lorry drove away.

Dave put an arm round her shoulder as he led her to the Land Rover. "A hard day my love...a hard day." He started the engine and joined the queue to leave the sale without the twenty ponies they had arrived with twenty-four hours ago.

As he drove his thoughts turned to the future; they had made enough money now to see them through this winter.

That damn foot and mouth! Morgan would still be alive. His eyes filled with tears, so many farmers had gone under. He was one of the lucky ones, he at least still had his flock of Buelahs.

Anwyn was a bit down at the moment, she had really loved that black pony, but he thought he would find her another foal to bring on as soon as things settled down.

Dai was off to Agriculture College next week! The twins would be moving on in a few years; Rhys, a lawyer, diue diue!

Tomos? Well people seemed to think he had talent for art, a hard road to travel if he takes *that* course.

He suddenly woke from his day dreaming and realized he had driven all that way with no memory of it!! They were almost home!

ELEVEN

Sue and Steve arrived at Lambourn just as it was getting dark. The lights were still on in the yard and her Dad was just finishing his evening inspection and waiting for Sue to get back from Wales, so was relieved when the lorry turned into her little yard.

He had sent his apprentice to feed Sue's two youngsters and check that they were OK.

Peter Church was the lads name; he was very small weighing only four and a half stone and looked only ten years old! He was a good lad, worked hard and could ride well. Steve said he had lovely soft hands and would make a good jockey, if he survived the training at the Newmarket Racing School!

The lads in Pat's yard called him 'Mouse', due to his minute size. Sue called him Pete; he was her favourite lad, always polite and kept himself clean and tidy.

Pat walked over to Sue's yard. "Everything OK?"

"Yeah...paid a hell of a lot. Take a look; she's in the end box. I'll have to-do something about the door, I didn't realize how small she would be....she can't see out!"

Pat was curious, it seemed strange for Briggs to be so insistent that they buy this particular pony when you could buy a kids pony anywhere, and cheap too, some of them, why go all the way to Wales?

He unbolted the stable door and went in. Cilla looked round at him. Friendly, kind eyes, a very pretty head. She walked to him, a lovely neck and powerful shoulders, if she'd been sixteen hands he would have bought her himself! Cilla licked his hand.

"What do you think Pa, was she worth one and a half Grand?"

Pat coughed "*That* much!"

"Yep...that much."

They stood admiring her.

"Well...you'd better go and phone the man, he's been on the line all afternoon... *'are they back yet?'*... *'when do you expect them?'* he's driving me mad!"

"He can wait a bit longer then, I'll make sure she's settled down, it's been a long, long day for her."

108

Sue and her Pa left Cilla to her feed and hay net, bolted the stable door and went in for a meal.

No sooner had she taken her jacket off than the phone rang.

"That'll be Briggs."

"OK Pa...I'll get it.....'hello O'Rourke racing, Sue O'Rourke speaking.......Hello Mr Briggs, yep, every thing's fine........fifteen hundred............yes, tomorrow'll be fine....I'll tell Pa..bye'......He's coming to see her tomorrow Pa. What'll I charge him for breaking Cilla, it's a long time since I got paid anything for it!"

Her Dad smiled, he hadn't paid her for breaking in his horses for years. "You'll think of something I've no doubt. I'd better phone Odd Job Bob and get him to alter that stable door first thing."

Sue was in the kitchen looking for something to cook, she was famished. There were some steaks and oven ready chips in the freezer, that would do for now.

She hummed away as she prepared the food, she'd have to go into town soon to stock up the fridge. How do I find time, she thought, with a pony to break in and make bomb proof by Christmas, Pa's two two year olds to finish off; there wasn't going to be much time for shopping. Also there was something else she wanted to discuss with her Dad concerning Briggs' Serpent.

The horse was causing a problem and she had an idea on how to remedy it, she would tackle him tonight. First though she would cook him a good supper.

Pat lit the log fire while Sue was doing the washing up, then when her Dad had settled down and was comfortable, she poured him a whiskey.

"So now my dear, what is it you want?" Sue was taken aback, how did he know. "I can read you like a book my love; you've got something on your mind, so let's have it."

She had to smile; there was no fooling her Dad. "Well it's not money Pa, don't worry about that. No, it's Serpent. I think he's totally bored."

Pat listened; she was very observant and very often saw a problem with a horse before anyone else. "Go on then."

109

"Well for starters he hardly ever has his head over the door; he's always standing in the corner. When he goes out he just plods along, head down, ears floppy. The food you pump into him; he should be jumping out of his skin! Out on the gallops he never grabs hold of the bit, he just goes along with the crowd." Sue stopped looking at her Dad.

"Go on, I'm listening."

"I wonder if I should hack him out on his own for a bit, up through the woods and onto the Downs, give him a change of scenery, perhaps a day's hunting. Something new to get him interested in life."

Pat laughed. "Your sure about the hunting bit, he's a big powerful horse...he'd drag your arms out!"

Now it was Sue's turn to laugh."I wish he would, I'd know he was getting keen again!"

Pat was quiet, thinking. "You could be right girl; he does look bored I agree. I'll have a word with Briggs tomorrow." Sue sat back satisfied, she was sure she could get Serpent going again. He had been such a good horse a couple of years ago, had a couple of bad falls and lost his confidence.

His previous owner gave up on him and sent him to the Ascot sales. Briggs bought the horse when he was told it had promise, and anyway he was keen on owning a race horse.

Serpent came to Lambourn with less promise than Briggs had assumed, and discovered that O'Rourke was the only trainer who would take him on.

Sue was glad. Her Dad was a good trainer, and she felt sorry for Serpent, he was basically a kind genuine horse that had just lost his way a bit, maybe she could help him regain his confidence and interest in racing again, she would give it a damn good try if Money Bags would agree.

A long day was drawing to a close, she'd just check Cilla was OK and then bed.

Sunday morning. At seven o'clock it was bright and clear, it looked as if it was going to be a lovely day. Sue was out in her yard, a cup of tea in one hand and a hot croissant in the other.

Briggs was sure to come this afternoon, and she wanted to have worked on all three of her charges before he arrived when

110

she would speak to him about Serpent, if she got the chance. First a check on Cilla, then the two year olds.

She was greeted with a whinny from Cilla, she looked happy and relaxed as if yesterday hadn't happened, and ready for some food. That was problem number one, what to feed her?

Plenty in the food shed, but all high protein, designed for race horses, it would be like feeding a little pony dynamite, *not* a good idea.

Her neighbour had children's ponies; perhaps she could borrow some pony nuts just for today. The corn merchant would be open tomorrow and then she would stock up with Cilla type food!

As soon as she got back indoors she rang her friends at the next door farm. Charlotte laughed and said she would bring a sack of pony nuts down as soon as they had breakfast, they'd like to see the pony anyway; why didn't she turn Cilla out in the paddock, she would probably enjoy a bit of grass and a run around to stretch her legs?

She put the phone down feeling an idiot, why on earth hadn't she thought of that! There was a little Shetland pony out there already, Twinkie, her very first pony, very old now but Sue couldn't part with her. Twinkie earned her keep these days by acting as nanny to any of Dad's race horses who needed a quiet companion for one reason or another.

Odd Job Bob was working on the stable door when Sue went out again. Cilla was in the stable so that made her mind up for her.

"Please don't do anything silly" she said to Cilla as she let her go. She bounded away and then set off at a trot around the paddock floating across the grass, startling Twinkie who was still half asleep!

"Bloody hell...look at her go!" Mr Briggs had arrived very early and crept up unnoticed.

"Mr Briggs... you scared me half to death!" gasped Sue.

They stood watching Cilla in silent admiration. The pony knew she had an audience and was really showing off!

Sue was transfixed, she'd only seen her trotting briefly at the sale, but now she had her freedom, well! She looked at Mr Brigs

111

who was standing there with his mouth open unable to utter a sound.

"Bloody hell....bloody hells bells!" he slapped Sue on the back so hard she nearly fell flat on the ground. "Aint she just lovely...you little beauty."

Cilla stopped and looked at Money Bags, tossed her long black mane and walked boldly up to them standing at the gate.

Much to her surprise Briggs was very gentle with the pony, stroking her head and patting her neck. "Oh I'm goin to love you me darling," he whispered. Sue felt unwanted and backed quietly away, the man had paid a lot of money for the pony, he deserved a bit of privacy.

Odd Job Bob was getting on well with the door. "About an hour Sue....then it'll be done."

"Thanks Bob." She hurried on to feed the two year olds. The morning was flying past and she'd done nothing and now she had Briggs to deal with. Blast it!

The two year olds were getting impatient, kicking at their doors, why was breakfast so late, they were hungry and didn't like waiting.

She calmed them down and a quick muck out today. Pa wouldn't pass that she knew, but time was flying, so needs must.

She had just about caught up with time when Charlotte arrived with the pony nuts. She could see that Sue was busy and didn't hang about.

"Is that the new pony?"

"Yea, that's the owner just arrived!"

"OK. I'll have a nosey tomorrow, that all right?"

"Thanks, things have gone a bit wild this morning. Tomorrow will be fine."

Money bags came walking back from the paddock grinning like a Cheshire cat. "Aint she just perfect. Just perfect!"

Sue smiled. "Yes Mr Briggs, I think she is. Perfect!!" She steered him towards the house, she was anxious to talk about Serpent while he was still in a good mood.

"Wha' ever you wan' for 'er, just you get it an' send us the bill. She'll need a saddle an' 'fings. Rugs an' all that stuff...just ge'it an stick it on the bill, there's a good girl."

"Yes I can do that, no trouble."

Sue opened the back door to find her father in the kitchen.

"Hello Mr Briggs...you're early, wasn't expecting you till this afternoon. Want a cuppa? tea or coffee?"

"Tea'll be fine..thanks."

He sat down at the table and helped himself to biscuits.

It's now or never. She put her idea about Serpent to him. 'Would a change of scenery and a different routine awaken the horse's interest in racing?'

Briggs thought about it while munching on biscuits and slurping at his tea. Pat and Sue waited.

"You wanna take im 'untin' wiv all them dogs!?" He asked, not sure he was hearing right. He looked at Sue, nine stone he guessed, as slim as any of the lads in Pat's yard. "You'll never stop im girl, 'e'll pull your arms orff!"

"No I don't mean straight away, not until I'm sure I can cope with him. I'll use a strong bit anyway, that'll make a big difference."

"You been finkin 'bout this about this aint ye missy? Ye never said a word 'bout it afore."

"No I'm sorry, I wanted to talk to Pa about it first."

Silence as Mr Briggs looked from Pat to Sue thinking. "Right then missy, you try. Only till Christmas mind. I want a race 'orse, not a bleeding 'unter! Just till Christmas."

Yipee! Thought Sue. "Thank you Mr Briggs, I'm sure it will do him a world of good."

"An I wan' that pony broke an ready for my princess by Christmas day. Don't forget......Now ven, where's me 'orse? I aint got round to seein im yet.....Come on girl, show me me 'unter!"

Sue walked him across the yard to the stable block. The lad that was looking after Serpent had seen the Range Rover and recognised it at once. He'd been busy putting a final shine on the horses coat and was brushing out his white tail as Mr Briggs approached.

113

Proudly he led Serpent out and walked him round the yard for Briggs to admire. Serpent plodded along, head down and ears flopping. He looked magnificent...but bored.

"He looks a bit down don'ee" Briggs muttered. "Ee's fighting fit, all credit to your Dad. But your right, 'ee does look bored."

They watched Serpent plodding round the yard. "OK missy, you try an sort 'im out, I wana 'orse that can race after Christmas don' forget."

"I'll do my very best, p'raps Pa will give him a run at Wincanton or Newton Abbot in the new year, the jumps aren't so frightening there, give him an easy race to get his confidence back."

"You do wha ya fink is best, I'll trust you an ya Dad!"

The lad was standing still stroking Serpents neck who was looking at them with dreamy eyes.

"Thanks Joe, put him back and rug him up please."

"Ere you are lad." Briggs slipped him his usual tip.

"Thank you sir." Said Joe, thankful he had such a generous owner.

"How's Lizzie?" asked Sue as they walked back to the car.

"Oh she's a good little'un. I 'ad a'ell of a job getin out wiv out 'er this mornin, 'ad to get out afore she woke, That's why I was so early! He laughed. "We'll 'ave to work sumut out so as you can 'ide Cilla when she wants to come an see Serpent!"

"Yes we must have a code or something so I can hide her!" They both laughed.

"Look after me 'orse girl, see ya next week!" He waved at Patrick who was just coming out of the house and drove off.

"That went well then" said Pa, "I hope you know what you're doing with that one, he's one of our best owners, can't upset him you know!"

"I know Pa, I'll be careful; I'm sure I'm right, that horse is just bored stiff, I know I can persuade him to enjoy life again".

She went back to her yard to work on the two year olds in her schooling paddock. One was ready to go out with the string, it was quiet to ride and well balanced, knew how to turn left or right with just the slightest touch on the reins, and was quite confident to go out alone, walk trot and canter. The rest was up to her Pa.

She would suggest that Serpent took the place of the two year old in the empty stable, it would give the horse a change of scenery, something to look at, chickens scratching about, Patch, her Jack Russell, was always hunting for rats or chasing the cats! Cilla would be his neighbour; she might turn them out with Twinkie if things were going well.

Serpent changed his lodgings and took up residence in Sue's yard. She had ridden him out with the first lot at about seven o'clock under the watchful eye of Steve who insisted he rode beside her once they were on the gallops.

She hadn't ridden the horse before and was amazed how powerful he felt, even just walking round the yard while Pa checked the other horses, she could feel the muscle power underneath her! She would need to have a good handful of reins when they got up to the gallops, but once the string moved out of the yard Serpent dropped his head and lost all interest in the proceedings.

They did the necessary half speed gallop without any trouble and walked back in line with the other horses. Sue rode him into her own yard and took his saddle and bridle off and replaced them with his quilted rug.

He looked quite interested in his new stable, sniffing and pawing at the clean straw bedding. Sue closed the door.

Suddenly his head appeared over the stable door, he pricked his ears, whinnied once and got a high pitched reply from Cilla in the adjoining stable!

Her little black head shot over the new low door. Serpent whickered to her and reached as far as he could in her direction. Cilla was obviously entranced by her over sized neighbour.

Sue smiled, she was right; the horse was just bored, now, at this very moment his recovery would begin.

TWELVE

Sue went shopping for Cilla. First the corn merchant for pony sized food and then on to the saddlers in the High Street for tack to start her training as a riding pony.

She got a lot of leg pulling from the saddler when he saw the size of bridle and head collar she was buying. Racing saddles and bridles he had in plenty, but small pony tack was in short supply. A lunge rein and a good English leather head collar was all she could buy today, tomorrow she would have to go into Marlborough or Hungerford for the rest.

On the way home she met Charlotte who wanted to know if they could come to see the new pony. Sue was glad to see her and thanked her again for the pony nuts.

"Come and have a look and bring the kids. I haven't managed to get any pony nuts here, so I'm off to Hungerford tomorrow, I'll repay you when I get it".

"Oh don't you worry about that Sue. I've got to go shopping soon, I'll get you some nuts, anything else you want?"

Charlotte and the kids came soon after Sue was back.

"I'm just about ready to do some basic work with her. I bought myself a new lunge rein and head collar, but they didn't have any pony saddles in the High Street; not surprising really with all these race horses about!"

She led Cilla into her schooling paddock.

"Oh Sue, what a lovely head and just look at those big eyes!"

The children climbed up onto the wooden railings. "Can she trot?" One of them wanted to know.

"Haven't tried that yet, but here goes". She flicked the end of the lunge rein. "Trot on Cilla, trot on".

Cilla recognised those words from when she was just a foal. She tucked her head in, pointed her toes and floated around at the end of the lunge rein.

Charlotte couldn't believe what she was seeing. "Wow! Does she always go like that?"

"Steady Cilla, steady girl...walk on". Cilla duly obeyed and dropped down to a walk.

116

"Stand...stand Cilla". She came to a halt and looked round waiting for the applause, or a bit of carrot, either would do!

The children walked over and patted her. "What a gorgeous mane" said the little girl, her brother seemed less interested. "Look how long it is!"

Their mother was silently admiring Sue's new pony."She's certainly a lovely, lovely pony Sue. Been well handled by the looks of things, shouldn't take long to break in?"

"No, you're right, she's done a lot of showing in Wales so is used to people and being led around. She's for a four year old girl, so I have to get her bomb proof by Christmas!"

"I'll help!!" said Charlotte's daughter looking at her mother pleadingly. "Can I mum?"

"Ask Sue, it's her pony."

The little girls offer took her by surprise; she would certainly need a small rider later on. She had been planning to ask Peter when the time came, but..... "That would be lovely, I'll tell Mummy when Cilla's ready."

"I've got a tiny felt saddle that would fit her, do for breaking her in I would have thought. I'll drop it in if you like?"

"That would be great Charlotte, just the job."

Charlotte gathered up her two children into the Land Rover and drove off. Sue thought how lucky they were to have such nice neighbours, all be it two miles away. The felt saddle would be ideal and safer for Cilla than a new stiff leather one.

Now Serpent. He was used to daily exercise and it was important that routine didn't change. He had to be kept racing fit, so that if Sues plan worked he would be ready to race again.

She groomed him and then tacked him up with her own saddle, not the little racing saddle he usually had on, and she changed his bridle, a nice eggbut snaffle and grackle nose band that would give her better control if things got out of hand!

The horse stood quietly, a bit too quietly for Sue's liking as she adjusted girths and noseband. Steve insisted she put a neck strap on as well, just in case she needed something to grab quickly. She scoffed at the idea, but Steve insisted, no neck strap, no horse! She didn't want to upset Steve; so on went the neck strap.

117

Now she was ready and Serpent was standing waiting. She stood back and looked at him; he was *big!* She hadn't realised just how tall the horse was.

She led him over to the garden wall and used that as a step to get on him. It was a long way down, she must be sure not to fall off; it would be a long walk home.

"Come on then laddie, let's go walkies." Serpent flicked his ears and plodded towards the gate.

He felt awful. Sue was sure he was half asleep; usually Pa's race horses jigged and danced about when she got on in anticipation of what was to come. This fellow showed not the slightest interest. She shortened her reins and tried to get his head up a bit higher. This was going to be a very boring ride unless something woke him up.

At the gate Sue wanted to turn left and take him to the woods, but Serpent was intent on turning right.

Pa's string always turned right, through the village and out onto the gallops, every day the same routine. Serpent knew the way backwards.

"Not today my lad, we *are* going left", she said firmly. "Something different today, come on, trust me, you'll like my way much better."

They turned left down the lane away from Lambourn and the traffic. Did his head come up an inch or two? Sue wasn't sure.

Autumn was in one of its beautiful, peaceful periods, warm and sunny, just right for a ride. They turned off the lane onto a grassy track. This time she was sure, his head did come up and he snatched at the bit.

Keep calm she said to herself, just relax, don't do anything silly. She started humming her favourite pop song.

The floppy ears came erect, he was listening! Gradually she noticed he was looking about him, his step was lighter and he was walking faster.

Its working she thought, my plan *is* working, he's just bored, he wants a bit of fun in his life. p'raps not today! I'd better not wake him up too much; I don't know what his brakes are like.

118

Sue turned into the woods; he was quite willing to try this new path and she was beginning to enjoy the ride, the ground was soft with a covering of autumn leaves.

Should she try a trot?...yes, she should. "Trot on Serpent" and squeezed with her legs, nothing happened...try again. "Trot on" she said with a sharp kick. His head shot up and they were off! Flat out gallop through the trees.

Help! She had nearly fallen off when he leapt forward and was glad of Steve's neck strap.

Gradually she shortened her reins and got some sort of control over the mad pace.

"Steady now...steady up" she gasped, pulling with all her strength. "Steady up you old fool". Serpent flicked one ear backwards.

Sue was beginning to realize how 'brain washed' the horse was, for years he would walk every day from his stable to the gallops. Charged up the gallops when he got kicked and then walked all the way home again. Day after day, year after year no one had ever asked him to trot, and a canter was unheard of. She was going to have her work cut out to get this fellow ready to go hunting.

He was under control again now, so Sue decided the best option was to walk the rest of the way. Tomorrow he would have some schooling. Lessons in trotting, and then maybe try a canter!

Now she was sure her plan to get him interested in racing was going to work. Even now as they walked home his head was up and there was a spring in his step.

She patted his neck, he was a good horse, it would be lovely to see him at Cheltenham, if only she could untangle his brain!

Her Dad was sitting in the yard when she got back trying to look unconcerned, but Sue suspected he was worried in case Serpent came home alone. He was delighted to see the horse with his head up and walking with a bit of life in him. "How did he go then?"

"Oh pretty good." Sue said nothing about the escapade in the woods. "He's very much a baby in some ways. I'll work him in the school tomorrow. He doesn't seem to know how to trot...funny that!"

119

Pat opened the stable door for her as she led him in and piled his rugs on.

"Now I've just got time to work your two year olds Pa, got time to watch? The bay's practically ready for you to start training him in your yard". He was a big colt, a bit naughty, very much a young stallion. Sue had broken him in during the summer; he had been a bit headstrong and took quite a while to get him settled having a rider on his back. Peter had been the reluctant 'volunteer' to be the first, and the first to come flying off, and not just once! Thankfully the boy just seemed to bounce and came back again and again until the horse suddenly gave in and had been pretty good ever since.

Pa was so impressed with Pete's courage and stick-ability he had promised the lad he could have the colt in his care when he was ready to go into training.

Steve didn't agree. He said the boy was too small and light weight to be in charge of a two year old colt. The horse was going to be too big and powerful, there were bigger and older lads who would be more suitable.

Pat agreed to think about it before the horse came to the main yard to start his racing career. Sue didn't think he would change his mind.

He watched Sue work the colt in the schooling paddock, he was going very well for a youngster, and you could see there was a lot of fire and spirit in the horse. He wasn't the easiest of rides; he kept throwing his head about, snatching at the bit and pulling a lot.

"He looks strong Sue."

"Yeah...he's quite a guy...ready to go now I reckon Pa."

"What about young Pete, think he'll manage the horse?"

"Dunno Pa, he's very small and not much of him. If it came to a struggle I think the horse would win."

Pa had to agree, there certainly wasn't much of him, but he had ridden the colt here in the paddock quite well. He seemed to have a way with the young horses, perhaps he'd let the lad have a trial session riding out beside Steve, see how they got on together, then make up his mind. "Does he jump?"

"Haven't tried Pa".

120

No time like the present, thought Pat and pulled out some white poles. He made a small jump, two foot high at the most. The horse was full of life, ready for anything.

"OK Pa, I'll bring him in at a canter...see what happens!" She shortened her already short reins. My word, she thought, as she turned him towards the poles, this horse is strong!

He saw the jump, snatched at the bit and flew. It was nothing to him; he could have jumped far higher. He put in a playful buck and came back to a steady canter.

"WOW....he's a National Hunt horse if ever I saw one!"

Pat was laughing. "My God Sue, I think we've got a winner here!"

Sue pulled up and patted the horse. "What a jump, he just loved that", she was almost speechless with excitement. "I'll cool him down and stick him back in his stable". The colt pranced around the paddock as cocky as ever. "What a horse you've turned out to be," she said to him.

Pete was watching Sue schooling the colt from a corner of the yard. If only the governor would let him ride that horse. "Shall I put him away for you Sue? He's certainly a jumper isn't he!"

"Thanks Peter, fill his hay rack will you. Yep I think we might just have a winner here!"

"Think I could ride him out for the guv?"He felt he knew the horse and was sure he could manage him.

"Well *I* know you can handle him in the paddock...see what Pa says".

Over supper that night the talk was all about the colt, Pa was as excited as Sue. The horse was a natural jumper, such potential already there, and he was only a baby, what would he be capable of when he was four? Perhaps they had their Cheltenham horse at last.

Sue hoped so for her Dad's sake, he worked so hard and was such a good trainer. They just needed one good horse and people would recognise his talent, maybe the colt *was* that horse.

In bed that night sleep eluded her, her mind was racing away, first she could only think of the colt, how exciting he was and such potential. Then Serpent, a lovely horse with a tangled up brain, he would come right and get back to racing, just time and patience plus a lot of TLC. What of Cilla? A beautiful Welsh Section A pony, kind and sensible, she would be easy to break in, but would little Lizzie learn to ride well enough to justify having such a wonderful pony?.

She decided on a routine for her three charges. She would ride Serpent first as soon as it got light. He would need a fair bit of work and she didn't want to be rushed to get home before it got dark. Then the two year old colt, if he hadn't gone to Pa's racing yard, after lunch an hour with Cilla.

Kate, Charlotte's daughter, had called in with the felt saddle, and to give Cilla a big cuddle, so now Sue was anxious to get down to some serious work with the pony. The sooner she could get her rideable the better. Then she could be introduced to the outside world, traffic, barking dogs, plastic sacks, a hundred and one things a young pony would never have encountered before.

At eight o'clock Pa's racing string set out for the gallops. Sue took Serpent in the opposite direction away from Lambourn towards the woods. The horse was eager to get going, fidgeting about as she tried to climb aboard, she smiled, her psychiatric method appeared to be working.

They set off; his head was up and looking about, taking an interest in where they were going. Such a difference already, she patted his strong neck. "Good boy" she whispered. He felt so powerful and without a doubt very fit.

She relaxed a bit and felt Serpent settle into a long striding walk, his ears pricked. Such a difference she thought again. She squeezed with her legs, trying to get a faster walk, or a few steps of a trot if he couldn't walk faster.

His ears flicked back and forth, no kick this morning, she had learnt her lesson yesterday. Another squeeze and shorten the reins slowly.

"Trot on Serpent...trot on". His ears flicked back again. One more try. "Trot on...trot on you old fool". A very slight kick.

The horse was immediately alive, but so was Sue. He plunged forward and snatched at the bit, but his rider was ready and had a firm grip of his head. *"No you don't old fella...not today"*. She muttered. "Trot on now...trot on".

122

His reply was a shambling trot, not sure what he was supposed to be doing. Stumbling and tripping at almost every step!

Sue kept him at it and gradually the hesitant trot grew into a long swinging stride as he understood what was required of him. She gave him a longer rein and they trotted up through the woods onto the old Drover's road.

The landscape suddenly opened out as they emerged from the trees. She pulled up, you could see for miles and miles up here. It was one of Sue's favourite places. Way to the left she could see Pa's string working on the gallops, in their green jumpers and crash hats. Further to the right one of the bigger yards had about forty horses circling at the bottom of another gallop, the lads in blue.

Serpent watched with interest as another string of race horses appeared close by. He fiddled with his bit and shook his head but made no attempt to join them.

Time to go thought Sue, plenty to do at home. Shame really, it was so lovely up here with the wind blowing through her hair and lifting Serpents white mane.

She turned away from the Drover's road and headed back through the woods. Serpent started jogging so Sue let him break into a trot, a lovely swinging trot that covered a lot of ground.

"I knew you could do it". She said as she patted him down his neck. The horse seemed to listen; he tossed his head enjoying himself up here in the woods.

He walked the last half mile or so on a long rein, but he was still awake, head up, ears pricked.

Pa watched them coming from the kitchen window. He couldn't believe it was the same horse that a few days ago looked so listless and bored. Perhaps she should have been a psychiatrist...a *horse* psychiatrist!

Sue put him away and rugged him up, he had done well today. She was about to open the stable door when she was pushed aside by the horse looking for Cilla, his new found friend, a bit small but very pretty.

The first job done and dusted. Now for the two year old colt, he didn't need a lot of work, he was only two years old and still a baby he just needed to improve his manners and learn to be more obedient.

Sue thought of that jump yesterday, she hoped and prayed he had the speed to match it, but they wouldn't know that until Pa took over his training and gave him a run on the gallops. She would go on with his education turning him into a well adjusted youngster, balanced and well behaved, unlike so many horses coming into training who knew nothing at all except walk and gallop! Brainwashed from day one, what sort of a start in life was that? It made her quite angry.

Now for Cilla. After a quick lunch she would play with her for an hour or so. Grooming her was a joy; she had a superb coat and such a long glossy mane and tail, Sue imagined Lizzie brushing away at it for hours.

Charlotte's little girl was dying to come and help, maybe having her play about brushing Cilla would be a good thing, but Sue had to be very certain the pony was really genuine and as kind as she looked before she let a very enthusiastic child loose on her. She would wait and see how Cilla behaved before she introduced Kate to Cilla!

Today she would put a saddle on her and see how that went, but Cilla was used to wearing a rug most of the time, so putting on the little felt saddle and tightening the girth was nothing to get worried about.

In the event she took it all in her stride, even with the bit in her mouth. Sue wasn't that surprised, she knew the previous owners had done a lot with her, but she couldn't believe how well it was going. She had expected a few squeals at least when she pulled up the girth, or some head tossing when she slipped the bit into her mouth and pulled the bridle over her head, but nothing, just a nice calm pony ready to do some work. "Let's go then Cilla my girl" and she led her into the schooling paddock.

Sue knew she would lunge alright, they had found that out on the first day. She knew walk, trot, steady and stand, but how would she accept the saddle flopping about on her back? The stirrups were rolled up tight so that they wouldn't slap her sides when she trotted, that was the only thing Sue altered on the saddle.

Cilla didn't fuss or fool about, she walked and trotted when asked, stood quietly waiting for the next command...she was unbelievably good! now for the next lesson.

Lunging her with two reins, one on each side with Sue behind her out of her sight, just relying on voice commands and control.

Cilla was completely confused. She spun round trying to see Sue and not being used to being alone, the two long reins touching either side of her seemed to scare her, and she was really frightened.

In the confusion one of the reins got wrapped around her back leg which scared her even more. Kicking and spinning she was getting completely out of Sue's control, she couldn't get close enough to steady her and untangle the reins. She let go of both reins in an attempt to calm her, keeping clear of Cilla's back legs.

Suddenly a small figure dashed across the paddock and grabbed her head. "Steady now....whoa my lovely.....steady now..it's OK".

Peter had arrived just in time, but where had he come from, Sue had no idea. He talked to Cilla stroking her neck until she stopped kicking and began to relax.

Sue quickly untangled the reins and collected them up "Thanks Pete" she gasped, "where the devil did you spring from?"

Pete went on talking quietly to Cilla, then suggested to Sue that she pick up the reins again. "I'll lead her around for you....she's just a bit confused that's all!"

"OK...when you're ready". How on earth did this lad know what to do? He'd obviously done it before somewhere. He was a mystery to Sue. "Walk on Cilla".

"Come on my love....walk on", he said putting a hand on her bridle. "Walk on...it's OK now".

Cilla took a hesitant step forward and then another. Pete walked with her a gentle hand holding the bridle, always talking to her gently. After a few steps he relaxed his hold but continued walking with them.

"Try a halt!"

"Steady Cilla...stand!" The pony stopped obediently.

Pete stroked her neck making a fuss of her. "That was a bit better, it won't take long I reckon. Want to try again?"

"Yeah". Now for it thought Sue, was the pony confident with Pete at her head to try again. "Walk on Cilla...walk on girl".

She stepped forward, and then waited for Pete. "I'm here" he whispered and walked with her. No hand on the bridle this time, just being there with her was enough.

Round and round the paddock Sue holding both reins gradually taking control while Pete gradually moved away from her head.

"Stand Cilla"

Cilla stopped. Pete stopped, ready to go to the pony if she panicked.

"Walk on", this time with a toss of her head she obeyed, without Pete and quiet happy, now she understood what was wanted!

"I must go Sue. Steve will kill me if I'm late for evening stables".

Sue watched him scamper away. Tomorrow she would catch the young monkey and find out exactly where he was from and how he came to know so much.

Cilla stood waiting for the next command. "Let's go in now Cilla, you're a good girl!" Lesson completed and well learnt.

After supper Sue asked her Dad about Peter. Where had he come from? Why was he working as a stable lad when he was already very knowledgeable around horses?

Pa puffed on his pipe. He couldn't remember much about the boy. He had written to see if there was a vacancy with us and turned up for an interview. When asked when he could start work he replied 'now' and he had been with us ever since. He suggested she looked in his office, the boys application letter would be in his folder that might answer some of her questions.

She found the lads folder holding his reference letter and health details, also weekly reports on his work from Steve, and finally his application for work letter. The letter was beautifully written, correct spelling and punctuation, obviously a well educated boy, unlike some of the lads who could hardly read. His home address was 'Valley Farm Oakhampton'.

126

The folder was replaced in Pa's desk. She hadn't learnt much, except he was intelligent and could write a good letter; tomorrow she would corner 'Mouse' and fire some questions at him.

Pa said not to upset the lad; he was a good worker and a promising rider. He had already put the lads name down for the British Racing School at Newmarket, hoping there would be a vacancy after Christmas.

Sue was determined. Tomorrow she would find out a lot more about young Peter Church. *Church Mouse,* what a stupid nickname!

Heavy rain and a howling gale woke Sue to a typically autumn morning. The rain was lashing across the Downs and soaking everything and anybody who ventured out.

The horses wouldn't be going out in this weather, but the stable chores still had to be done. The lights were on in the racing yard, the lads clad in a variety of weather proof clothing scuttled in and out of the stables. Which one was Pete? She had no idea; they all looked the same in the pouring rain.

She shuddered in the damp dawn and pulled on her own oil skins. Her intended interview with Pete would have to wait for another day. How nice it must be for the famous trainers in the village with their huge yards, enormous indoor schools and covered gallops where horses could be exercised no matter what the weather. Most of them had swimming pools and solariums to dry them off! Not forgetting multi millionaire owners. That must be a big help.

The rain lashed down relentlessly, puddles grew and gutters overflowed, not a day for riding. A good day for tidying the food shed and cleaning tack.

Cilla popped her head out briefly as Sue splashed across the yard, she whinnied a high pitched feminine whinny. Serpent mumbled a reply from his stable next door. The two year old colt stood at the back of his stable, He had the right idea thought Sue, keep well away from the wind and rain in a nice warm stable!

After she'd done the mucking out, dodging the ever growing puddles with the wheelbarrow on her way to the muck heap, she hurried back and forth with feed buckets, spending a few minutes talking to each horse. Later she planned to give them all a good grooming. At the moment it looked as if it would never stop raining. It was nice in a way not to have to hurry to get on with exercising the horses.

Tomorrow would be a better day, it must be.

Daybreak the next day the main yard was busy, the sky was clear, and everything had that just washed appearance.

Two horses were racing today and they had to be off early for Newton Abbot. Not that far, but they needed to be there early enough for a quick canter to loosen up muscles after standing in all day yesterday.

Steve was busy supervising the two runners with his assistant who would take them and be in charge for the day. Pat was going later in his car to watch them run. He had high hopes for the hurdler, a fast little filly, but the chaser wasn't all that genuine, if he had an off day he could be a real pig!

The sun was just up when Sue got cracking in her little yard. She wanted to take Serpent into the woods again today and then ride along the Drovers Road for a change. To keep the horse interested in new things was very important. He was improving nicely now and she was determined to get him right for Money Bags.

She had forgotten he would be coming to see his horse on Sunday and probably Lizzie would be in tow hoping to have a sit on her Dad's big 'orse'. Cilla must be hidden away for a few hours. The paddock with Twinkie seemed the obvious choice; it was well away from the yard, and as long as she could keep an eye on Lizzie, making sure she didn't wander off, all should go well.

Serpent was looking over his door as Sue got his saddle and bridle ready. He fussed and fidgeted as she pulled his lovely warm rug off, and aimed a playful kick in Sue's direction.

"You're full of yourself this morning aren't you?" She laughed and gave him a hard slap on his quarters. He squealed and laid his ears back in protest. "Come on then, let's go."

128

Serpent jig- jogged across the yard to the mounting block that Odd Job Bob had repaired after seeing Sue struggle to get on the big horse. He was getting impatient; keen to get going that in itself was a massive improvement!

Sue mounted him quickly and just circled the yard while she checked everything was tight enough. *"My golly...he's a powerful brute.....when he's awake!"* She thought.

Pa happened to come out at that moment and automatically walked up and checked the girth; he did the same thing every morning before they went out for exercise, a lifelong habit. "You be careful up there my girl" he laughed. "You might have woken up a hornet's nest!"

Sue wasn't sure what she had woken up. A long quiet ride was what she hoped for. "I'll be careful Pa....don't worry" she shouted as Serpent danced his way out of the yard. "Come on now old man...settle down will you" she muttered trying to appear relaxed and happy, "You're pulling my arms out ...and we're only walking!"

He did settle down after a little while and strode out well. She could feel the power and muscle of the horse, nearly eighteen hands high and in the prime of life. *'Hang on..this is some horse'* she told herself!

They went along the lane more or less in control and turned onto the track that led to the woods.

Serpent remembered this path and snatched at the bit. "Not yet Serpent" she whispered, not too sure she would be able to stop. "In a bit we'll try a trot". He heard the word trot, he was no fool this fella...he learnt *trot* yesterday!

Off he went, a long striding trot covering the ground with ease. Sue had to quickly shorten her reins. He was well under control, just happy to be moving on, not pulling, just head up, ears pricked enjoying himself.

A pheasant flew up from under his hooves with a squawk and flapping of wings! He jumped sideways and bucked, Sue hung on desperately...to fall off now was not an option. "Whoa, steady you old fool, steady now....steady up...whoa" Dragging with all her strength on the reins she gradually had him back under control. "Whoa you silly bugger!"

She was just letting out a sigh of relief when she spotted another rider blocking the path a few yard ahead of her.

"I was just about to try and grab him as he shot past...that was close Sue!!" It was Charlotte mounted on a smart looking hunter. "I thought you were a goner".

"Yep...so did I. he's one of Dad's horses....I'm giving him a break from his usual routine....trying to wake him up a bit".

"I think you've succeeded.....is he the horse that was so lifeless and bored?"

"He's the one. I reckon he's enjoying life more now!"

They rode along quietly for a while until the path came out onto the downs.

Serpent having had his fling was behaving well, walking beside Charlotte's horse with a spring in his step.

"Which way are you going? I thought I'd go along the Drovers road for a bit and then drop down towards Upper Lambourn. Don't want to take this guy here anywhere near the gallops".

"No...better keep clear....mind if I ride along with you?" So they rode along the Drovers road chatting, enjoying each other's company.

Serpent was a different horse; he was loving it up here on the chalky downs, tossing his head and chewing on the bit. Sue had him on a loose rein, he was totally relaxed.

"Shall we have a little canter?" suggested Charlotte.

"Well....er. He doesn't have a canter...yet. Only a walk, trot and flat out gallop!"

"Oh I see" Charlotte laughed. "What happens if we trot faster and faster until he can't trot any faster, will he canter then do you think?"

"I've no idea" Sue looking apprehensively at the miles of open country ahead of them, "but we'll never know if we don't try!"

They walked on a little further, Sue looked at her friend. "If I take off pray for me!....OK I'm ready if you are".

"Hang on then Sue!"

"Trot on Serpent". The big horse didn't need asking twice, he knew what 'trot on' meant and was only too happy to oblige, he broke into his long swinging trot. Sue shortened her reins.

"Faster?" Charlotte asked smiling as her horse trotted easily beside Serpent.

"OK". Sue squeezed with her legs; his ears flicked back, but lengthened his stride obediently.

"Bit more?" She laughed keeping beside Sue.

"God help me...come on then Serpent..faster", and she squeezed harder. This time his ears flicked backwards and forwards several times. She felt the horse grab the bit, but instead of throwing his head up, he tucked it into his chest and *cantered!!*

Charlotte had the sense to drop back apace or two, she didn't want Serpent to think he had to race her hunter.

Sue let him canter for quite a long way before she gradually got him to slow down and walk. She was laughing when Charlotte caught up. "WOW...that was fun!"

"My word Sue he's a powerful brute your Serpent, just look at those muscles on him.....however did you stop him?"

"With great difficulty...my arms were just about dropping off!"

They turned for home both would have liked to go further but Sue had Cilla and the young colt to work on and the days were getting shorter and shorter.

"We must do this again" Charlotte said as they reached Sue's yard.

"Yes we must....I'll give you a ring when I take Serpent out again, bye for now".

THIRTEEN

Pa had suggested that Sue tried young Pete on the two year old colt, only in the schooling paddock.

The colt was ready to go into proper training now and he had half promised the lad he could have the horse to look after and perhaps ride.

Steve didn't approve, and told Pa there were bigger, stronger lads who would be delighted to look after the colt. "We'll see....I want to give the lad a chance...ride up side him a few times, see how he goes"

Pete would be coming across to Sue's yard any minute now so she had better get the colt ready. She would ride him herself for a few minutes just to get the tickle out of his toes!

She had only just got him out when Pete was there, crash hat in hand. "Get a body protector on Pete", there was no point in taking chances. "And do that crash hat up properly".

He was back in seconds fastening the protector on. "I hate this stuff...do I have to wear it? I feel like a black beetle".

"You look like one too, and yes, you do have to wear it".

The colt was being good. Pete rode him quietly round the paddock, no trouble at all; the boy looked as if he'd been born on a horse! He was a natural rider, probably the most promising lad in Pa's yard.

"Move him on a bit Pete...try a trot". He leaped about a bit but Pete had a steady hold on him, he was quite safe and didn't look at all fazed. "Shorten up a bit and try a canter".

He shortened his reins and got into the crouch position. The colt was strong, very strong for a five stone lad, and for a couple of seconds she thought she had asked too much of him, but quite unflustered, Pete had him under control again as they circled the paddock a few times looking completely at home. Steve would have nothing to worry about with this young lad.

"He's come on really well hasn't he Sue?"

Sue smiled. "Want to try a jump then?" expecting the boy to refuse.

"OK....but not too high....he's only a baby yet".

132

She was stunned, she wasn't expecting that reply. *'I must find more about you my lad'* she thought. "Walk him round a bit while I find a hurdle"

There were some old hurdles in the corner of the school and in no time she had erected a smallish jump.

"Now take it easy...canter him round and when you feel he's settled turn him into the jump, there's no hurry....take your time". *'And hang on'* she said to herself.

Pete set off at a canter; the colt was too keen and fought for his head. Sue's heart stopped beating, but the boy's hands never moved from the horse's withers and the colt soon gave in and stopped fighting.

"Steady now.....steady". Pete had quietened him as they circled the paddock again; he wasn't going to let the horse jump until it was quite settled. Then when they did turn in to face the jump, the horse had time to look, measure it up and fly.

Sue's jaw dropped! The colt had put in a tremendous jump, Pete had placed him on exactly right spot to take off. The jump was perfect.

Slowly they came back to a walk; the horse appeared to want to go again, but once was enough for today. Pete jumped off and patted the colts neck. "Good lad" he murmured "good lad!"

Sue was speechless, this boy was something special. "You've done that before!?"

"Just a few times yes....a few times" He replied as he walked the colt casually back to his stable and rugged him up. "Are you going to work Cilla now?"

"No, after lunch I think...You'd better be off now or there won't be any for you at the hostel!"

"Can I give you a hand then? There's nothing else I have to do until three thirty".

Sue could see he was hoping she'd say yes, and she was glad he'd offered. With his help they could back Cilla and start riding her. "All right Pete...and thanks....two o'clock then".

He hurried off back to the hostel and lunch, smiling, thinking of the colt, how wonderful it felt riding him. This afternoon he would help with Cilla, maybe even ride her, which would be something to tell his mum when he wrote home at the weekend.

He was back before two and started grooming Cilla while he waited for Sue. He was sure he'd seen this pony before somewhere, he never forgot a pony, but where had it been? She'd come from Wales, he'd never been there, so where? The answer never came.

"Oh there you are Pete....thanks for getting her ready. I'll get her tack".

Sue lunged her for a few minutes and then put the long reins on and drove her round the schooling paddock. Today Cilla didn't need to be led, she boldly walked on by herself, well balanced and willing to turn left or right at the slightest touch.

Pete put his crash hat on and fastened the chin strap; he didn't need telling what was coming next. He walked over to Cilla and made a fuss of her. "Don't worry little one it's only me" he whispered.

Sue got him to lay across the saddle a few times so that she got used to the boy's weight. "OK Pete, now throw your leg right over...mind you don't kick her!" She gave him a leg up and he slid gently onto the saddle.

Cilla twitched her ears and looked round at Pete.

He was sitting crouched forward whispering to her. *'It's only me sweetie...only old Pete, don't you worry now'* and he gradually straightened up sliding his toes into the stirrups. "Walk on Cilla.....walk on girl".

Cilla hesitated a moment, this was very different, but she understood the command so obediently walked on carrying Pete and leaving a bewildered Sue behind.

The further they went the more confident she became. Pete kept talking to her and stroking her neck. Gradually she relaxed, tucked her head in and her neck arched.

"She looks good Pete!" Sue shouted sitting on the gate.

Pete smiled, he was enjoying this! Should he try trotting? Cilla seemed quite happy so far and not at all worried. What the hell, it's not very far to fall if it all goes wrong. "Trot on Cilla...trot on my love".

Cilla tossed her head and swished her tail, she wasn't sure about this.

134

Pete shortened the reins; a slight tap with his heals. "Trot on Cilla" not a question this time but a definite command. Cilla was definately *not* happy and swished her tail showing she wasn't! But she did break into a trot!

Pete tried to move as little as possible until she grew accustomed to the change of position, then finally she got into her lovely floating trot. Her white socks seemed to dance over the ground as her mane and tail streamed out behind her.

"*Now* I know you, you beauty, now I know where I've seen you before!" he laughed as he slapped her arched neck.

Sue watched in admiration, what a wonderful pony she had bought, and what a wonderful rider young Pete was. She could have sat on the gate all afternoon watching the Pair, so graceful, so correct. But time was rolling on; the sun was dropping behind the trees.

"That'll do Pete...that's enough for today" She jumped off the gate and opened the gate for them.

Pete dismounted slowly doing his best not to startle Cilla. "Isn't she just lovely" he said to Sue as he led her back to her stable.

Sue was about to pounce on the boy, she had even more questions for him now. Pete saw her coming and guessed he would have to find some quick answers.

"Sorry Sue...I've got to fly...evening stables....Steve will not be pleases if I'm late again...sorry". He dashed away before she could get one question asked. *'I'll get you one day Church Mouse Pete. I will find out how you know so much and ride so well. I will find out one day!!'* she said to herself.

Pete was early for evening stables and spent the extra time grooming the three year old filly he rode and looked after. He put a lot of effort into brushing and polishing her coat. The Guv had a nasty trick of rubbing a white handkerchief over the horses backs when he did his evening inspection, and woe betide any lad whose horse left a greasy mark on it. Pete brushed and polished...it mustn't happen to him.

Steve rang the bell for feeding time and the lads rushed out to the feed shed to collect their allotted buckets. There was a lot of pushing and shoving to get in the shed, but it was mostly just fun,

135

Steve didn't allow any bullying; he was very strict and kept an eye out for that sort of behaviour.

After the horses had been fed the Guv would come to inspect them and the stables, after which the lads would be off.

Pete waited anxiously, he was sure his filly would pass tonight, he had one or two grooming tricks up his sleeve and he often used them on her.

The Guv came in looking round the stable, checking bedding and water. Then asked Pete to take the filly's rug off. The little horse gleamed under the stable lights, her coat shone like satin and her hooves were black, clean and shiny.

"Well done lad, rug her up again, it will be a chilly night".

Pete sighed with relief...but the Guv wasn't finished.

"I hear you rode the young colt today?"

"Yes sir"

"And I also heard you jumped him?"

Now he was in trouble. "Yes sir. Only the one jump sir".

"And how did that feel?"

"Bloody marvellous sir. Sorry, very good sir, he's a Grand horse".

"Well done lad, the filly looks fine. Tomorrow bring the colt over here, be careful how you ride him. I'll be watching and so will Steve" The Guv put his hand on Pete's shoulder. "Well done lad, well done" he said again.

Over supper the talk was about the races at Newton Abbot. The filly Manor Maid had run really well and won against poor opposition, the owners were ecstatic. The other fellow was having one of his bad days and was a real pig at the start, he was the last to jump off and sulked at the back of the field for most of the race, the jockey tried everything he could think of, the whip didn't help, if anything it made him slower! Then with about three furlongs to go he suddenly woke up and got interested, started jumping well passing one horse after another. He powered up the final straight going like a train, ending third in a tight finish. Pa said the jockey was happy enough to have survived the race, the horse was going like an old dog most of the way.

"I asked him what had happened to make the horse suddenly pick up and start racing. He said he thought that maybe the horse

136

needed a longer race; he was certainly full of running at the finish. Apparently he dropped his whip and would have to go back and find it".

"How far back, did he say?" Sue asked.

"At the last corner, three furlongs out, just before the straight. He was just changing hands to give him one up the ribs when he dropped it! Then the horse took off and he didn't need it. I thanked him for riding as he went to weigh in. What do you think Sue?"

"I think he could be whip shy. I can't think of any other reason for the horse to suddenly take off. I've *never* used a stick on any horse, so don't know really".

"But when he lost his whip the horse started to race" said Pa. "Must be the reason surely, don't you think?"

"Yeah...must be Pa".

"The jockey was so impressed with the power and speed he showed. It was just incredible he said".

Pa was a happy man. The horse was whip shy! He said he would give him a trial run on the gallops without the whip. They were both sure it would work, and if it did then he could race again as soon as they found a suitable meeting.

Sue yawned, "I've had enough excitement for one day...I'm off to bed. Did the owners name the horse Bunny? Terrible name for such a big horse!"

"I think so, don't ask me why. Its full name is *Jungle* Bunny! Even worse. Oh by the way....there was a phone message for you. Briggs said to tell you he'd be here tomorrow about two....with daughter. Does that make sense to you?"

"Yeah....he'll want to hear about Serpent's progress, and I must hide Cilla away if Lizzie's coming. You should have seen young Pete ride that pony Pa......there's a lot about that chap we don't know".

"Yep he's a good lad. The filly looked immaculate this evening, don't you go upsetting him now"

"As if I would....night Pa".

Pat and Sue were enjoying their usual early breakfast when he suddenly remembered he told Pete to take the two year old colt to the training yard first thing.

"I think we ought to have that colt gelded before he goes into training, don't you Sue? He'll cause havoc this spring if he's entire!"

Sue agreed, he was randy enough already and by spring he would be a three year old stallion, big powerful and very excitable. Pete would have to wait a few weeks before he got his hands on the wonder horse.

It was Pete's weekend off, but he was waiting in the yard when Pa went out. He understood the change of plan, and readily agreed it was probably for the best, but he was disappointed, that was easy to see.

"I'd like to see you ride that black pony if you've got time. We'll go and see what Sue says". He walked with Pete to Sue's yard and went to find her.

Pete had Cilla tacked up by the time Sue and her Dad were back.

"We mustn't be too long Pete. Old Briggs is coming with his daughter so I have to hide Cilla away"

He vaulted on to Cilla, one quick swift movement that surprised Sue and Cilla alike. "Walk on Cilla" he whispered, a slight pressure with his heels and away they walked   . Pete sat perfectly on the pony, everything correct, a real show rider.

They trotted round the schooling paddock several times, the pony happy with her rider and trotting like a dream. A few figure of eights, perfectly balanced, no break in the rhythm and flowing along nicely.

Pete slowed down to a walk and stopped in the centre of the paddock facing Sue and Pa, he did a polite bow, force of habit, and then laughed. "I wish I was six again, I'd have loved to ride this pony!"

"Put her away Pete" said Sue "She's not ours....more's the pity".

Pa said nothing, he just smiled thinking it was a shame that a lovely rider like Pete wanted to be a jockey, such a shame. "Well done boy" he said at last, "you sure you want to be a jockey?"

"Oh yes sir, I'm sure!"

FOURTEEN

Mr Briggs arrived bang on two o'clock. The big car had hardly come to a stop before little Lizzie jumped out.

"Where's me big 'orse then?"She shouted, he wasn't in the stable where she had last seen him. "'ere where's ee gorn then?" horror written on the little face. "Wot you done wiv im?" she said looking at Sue.

Her Dad was laughing. "Ees gorn on 'is holidays".

"Come on Lizzie....I'll show you where he is" Sue couldn't stand seeing the child so upset. "He's in my little yard....come on, he'll be pleased to see you".

"You 'fink ee will?"

"I'm sure of it". And they walked off hand in hand. "I like your green jumper....and the green bobble hat.....you look like one of Pa's stable lads now don't you?!" Lizzie just grinned.

Serpent whinnied when he saw Sue coming and tossed his head up and down. "There.... you see..he *is* glad to see you!"

She opened his stable door and they went in. The rugs came off quickly and then Lizzie hugged a front leg!

"Allo big 'orse...'owe you feelin today?" The big horse looked slowly down and very gently removed Lizzies green hat! "Ere 'ees got me 'at" she shouted "Give it me back".

Serpent held her green hat just out of reach and shook his head from side to side.

"It's mine...give it back big 'orse!"

"Say please" suggested Sue.

"Wot?"

"Say. *'Please may I have my hat back'*" Sue noticed her father doubled up laughing just outside the door.

"Wot ya mean?"

"Ask him nicely".

"Can I 'ave me bloody 'at back pleeease?"

Well, it was a start thought Sue. "Come on Serpent, be a good boy, give it back please". The hat was politely dropped at Lizzie's feet.

"Fank you" she said looking sheepishly at Sue. "Can I......you know" she said looking at Serpents broad back. "Can I 'ave a sit up there?"

"Why not" and she was whisked up onto the broad back! "There now, how's that?"

"Ees lovely aint ee". She patted the big strong neck.

"Want a ride then?" Not waiting for a reply Sue led Serpent out into the yard.

"Oere Dad....'old me!"

"Your safe enough" said Sue...."Sit up there and enjoy the view".

Her Dad was still laughing. "Go on girl....let's see you ride me 'orse". He wasn't going to come to Lizzies rescue!

They went slowly round the yard, Serpent patiently plodding along beside Sue.

"Aint 'ee a good 'orse Dad..ee's sumut special aintee Dad?!" Sue was doing her best not to laugh, the little child was so happy, her face bright red, and the biggest smile you could imagine.

After a few more trips around the yard Sue sensed the horse had had enough babysitting and had better go back to his stable.

"That's enough for today Lizzie, you'll tire him out".

"Oh all right then....'elp me down Dad". He gently pulled his little girl down.

"Say fank you to Sue an' the 'orse".

"Fank you big 'orse...I love you". Mr Briggs nudged her. "Oh..fank you Sue".

Serpent looked over his door; the child was still there holding Sue's hand. Very quietly he stretched his neck out and gently removed the green hat again, held it up high and shook it!

"Ere ee's pinched me 'at again!"

"We gotta go girlie....Mum'll be watin in that cake shop, she won 'alf be cross if were late".

The thought of the cake shop in Marlborough changed everything.

"Pleeease big 'orse...give us me 'at back". The hat dropped at her feet. "Fanks big 'orse....see ya next week".

"Fank's Sue" said Mr Briggs "you've made 'er day!"

"Only too happy".

"By the way, 'ow's the other busyness coming on?" he asked with a wink.

"Just great....really great. No problems there!"

140

"That's good....fanks again Sue. Were orf now. Got'ta collect Willam. He don like that new school too much, too many toffee nosed snobs ee says.....see ya next week. Fanks for every fink".

They drove off in the big shiny car, both happy. Briggs amazed at the difference in Serpent and Lizzie having had a ride on her 'big 'orse'!

Pa had been watching proceedings from the food shed out of sight, so when Briggs had driven out of the yard he walked with Sue back to the house slipping an arm around her shoulder.

"And how long did it take you to teach the old horse *that* trick?"

"Oh not very long...he's pretty cute that animal! Come on Pa, let's have a cup of tea before evening stables....I'm parched".

The two year old colt had his operation and was now a gelding. He would be a bit sore and stiff for a few says, but being young and fit would be ready for some gentle exercise soon. Pete couldn't wait for him to be fit enough to go out with the first lot to begin his serious training.

Steve would ride beside the horse on a quiet old hack belonging to Pat who wanted to be sure Pete was strong enough to handle the two year old.

He was a lot stronger than he looked, Sue knew he went to the local gym to do weight lifting in the evenings and she had seen him cycling for miles on a bike that had no saddle to strengthen his leg muscles. It was certainly making him fit!

Steve took Pete and the gelding, who had recovered from his operation, up onto the gallops. They only rode at half speed for the sake of the horse and so that he could watch Pete closely. The boy rode the young horse well, he had lovely soft hands, he didn't hang on to the reins too tightly, just enough to feel the horse's mouth and keep him steady.

He was impressed. He told Pat the first time he saw him ride that the boy was a natural, probably the best lad in the yard. Now he was sure.

Pat had a good look at the gelding on his evening rounds and told Steve to send him out tomorrow for gentle training.

Pete was excited to be riding the young horse on his first training run. Steve gave the boy a leg up. "Be careful" was all he said.

He rode off with the other lads happy to be on the big gelding and pleased that Steve trusted him.

They walked to the gallops, laughing and joking. The lads still called him 'mouse', having dropped the 'church' bit, but it didn't worry him a bit. The governor had trusted him with this potential chaser, and it made him feel good. Maybe one day when they were both older he would even race the horse! That was something to look forward too.

The Guv' was waiting when the string arrived at the gallops.

They walked round in a big circle while the boss paired them up, then off they would go, two at a time.

The first few pairs went up the hill at racing speed; they were the horses running that week. Then Pat sent a few more with instructions only to race them for the final two furlongs where they should push the horses on and see how they coped.

Now the youngsters were sent off, still in pairs and only at half speed. Pete could feel the power of the horse under him, he would have loved to drop his hands and whisper 'go boy go'. But not today, their turn would come, he could hardly wait!

By November Sue had got Cilla going really well. Pete came and rode her in the afternoon if he wasn't needed in the main yard. Together they had built an obstacle course in Sue's schooling paddock. Everything Cilla might meet out on a ride that might frighten a young pony, plastic bin bags were a must, and a blue tarpaulin pegged out on the ground. She didn't like the look of that at all; it took a lot of carrot lumps to persuade her to walk over it! They put flags fluttering on the fence and a string of old tin cans which made a lovely noise, enough to startle any one.

After a week of this she could pass them all and not turn a hair.

142

Then came the day when Sue decided to take a big step forward and take Cilla out of her yard and introduce her to the outside world. Pete would ride her, and Serpent, who had changed so much in the two months Sue had been schooling him, would keep her company. He was good in traffic and steady enough to give Cilla confidence if anything frightened her.

Sue and Pete took them cautiously along the lane, She was a bit spooky to start with, it was all so new to her, but Pete talked quietly to her; she soon relaxed and walked along beside Serpent quite happily.

They turned off the lane onto the grass track. Serpent wanted to go; he could trot and canter wonderfully now, but today he had to be patient. He snatched at the bit and humped his back. He wanted to canter up the track!

"Steady old man....don't you drop me off today" laughed Sue "just a short trot then....you OK Pete?"

"Sure thing Sue". The pair trotted along the soft grassy track and into the woods. Cilla was loving this, she arched her neck and kept pace with Serpent.

"She's enjoying this...just look at her" shouted Pete who was enjoying it as much as Cilla. The daily trip to the gallops and back was a bit boring. "I've missed this" he said as they dropped back to a walk.

"Done a lot of riding then" asked Sue probing into the boys Past.

"Yeah....almost every day for as long as I can remember....only ponies though......I never rode a horse 'till I came here". They walked on in silence for a while. "That's how I knew Cilla before"

"How d'you know her then?" Sue was suddenly very interested. "You come from Oakhampton don't you?"

"Yep.....but promise you won't tell the other lads Sue.....promise me".

"Alright I promise...cross my heart.......but *what* must I promise!"

"Well my Mum breeds Dartmoor ponies; they're officially a rare breed now. We show them, the young ones in hand....I ride some of the older ponies. Well last summer we had a lovely three year old filly, she had won quite a lot and we took her to her to

143

the Mountain and Moorland class at the Devon county Show. I thought I'd won....and then this Welsh pony came trotting past, a bit late coming into the ring, I hadn't seen her before; she just took your breath away! It was this young lady. She beat me..I didn't recognise her at first when you got her. I thought the one that beat me came from the West Country. You bought Cilla in Wales, that threw me at first 'till I saw her trot; you don't forget a thing like that, especially when it takes the championship from you". He laughed "I told my Mum when I phoned her, she said it's a small world!"

Now Sue understood. He was a show rider! "Does your Dad run the farm?" she asked as they rode back to the yard.

"Haven't got a Dad, he got killed in a plane crash". Silence for a while. "My mum crashed the car coming to collect me from school; ran into a tractor, that was some time ago. She's Ok now" He murmured. "It leaves a big hole in your life".

"It certainly does". She was sorry she'd asked about his father, he was visibly upset. "Does your mum run the farm then, on her own?" She was trying not to upset Pete any more, she knew exactly how he felt, it had taken a long time to come to accept that *her* mum had gone for good after *her* car crash.

Pete sniffed and rubbed his eyes. "You might as well know....I promised mum I'd give racing a year, if I hadn't ridden a winner in that time I would come home and help run the farm. So you see I've got to make it as a jockey or go home and raise sheep".

They were back in the yard now, both had been thinking of the past and future.

"I'm sure you will ride a winner Pete" she said at last. "You're off to Newmarket after Christmas. Then you'll have your apprentice licence from the Jockey Club. You're so light weight every trainer here in Lambourn will want you to ride for them!"

"I hope so, otherwise its back to Dartmoor ponies for me...not quite the same".

"Cheer up Mighty Mouse, it'll come right in the end" Sue laughed "let's get these nags rugged up, then I'll make us a cup of tea. I think we've earned that"

144

Later that night Sue and her Dad were relaxing in front of a roaring fire Sue told him what Pete had said on their ride that afternoon.

"He's a very determined young man is our Pete" said Pa. "I'll do my best to help him once he's been to Newmarket. Can't do much till then, except put him up on some good horses. I wish he wasn't quite so small though".

"Good things come in small packages" Sue reminded him.

"Yes I know that....but think girl, how many jump jocks do you know who can ride at five stone? He'll need to carry another four or five stone in lead, dead weight, if he is going to make the minimum ten stone! No our Pete is going to be a flat race jockey, and I don't have any flat race horses in my yard....yet".

"We could feed him up a bit" suggested Sue laughing.

'Or buy some flat horses at the Newmarket sales' Pa thought. "Maybe a yearling or two for you to break and race next year?" he said.

Sue had thought along these lines herself but hadn't dared to suggest it!

"I'll have a look at the accounts; see if we could afford it". Pa sat in his chair for another hour thinking about Chepstow tomorrow; Jungle Bunny, the whip shy horse was running.

He had tried him out on the gallops with a different rider *without* carrying a whip. The horse was a reformed character, he put his best effort into the gallop and he flew over some practise jumps.

The jockey was most impressed; he'd ride the horse without the whip whenever Pat thought he would be ready.

Chepstow would hopefully confirm that Sue's diagnosis was right. He was quietly confident the horse would perform...maybe win?

"Fancy a day out tomorrow; see that whip shy horse run again without the whip? I'm sure you will be proved right!"

"Sure thing Pa; I'll get my lot done early. They can have a day off".

Sue hurried round her yard feeding. Mucking out and grooming, Cilla in particular.

145

Thankfully Chepstow was only down the M4 a bit, about an hour in the lorry. Racing didn't start before one o'clock so there was plenty of time.

She went straight over to the main yard just after the first lot had got back from the gallops.

Jungle Bunny knew there was something different going on, he should have gone with them. He stomped around his box and wouldn't settle.

Sue found Pa talking to him, trying to calm him down. "No good getting het up yet old fellow, save it for this afternoon".

Jungle Bunny was a daft name for such a big horse which would inevitably become just Bunny. The lads called him something else, not very complimentary.

The owners were coming to see their horse run, he'd so nearly won last time out, and they had high hopes for today.

At last he was lead into the lorry; best rug on today, bandaged and a head guard, Sue supervised the loading and wished him 'good luck!'

The assistant head lad was driving and the lad who looked after Bunny was going to see to the grooming and lead the horse round the parade ring. He certainly looked a chaser, a big powerful horse, tremendous quarters and strong legs.

Sue hoped her Dad was right to run the horse without the stick; she felt responsible in a way for agreeing with him. *'Oh well, only time would tell'* she thought.

A quick change of clothes and a warm sheepskin coat; Sue was ready to go. She hadn't been to the races for some time and was determined to enjoy her day out.

They met the owners and had lunch in the member's restaurant; nice country people who loved their racing; the sort Sue liked! Bunny was their pride and joy; they had had him for some time but without much luck.

Pa was convinced that Sue was right; no jockey would ride without a whip and this fellow didn't like it one bit...that was it, he was whip shy...plain and simple!

In the parade ring the horse was getting admiring looks from the excited crowd, only eight runners, not a big field, just what

Bunny needed. He wasn't favourite, or second, but well down the list. He had a bad reputation to overcome!

Sue studied the other runners, a pretty rough lot in her estimation. Should she have a bet on Bunny?...Yes! Fifty pounds, a lot of money for her, but at twenty to one it was worth the risk......now she was worried!

Pa had a last word with the jockey who gave Pat his whip to hold. "I'll have it back after the race. In the winner's enclosure!" he said half joking. Sue was chewing her nails, an old habit.

"He seems happy enough" said the owner's wife.

"Stop chewing those nails girl...you'll have none left". Pa said. Sue smiled, she remembered her mother saying exactly the same thing many years ago.

Bunny danced and pranced all the way down to the start. He really looked terrific.......after a bit of milling around the starter climbed up on to his rostrum and they were off!

Bunny hung back a bit at the start. The jockey told Pat he thought the horse was waiting for the whip, but this was going to be a hands and heels race today.

After the first jump which he cleared with ease with no use of the whip, he started to get into the race. His jumping was faultless and by half distance he was ahead and jumping for joy!

He powered up the final hill still pulling like a train and raced across the finish with his ears pricked!

The jockey said afterwards he could have gone round again...no trouble.

Proud owners led him in to the winner's enclosure to the cheers of the crowd. Pat was waiting for them, a big grin on his face.

One of Pat's neighbours from a yard in Lambourn who had a runner in the same race patted him on the back. "Well done Pat, wouldn't have believed it was the same horse I saw last time you had him out...well done!"

The horse had won, he was right to run him without the whip, the transformation in his performance proved it.

147

The jockey, all smiles, waved at the crowd as Pat gave him his stick back. "I'll ride him again any time Mr O'Rourke...what a jump he's got" He rushed off to the weighing room.

Sue was so excited she was jumping up and down and dancing with the owner! "Oh help" she said waving her betting slip. "I've won a fortune!"

As the travelling head lad led Bunny into the horse lorry Pat said to tell the lads when they got back to Lambourn, he'd be in the Lamb at eight o'clock, the drinks would be on him!

"Thanks Pat...I'll tell them".

FIFTEEN

There were a few bleary eyes and sore heads next morning when the first string walked out of the yard and up to the gallops, spirits were high, a winner made a big difference.

Sue, who *wasn't* bleary eyed, tacked up Serpent thoughtfully, he'd had a long rest from the normal routine yesterday and he was such a changed horse. Today she was on a mission; she would try and find some jumps for him!

She had phoned Charlotte first thing and arranged to meet; it might be wise to have company when she jumped the big horse for the first time.

As they walked up the lane towards the woods Sue asked her if she knew where they could find some logs or something to jump.

Charlotte had a much better idea. The Drag Hunt had built all manner of jumps beside the Wantage Road, big ones if you were bold enough and small pony sized if you lacked courage. She was a member of the hunt and was sure it would be OK to jump a few first to see how Serpent behaved.

Sue was excited, she had been planning to find a few logs in the woods, but proper jumps would be just perfect....depending on their size!

They rode along chatting away about horses and children, Charlotte laughed when told about Lizzie and her hat with the bobble.

Sue mimicked her cockney accent; *'Oi 'ees got me 'at'*

"I wish I'd seen it! Does she ride yet?"

"Not yet, it's a pity 'cos she loves sitting up here on this fella. Still it'll soon be Christmas and Cilla will be ready for her".

"Yeah...lucky girl......Here we are Sue...just through this gate and then we can try a few jumps".

Sue looked at the jumps, all well made and inviting. It seemed that Serpent thought so too, he tossed his head and Sue felt his muscles bunch up in his quarters. "Steady old chap, steady now...I'm not ready yet!"

149

He wasn't listening. *He* was ready, ears pricked and dancing sideways!

"You OK Sue?......Want to pull out?"

She couldn't answer; she had no option with her hands full of a heaving pulling horse. "No, I'll have to let him go in a minute!"

"Keep close to the hedge; they're in a straight line".

They were smallish jumps all tight against the hedge, he should manage those thought Sue. She turned his head towards them. There were bigger jumps built alongside that looked pretty substantial, *another day p'raps,* she thought.

Serpent literally leaped forwards grabbing the bit. Sue had lost control. She tried to keep him facing the small jumps, no chance, he had other ideas.

He took the first of the big jumps at a gallop, she hung on desperately, the second loomed up and he treated it with scorn. On to the third, Sue was beginning to enjoy the feeling of flying and stopped trying to fight him! He was so bold and sure footed, more important, he was *loving* it.

They galloped on up the hill, jumps four five and six disappeared beneath his pounding feet. Suddenly there were no more jumps. He pulled up without much of a struggle, which was just as well because Sue's arms were dropping off and her hands were raw.

Serpent was blowing hard throwing his head about and skittering sideways ready for another go! Charlotte cantered up white faced.

"You alright" she asked and took hold of Serpents bridle. He looked ready to dash off again, she could see that Sue wouldn't be able to hold him a second time.

"Yeah....I think so! Crikey Charlotte what a horse....I don't think I'll try that again. Can you hold him a minute while I get my breath back?"

"I thought you were going to try the little jumps?"

"That *was* my idea....he made up his mind otherwise!!"

They walked away from the jumps back to the gate; Serpent seemed to be a bit reluctant,

"He certainly can jump Sue; you must be over the moon".

"Pa will be.....if I have the courage to tell him!"

150

Serpent was under control by the time they reached the lane and Charlotte's farm.

He had a new spring in his step as they arrived back at Sue's yard. Pat saw them coming and guessed something had happened. "Have a good ride?"

"Great..thanks Pa" she said as she tried to hide her raw hands in her pockets.

"You look a bit flushed". He knew she wouldn't say anything, not now, maybe after supper. They were both back safe and sound, that was the main thing.

Sue put Serpent back in his stable and put his warm rug on. He was still quite excited and kept moving just as she was trying to do the buckles up. "I wish you would stand still you old fraud" she shouted at him.

Pat heard her and wondered what had gone wrong; usually she came back from a ride in a good mood. It wasn't like her to shout at the horse. He went back and looked over the stable door. "What's up Sue, what's been going on?"

Sue looked up surprised. "Oh nothing really....it's this horse, he's so strong".

"But you knew that girl before you took him on....come on, what happened out there today?" He was concerned in case they'd had an accident. "Tell me now. What's gone wrong?" Pat wasn't cross but getting more and more worried.

"Well.....I took him over some jumps".

"You did *what*?" he exclaimed.

"I tried him over those jumps beside the Wantage Road".

"I've seen them....how did he go?"

"Like a bloody bird Pa. He flew them......but I just couldn't hold him, he's so strong!" She looked at her hands covered in angry looking blisters. "But what a horse Pa...*what* a horse" she smiled, "I love him...but I think you'd better have him back in training!"

Pa slapped Serpents neck. "Hear that old fellow...your holidays are over....it's back to work for you tomorrow!"

Steve was glad to have Serpent back under his care, he hadn't been too happy about Sue taking over his welfare, but he had to

151

agree, the horse looked alive now, much better for the change of routine.

He put him in a different stable from where he could see the house and everything going on outside in the lane, anything to keep him interested.

When he went out for exercise he went with just one other horse, and they only used the gallops when everyone else had gone back. He usually had Bunny for company and twice a week the Governor would watch them over the training jumps. Everything seemed to be going well; the two horses were pretty evenly matched.

Mr Briggs arrived very early one morning to watch them go over the jumps.

They drove up to the top of the hill in Pat's four by four and watched through binoculars as the two horses paced each other for eight furlongs and then turned into the line of jumps.

Serpent was an extravagant jumper, he cleared everything with ease. Bunny was more careful and saved his energy for the last uphill gallop. Over the last furlong there was nothing between them.

The lads pulled up slowly and walked the two horses over to Pat and Briggs. They were blowing a bit, not too much considering they had just done one and a half miles and jumped six big jumps at near racing speed. They both looked and were supremely fit.

Mr Briggs was beside himself with excitement, he had never seen his horse run with so much enthusiasm. When could they race him, where was there a meeting he could enter?.

Pat had to calm him down and explain about entries etcetera, but promised it would be as soon as he could find a suitable meeting.

Jungle Bunny was running again next month and again at the Cheltenham Spring Festival. Serpent had run beside him today easily, he was ready to go.

"Walk them home now, careful on the road" He told the two lads as he climbed into the Land Rover with Briggs. His two problem horses were coming right, the future was looking good.

"I 'aint never seen me 'orse go like that...never! your girlie sorted 'im out din' she...blimey can't 'ee go!" He didn't stop talking until Pat drove into the yard when Briggs looked at his gold Rolex and said he must 'Get 'ome quick'.

He blew Sue a kiss as he got into his shiny new car and shot away. Still muttering about his big 'orse.

Pat went into the kitchen and made himself a strong cup of coffee.

Sue joined him. "Well...how was it, how'd he go?"

"Bloody marvellous. Christ what a horse he is!"

Sue laughed "Told you he was something special. I'm not just a pretty face you know".

Pa chased her out of the kitchen. "Get back to work girl" he teased her. "Go and ride that pony".

She didn't go and ride the pony, but went into Lambourn to the saddlers, who had phoned to say he'd got a lovely small saddle, just come in.....did she still want one? Yes she did and would be in later.

It was a lovely leather saddle, not new but had been well looked after, soft and supple, just right for Cilla. Sue managed to get tiny safety stirrups and short leathers thrown in to complete the purchase.

As she was leaving the shop she bumped into Charlotte and her daughter Kate who was anxious to know when she could come and help. It was half term, so she could come any day. It was a good idea to get Cilla used to children, little girls particularly. So Kate went back with Sue to 'help' with Cilla

"Just play with her Kate, brush her if you like, and pretend you're only five! Lizzie doesn't know a thing about ponies yet, so I've got to be sure Cilla can cope with being messed about with".

Kate was in her element fussing over Cilla. The pony seemed to enjoy having a little person handling her. Her mane got a lot of attention and then her tail. Sue remembered how she used to spend ages brushing her pony's tail when she was young.

"How old are you Kate?" Sue asked looking over the stable door.

153

"I'm eight, nearly nine...why?"

"Well...I wondered if you could pretend to be five again and ride like a beginner....being led. You know, all floppy and almost falling off!"

Kate laughed "I expect I could do that....do you *want* me to fall off?

"Heavens above no...that's the last thing I want!"

"Shall we do it now, before I go home?"

Sue hesitated; she didn't want to try Cilla's patience too much on their first day. "No tomorrow will be fine, if you can spare the time" she said at last. "But you could put her out in the paddock for me if you like".

Kate soon had the head collar on and the lead rein attached. "Do you leave the collar on Sue?".

"Yeah. Leave the rope on the gate". She watched the pony go quite happily with the child. Lizzie would be sure to want to lead Cilla about, it was just as well to let Kate get her used to being led by a little person.

Tomorrow they would teach her the art of being a good lead rein pony.

Kate arrived early on her lovely red bicycle, her mother had insisted she wore her body protector when she rode Cilla, it was pushed into a basket on her handlebars.

As Sue wasn't quite ready Kate got the brushes out and started grooming Cilla. She could hear her chatting to the pony as she brushed away, making the black coat shine like satin. "I wish my pony was as shiny as you Cilla, he's all fluffy".

Sue smiled; it was always difficult getting little fat ponies looking decent at this time of year. She had been lucky; all her little ponies had warm stables to live in during cold winters, so never grew long coats natural to ponies.

"We'll try the new saddle today Kate...can you put it on her?"

"Oh...I didn't know you were there! OK I'll try"

Sue watched carefully, she wanted Cilla to get used to a child doing everything. She was perfectly good until Kate pulled the girth up quickly and got a nudge from Cilla, just to reminder her not to be rough or take too many chances.

154

"Careful now Kate she's only a baby still. You have to be gentle; she's still got a lot to learn".

"Sorry Cilla.... I won't do it again..promise".

Sue checked everything was on correctly and then Kate led her out of her stable. She stood perfectly still while Kate hopped about on one leg and finally scrambled up onto the saddle.

Pete had taught Cilla to stand on command, envisaging Lizzie trying to climb up when the pony was given to her on Christmas day. Kate was acting as any small child would do.

Sue admired her efforts. "Well done Kate, now she'll have to learn to walk at the end of the lead rein and not just follow me.....Can you keep her level with me but about three feet away?"

"OK Sue".

It wasn't quiet that easy! Cilla had always been led beside her handler on a short lead rein, now however, she had to walk on a long lead rein. Not in front of the handler, and defiantly not behind, just level with the lead rein loose enough to look like a big smile!

Kate had to keep her in the right position and keep her there, while they were led around the schooling paddock.

Sue could foresee all sorts of problems when they progressed to a trot!

At shows with Cilla's previous owner she had set the pace at the trot and Anwyn had run with her keeping close to Cilla's shoulder, she loved to trot freely and not have her head tampered with.

Her best action only showed at a fast pace. Unfortunately lead rein ponies must *not* trot fast, just a slow gentle trot that wouldn't alarm a tiny rider.

So marks were lost for being in front of the handler, or being behind the handler and trotting fast!! A lot to learn.

It would be difficult to get Cilla's lovely floating trot at a gentle pace, but Sue and Kate had to find a way. It was that wonderful trot that caught the judges eye every time and won her so many prizes.

On this first day of training the potential lead rein pony Sue was happy to get the walk correct. Kate was doing a good job in keeping Cilla in the right position, but any laps of concentration and the pony would close the gap and walk beside her. Lizzie couldn't ride at all and would have no idea how to keep Cilla in the correct position. Sue would have to tackle her riding, or non riding, before much longer. Yet another problem for her to sort out.

Overnight Sue had thought of a brilliant idea. She had taken one of her father's walking sticks and wound the lead rein round it with just the clip at the end loose. When the end was clipped onto the bridle the walking stick would keep the pony at the stick length away from the handler! So if Lizzie forgot to concentrate the stick would gently push Cilla's head away.

She thought it would work, but at first Cilla couldn't understand this new addition to her bridle and protested by standing still, not walking at all.

With a lot of encouragement from Kate they got over the problem and the 'walking stick/ lead rein' worked perfectly!

It was difficult for Kate to pretend not to be able to ride, there were so many things she did naturally that Lizzie wouldn't know about, but they worked on and gradually Cilla began to accept her new vocation and learnt quickly.

By the end of Kate's half term they had quite a well behaved lead rein pony, there was still a long way to go and lots to learn. Sue was quite hopeful now that Cilla would be ready by Christmas day.

Kate agreed to come every Saturday morning, while her mum went shopping, to continue Cilla's education. She also offered to lend her old lead rein pony to Sue so that Lizzie could learn the basics of riding.

This seemed a good idea and was gratefully accepted. Kate would ride Barny to Sue's yard when she came on Saturday mornings and take him home again on Sunday afternoon, when Mr Briggs and Lizzie had been and gone. That would give Sue about six sessions with Lizzie, just about enough time to teach her the very basics of riding.

Serpent was causing havoc in the racing yard with his newly acquired trick of removing hats! Several of the lads had been surprised by their hats being removed from their heads as they passed Serpents stable. His pranks had to be stopped when one of the new and innocent lads was persuaded by the older and questionably wiser boys, to walk past Serpents door. The young lad had his crash hat on, securely fastened with the chin strap, but unfortunately with the green silk cover tied tightly on.

Serpent saw the green hat coming well within his reach; he grabbed the green cover and lifted hat and boy clear off the ground. He was nearly strangled by his chin strap before Serpent was persuaded to let him go!

Steve said the trick must stop before someone got hurt. No one told Serpent who seemed to think it was great fun and occasionally caught an unwary passerby!

His behaviour on the gallops was much improved since his 'holiday' in Sue's yard. He worked most days with Bunny and was getting faster in the trials and over the practice fences.

Pat was looking for a race to enter him, not too far away and a course where the jumps didn't look to formidable. Chepstow was a possibility, just after Christmas, or Wincanton?.... Cheltenham? No..not Cheltenham just yet!

Manor Maid, the little filly Pete looked after, was going well, she was three years old and destined to be a hurdler. She had run twice in flat races as part of her education, and was now ready to take the next step over hurdles. Pat had entered her for a novice race at Newton Abbot. Both Pat and Steve agreed that Pete should take her as he was her lad, and lead her round the parade ring.

Steve told him to ride her on her last early morning on the gallops, before the race; he was very impressed.

"That was fun eh lad" he said as he walked back to the yard with the horse jig-jogging along the road beside him.

"Oh yes, crikey she's fast isn't she! I hope she jumps well tomorrow"

"By the way..there's a turnout prize for that race..see if you can win it for us eh?"

A turnout prize! Pete made up his mind; Manor Maid was going to win that even if she couldn't win the race.

157

He was in the yard very early, even before Steve, with his special grooming box his mother had given him when he left the farm. It had everything in it you could ever need to produce a horse to show standard; brushes, combs, dusters, oil, chalk, everything, but best of all it was made of oak, very solid and strong.

The lid had a rubber grip on it so that he could stand on it and reach even the tallest of horses. He hadn't used it in the yard before in case it got 'nicked', but today he meant to make full use of it.

It took about an hour to get the fillies coat looking good, and then he set about her mane. Steve usually did the platting, he was quick at it, but Pete's plats were a work of art. Each one exactly the same size and length, carefully sewn in with black thread and finished off with a dab of baby oil. His little fingers could coax even the most awkward bits of hair into a stylish neat little plat.

Manor Maid's tail, washed the night before, got the same care and attention, the top half platted tightly and the lower brushed, combed and oiled to perfection.

The yard was alive with early morning action by the time he had finished. He was so busy he nearly missed the bell for feeding up time and was the last lad to collect the fillies rations.

"Got your filly ready?" asked Steve, "we'll be away soon".

"Yes...she's ready".

"Hope so...the Guv will want to see her before you go. Come to the tack room when you've fed her and I'll give you the travelling boots and rugs"

"Yes Steve".

"Put your best jacket on, can't have you looking scruffy now can we?!"

"Yes Steve....I mean no Steve!" The poor lad, he was so worked up the last thing he needed was Steve teasing him.

The filly had just finished eating when Pat came striding across the yard. Where are the two runners Steve?"

Steve came running. "Here's Silver" He said opening the stable door to reveal a dapple grey horse. The lad doing the horse held its head while the Guv looked it over carefully.

"Not platted yet!"

158

"No" answered Steve, "His jockey likes a bit of hair to grab hold of over the jumps".

"Bah...rubbish!!" The Guv was not pleased. "Now where's Manor Maid?"

"Here sir" Pete opened her door. He stopped in the doorway and stared. The filly looked round patiently waiting with Pete holding her head. *What was wrong, what had he forgotten to do?*

"Did you do this Pete?"

"Yes sir". *What hadn't he done?* The Guv reached up and felt the plats, each one identical to its neighbour, neat and tight. He ran his white handkerchief over her gleaming coat, spotless! The hand went over her quarters....*Pete was almost in a state of collapse!*...the tail platted down half way the bottom half shining like silk.

The Guv stood back and surveyed the filly...then he surveyed Pete. "You did all this yourself lad?"

Steve was smiling.

Pete was about to die.

"Bloody good lad...bloody good!" he ruffled Pete's hair. "I'm going to miss you when you go to Newmarket....carry on Steve....let's hope she runs as well as she looks!"

The Guv left Steve and Pete staring after him. "Come on 'mighty mouse', let's go to Devon. I might even buy you a cream tea!"

The two lads stowed their best clothes in a locker on the horse lorry and climbed into the cab with Steve. The other lad was older than Pete and had done all this many times before, but for Pete it was all very new and exciting.

Before long they were driving through the Devon countryside. It wasn't a brilliant day; there was a lot of fog drifting over the moors.

"You live down here don't you Pete?" Steve asked.

"Yep...near Oakhampton".

"Is it always as foggy as this?" He had to concentrate on the road.

"No ..not always...it comes down very suddenly....goes just as fast!" To prove Pete right they were suddenly out of it in brilliant sunshine.

"That's better...I can see where I'm going now". Steve relaxed a bit.

The other lad who had been half asleep, sat up and after a pause he said "What happens in a race if the fog comes down and the 'orses go the wrong way?"

"They get lost!" Pete joked and Steve laughed.

"Let's hope we don't find out today".

They arrived at the race course safely and in good time. Steve helped Pete find the correct stable for Manor Maid and checked that the other had found *his* horses stable.

"Now you two don't go wandering off...you are in charge of these horses today. *All* day. I don't want any accidents...Stay here with them.....I'll come and collect you in plenty of time to go to the saddling up boxes. Don't let *anyone* near our horses...*no one*....is that clear?"

"Yes Steve" they both said in unison.

"Right. I'll go and get you something to eat...won't be long". He strolled off in search of Beef burgers and chips.

Pete's filly was a bit excited, strange stable, strange horses walking past and a lot of noise. She was fidgeting, pawing at the ground and whinnying a lot. Pete was getting a bit anxious and hoped Steve wouldn't be too long.

He tried talking to her and stroking her neck. It helped a bit but she was still not settling down.

The other lad was an old hand at the racing job and came to help. "Play her some music Mousy," he had a transistor radio in his hand. "Find some Mozart, something quiet, they like music. It works sometimes!"

Pete took the radio rather dubiously, he'd never heard of this before, but he was new to the game and this lad seemed to know what to do.

"Here...give it me....I'll find some music. 'Aint you got a transistor?...Where was you brought up?" Very soon the stable was full of loud music.

"Turn it down mate" someone shouted, and quickly the volume decreased.

"There you are Mousy, see, it works wonders does a bit of Mozart!"

160

Pete doubted whether Mozart had anything to do with this music, but Manor Maid seemed to like it and began to relax standing quietly listening.

"Gee thanks...just look at her!"

"'Aint nothing Mousey...by the way my name's Jim.....Slim Jim...that's me!"

Pete smiled. "Thanks Jim, I'll have to get one of these things. You learn something new every day!...Look out Steve's coming". The boys grinned at each other; they were ready for their Burgers and chips.Pete's spirits rose. He had found a friend at last.

The lads sat outside the fillies stable on a bale of straw eating greasy chips covered in tomato sauce. "Don't get grub like this in the hostel do we mate, all that salad stuff...don't do a lad no good at all!" Jim elbowed Pete so hard he nearly fell off the bale. "Wanna come down the chippy tonight after stables?"

"Yeah...if my filly wins I'll treat you".

"You're on Mousey...look sharp the Guv's coming". Burger wrappers quickly vanished under the straw and two innocent looking lads leapt to their feet.

"Horses travel alright?" asked the Governor.

"Yes fine sir...they've settled down well".

"Good...tidy them up before they go to the parade ring...you too...you look like two stable lads who've been eating chips and tomato ketchup!" Jim wiped his mouth with the back of his hand; Pete had a clean handkerchief that did the same job. "I'll want you to meet the owners, so be polite...and get that ketchup off your nose Jim!"

The boys looked at each other and as soon as the Guv had walked away burst out laughing. "Best we clean up Mousey if we've got to meet the owners".

Pete disappeared into the fillies stable; he gave her a final polish with a duster, checked her plaits and tail, oiled her feet and then did a quick change himself. Under his work jeans he already had his clean trousers, fawn best quality cavalry twill; the jumper came off and was thrown on top of the jeans, a clean white shirt underneath with an orange tie, the owner's colours he'd had it in his pocket, tied neatly round his neck. His best tweed jacket was hanging on the door.

161

"Blimey Mousey you look a real toff" exclaimed Jim, "where'd you get all that gear...Mothercare!?"

Pete was about to pounce on Jim when Steve arrived. "Now then lads lets be having you. Pete, you and me go first. Jim you're not on for another hour...stay with Silver Circle, I'll be back for you after the fillies run, OK?"

"OK, I'll be here *don't get your knickers in a twist"*, he said under his breath.

"I heard that! Just you watch it young man or I'll box your ears".

Pete led Manor Maid out and followed Steve to the saddling up boxes.

The saddle and weight cloth went on quickly, then her number cloth, number seven. Pete smiled, *that* was his lucky number! Her usual bridle and breast strap followed She was ready for the parade ring.

Pete straightened his tie, put on his soft leather gloves and proudly led her in.

Pat was there with the owners talking to the jockey and looking at Manor Maid walking round, head high and ears pricked.

Pete knew she looked spectacular, his years of showing ponies for his mother gave him a big advantage, and he had the filly moving beautifully.

The other runners, there were eight altogether, looked fit and well, but lacked that final polish.

The turnout prize was announced over the public address speakers.

'TURNOUT PRIZE HAS BEEN AWARDED TO NUMBER SEVEN MANOR MAID TRAINED BY PAT O'ROUKE LED BY PETER CHURCH.

A big cheer went up from the crowds of spectators round the parade ring.

Pete was handed his prize of £50. He hardly had time to say 'thank you' when the 'jockeys up' bell rang and he had to hurry back to his filly in the middle of the parade ring.

"Well done lad" said the Guv patting him on the back. "You deserved that, she looks a picture!"

"If you get tired of working for Mr O'Rourke" said the owner. "Come and work for me". The owner's wife had a number of show horses. "Make our horses look like that and no one would beat us!"

"Thank you sir, but I'm aiming to be a jockey".

"Oh well, such a waste of talent" the owner laughed. "Here's a little something for all your hard work". A twenty pound note was pushed into his hand.

"Thank you very much" he stuttered "thank you". But the owners were off to watch the race.

"Pick up them rugs lad and stop daydreaming, we've still got work to-do!" Steve was bustling about picking up lead reins and arm bands. "Come on now, jump to it or we'll miss the race".

Pete was brought down to earth again with a bump! He was daydreaming. Steve was right, but in the space of a few minutes he was £70 richer, for a sixteen year old not long out of school, life looked very rosy.

The filly ran well, very well really. She bounced along in the middle of the runners for most of the race. Ten hurdles were nothing to her, then two furlongs from home when the jockey asked for a bit more, she responded quickly and gained a few places. Turning into the final straight she was level with the leader and still going easily taking the lead for a few strides, then when she came in sight of the Grand stand and the winning post she seemed to check her stride for a split second to allow the other horse to slip past her on the line! A photo was called for, but the jockey knew he had lost the race.

Afterwards, talking to the Guv, he said he had the race won, she was going so well, she just seemed to hesitate as they came level with the Grandstand.

The owners were somewhat disappointed, Manor Maid had run really well to finish second after a photo. They were sure next time she would win!

Pete took her back to the stables, he hadn't led the winner in after all.

163

He washed her down and led her round the stable block until she was dry...why had she given the race away...it really bugged him.

The other horse, Silver, ran like an old dog and didn't get into the race at all. Jim was of the opinion the going was too soft whereas the little filly seemed to relish a bit of mud.

They discussed the merits of both horses all the way home, but still couldn't fathom out Manor Maids unusual behaviour. Maybe it was the sight of so many people cheering and shouting, she had run so well out in the country, it was only when they got within sight and sound of the crowed she hesitated.

Pete smiled, he'd got it! He was sure he knew the reason and felt he should tell Steve when he had settled the filly down for the night, or p'raps it could wait till morning? But it didn't!

The Guv and Steve came to check the filly just as Pete was rugging her up. They looked her over quickly; she looked fine eating her 'supper' quite happily. They felt her legs and checked her feet, nothing unusual there.

Steve scratched his head. "I don't get it Guv...she seems fine"

It wasn't Pete's place to butt in on their conversation, but he was sure he knew the reason and the cure for her behaviour. "Excuse me sir" he swallowed hard "Excuse me Guv, I think I know why she checked suddenly!"

Steve was about to tell him to mind his manners when Pat turned and looked hard at Pete.

"Well lad....what's your theory, it's got me puzzled".

"She doesn't like the loud noise sir".

"Go on then".

"All the cheering and shouting as she got near the Grandstand...it startled her".

Pat looked at Steve. "What do you think Steve? She was certainly going sweetly enough till that bend and came in sight *and* sound of the crowed.

Before Steve could make his reply Pete took his courage in both hands and went on. "We had a stallion at home that couldn't stand the noise of the crowd and worse, the loud speakers at shows. So we stuffed his ears with cotton wool...then he was fine!" He was so embarrassed; it wasn't his place to presume to

164

tell them what to do. "I'm sorry sir...I should have minded my own business...I'm sorry!"

The Guv was staring hard at Pete, slowly he grinned, then burst into a hearty laugh coming up from his boots! "Cotton wool in her ears!" he laughed even louder, Steve joined in. "Lad....you'll be the death of me!"

Pete stroked the filly's nose.

"Try it Steve next time she runs. The lad might well have the answer. Cotton wool! At least it's a cheap remedy". Pete felt a lot better. "Off you go Pete...I see young Jim waiting for you by the gate. Going out on the town are you?"

"No sir, just to the chippy...it's my shout tonight".

"Good boy. Oh....by the way, tell Jim he's going to the racing school at Newmarket with you? I just got the letter today, it was waiting for me when we got back!"

"That's great news sir..I'll tell him now". He turned and dashed across the yard. It would be good fun to have his friend at the school with him. They set off at a run, heading for the chippy to celebrate.

"They're a most unlikely pair eh Steve?"

"Yeah, like chalk and cheese, but it's good they've palled up".

The Guv pulled out his pipe and thought about lighting it. There was a sign over his head that read 'NO SMOKING'. He put the pipe reluctantly back in his pocket. "I'm off then Steve...see you in the morning. Oh, and Briggs is coming to see his horse after lunch tomorrow...see the lads know will you....good night then". He walked slowly back across the yard, Sue would be busy getting the supper. She would laugh when he told her about Pete and the cotton wool. Damn it all, the lad could be right, what a joke that would be.

SIXTEEN

Sunday was cold and damp. Kate had ridden Barny over the day before as arranged and now he was waiting for Lizzie to arrive.

Cilla was tucked away out of sight and covered in rugs from head to toe! Kate had played with her on Saturday morning and rode her in the schooling paddock later.

They had fun riding round the obstacle course. Cilla would pass the flags, plastic bags etc without hesitation, but Barny, when shown the obstacles had pretended to be scared witless, until Sue told him to behave and stop being such a baby!

Mr Briggs arrived with his daughter about two o'clock, the sun was shining weakly through an overcast sky. Lizzie leapt out of the car and ran to find the big 'orse'. Her father was smiling as usual; he loved his little girl and delighted in seeing her fondness for his horse.

Serpent saw his pint size friend coming, and duly obliged by removing her woollen hat!

"'Ees got me 'at Dad...'ees pinched it again" she squealed with delight.

Steve watching from a distance shook his head.

"Give it back *pleeeease*" squeaked Lizzie and with a final shake of his head the horse dropped the hat at her feet. "Ee remembers don't ee!?" Lizzie was so happy and delighted to think Serpent had remembered his trick; her little round face was a picture.

Sue was equally delighted the child had remembered the magic word please; at least that was a step in the right direction. "Come on Lizzie, there's someone I want you to meet" and took her hand.

"I aint 'ad me ride yet on the big 'orse"

"He's a bit grumpy today...I want you to meet Barny".

"I don' like boys" she said in a sulky voice.

"You'll like Barny...I promise" She trotted beside Sue reluctantly.

"I 'ate boys" she muttered.

166

"You'll love Barny" Sue was smiling, "He's very fat and hairy".

"Wot!....I aint coming no furver".

"Come on Lizzie....I'm only teasing. You'll really love him, I know you will".

Barny hearing his name popped his head over his stable door and whinnied.

Lizzie stopped dead in her tracks and stared.

"See...I knew you'd like him" laughed Sue. The Childs face changed from sulky to surprise, to delight in a matter of seconds!

"Can I touch 'im?" she asked timidly. "Will 'ee let me stroke 'im?"

"I'm sure he will....come on..he's very friendly". She was in his stable as soon as Sue opened the door.

"Oww" she whispered. "'Ees lovely.......ee's just my size 'aint 'ee?"

"He's more your size than Serpent that's for sure!"

"Will 'ee let me sit on 'is back...'ees got one of them leather seats on 'aint 'ee Sue?" Lizzie was getting quite excited now. "Can I Sue? Can I 'av a sit on 'im?"

"You can...and Lizzie, I'm going to teach you to ride....what do you think of that?"

"Blimey...you gonna learn me 'ow to ride proper...like them boys in the yard?"

"Well more or less like the lads...yes. My friend Kate has let me borrow Barny to see how you get on".

"'elp me up Sue".

"I didn't hear the magic word!"

"Oh...pleease Sue 'elp me up..I'm ready....can we get on wiv it".

"Use the mounting block, Odd Job Bob made it for me...come on, lets go outside". Lizzie skipped across the yard.

"Up them steps?" she asked.

"Let me get Barny standing next to them first...then you can climb on!" He was a good pony and stood patiently by the steps while a very excited child climbed up and down several times.

"Whose Odd Job Bob Sue?..It's a very funny name".

"He's a man who does odd jobs around the yards; we've known him for ages. I think his real name is just Bob. He can mend most things when they go wrong, that's why we call him *Odd Job* Bob".

"Oh I see", satisfied, Lizzie was keen to climb onto Barny.

"Put your left foot in the stirrup". She struggled a bit. "That's right....now..throw your other leg over his back and sit *gently* down. There you are.....that wasn't difficult was it?"

"No....nuffin to this riding is there!".

"Well your only standing still....it does get a little more difficult later on".

Lizzie wanted action, so Sue led her round the yard...slowly, and showed her how to hold the reins properly and where to keep her feet. She was quick to learn and sat very confidently on Barny's back.

They progressed so quickly Sue took them into the schooling paddock. Lizzie loved the obstacle course and squealed with excitement when Barny had to walk over the blue plastic that was supposed to represent a lake!

All too soon Mr Briggs came to find his daughter, he was amazed to see his little girl riding so confidently.

"Watch me Dad....watch me ride Barny" she shouted as Barny went round the obstacle course yet again!

'What a good boy you are...what a good boy' she whispered as he plodded on."Watch me cross the lake Dad". Barny obediently crossed the blue plastic lake.

"We really must go now luv, Mum will be waiting in that cake shop". He shouted across the paddock.

'She can wait' muttered Sue trying not to laugh. "We'd better put Barny back sweetie....would you like to ride him next Sunday when your Dad comes to see my Dad".

"Oh yes *please*" remembering the please word.

"Good girl, I'll see if we can borrow him again".

Lizzie rode Barny back to his stable and helped Sue close the door. She had to be dragged away; even the cake shop in Marlborough didn't seem as attractive this week,

"Can I 'ave some of them proper riding trousers wot Sue 'as on Dad, can I?"

"Ge'in the car Madam! You're as bad as your Mother...always wanting new clothes" he winked at Sue.

"She'll need a crash hat too" said Sue quietly.

"God...you women, you're all the same, always wanting something new!,,,,,I'm off before you think of some'ut else......bye, thanks a lot" and with that the big black car roared off.

Sue breathed a sigh of relief. Lizzie had done very well, but it had tired her out, it was time to have a few minutes rest.

"I'm ready for a cuppa" she called to Pa who was about to go indoors.

"Good idea love, I'm parched" he replied as they went into the kitchen. Sue put the kettle on. "Briggs says he's looking for a house down here, a weekend cottage, so they can be near that school in Marlborough" he reached for the biscuit tin. "I can't imagine a young edition of Briggs at that Public School, can you? They'll wonder what hit 'em if he's anything like his Dad!"

"I imagine he's a lot worse from what I've seen of him" laughed Sue.

They sat quietly enjoying a few minutes peace before evening stables started.

The lads were beginning to drift back to the yard and the horses were whinnying knowing it was time for their food. Sunday was nearly over; it had been a good day, not too many visitors, just three owners plus Mr Brigg. Lizzie had had her first riding lesson and had proved to be a good pupil. Barny had been very patient and behaved beautifully. He went home to Charlotte's farm just as it was getting dark. He was coming back next weekend.

Sue stretched out in her armchair, she had changed her mind about Briggs, she quite liked him now, but she wasn't sure she wanted them as neighbours. Perhaps he'd find a house in Marlborough. That would be close enough. Another five minutes and she would go out and help with evening stables, but in five minutes she was asleep.

SEVENTEEN

Christmas was getting very close, the square in Lambourn had a tall Christmas tree in the centre decorated with flashing coloured lights. All the shops and the pub had joined in and decorations hung from every nook and cranny.

Work went on as normal in the racing yard. Pat asked for volunteers to work on Christmas day, a list had been hung on the tack room door for ages, but so far only two names had declared they would work that day. It didn't look too promising, Sue had visions of herself mucking out and feeding some twenty horses before getting the Christmas dinner in the oven!

Her father had other ideas. He would treat Sue to a Christmas dinner at the Lamb and all the lads that worked that day. The list on the tack room door filled up quickly! Too quickly for Pa, it was going to cost him an arm and a leg, but it would be fun and he booked them all in before the pub got over booked.

As the twenty-fifth drew nearer Sue spent more time on Cilla. Kate came and rode her whenever she could. The pony was perfect in every way.

Mr Briggs brought Lizzie most weekends to ride Barny. Kate had met her and they got on very well together sharing the riding on Barny. If Lizzie couldn't manage something Kate would demonstrate how it was done. After just three lessons with Sue Lizzie could manage a rising trot, with only an occasional bump, largely due to Kate's help.

As expected the little girl had got her riding trousers, Jods Kate called them, proper boots and a velvet crash hat.

Sue couldn't wait to see her face on Christmas day when Cills was produced, saddled up and ready to go. The pony was looking lovely although a bit woolly and a trifle fat but she was sure that wouldn't matter.

The Briggs family were renting a big house near Marlborough and would be there over the holiday so sneaking out on Christmas day shouldn't be a problem. Would Lizzie like Cilla? That no one could tell.

Sue was planning to take some photos of Lizzie on Cilla and send them to Anwyn at Sibbertswold farm. She had promised to

170

let them know how Cilla was getting on but so far had done nothing about it.

Christmas morning was wonderful in Lambourn. The sun shone in a cloudless sky, the air crisp and fresh. Sue and the staff who had offered to come in and work, fed the horses, cleaned the stables quickly and left to get back to their friends or families. Most would be at the Lamb at lunch time for their Christmas dinner and most would be practically drunk by then.

Sue had other things to-do. Cilla's stable was to be decorated with paper chains and tinsel with '**Merry Christmas Lizzie from Daddy**' chalked on her door. *'Please let her like the pony'* thought Sue, so much money and thought had gone into this present. She couldn't bare to think how Briggs would feel if his precious little girl didn't like Cilla

Soon she would find out, the shiny black car was coming into the yard. Lizzie jumped out almost before the car had stopped. "I got you a present" she shouted, "Merry Christmas Sue...look....I bou'it meself!" She scrambled into the back of the car and came out with her arms full of a wriggling golden puppy. "'Aint 'ee cute Sue....say yer love 'im!"

"Is he for me!?" exclaimed Sue. "He's gorgeous...oh Lizzie, you are so kind".

"It's nuffin, but you like 'im don't ya?" Her face was suddenly anxious.

"I love him Lizzie....he's the best present I've ever had".

"I fink 'is name is Barny" Lizzie said laughing. "'Ee's fat an woolly". They were both laughing and hugging each other.

"Come on me darlin" said her father, "I've got sumut to show ya".

"Wot..anuver present...where is it....where Dad?" She skipped into Sue's yard and stopped suddenly. Cilla's head popped over the door.

"What does it say on the door?" Sue asked.

"Dunno..can't read yet".

"Yes you can...try hard now...what does the first bit say?"

"Merry Chris..mus".

171

"Good girl. Now the next bit". Lizzie was staring at Cilla, tears slowly trickling down her checks.

"Is it for me?" she gulped, "is the 'orse for me...fir Chris..mus?"

Her Dad picked her up and kissed the tear staind cheak. "She's all yours me darling...all yours...lets go an' say 'allow".

Sue had to turn away before she had a little cry as well. She cuddled and fussed the puppy to hide her embarrassment.

Pa laughed at her and took the puppy. "Go and give her a ride my dear....I'm sure she'll want one".

Briggs planted his smiling daughter on the saddle and Lizzie tucked her feet in the stirrups, picked up the reins and said in a confident voice, "Walk on....watser name?"

"Cilla".

"Walk on Cilla". And Cilla obediently walked on into a beautiful sunny Christmas morning.

Lizzie and her father stayed a long time playing with Cilla but eventually they had to go

"Can we trouble you tomorrow; I know Lizzie wants to come?"

"Sure thing...Dads got to go to Chepstow, we've got a horse running, but I'll be here". She sighed as they drove off. It was lovely to see them both so happy.

Now...what to-do with the puppy? She looked round...it seemed to have disappeared, he couldn't have gone far.

Pa was nursing him in the kitchen when Sue burst in desperate to find the puppy.

"He's rather cute isn't he Sue..what's his name...Barny did Lizzie say?"

"That's right Pa. Wasn't that nice of them? But what *am* I going to do with him Pa...I've nowhere to keep a puppy!"

"Oh I don't know love, we'll think of something...he's very sweet isn't he!.....Lets go to the Lamb shall we, the lads will be there by now, it must be lunch time".

"Yes..but *where* can I leave him Pa?"

He was still playing with the puppy on the kitchen floor. "Well take him with us, he'll be fine on the back seat of the car, probably sleep most of the time....don't fuss girl. He'll be fine wont you Barny?"

So Barny sat on the back seat of the car and went to the Lamb for Christmas dinner.

Sue had to drive home as Pa was somewhat over the limit! The Lamb had put on a marvellous meal, all the lads enjoyed the feast and many of them bought the Guv a drink. Sue had to stop them plying him with whiskey before he became legless!

Fortunately pup had slept soundly on the back seat, but as soon as they got home he was ready to play again. One of the lads said he was a Golden Retriever, very intelligent and easy to train, *and* they made good gun dogs. Pa was at once very interested. He loved shooting and envied the men who had well trained dogs to fetch the fallen birds.

When it was time to do evening stables Pa was fast asleep in his arm chair, Barny squeezed beside him. Sue left them, pulled on her anorak and went out to help feed up. Most of the volunteer lads had made it back to the yard safely, they all laughed when she told them the Guv was snoring away in front of the fire with the puppy on his lap.

There would be no inspection tonight so Sue was about to lock up when Steve arrived just to check on everything.

"It's supposed to be your day off" she chided.

"I know love, but I couldn't rest till I made sure they were all OK and eating their grub".

"Go home Steve...they're all fine. Go and enjoy your tea. Back to normal tomorrow....mind you, Pa will have a sore head I'm sure, so we'd better look out!....Go on home Steve...Merry Christmas!"

'*What a Christmas*' she sighed thinking of the day's events.

Mr Briggs had been so happy to see his little darling riding the lovely Cilla. She had immediately fallen in love with her; there couldn't have been a happier child.

Pa had got a little drunk and made the lads laugh. She had got a puppy that she really didn't want, but her Dad had taken him over and would soon have a well trained gun dog.

173

She smiled when she went up to bed; the pup was asleep on Pa's bed...so much for the gun dog theory!

Christmas over and quickly the evenings were drawing out, it was no longer a rush to get evening stables done before it got dark.

Pete and his friend Jim would be going to the Jockey Racing School in Newmarket at the start of the coming year. Jim being a bigger and heavier lad was destined to be a jump jockey. National Hunt racing beckoned him, Pete on the other hand could only make the six stone mark on the scales, even carrying his heavy saddle. He would be in great demand as a flat race jockey, so long as they both came up to the standard required by the jockey club to win their apprentice licence. Competition was keen, it wasn't going to be easy for either of them.

The day before they left for Newmarket, Guv put Pete up on the young gelding that he had got to know in Sue's yard. He was now called 'Asktheboss', and officially a three year old. Steve and a work rider went out with him, up to the two mile gallop. They usually gave a horse its final gallop at racing speed, a day or two before a race. Work riders rode for any trainer and moved freely amongst the Lambourn yards, Pete had seen him a few times last year.

Pete often rode Bossy on the gallops but only ever at half speed and only over eight furlongs. He got a bit suspicious when the work rider vaulted up onto Serpent and the Guv gave Steve a leg up onto Jungle Bunny.

He kept Bossy walking round the yard while the Guv had a whispered conversation with the other two. They all had a laugh at something and eventually joined Pete walking his horse round and round the yard.

Pat came over to check Bossy's girth and surcingle before letting them out of the yard. "Be carful Pete, listen to what the others tell you. I'm trusting you with my best horse today". He turned to Steve. "OK Steve take them away...I'll see you at the top of the hill".

Pete knew for certain this wasn't going to be the usual half speed gallop. Why were Steve and the work rider smiling? He

174

knew Serpent was running next week at Newbury, everyone in the yard was talking about it. His brain was whizzing round and round, Serpent should be having his last pre-race gallop in a day or two and Jungle Bunny was fighting fit as always. Suddenly he thought he understood, could it be possible, would they let him.

He wanted to ask Steve, but he might laugh at him and tell him not to be daft. The work rider he didn't know that well and couldn't ask him!

They had arrived at the start of the two mile gallop. Steve rode up beside him. "How many times have I told you boy? Put your toes in them stirrups and keep them flat against the horse.....I could come up beside you and kick that stirrup away while it's sticking out like that. Then where'd you be...on the deck!!"

"Sorry Steve, I just forgot...wasn't thinking". Pete was embarrassed to be ticked off in front of the work rider, but he winked at him.

"It's OK lad...just watch yourself, I'm going to be on one side of you and Steve on the other. Try and stay with us, close as you can until we get to the four furlong mark, then drop your hands and see if you can lose us....drive him on hands and heels...see what he's made of. Can you do that? My names Paul by the way!"

Yeah...I can do that....I dunno if I'll stop though!"

"He'll stop after two miles don't you worry....ready then?...come up close to me...let's go"

At first he thought he would never hold Bossy, the young horse leapt forward and dropped his head which nearly yanked Pete out of the saddle, but a firm hand gripped his jacket and pulled him back into the right position.

"Bridge your reins lad like this". Paul was close beside him and Pete copied his hold on the reins. "Good. Now....put all your weight on your hands and lean on them....you've got it.....now you've got a hold on him laddie!"

Pete felt much safer now. How could Paul be so calm when they were going so fast, he was chatting away as if they were walking. He decided then that he had an awful lot to learn!

Steve was at his elbow. "You OK Pete?"

"Yeah I think so".

175

"Good boy....keep your elbows in, your flapping like an old hen".

"Yes Steve" he gasped. They were approaching the last four furlong marker and he was nearly exhausted, but the adrenaline was pumping so he didn't notice the aching arms or the biting wind in his face.

"Right Pete". Paul was still close beside him. "Let's see what Bossy has got left in his tank....push him on boy...pass me if you can!"

"Oh boy.....This is what I've been waiting for. I was right!" He crouched lower on Boss's neck, dropped his hands and whispered "Go boy..go!"

Boss stretched his neck and increased his speed, but Steve and the work rider were still with him. He pushed with his hands and kicked hard. "Go boy..get moving". He found he was shouting. The horse pricked his ears and found another gear, gradually he inched away from the other two horses and was flying up the hill past the Guv!

Now he had to stop! He thought it would be a problem, but Bossy was blowing hard, he'd had enough and pulled up quite quickly. "Well done Bossy....well done old boy!" He slapped the horses neck. "I've wanted to do that since the first day I rode you". He walked the horse quietly back to the Guv where Steve and Paul were sitting on their horses.

Paul slapped him on the back. "No wonder they call you 'Mighty Mouse'" he laughed "you're tougher than you look!"

"Well now Pete....how was that?" asked Pat.

"Bloody marvellous, fantastic". He was so excited he forgot 'sir'.

"Walk them back Steve, quietly now and mind the road. Oh, and Pete, take the rest of the day off and get yourself ready for tomorrow. I'm taking you both to Newmarket; I want to be away by eight". Steve and Paul looked at each other and smiled.

Pete was going to make it alright.

EIGHTEEN

Bitterly cold weather came with the New Year. Wind blew straight from the Arctic, day after day, freezing the ground until it was rock hard! The gallops were dangerous and out of use, the all-weather had to be rotavated every morning so that the surface was broken and the horses could be exercised. The gallops man was kept busy, week after week, keeping the gallops useable. His tractor could be heard grinding away long before the lads arrived for work, muffled up and stamping their feet to keep warm.

Most yards had 'Horse Walker' machines that allowed trainers to keep horses fit in these conditions. The richest trainer had the latest model of 'Walker', unlike the usual design that walked the horses round in a circle; this was about forty yards long and could accommodate twelve horses turning at the end and back again either at a walk or trot depending on the exercise needed. He was the envy of every one!

After an age of freezing temperatures, Lambourn woke one morning to thick snow! The village came to a complete stand still; it fell all morning and into the afternoon, so by four o'clock it was lying a foot deep over the downs and several feet where the wind had blown it into drifts

The horses looked out miserably onto a white world; they wouldn't be out again until the snow melted!

Steve and the lads hustled around the yard, feeding and grooming their charges and then it was a case of finding shovels. They managed to clear an area in front of the stables and Odd Job scattered sand which gave the lads a bit of safe ground to walk on.

The snow was still lying next day, showing no sign of melting, crisp and white, very pretty but the last thing Sue and her Dad wanted to see.

All the staff huddled in the tack room, Sue providing unlimited cups of tea, coffee or hot chocolate, while everyone discussed what could be done!

Racing was cancelled everywhere, except for a few all-weather tracks, but who could get to them with so many roads

177

blocked? No, it seemed that all they could do was sit it out and hope there was a quick thaw.

Sue rugged Cilla up in her water proof rug and turned her out for an hour or two each day, the pony loved the snow, rolling in it and galloping around tossing snow aside with her nose until she tired of that game and waited at the gate to be put back in her warm stable.

Pa stood watching her with Barny at his side puffing on his pipe. He was thinking; dare he risk putting *his* horses out, one or two at a time, just to play and stretch their legs? It would be an almighty risk, but they were becoming decidedly restless standing day after day in their stables. Cilla seemed perfectly OK, even when she slipped over. she was back up instantly, bucking and prancing.. He must talk to Steve, see what he thought.

More snow fell during the night!

Steve and Pat had decided to let two horses at a time free into Sue's paddock. The lads were to watch them for half an hour and then the next pair could have a play...under supervision. By evening stables nearly all the horses had been out.

Sue's exercise paddock looked like a battle field, she was dismayed at the damage, but Odd Job Bob assured her that once he got on to it with a roller, it would be as good as new! But she wasn't at all happy. The race horses however had enjoyed their little bit of freedom! All looked content and refreshed, eating their meal with enthusiasm, which pleased Steve.

The ground remained frozen for the best part of a month, then at last the air turned a few degrees warmer and the thaw set in. Ditches and gutters were soon full to overflowing. Eventually the Gallops man was able to get onto the all weather tracks and things soon were back to normal, with the horses working again.

Lambourn High Street had loose horses trotting back from the Gallops with a few sore lads running to catch them! No one could blame the horses, they were all fighting fit when the snow came and confined them to their stables. It was just bad luck on the

178

lads who had got bucked off. The shouts of *'Loose Horse'* could be heard anywhere up on the gallops.

Pat was lucky, only one of *his* charges came home alone on the first day the gallops were open! The unfortunate lad limped home later, trying to keep out of Steve's way, not because he'd fallen off, but because he'd let go of the horse which had galloped off on its own.

Pat tried not to laugh when he heard Steve lashing out at the lad. He'd probably been talking to a mate and not paying attention to his horse. Horses are great levellers, and this one had grabbed the opportunity to put in a quick buck. The lad would have been riding short with his knees almost on the horses neck and stood no chance of hanging on. He would keep his mind on the job next time he rode out. Which would not be for another week, he was demoted to yard sweeping, such a disgrace for a 'would be' jockey.

Mr Briggs visited again as soon as the roads were clear. Lizzie, wrapped up in a sheepskin coat, looking like an Eskimo, trotted along beside her Dad.

Sue had got Cilla groomed and ready for Lizzie and had grabbed the smallest lad in the yard to ride her for a little while to take the tickle out of her toes before Lizzie arrived for her lesson. Cilla had been as good as gold; the lad had had no problem with her.

She decided to take Lizzie out along the lane for her ride, the paddock was still a slushy mess and very difficult to walk on. Lizzie was thrilled at the idea of riding along the lane, they would pass Kate's house, and maybe they could stop to say 'allo.

Sue brought Cilla out into the yard. Lizzie rushed to get on the mounting block; climbing up and down the steps seemed as much fun as riding! She could manage to mount by herself now and Cilla stood quietly while she tucked her feet into the stirrups and sorted out the reins, just short enough so that she could feel Cilla's mouth at the other end, one in each hand and thumbs on top.

When all was done correctly to Sue's satisfaction Cilla was told to 'walk on', and with a toss of her head and a swish of her

179

long tail, they set off. The air was very cold and before long they both had red checks and noses.

Cilla walked briskly, she was glad to be out again, so it didn't take long to get to Kate's gate.

"Can I go and say 'allo Sue?" There was no sign of her in the yard but lights were on in the house.

"Well you'll have to be quick, it's freezing standing here. Just say 'H-H- Hallo' and then come back". Sue was trying to make Lizzie talk properly, not dropping her H's and T's.

"OK...I'll just say...H...Hallo!" she slid off Cilla laughing. "Don't wait for me" sounding the T's correctly. "I'll only be a little while".

It was Sue's turn to laugh. "You cheeky monkey..hurry up or I'll be frozen to this spot!"

Kate's mother insisted they came in for a hot drink, so the girls put Cilla in an empty stable, threw a rug over her and hurried indoors. Kate grabbed Lizzies hand and they rushed up to her bedroom to look at all the presents she had got for Christmas.

Sue always found it easy to relax and chat with Charlotte who immediately set too and made hot drinks for them all.

Her kitchen was old and comfy, oak beams and a huge range with two dogs stretched out in front of it. It made Sue realize how cold and masculine her kitchen was. Pa didn't seem to notice how few luxuries there were, how cold and bare the walls looked. Here, in Charlotte's kitchen the walls were covered with photos of children, dogs and ponies. The dresser was a mass of silver cups and rosettes they had won over the years. It was all so homely. Maybe if her mother had lived their kitchen would have been as warm and welcoming as this.

"I must go Charlotte...Lizzies Dad will be going frantic, he idolizes that girl!" she called up the stairs for Lizzie. "Oh by the way, Serpent is running next week at Wincanton. Do you want to come? Goodness only knows how he'll run, I just hope he starts with the others!"

Charlotte laughed. "I'd love to come Sue, but I'd better see how things work out here".

The girls clattered down the stairs. "Do we have to go Sue?" Lizzie whined remembering the H.

"Yes we do...come on your Dad will be tearing his hair out".

"'Ee 'aint got much 'as 'ee! Thanks for the 'ot drink" she giggled forgetting all the H's.

"It's getting better; you'll get her talking 'proper' one day!"

They walked out into the cold air again, shivering after the warmth in the kitchen.

"Come again Sue, the kettle's always on the hob".

"Thanks Charlotte, I certainly will" she said as she helped Lizzie get back on Cilla. Kate opened the gate for them.

"We'd better trot a bit; we've been gone a long time".

"Bye Kate, bye Charlotte" shouted Lizzie.

"Trot on Cilla, I'm freezing" said Sue starting to run beside the pony. Cilla knew she was on the way home and set off at a spanking pace.

They were back in record time, Sue gasping for breath. But they needn't have hurried; Pa and Briggs were in the kitchen, a bottle of malt whiskey on the table, laughing and joking.

"Have a good ride my love?" asked Briggs.

"Yeah lovely....you 'aint 'arf gonna cop it if you drive like that!" she said shaking a finger at her Dad. Sue sighed, would she ever talk properly, she had her doubts.

Briggs got out of his armchair a little unsteady on his feet. "Should I drive him home Pa?" Sue was a bit worried by Briggs's erratic progress walking to his car.

"No I guess he'll be OK once he gets some fresh air...by golly but it's cold out here!" Pa stamped his feet, "let's go back indoors..he'll be alright, his a tough old devil".

Sue watched the big black car drive slowly out of the yard, he should be safe enough, Marlborough wasn't very far with no busy roads to cope with.

Pa piled logs on the fire. "I'll be glad to shut up shop tonight Sue; this cold gets right into my bones".

"Yes I know! Still the days are getting longer..Spring must be coming soon and then Cheltenham Festival!! Will Serpent be running?"

"Well I've entered him, have to see how he runs next week...Briggs is like a child with a new toy, heaven help us if he wins!"

"He'll go mad!" They stood warming themselves in front of the fire. She tried to imagine the kitchen with pictures on the

181

walls and brightly coloured curtains hanging on the windows. She made up her mind to talk to Pa about it.

"You do what you like my dear. Bob can do the painting...Yep, it's time we had a change...you do whatever you want, it's a good idea".

So she got her way and decided to talk about it with Charlotte, who *was* coming to Wincanton with them to see how the reformed Serpent behaved.

There was a touch of frost early the day of the Wincanton Races, the grass around the yard sparkled in the sunshine. "Looks like a good day" Steve said as he hurried the lads around the yard. He'd got in early to plat Serpents mane and tail. The horse knew as soon as the first plate went in that today was a special one. He must be going somewhere!

The daily routine went on as usual. The first lot went out, did some slow speed work on the gallops and came back, the lads all chatting and laughing. Then the second lot mounted up and were sent off followed by Pa in the car.

Serpent whinnied anxiously as he was left behind; he kicked the door in frustration. Sue came over to talk to him; it wouldn't do for him to get to excited and sweated up. He did seem to calm down a little, but she was relieved when she heard the second lot coming back down the lane.

They loaded him and headed for the race course. Not a long trip, but far enough with a horse that was stamping and kicking all the way.

When the ramp was lowered he came roaring down like a young stallion, the lad in charge had his hands full holding him. Sue helped getting him settled in his stable and stayed with him, talking, while he calmed down. He knew exactly where he was and why...he was ready...bring on the opposition!

Mr Briggs arrived at lunch time with an army of friends and well-wishers, all having consumed a lot of alcohol. Sue's heart sank when she saw them heading for the bar.

182

Pa managed to drag Briggs away in time to get him to the parade ring before the race.

Serpent looked truly magnificent, his coat shone like silver and his muscles rippled as he walked. He was very fit and obviously ready to race. The bookies took one look at him and dropped his starting price radically!

Sue and Charlotte had already placed their bets, and at a good price of twenty five to one.

"He does look good", Charlotte said. "All that hacking did it Sue, it has done him the world of good"

"And those jumps!! I'll never forget that ride, never ever. I felt as if I'd been launched into space!" laughed Sue.

"Does the jockey know what he's sitting on?"

"He soon will...come on Charlotte, let's get into the Grandstand and watch the fun!" They slipped away from the Briggs Army and left Pa with the over excited Briggs and his barmy army.

The horse danced and pranced all the way down to the start. The jockeys kept their mounts well away from the big white horse, they knew a good horse when they saw one.

The starter quickly called them into line and sent them on their away. Two and a half miles and eighteen jumps before they galloped to the finish.

Sue watched the start anxiously, would he start with the others? But Serpent was ready and leaped into the lead. Thankfully the Jockey was very experienced and soon had the horse tucked in behind the front runners. Sue was able to breathe again!

The first fence loomed, the jockey had moved Serpent to the outside of the leading group, so he had a good view of the jump. He flew it, ears pricked and going easily. *'Good Jockey'* thought Sue, as they came charging past the Grand stand for the first time, he was giving Serpent a careful ride.

They were running in about fifth place and going well on the outside. "Looks good" shouted Charlotte over the roaring of the crowd. Sue had forgotten Charlotte was with her as the horses turned away from the Grandstand and set off down the back of the course.

183

One horse came down at the next fence and brought another down with it. Sue gasped, but Serpent was OK.

"I can't watch this", said Sue. She had never felt so concerned about one of Pa's runners before.

Charlotte had her binoculars trained on Serpent, watching every jump, while Sue had her eyes closed. The commentator kept up a running commentary and every now and then the crowed groaned as another horse fell.

"The Grey, Silver Serpent still going well on the outside". The commentator shouted, he was getting quite excited now. *"Only six still running".*

"You must watch Sue", Charlotte screamed. "He's going so well".

"I can't" mumbled Sue. *'Please bring him home safely'* A silent prayer.

Two more jumps and a long run to the finish. "Here take my glasses".

"The grey is moving up smoothly on the outside" The loud speaker roared at Sue. *"What a jump, he's gaining on the leader with every stride!"*

Sue had to look, only one to jump and he was going easily. She started shouting. **"Come on Serpent. You can do it...stay on your feet,,careful now,,,,measure it..take your time".** Could he hear her? He seemed to; he took an enormous leap at the last and past the leading horse in mid air, galloped on without a break in his stride, to the winning line still going easily.

Sue was shaking from head to foot and had gone very white.

"You OK...you're not going to faint are you?"

"He won!" Sue said softly. "The bugger *won!*"

"Didn't he just" laughed Charlotte, "by a good few lengths!"

They pushed and shoved their way out of the Grandstand and over to the winners enclosure.

Mr Briggs led his winner in, a dream come true for him.

Sue laughed and cheered with the crowed, it was a moment to remember for all of them as Serpent walked sedately round while the photographers did their bit.

184

He looked well, not blowing much and still quite fresh. The jockey was all smiles. "Just like a ride in the park, the horse was loving it!...I'll ride him again if you like, any time".

Pa just smiled and stood back, it was Briggs's big day, let him enjoy it.

"Take the horse home quietly Sue" Pa said as he was being led away from the winners enclosure. I'll find Briggs's driver and make sure he gets back safely....I might be some time yet!"

Charlotte and Sue collected their winnings, a tidy sum between them, much to the bookies dismay, and went to find Serpent to take him home. He had done well and would run again at Cheltenham.

Sue took Serpent for a relaxing ride through the woods and out onto the downs the following day. She had arranged to meet Charlotte to enjoy a nice quiet ride together. She wanted to ask her about redecorating the kitchen; this morning would be a good time. It turned out she was an expert, having studied interior design at university. She jumped at the prospect of helping. "Your house is quite old?"

"I suppose it is...I don't know exactly, I've never thought about it".

"Well...if it is we might find some old beams or an inglenook!", Charlotte was getting excited.

"Oh I don't know if it's as old as that. Pa will know, I'd better ask him before we start knocking holes in the walls looking for an inglenook! But it would be exciting". They rode on over the downs thinking of plans for Sue's kitchen.

Serpent was none the worse for his race the previous day, in fact he had quite a spring in his step.

"Will he go to Cheltenham?" Charlotte asked after they had been riding for a while. "Bet we won't get those odds next time he runs".

"No that was fun...I've never won that much before".

"How much did you bet on him? Come on tell me!"

"Well...I had £50 put aside for his first race" Charlotte puffed out her cheeks. "But then Briggs gave me £100. For 'good luck' he said".

185

"Crickey....so what does it feel like to be a millionaire?" She laughed.

"It feels pretty good. No...*bloody* good..that's for sure!"

Charlotte suggested she came back later with her tape measure and sketch pad to look at the kitchen. "I can draw up a few ideas for you to look at later. If your Dad is out of the way we can look for old beams, and *maybe* an inglenook in that fireplace!"

"That would be great...I'll send Pa to the food merchants, that always takes him ages".

"Right then, straight after lunch, bye for now". And she trotted off heading for home, her mind already full of plans for Sue's kitchen.

As soon as she had gone Sue handed Serpent back to Steve. "He was good today; we had a lovely ride up on the downs". Barny, the half grown pup came bouncing up to meet her, his tail wagging glad she was back.

"Better keep the puppy out of the yard Sue...he's got no sense around horses yet, your Pa won't be best pleased if he gets kicked".

"Your right Steve, he's a bit stupid yet, but he's very loveable aren't you pup?" They headed for the house as Steve walked Serpent back to his stable, the pup dashing around in circles he loved attention, especially from Sue. He would learn in time to keep his distance from horses, but he was a liability at present in the yard.

She surveyed the area in the kitchen she wanted to alter. She went round taping the walls; what was hidden under the boring Magnolia plaster, and the fire place, was there an inglenook there bricked up many many years ago? Certainly the chimney breast was too wide for the existing fireplace...why hadn't she noticed it before? Could there be lovely old beams under the plaster board ceiling? Sue grabbed the torch and raced upstairs to her bedroom; there was a loose floor board under her bed, as a little girl she had hidden her treasures in the gap between floor and the kitchen ceiling. If she shone her torch in the space perhaps she would be able to see.

186

She pushed the bed to one side and prized up the loose board. There were still a few treasures, her favourite hair ribbon, an old stuffed toy... and a photo of her mother.

Sue sat back on her heels and looked at the smiling face she remembered so well. After all these years she still missed her; she could remember vividly the day she crashed the car, the quiet way the head mistress at school had told her about the accident, that her mother wouldn't be waiting for her after school...ever again.

She sniffed and wiped away her tears. It was a long time ago. Sue had been eight years old, but the pain and anguish was still there, just below the surface. As she had said to young Pete, it left a big hole in your heart.

Sue sat a moment longer looking at the long forgotten photo and then put the floor board back and placed mother's photo on her dressing table. It had been hidden away for too long. Tomorrow she would find a nice frame for it and look at the smiling face every day.

Pa was back in the yard shouting for Steve, he would be in for his lunch any minute now, so she hurried back down stairs and got busy in the kitchen. She had to get Pa out of the house for an hour or two this afternoon so the two girls could rummage round the kitchen looking for oak beams and the elusive inglenook! It would be an exciting afternoon.

He was dispatched straight after lunch with a long shopping list. His car was barely out of the yard before Sue was on the phone to Charlotte. "He's gone, the coast is clear!"

"OK, I'll be with you in a few minutes".

The collaborators got to work! Charlotte was very professional, she measured walls the width of the kitchen etcetera, and drew a rough sketch. The fireplace quickly drew her attention. "It's too big for an ordinary chimney Sue", she said at last. "Has it always been like this, it seems to me the tile surround is relatively modern?"

"I don't remember it being any different...it's always been the same from when mum was here".

"Well Sue...with your permission I would like to try something". She got busy measuring the chimney breast and

187

gently tapping the plaster so as not to leave a mark. She opened her bag and took out an electric drill. "Now don't worry...I'm going to drill a minute hole here about five feet above the hearth. "First of all the dust coming out will be the white plaster. But then, I'm hoping, it will turn to saw dust.....in which case we will have found the old oak lintel above your inglenook!"

"Wowee.....how exciting is this?......go to it Charllote!"

"I'll cover the hole up when I've finished so it won't notice". The drill whirled away shooting white dust everywhere. "Sorry about the mess".

"That's OK"

"Aha", the sound of the drill suddenly changed. "Now we'll know". They both peered anxiously as the drill went deeper, then slowly the plaster dust turned to wood,

"Its wood!!" shouted Sue

"That's it Sue...I reckon you have an inglenook, there must be an old beam behind the plaster".

"What about the ceiling?" she was really excited now. "Do you think there are oak beams up there behind the plaster?"

"Almost certain to be I should think". And she set about tapping the ceiling. "Listen the sound Sue, listen, its hollow here and solid over there....I reckon you have beams up here......shall I try the drill again?"

"Oh lord, what will Pa say, he'll think the house is full of wood worm!......Oh go on then, somewhere he won't notice". The beams *were* there, just as Charlotte thought; Sue's imagination was racing away!!

"This is not going to be just decoration is it Charlotte...this is looking like major renovation!" Sue said at last when they were enjoying a well earned cup of tea.

"It'll make a mess for a while, that's for sure".

Would Pa agree to so much upheaval, that was the question? "I'll draw up some sketches tonight when the kids are in bed, see what you think....I must be off now Sue, things to do at home. See you tomorrow". She drove off just as Pa got back from the shops.

"Make me a cuppa love before I have to do evening stables". He said as he dropped the shopping on the table...Was that Charlotte I saw driving off?"

"Yep..we had a cuppa and a chat". How could she ever tell Pa she wanted to pull all the plaster off the ceiling and tear the tiled fireplace out? It would have to wait for another day, she hadn't the courage now.

Carefully she made the tea and cut him a large slice of cake; her head was full of wild plans for the house.

"You alright love? You look kind of distracted".

"It's fine...just something Charlotte was talking about. I'll get on outside if you've got enough tea there" She made a hasty exit. Odd Job Bob was sure to know how old the house was, he was a mine of information about anything and everything in Lambourn, where could he be this time of day.

It was a touch early for evening stables, so there weren't many lads about yet. "Have you seen Odd Job about Tony?" she asked the only lad she could see lounging against a wall.

"He was here just now...I think he's in with Steve Sue".

"Thanks". Of course, that's where he'd be, huddled over the stove, a cup of tea in his hand chatting away about nothing in particular! She would just have time to talk to him before the yard got busy.

She opened the door to Steve's office. "Excuse me Steve, can I have a quick word with Bob?"

Bob looked up "What's up Sue?"

"Do you know anything about our house Bob, like how old it is?" She waited patiently, you could never hurry him.

"Well now young Suzie...why you want to know 'bout that?"

"Just interested" she tried to be casual, not too excited.

"Now let me think". There was a long pause, Sue was itching for him to get on with it! "When I was a young lad it were a flint cottage with a thatch.....why..it must be all of two 'undred year old...bit older than me!"

"Wow, as old as that Bob! But when did it all change....there's no flint or thatch".

"No, that would've been when that smart, young, developer from Lon'en got it. Ruined it 'ee did. Covered the outside wi'v that there pebble dash stuff and painted it all white". He took a mouthful of tea. "Ripped off what was left of the thatch, mostly gone anyway, and put a new roof on....proper smart it looks now don'e it Sue".

189

"Yes yes Bob, but what about the inside?" Sue was trying not to get impatient; he was quite an old chap really.

"Well I duno 'bout the inside. 'Ee made a bathroom and a new kitchen I knows that Sue". He paused, thinking again, trying to remember. "'T'was a shame 'ee covered up the inglenook though, you could sit inside and look up the chimney, see the sky!" He took more tea.

Sue was ecstatic, a big inglenook, big enough to sit in. She hugged the old man. "Bob...I love you....I really do!"

Odd Job Bob was so surprised, he spilt the remainder of his tea.

Sue dashed out of Steve's office. Charlotte must be told, but she ran straight into her Dad. Evening stables had started and Cilla was still in the field, it would have to wait until tomorrow, horses came first!

It was getting dark by the time she went out to the field to catch Cilla, nothing worse she thought than looking for a black pony in the dark. But thankfully Cilla was waiting by the gate. She had soon learnt when it was tea time and was usually ready to come in.

These days it was a bit quiet in Sue's yard, her two youngsters had gone over to the main yard some time ago and so far Pa hadn't been to the sales to buy replacements. Something else to talk to Pa about, but which should come first, house or horse? Why was life so full of problems!

Cilla was soon fed and tucked up for the night. Sue stayed with her for a while stroking her lovely black main, "Lizzie will be here tomorrow my love" she whispered, "We must start thinking about some shows soon". Will I get her ready in time I wonder? Will she ever learn to say 'thank you' and not 'ta' or 'fanks'. She smiled at the thought

"Good night Cilla, sleep well!" With a final pat she turned out the light and headed for the house, Pa, and supper. Would she talk to him tonight about the house, or new horses? It all depends on whether he was in a good mood or not!

He appeared to be in a very good mood and brought up the subject of new horses himself. While he was in town he had seen

190

the bank manager. The accounts were doing well, so Pa thought they could afford one or two yearlings...if Sue agreed.

"Wow Pa, that would be great, I've got room for two in my yard". She was delighted at the idea of having two youngsters to break in. All thoughts of the renovation and inglenook disappeared like a puff of smoke!

"We'll see what we can afford then shall we Sue?"

As promised Charlotte arrived in the morning with sketches of possible alterations. Sue explained about the purchase of some yearlings, and they agreed the plans could be put on hold. She was pleased to hear about the inglenook and that Bob remembered the cottage as it was before 'modernisation'. It would all help when they started ripping the plaster boards away. Sue looked at the plans lovely, especially one that had the imaginary inglenook and all the oak beams exposed.

"I'll show them to Pa. I hope he likes this one of the inglenook, it looks wonderful". She put that sketch on top. "But he will want to get the yearlings before I dare ask him if we can get to work on the cottage".

Charlotte agreed and put the sketches away in a folder, "Here...you keep them Sue and when the time's right we'll get on with it!" She was a touch disappointed but it wasn't the best time of year to be pulling the kitchen apart anyway.

Sue put the folder in a draw, the plans could wait, first must come the new horses.

Pa started looking around at various yearlings during the next few weeks.

The yard was very busy with horses running two or three times a week and the preparation of the forthcoming Cheltenham Spring festival...Serpents next race. How would he run? Was he ready or brave enough for those huge jumps? Sue worried about him, he was such a loveable horse, she couldn't bare thinking of him falling getting injured. She told her Dad she wasn't going to watch the race this time. He laughed. "You'll have to come, Briggs swears your his 'good luck' charm, he'll be most upset if I tell him you won't be there".

191

Sue was adamant, she couldn't go and watch her lovely Serpent face those jumps, gallop for two and a half miles against top class horses and then face the gruelling last half mile all up hill.

Pa smiled, he knew, come the day she'd be there, cheering and shouting alongside Briggs, it was all due to her patience and understanding that the horse was racing at all.

Sue concentrated on Cilla and tried to ignore the excitement in the yard. Lizzie was coming on so well now with her riding that Sue had taken to riding her Dad's old cob, Steady Eddie, alongside when they went off on longer outings through the woods and onto the downs.

Lizzie loved going through the woods. Sue would point out the various wild flowers as they came into bloom and name them all. The Badgers set, very old and well used, was a source of great excitement, although, despite sitting, and watching quietly, Mr Badger never appeared. Rabbits though, hopped and skipped everywhere, and even the mad March Hares ran across the short turf on the downs.

"You 'aint 'arf clever Sue" Lizzie said one bright morning. "Ow'd you know all that stuff 'bout flowers an 'fings?"

"Oh I read a lot, and anyway I'm a bit older than you!"

"Yeah, but still I 'fink your ever so clever".

"Well thanks Lizzie, that's very nice of you". They rode on in silence for a while.

"Why's there no 'ouses up 'ere then...where people live?

Sue smiled to herself, Lizzie never could get over the wide expanse of the Downs, at first she thought it was a park, but there were no iron railings, or gates, and no Park Keepers, to chase you off the grass. It was all a bit strange for a little girl who'd lived all her short life, surrounded by tall buildings and busy streets. So much space and the silent woods, it was like another world! Sue was so thankful she had been born and brought up here.

"Come on shorty, we'll go down to Lambourn where there are some pretty cottages you can see".

"'Ave they got shops down there...I'm starvin'"

"No...sorry Lizzie, there's a pub but nowhere to buy food".

"W'ot no MacDonalds...can't be much of a place". Pretty thatched cottages belonged on the lid of chocolate boxes as far as

192

she was concerned. This child certainly lived on another planet thought Sue.

They trotted through the village, the pretty thatched cottages and their neat little gardens hardly got a second glance.

There was a chippy and an Indian take away, the height of luxury and modern living in Sue's mind. No MacDonald, well well, how did they manage to survive!

They had been out longer than usual and Mr Briggs seemed unnaturally worried when they rode back into the yard.

"We've bin up in them 'ills" shouted Lizzie pointing up at the chalk downs. "It 'aint 'arf lovely up there Dad, you out'a come wi'v us one day".

"Yes my lovely, one day maybe, but we gotta go now. Say fanks to Sue...come on 'urry up!"

"Fank you Sue" she said speaking carefully. "Fanks for the ride".

"Come on Liz, 'urry up now". Briggs was in the car and ready to go.

"Bye Lizzie...you rode really well today, see you soon". Sue waved to them as the car raced off.

"He's in a hurry" Pa said coming to take Steady Eddie back to his stable. "I wonder what the hurry is today".

"Can't think, we.ve not been out *that* long". But it did seem a bit odd.

Cheltenham Spring Festival was upon them at last. Pa had a couple of runners early in the week while Serpent raced on Thursday. The tension in the yard was Palpable. Steve shouted and cursed at the lads although they worked endlessly to keep everything running smoothly, even Barny felt Steve's boot when he got too close to one of the two year olds.

"Get that dog out of my yard!" One of the younger lads quickly caught the pup and pushed him through the gate. Tempers were short, waiting for Thursday and the big race, all the stable staff were on edge.

193

On Wednesday Sue could stand the tension no longer. "I'll take Serpent out for a quick ride" she said to Pa. "It will relax him a bit, all this tension will only upset him".

"For God sake be careful, nothing must go wrong now, Briggs will kill us both if the horse goes lame or something!"

Steve was furious; he didn't want the horse out of his sight for a moment,

"Come with me then" Sue said cheekily

"I might just do that young lady",

"You could ride Steady Eddie, he's quiet enough", she laughed.

The lads who could hear the conversation were convulsed with the giggles, no one ever dared speak to Steve like that. Sue realised she had probably gone too far and said more then she should

"Sorry Steve....come on, a nice ride will calm us all down".

"You go if you must, be bloody careful that's all. He's fighting fit and full of his self....here Kevin, take the old cob and go with her!" He turned away and stomped back to his office. "Wot you lot standing about for...get on with your work".

"Phew, I'll be glad when tomorrows over" Kevin said "I've never seen him so worked up!" He quickly tacked up Steady Eddie and vaulted on to the cob, and then they rode out of the yard and headed for the woods.

Serpent strode along easily and Sue could feel the power in the horse. I hope he runs well tomorrow she thought, he feels so strong and fit. Those fences are huge...will he face them or chicken out at the last moment? No, he wouldn't do that, or would he! Her mind was in turmoil.

"He looks great don't he Sue" Kevin broke into her thoughts.

"Yeah....he *feels* good too". She smiled to herself. "He won't let us down Kev".

"I hope not. I've put me weeks wages on him!" They both laughed breaking the tension.

Serpent walked on, ears pricked, loving the early morning out in the woods. Sue was right, a nice quiet hack out was just what he needed to calm the nerves. Tomorrow he would come out fresh and eager to run.

The second string had gone out when they got back to the yard, Steve had gone with them. Pa was walking around the yard talking to the lads that were left working there. He came over to Sue and helped her with Serpents tack.

"What's the matter with Steve, he nearly bit my head off when Barny came out with me".

"I think he's having a bad day" laughed Sue

"I'll be glad when today is over, my nerves won't take much more". The day however just ground slowly on.

Steve's temper didn't improve. After the lunch break he caught a young lad and told him to bath Serpent. The lad scurried away to find some buckets and shampoo.

Serpent was a tall horse by any standards; standing close to eighteen hands, seventy two inches. The lad was less than five feet tall, sixty inches at the most! A box was needed to reach Serpents back, but he set about it happily enough.

The horse knew something was up, he fidgeted and stamped his feet making the lads job twice as difficult. He was practically finished when Steve came back to check the horse. Unfortunately there was a stain on his long white tail. He cuffed the lad round his head and really tore him off a strip.

"I'm sorry Steve" the lad was almost in tears. "I'll do it again".

"Too bloody right you will. Get it clean this time!" He walked angrily back to his office. The unfortunate lad ran off for more water.

Sue had seen all this going on and felt sorry for the lad. She quietly went over to the sparkling Serpent to help. "Here Rod let me do it". She sprayed the offending tail with a special shampoo she had for white horses....The tail turned blue!

"Christ Sue he'll kill me now" cried the terrified lad. "Wot you dun to 'im?".

"Don't panic Rod...get me some clean water" Sue said calmly as she rubbed the tail furiously. It was a mass of pale blue bubbles. "There you are Serpent, that looks ever so pretty" she laughed.

195

Rod came dashing back, a bucket in each hand, his face deathly white. "Do something quick Sue" he stammered "Before Steve sees wot you dun...he'll kill me!"

Sue laughed. "Don't worry" she said as she stuffed Serpents tail in the bucket of water, a quick swish round and the tail was pulled out. It was sparkling white....not a stain in sight! She stood back to admire the dripping tail. The boy was struck dumb.

"'Owd you do that?"

"Just the tricks of the trade Rod, and a special shampoo!" Sue slapped him on the back. "Don't tell Steve though....it's our secret".

At last it was time for evening stables and the Guv's usual inspection.

The horses were all eating well and had all been carefully groomed. No one wanted to fall foul of Steve tonight!

Pa looked Serpent over carefully; young Rod was holding his head with anxiety. "The horse looks good" he said rubbing his white handkerchief over Serpents back. He shook out the dazzling white tail, each hair silky and clean. "Did you do this?" turning to Rod, "By yourself?"

"Well not quite Sir...I had a little help" gulped Rod.

"Never mind lad, well done. Full marks I'd say Steve!" He passed on to the next horse.

When the last lights went out in the yard and Serpent was safely tucked away, Sue and her Dad went into the house.

"I don't know Sue...I think we deserve a trip to the Lamb. I could just do with one of their T-bone steaks tonight, how about you?"

"Give me ten minutes Dad and I'll race you there!"

NINETEEN

The day of the Cheltenham race dawned grey and damp. Not good for racing, but the forecast was an improving day with bright periods in the afternoon. The going was predicted as being firm with soft patches. Serpent was OK with a bit of mud; his big feet could plough through most he was likely to face.

Steve was taking the horse in the small lorry, along with Rod, and one of the bigger stronger lads, just in case Serpent got a bit excited and proved to be too strong for the slightly built Rod to lead around the parade ring.

They set off early to give the horse plenty of time to settle down once they got to the race course.

The assistant head lad took out the first string and supervised their work on the gallops, then the Governor drove up to watch the second string after which Pa was free to go to Cheltenham himself. Sue and Charlotte were ready and waiting when he got back.

Briggs phoned just as they were leaving to make sure his horse was OK. He was already at Cheltenham booked in at the Grand Hotel for two nights.

"He's fine", Sue told him. "He looks terrific, don't worry, we'll see you soon". Now they could go,

As usual the crowds were enormous, noisy, jostling. Some country folk in their tweeds and sheep skin jackets and townies in fashionable outfits, high heeled shoes, miniskirts and stupid hats. Sue said you could tell them a mile off, looking very pretty but hardly suitably attired for a damp draughty day at the races! Nevertheless every one joined in the fun and excitement that made the Cheltenham Festival world famous.

Sue wanted to put her £50 money on Serpent early in the day to get good odds, but early as she was he was only 12-1. She found an honest looking bookie and placed her money on Silver Serpent in the three o'clock race.

The bookie snatched her money and tucked it in his satchel. "Each way love?"

"No...to win" said a surprised Sue.

197

"Ere...do you know sumut I don't missus?!"

"I know a good horse when I see it" she replied with some scorn in her voice.

Charlotte laughed. "Come away Sue before he gets too curious". They went chuckling away to watch the first race.

Sue turned up the collar of her sheepskin coat; the wind had a bitter edge to it although the clouds were lifting on Cleeve hill as a weak looking sun was pushing through.

The crowd cheered and roared at the start of the first race as the horses and brightly coloured jockeys pounded up the long straight to the first jump. Who'd want to be anywhere else on a day like this, thought Sue, it made your heart beat faster and you had to cheer with everyone else, even though you hadn't got a bet on any of the runners.

The girls watched the first two races. Charlotte had won a little money on the second horse in the first race. Then after a quick cuppa they went to find Serpent in the saddling up box.

Steve was busy making sure the tack was on correctly. The number cloth, the weight cloth, saddle cloth, girths, circingle and all the other trappings a National Hunt horse needs to carry.

Pa was talking with Briggs, who was beside himself with excitement. He had brought two of his 'Boys' with him this time, both were about six feet tall and built like heavy weight boxers, close shaven heads and faces like Bulldogs!

Sue didn't like the look of them at all, reminding her of gangsters in American movies. Charlotte decided they must be his 'Minders'; because they positioned themselves either side of Briggs whenever he moved.

Serpent was enjoying all the attention; he even relieved Briggs of his new trilby hat and threw it up in the air. "Ere that's me new 'at you 'orrible 'orse" he laughed. "My Lizzie warned me about you!" One of the Minders retrieved it and keeping well out of Serpents reach handed it back.

When no one was looking Sue found herself pushed into a corner by Briggs. "Ere girl...put this in yer bag an' don't open it till you get 'ome". He pushed a bulky envelope into her hand and planted a big wet kiss on her cheek. "That's from my Lizzie...thanks for everything you dun for her".

"All ready Guv" said Steve.

198

"Let's go boys" Briggs shouted, and off he went smiling at Sue's expression. "Oh blimey. I nearly forgot" he rushed back rummaging in his pocket. "I put a bet on for ya Suzie my girl, 'ere, take the betting slip in case 'ee wins!"

Sue was struck dumb for a moment. "Oh thank you Mr Briggs, thank you very much" she mumbled at last, he smiled and blew her a kiss.

"So long luv" and with that he was whisked away by the 'Minders'.

Serpent strode around the parade ring as if he owned it; he looked superb and attracted a lot of attention. He was full of himself, bouncing about, but young Rod had a good hold and although he was in danger of being lifted off his feet quiet often he managed to walk calmly beside the big grey horse.

Sue watched the horse with pride; he had improved so much since he had come to Pa's yard. When he first arrived he was bad tempered and sulky, walked with his head down, ears flopping, bored with the whole racing routine. You wouldn't have given him a second glance. But now, six months later, he was a horse any trainer would be glad to have in his yard!

Charlotte and Sue stood a little apart from Briggs and Pa who was talking to the jockey, giving him instructions, he had ridden him in his last race and was only too pleased to be riding him again.

"Just keep him out of trouble" Pa was saying. "Let him see the jumps and try to stay away from the crowd,,,,good luck, bring him home safely"

"I'll do my very best sir" he said as the bell sounded for 'Jockeys Up' and walked over to the big grey horse. Steve gave him a leg up, *"Good luck Serpent"* he whispered and patted his neck.

"All right then?" he asked the jockey. "Take care of my little horse,,,good luck mate". He let the horse walk away round the parade ring and canter down to the start.

Sue stood silently as Serpent walked away; tears she couldn't hold back trickled down her cheeks. *"Take care of my big boy"* she thought.

Charlotte slapped her on the back "Come on Sue" she laughed, "Let's go and watch...here, have some tissue.....have the whole packet, but let's go and watch him win".

The girls pushed their way through the jostling crowd to get near the rail, it was almost impossible, but Charlotte managed to find a way.

All the horses were circling quietly at the start while officials checked girths and other bits and pieces.

At precisely three o'clock the starter called them into line. He dropped his flag and sixteen of the best chasers in the country were on their way with three miles to race and twelve jumps to contend with!

They galloped straight up the course towards the Grand stand, a mass of bright coloured jockeys, straining horses and pounding hooves.

Sue caught a glimpse of Serpent about half way down the group on the outside and going easily, the jockey sat quietly holding the horse, there was no need to push or kick, just letting him bowl along with the leading group, allowing him to see each jump clearly and keeping out of trouble.

They all cleared the first jump, Serpent put in a huge leap and gained a bit of ground. *"Don't go yet you old fool, take it easy you've a long way to go"* Sue said to herself.

The jockey steadied him and dropped back a place or two not wanting to be out in front yet.

Serpent was tucked in behind another horse now and still going easily. Just before each jump he was pulled out for a clear view with plenty of room. There was a bit of jostling and barging on the rails where most of the runners were.

Two horses went crashing out of the race; the crowd groaned and then cheered as both horses staggered up and galloped off after the other runners.

Sue had now lost sight of the field but the commentator kept the enormous crowd informed. It didn't matter to her who was leading or had fallen, she just needed to hear him say the big grey horse was going well.

They came past the Grandstand for the second time but now well spread out, some finding it a bit too far or having trouble with the soft going.

Serpent was still there in fifth, a bit muddy, but with ears pricked and seemed eager to get going! His jockey knew he had a powerful horse under him, he sat quietly, he could be patient a bit longer.

Charlotte was getting excited, jumping up and down. "Come on Serpent" she shouted as the leading group shot past. Sue was chewing her nails and praying. The next time they came past would be the fight for the winning post!

She caught the occasional flash of white as Serpent flew over fences, one after another, any minute now they would come back in view with only three more fences to go.

"Where *is* he, can you see him Charlotte?"

Charlotte handed her the binoculars. "See for yourself, he's moving up steadily!"

The commentator saw the sudden movement as the jockey asked for a little more speed and Serpent changed gear. "The grey horse Silver Serpent is cruising up on the outside...a gigantic leap...what a jump he made two out!" The commentator came alive, his voice rising with excitement, "One fence to go,,,, the grey is gaining on the favourite with every stride, surely he won't be denied!"

"Oh my word Sue, they're neck and neck!" Sue couldn't look as the last fence loomed up.

Serpent saw it, measured his stride and jumped passing the leading horse in mid air, landed safely and set off on the last gruelling half mile, the 'Cheltenham Hill', infamous for sapping the strength of most horses.

The jockey urged him on giving him more rein but not raising his whip, just hands and heels. "Come on old fellow...you can do this" he said to Serpent.

Serpent took hold of the bit, pulled at the jockey and pounded his way up the hill. No horse made any attempt to catch him, the favourite dropped further and further behind. Serpent had run them all off their feet!!

Sue and Charlotte were ecstatic and hugged each other. "He won...he won, he did it!" cried Sue. Charlotte was crying.

"Here...give me the tissue's back..I need one" she said laughing. They linked arms and went to watch Serpent being led in.

Briggs grabbed the horses bridle and kissed him repeatedly leading him proudly all the way into the winner's enclosure. He laughed and hugged everyone; he was a *very* happy man.

The crowd in the enclosure pushed and shouted, they all wanted photos of Serpent his owner, jockey and trainer who had ridden such a brilliant race.

Steve was happy Serpent had come back in one piece and the yard had at last had a winner at the Cheltenham Festival. However he wanted the horse checked over.

"Sue, would you take him back to the stable...he's just about done in. I'll be with you in a minute". He didn't look a bit 'done in' and cheekily removed an admirer's hat and tossed it in the air on his way out of the winners enclosure!

"Can you get him to do that again" asked a press photographer, "It'll make the front page in the Racing Post".

"Sorry, it's an old trick he learnt somewhere" and laughing she led Serpent away to his stable. She washed him down and looked for any cuts. He was fine, just a few minor scratches where he'd got too close to the birch fences.

Steve came hurrying back, red faced and out of breath. There was something wrong.

Sue looked up at him anxiously. "What's the trouble?"

"Christ Sue, there's chaos down there, Briggs has gone missing. Done a runner, his two bully boys with him!"

"Gone missing? He was there when I left with his horse"

"Well he *should* be, to collect the trophy, but no one can find 'im, not nowhere!" He thought it was funny and kept chuckling to himself while he got Serpent ready to travel home. "Oh yeah. I nearly forgot" straightening his rug. "Your friend's waiting for you by the gate; she can't come here without a pass".

"Oh Lor. Thanks Steve, I'd almost forgotten her, and I must go to collect my winnings. I'll be quick, wait for me". She dashed off, dodging horses and grooms, running back to the gate.

Charlotte saw her coming and laughed. "You missed all the excitement Sue. Your Dad had to collect the trophy. Briggs has disappeared!"

"So I hear, but I was only talking with him half an hour ago. Unlike him to miss his trophy! I nearly forgot to collect my winnings, which bookie was it Charlotte?"

"That fat one with green umbrella". She wasn't too sure either.

"Yep, that's him I think, come on".

The bookie handed Sue a lot of money. "Fifty quid at twelve to one on the winner!" he croaked. "Ere, do us a favour missy, go to some other poor sod next time you have a hot tip!" They both laughed, the bookie didn't, linked arms and walked away.

"Hang on a bit Charlotte. Briggs said he put a bet on for me. What did I do with the slip?" She rummaged around in her bag and at last found it in her pocket.

"That's at the Tote..over this way" Charlotte said pointing. "Come on".

There was a long queue at the paying out counter so they had to wait until Sue handed over the betting slip.

The cashier looked flummoxed and taken aback! "Will you wait here a moment madam, I must see the manager, I don't have this much money in my till!"

"What do you mean?" Now it was her turn to be flummoxed. She tried to grab the betting slip but the cashier was quicker.

"This bet is for one thousand ponds to win at eleven to one!! That's a lot of money...will you step this way please!"

On the way home she was convinced she was dreaming! What was Briggs up to? The money in a linen bag supplied by the Tote manager lay heavy on her lap. Then the bulky package he had thrust in her hand. *"Don't open until you get home"*. She could feel the package in her bag. What was going on??

Sue and Charlotte chatted away while Steve was very quiet driving carefully, he had a Cheltenham winner in the back stamping about behind them, and he couldn't take any chances with the big horse. Give him a nice quiet ride home the Guv had said. He had a big smile on his usual grumpy face.

203

"He ran well didn't he Steve". Sue broke into his thoughts. "He's a brave horse, those jumps looked fearsome!"

"He did that alright....did you see the old bugger pinch that ladies hat?" He roared with laughter. "Thank God he didn't eat it...I nearly died I was so embarrassed". They all laughed.

"I missed that, He's got a wicked sense of humour your Cheltenham Winner!" Charlotte said as they drove into the yard. All the lads were lining the drive cheering, they had even written **'Well done Serpent'** in chalk over his stable door.

Sue jumped down first from the horse box. "OK lads..eight o'clock in the Lamb....drinks are on me, you youngsters can have a Diet Coke. She knew all of Pa's staff would be there, and probably half of Lambourn!

Charlotte went home immediately, while Sue helped out in the yard for a while, fussing over Serpent, making sure he had a good thick layer of straw and plenty of clean water. Then she left, leaving Steve and the lads to get on with the feeding.

She went indoors and took off her coat. The linen bag was flung onto the kitchen table. Bundles of high value notes rolled out. What on earth was she going to do with all this money? She emptied her bag and the money she had put on Serpent was added to the pile, another six hundred pounds, plus the original fifty pound stake money.

She had to sit down; her legs had turned to jelly. Whatever was she going to-do with it?

The package Briggs had told her not to open! What *was* going on!! She blushed at the memory of that wet kiss.

Sue stared at the mysterious package lying on the table half hidden by money. What was so important that he'd tried to hide it from the people around his horse?

A big brown envelope tied up with string and stuck down with selotape. Opening it carefully she reached inside. More money! All old crumpled notes, very old and dirty. Lots and lots of money.

She gasped staring at the ever growing pile of money, and then a neatly folded letter dropped from the package. Her hands trembled as she opened it and started to read.

Dear Sue

By the time you read this I'll be gone. I've made some bad decisions, got mixed up with some bad guys just recently and the business has gone belly up. A lot of unpleasant people are after me, including the police. So for my own safety and my family's lives we are going. Can't tell you where then you can't get involved sorry. I have been in touch with Weatherbys and changed Serpents ownership to you. I do not want him to go to t anyone, he is happy with you and I'd like you to keep him. The enclosed money should keep him in oats for a little while. Sorry we can't take Cilla with us so you'll have to sell her. Her registration papers are in the post as are Serpents paper Lizzie will miss you and your lessons she sends her love. Thanks for making her so happy. Keep anything you get for Cilla to pay for any expenses. Look after your Dad Sue he's a really good honest guy. I will miss you all Love from   Alfie Briggs

Sue was stunned; she was still holding the letter when Pa came home.

"What a day Suzie, what a wonderful day!" He laughed as he hung his coat on the hook. He turned to Sue puzzled by her silence. "Christ Almighty....what's that,,,real money?! He picked up a handful of notes. "It *is* real....what you do..rob a bank?"

Sue held up the letter. "He's gone Pa, he's gone for good and he's given me Serpent!" She broke down and cried.

Pa sat beside her, put an arm round her shoulder and let her cry. The shock of all the days' happenings had just been too much.

When the tears had dried up and she was just sniffing he passed her a tissue. "Now Sue....tell me what's going on. How much money is here on my table....where did it all come from!?"

"It's from Briggs....well most of it. He put a thousand on Serpent for me. I put fifty on him earlier and then he gave me this fat package just before Serpent went out to the start. He said I must not open it 'till we got home. It was full of these dirty bank notes and this letter". She held the letter out for Pa to read.

He pulled out a chair and read it quietly...twice. "Well my love. He was obviously in a lot of trouble, so that solves that mystery; he had to disappear to save himself and his family by the sound of it. Poor old devil he didn't deserve this. I liked him a

205

lot you know. He just wanted his horse to win one good race so he could be proud of him. He loved that horse".

Pa looked at the money piled up on the table and fingered the old grubby notes. "It must be legal currency or he wouldn't have given it to you, although no bank would hand out notes in this condition. So there is another mystery! Money that can't be traced? It seems he was in something very dodgy. So now my love, you are the owner of a Cheltenham winner and you owe me this month's training fee!!"

They both laughed sitting at the kitchen table looking at each other.

"How much is there?"

"I have no idea ..haven't dared count it...must be about eleven or twelve thousand *without* the old notes". Sue said looking bemused at the fortune she had so suddenly acquired. "What'll I do with it all Pa, where can I put it" She shuffled the pile of notes.

"I think we'll put it all in a plastic bag and shove it in my safe. Tomorrow we'll go into town and put it all in the bank. That should please our bank manager!"

"That sounds like the best idea, I'll have to count it first Pa".

"Not tonight". He laughed "I've booked us a table at the Lamb. Charlotte and her man are coming as well".

"I told all the lads to come this evening Pa, I told them drinks are on me!"

"That's good; I expect they would be there anyway. Come on my girl, get changed and cleaned up...we're all celebrating tonight!!"

The celebrations went on well into the night; Charlotte and her husband were good company. Everyone laughed at Sue when she discovered he was the Gallop Man!

"Don't you hear me driving past your cottage every morning about five in my old Land Rover; it makes enough noise to wake the dead!" He teased.

"My God, I had no idea you were the Gallop Man. *Charlotte!*"

"I thought you knew" Charlotte couldn't stop laughing.

"I feel so stupid I do apologise, how stupid can you get"

206

Another trainer was also celebrating two winners. He had overheard the banter. "We couldn't do without Dan, he keeps us in business! Where did you find that horse Pat? I don't remember seeing him before. I'm jealous".

"He's been with us for some time, had a bit of a mental problem to start with, but Sue sorted him out".

"I've got a few in my yard with mental problems, and they 'aint all horses!....Has he been entered anywhere Pat?"

"Not yet...have to see what the owner thinks". And I bet she will never enter him if I know my daughter. I wonder what she'll think when the owner's winnings drop on her lap.

There were a few bleary eyed lads the following morning, and two were late, Steve ticked them off loudly in front of all the other lads and put them on yard duties for the day. No riding for them.

Sue took her new horse out for a quiet walk. He was a bit stiff but otherwise his usual happy self.

What am I going to-do with you Serpent she thought as she rode him slowly through the woods. "You're not going racing" she told him "I couldn't watch you over those jumps again!" It was wonderful to have been given such a lovely horse, but it had its problems.

Charlotte, as usual, came up with some good ideas. "He's big and powerful with lots of stamina. Why not try him at endurance riding?"

"Or" added Dan, "Why not try him in the Drag hounds Team chasers that would be fun, he'd enjoy that...so would I" he laughed. "Fancy having a Cheltenham winner leading our team!"

"You'd never keep up with him!" Charlotte scoffed. "The most you'd see of him would be his back end disappearing out of sight".

"Yeah you're probably right" he sighed. "But it's a lovely idea".

Sue said nothing, she also thought it was a good idea though, Serpent would probably enjoy being in their team, he'd have to be the leader otherwise he'd be pulling like mad trying to get in front. She might give it some serious thought.

207

A few days later Sue and Charlotte were out for their usual ride, through the woods and out onto the downs. Sue decided to find out a bit more about Team Chasing.

"Charlotte...about this team racing, how does it work?"

"Oh don't tell me you're getting keen! It's fast and dangerous, but great fun".

"So I gather from what Dan was saying".

"You really want to know more about it? Why for heaven's sake Sue. It's not for Happy Hackers like you and me". Anxiety creeping into her voice.

"No, but it might be good for Serpent, stop him getting bored. He's not ready to be a 'Happy Hacker', not for a few years anyway". Sue was quiet serious.

"Well OK...but promise me you won't try it yourself".

"I promise".

"OK then....You have a team of four horses. You race against the clock over a course usually about two miles, cross country, jumping maybe fifteen natural jumps...you know. hedges, ditches, tree trunks, nothing very big. The fastest time by the first three horses count. You only need three to finish; the slowest of your team is not counted. The fastest team is obviously the winner!"

"Sounds exciting...I think Serpent would like a bit of that, stop him getting bored and moody again wouldn't it".

"It's not for the likes of you and me Sue" Charlotte said quiet concerned.

"No, but your hussy Dan might like to have a go on Serpent don't you think?!"

"He'd love to I've no doubt, he's a strong rider and Serpent would certainly spice up his Drag hunts team".

"Ask him then Charlotte, see what he thinks". They rode on in silence for a mile or so.

"What's going to happen to Cilla Sue?"

"Well I'll have to sell her I suppose, Briggs can't keep her, shame really, she's a lovely pony. I was looking forward to having Lizzie on her at some shows this summer........I miss that little kiddie, she was so much fun to teach".

"Yeah I know what you mean, even though you never did 'learn 'er to talk proper'!" They both laughed and jogged on home.

TWENTY

Easter holidays came all too quickly. It was lovely to see the spring flowers blooming Daffodils and tall Tulips seemed to suddenly shoot up everywhere, but it also brought a flush of rich grass and Katie's pony was crippled with Laminitis, a painful, sometimes fatal condition of horse's feet.

The poor pony could hardly stand, so Katie's Pony Club rally was quite out of the question.

"How would you like to ride Cilla" Sue asked the tearful child, "She needs some work and I must think about selling her now the weathers improved".

Katie's face lit up. "Could I mum?" she looked up at her mother. "Could I practise a bit and then take her to the Pony Club?"

Well, Charlotte couldn't refuse such an offer and was really grateful. "It's only a working rally, you know, just to get the kids and their ponies ready for the shows. Just a bit of schooling really".

"Ideal, just what Cilla needs, do you want to take her home with you or shall I keep her here?"

"Let's take her home mum pleeease, I'll look after her I promise".

Charlotte wasn't sure what to say, it would be more convenient to have Cilla at their farm, but she was a *very* expensive pony.

"She'll be fine with you Charlotte, I know you won't let her eat too much grass! Katie will be able to ride her more often if she's with you".

"Alright then Sue...but you young lady, get the broom out and really clean the spare stable. You can't have this aristocratic pony standing in a dirty stable. Get to it, NOW!" Katie dashed off, and then dashed back.

"Thank you Sue, thank you very much" and gave her a big hug before dashing off again to find the elusive broom.

Charlotte sighed "You're an angel, thank you; I'll take great care of Cilla".

"I'm relieved Charlotte. The pony needs the work and needs children round her, Katie will be fine".

210

So Cilla moved next door for the Easter holidays. Lots of riding and the pony club rally to look forward to. Katie was ecstatic to have such a lovely pony for the rally, but to have her to ride every day through the holidays was just fabulous.

She worked hard all morning sweeping out the spare stable. It hadn't been used for ages, not since her elder brother Sam had got tired of riding ponies and yearned for a motor bike. He still had a few years to wait before he could get his driving licence and a proper bike, but in the mean time he had a scramble bike to ride around the farm. More fun than ponies but not as reliable.

Sam offered to give the stable a fresh coat of paint and between them it was ready for Cilla the next day.

Charlotte went with Katie to collect the pony. Sue said she would ride back with her on Serpent. Cilla looked lovely, her new summer coat was growing through and it shone like velvet. There was just a touch of sadness in Sue's voice as she said goodbye to the pony she had admired for so long.

Katie would get Cilla going really well before the rally Sue was sure. They would certainly turn a few heads at the Pony Club, perhaps someone would want to buy her, she was after all going to be advertised fairly soon.

As soon as they got home Katie wanted to take her out for a ride up on the downs, or more likely show off to her school friends! Her mother was very firm about where and when she could ride her. Katie had to realize Cilla was only on loan for the school holidays and would then have to go back to Sue and be sold.

There were tears and tantrums to start with. She didn't understand why she had to go back and be sold. Surly they could buy her and keep her, she was such a lovely pony.

Charlotte had to convince her they couldn't afford another pony and that her own pony would soon be well again. Laminitis didn't last forever, and if they were careful with her she probably wouldn't get it again. Beside which Cilla was quite small and Katie would soon be too big for her.

Katie and her mum rode out every morning, through the woods and up onto the downs. It was easy to do some schooling, the downs were perfect too for getting Cilla to do a collected

211

canter, something she hadn't attempted with little Lizzie, and introduced her to jumping. She enjoyed jumping and would readily try anything they came across.

Sue was amazed with Cilla's improvement; she had only been with Katie for about a week when they had met Sue in the woods on their morning ride.

Katie wanted to show Sue how nicely Cilla could jump, so she led the way through the woods and over little jumps. The big horse followed trying not to overtake the little pony.

Serpent, embarrassed by the whole charade, crashed through every 'jump' scattering the flimsy branches in all directions.

Out of serious training and with a much stronger bit, he was better behaved and easier to manage, but these so called jumps were an insult to his pride!

Sue could understand the big horse trashing the so called jumps and patted his proud neck. "You'll have to do better than that when Dan takes you Team Chasing my boy!"

"What!" Charlotte turned in her saddle. What did you say Sue".

"I said" and she spoke very slowly and clearly. "I said he would have to jump better than that if Dan was going to take him Team Chasing".

"Do you mean it...do you really mean you'd let Dan jump him!?"

"Depends on what sort of a rider he is" she teased, "I'd have to watch him over those jumps by the Wantage Road, you know the ones I mean!" They both burst out laughing.

"Oh my goodness, just wait 'till I tell him. I can't wait, he'll be over the moon!"

"Got to see him ride first" laughed Sue, "Not a beginner's ride my Serpent, no indeed, defiantly not a beginner's ride".

Katie had gone on ahead and was practicing her collected trot and then asked Cilla for a collected canter. The little pony eagerly obeyed and went into a collected canter and then allowed Katie to bring her back to a nice smooth trot again.

"Just look at that pony" Sue gasped. "Hasn't she improved since Katie's had her?"

212

"Yep I think she has.....you know I'm going to have a problem with her at the end of the hols!"

"I'm sorry Charlotte...it's my fault really, I should have spoken to you first, stupid of me".

"Don't worry, she's having so much fun, it's keeping her from getting bored, and I've told her we can't keep her....they do look well together though don't they?"

"Yes damn it, they do!" muttered Sue.

Katie rode Cilla every day, and every day both pony and rider improved. It was so much easier to ride well when you had such an eager pony under you, and Cilla, not being hampered by a lead rein and an absolute beginner, was showing her true potential, and the fact that she enjoyed jumping, was an added bonus.

For Katie the Pony Club rally couldn't come soon enough.

Charlotte told Dan there was a chance to ride Serpent, and at the first opportunity he spoke to Sue about it.

"Are you sure Sue, he's a very valuable beast?"

"Dan, I'm sure Serpent will love it....but you might have to let him lead. He's been bred and trained to race as you know, and race he will if there's another horse in front of him!"

"I'm sure we can arrange that" Dan was smiling. "But I'd better try him over some jumps by myself first".

"You'll be in for quite a ride, we know, don't we Charlotte, because I tried it once, he was hardly fit then and you came to the rescue! Remember Charlotte?"

"I certainly do!"

"Are you trying to put me off now? *You* told me about the Wantage road problem didn't you Charlotte, so I'm as well prepared as I can be!"

A few days later it was arranged that Dan and Charlotte rode up to the infamous jumps with Sue. Dan road Serpent through the woods and up onto the downs to get accustomed to the big horse. He was amazed at the strength of the horse and couldn't wait to get to the field with the jumps.

Sue rode Charlottes hunter and Charlotte had the young horse she often road when they were just happy hackers.

213

Surprise surprise, when they got to the jumps, another member of Dan's team just happened to be there rolling the turf with a large tractor.

"Did you tell him we were coming?" Charlotte asked quite angrily.

"Well I might have mentioned it in the pub last night. I only said the field could do with some attention....I might have said something about trying a new horse".

"You're impossible....I think we'll just turn round and go back". She really was cross with her husband.

"Seems a pity to go home Charlotte. Serpent has seen the first jump, look at him, his ears are pricked! He'll be ever so disappointed if he doesn't jump at least one!!" She looked at Charlotte; they both knew what would happen if Serpent was allowed to get at the first jump, he wouldn't stop until he'd jumped all six!

"Oh go on then...but I'm not happy with you!"

Sue got the giggles and didn't dare look at her friend.

"I'll just go over the first...see what he feels like" innocent Dan said. Charlotte was trying very hard to look cross, but she had to turn away before she too got the giggles!

The friend driving the tractor had pulled to the side of the field and turned off the engine.

All was quiet except for the horses champing on their bits.

"I'll go then". Dan pulled his crash hat down firmly and turned Serpent towards the first jump shortening the reins.

Serpent responded as the giggling girls knew he would. A violent leap forward, he snatched at the bit and he was off, ears pricked and hooves pounding the newly rolled turf.

The girls thought they heard 'blimey', they couldn't be sure, it may have been something stronger as horse and rider shot away.

Serpent was enjoying himself, the sun was shining, the turf was soft and he had an experienced rider on his back, what more could a fit horse ask for.

Dan quickly recovered from the initial shock of acceleration and began to enjoy the experience of riding such a safe bold horse. There was never a hint he might fall or stumble; he was as sure footed as a mountain goat!

214

The girls watched amazed, Sue was so proud of her big horse, both horse and rider enjoying each other's ability. Dan was enjoying himself so much he went round the jumps twice!

Eventually he rode back to the girls beaming. "What a horse Sue, what a dream of an animal he is!"

"Yep...he's quite a boy...do you think he'd be any good in your team?"

The tractor driver had joined them, he was looking at Serpent admiring the big horse. "Where on earth did you find this one Dan?"

"He's mine...and before you ask, no, he's not for sale".

"Whoa...I only asked, I've not seen him out hunting or anything".

"Sorry" Sue apologised. "He's mine, Dan was just trying him out, he's too strong for me to jump".

"I can believe that, Barry's my name by the way". He reached up to shake her hand. "I captain the Team Chasers".

"Well well, there's a coincidence", Sue laughed. "Fancy you being here this morning just as Dan was trying out a new horse for your team!"

"It wasn't *quite* by chance I admit...but I wouldn't have missed that exhibition of jumping for anything". They went on discussing Serpents qualities when Charlotte put an end to it.

"Come on Sue, I must get home, lots to do for the pony club rally tomorrow".

"Yes I'm coming...nice to have met you Barry".

"See you again maybe".

"Perhaps" she laughed.

Charlotte smiled, why not indeed; he was a very eligible young man.

Dan dismounted at his farm gate and reluctantly handed Serpent back to Sue. "I really envy you Sue, but my word he's strong!"

"Well, if you want to borrow him for the team that's fine...but do look after him, that's all I ask". So it was agreed, He would have Serpent for his team.

Sue rode Serpent the last mile home; he strode out confidently his ears pricked backwards as Sue spoke to him. "You'll like that

215

old buddy won't you, a bit of fun on a Saturday eh! But please be careful won't you?" The big horse tossed his head; did he really understand what she was saying?

She put Serpent into his stable and went indoors to prepare a snack for Pa and herself. Tom the postman had delivered during the morning the usual rubbish that was immediately thrown away, but Sue noticed two official looking envelops, one addressed to Pa the other to her!

From Weatherbys! Apologising for the delay in sending the winnings but there had been a problem about ownership of Silver Serpent. She had completely forgotten. Of course, she was the owner so all this on top of the winnings at the Tote and the money Briggs had given to her. Pa also had earned a lot on that fateful day at Cheltenham. His racing yard was in profit!

Katie had been busy while her parents were riding out on the downs. She had bathed Cilla, scrubbed her white socks with the nail brush from the bathroom. Her tail had been carefully brushed and then washed in a bucket. She was nearly as wet as the pony when she'd finished! She was happy to have got Cilla looking as good as a little girl could.

Her mother was delighted to see the pony looking so clean and tidy. It was a shame the pony would soon be too small for Katie; they must just enjoy her while Cilla was with them.

Tomorrow would be fun for both Katie and Cilla; neither had ever done anything like a Rally before so it would be very exciting.

Katie spent the rest of the day cleaning Cilla's saddle and bridle. It was all made of the best English leather, beautifully soft and hand stitched thanks to Mr Briggs who had insisted the pony had only the best of everything. Her tack was the finest Katie had ever seen.

It was so very difficult for the little girl to understand why Lizzie had suddenly gone away without Cilla. Charlotte had tried to tell her she had moved a long way away and couldn't take the pony.

Katie was too young to be told the truth, and anyway no one actually knew where the Briggs family had gone. It seems they had just vanished without a trace.

Katie was up early. She rushed out to check on Cilla but her mother was already there feeding the pony.

"You'll need a white shirt and pony club tie my love. Do you know where the tie is?"

"Not sure...it's probably in my jacket pocket".

"Well go and look...you know you have to wear a tie".

Discipline in the pony club was very strict. Charlotte thought it was a good thing, too many people these days didn't care how they dressed for riding and the pony club children had to make sure their clothes were always clean and tidy. Jeans were absolutely forbidden.

Katie found her shirt and tie on a hanger in her wardrobe, her tweed jacket neatly pressed was there as well. She knew where her riding boots were since she polished them last night.

Everything seemed to be ready. She admired herself in the long mirror, just needed to plat her hair and they could set off for the Rally!

Her mother led Cilla into the trailer. Checked that they had everything needed and away they went.

The Rally was at Wantage, only a short distance to travel. Katie could have ridden there, but it was quite a busy road so it was safer, easier and more convenient to use the trailer.

Cilla was a bit unsettled at first, Charlotte was a little worried. The pony had never been to a pony club rally before and with so many children and ponies dashing about it was asking a lot of a young pony to behave well.

"I think I'd better lead Cilla around for ten minutes or so" she told Katie. "She'll never have seen anything like this before and I don't want you being bucked off! Go and find out which group they've entered you in love. I'll just get Cilla calmed down a bit for you".

Katie pulled a face. She desperately wanted to ride Cilla to show off to her school friends, but reluctantly walked off to look at the list of groups.

Charlotte put the bridle on Cilla and took her for a walk round. At first she danced about and whinnied a lot, a good job Katie wasn't on top, she surely would have come off!. They walked in between the trailers and horse boxes, people looking

217

enviously at the little pony, until she eventually began to settle down.

When Charlotte was satisfied Cilla wouldn't do anything silly she took her back to the trailer. Katie was there sitting on the ramp, her face as black as thunder. *'Oh no, what's wrong now'* thought her mother.

"Here we are!" she said cheerily. "Where's your saddle?"

"It's not fair" Katie spat out.

"What's not fair?"

"They've put me in the babies group 'cos I'm not ten yet!!" She was very close to tears; probably her pride had taken a big knock.

"Must be a mistake love...come on...get up on Cilla. I'll see what's going on".

Katie sniffed. "It's not fair...I don't need a lead rein. I'm nearly ten and I can ride better than those little kids".

"Get on now....ride your best. I'm sure it's a mistake. They'll see that and move you up a grade".

She was still mumbling and sniffing as she rode off to join the young ones group.

The ponies were already circling the instructor when Katie arrived and joined at the end of the line. "Help me Cilla" she whispered. "We don't belong here".

Cilla thought it was just another show. She tucked her head in and stepped out brightly. Katie sat well, hands in the right place and feet still in the stirrups looking relaxed and in control.

They caught the instructor's eye immediately; she watched the lovely pony and her sensitive rider walking quietly round to join the other ponies. *'Where did they come from!'* she thought.

The instructor asked the first child to walk their pony round and join at the back of the line so that she could watch each child, and consider how to help them improve.

Cilla stood at the end of the line, quite still, like an old hand at this showing game.

At last it was their turn, Katie rode forward, did a perfect halt in front of the instructor, bowed politely as mother had drummed into her. Then picking up her reins she set off at a brisk walk. Half circle to the right and break into a collected trot, Cilla pointed her toes and floated along. Complete a figure of eight

218

trotting, move up a gear and canter the first half of the figure of eight. Now, could they pull off the next move, very advanced, but they had been practicing secretly, *'let's do it'* she whispered to Cilla. The first circle completed they approached the centre. *NOW*...Katie shifted her weight, used a little leg pressure and a slight change of rein....it happened. A perfect flying change and they completed the figure of eight at a lovely collected canter!! Katie blew out her cheeks and sighed. They came back to a trot, then a business like walk straight at the instructor, a perfect halt and a polite bow. Katie knew she had done her very best.

The instructor smiled at Katie "My dear that was a perfect display, I can't think what you are doing in my beginners group...you should be with the advanced children! Come with me".

Katie gave her mum a quick grin as they passed her, she in turn gave her a big thumbs up, she was so proud of her daughter, all the hard work she had done with Cilla. That 'flying change' was quite advanced stuff and they had pulled it off to perfection. Charlotte was about to follow when her thoughts were interrupted

"Excuse me". She turned to see a woman in a car she was standing next to.

"Is that your daughter riding that beautiful pony?"

Charlotte was startled. There was an elderly lady sitting there with a pair of crutches propped up beside her.

"Why yes...yes it's my Katie".

"Lovely rider...lovely pony too! I was wondering if you would want to sell her....your daughter will soon be too big for her".

"Very true" Charlotte was taken aback a bit. "Actually the pony doesn't belong to me; she's on loan for the holidays. But yes, I think my friend is thinking of selling her".

"Good...help me out of this darned car; I want to have a closer look". Charlotte opened the car door and helped the old lady out. She was severely crippled and couldn't stand without the crutches. "Does she drive?"

"Pardon!" This woman was beginning to annoy her.

"Does she go in harness?"

219

"Oh..I see" a startled Charlotte gasped. "Well no, she's only four and just broken". Who *was* this abrupt woman asking all these questions?

"That's a pity....but it can be easily remedied". She hobbled away from the car leaving Charlotte who was looking bemused, what a woman!

"Where's the damned child got to on that pony".

Charlotte was getting more and more irritated. "I should think she's joined another group" she replied being deliberately polite. "I was about to follow her" she turned to walk away and bumped straight into Barry!

"Hello Charlotte. We meet again!"

"Oh Barry, what on earth are you doing here?"

"Had to bring me old Gran" Then added whispering "It's my turn unfortunately".

"I don't think I've ever met her?"

"Yes you have!" nodding towards the car.

"Oh my God Barry...I'd no idea. She's a bit of a tarter isn't she!? Sent me off to find Katie and her pony".

"That's my Gran, her bark's worse than her bite I promise you".

"I'll take your word for it...but I must find Katie, Did you see her ride just now, she rode *so* well. I must find her before your Gran does" They walked off together.

"Is your friend Sue here today?"

"No they're all busy....got a horse running at Newton Abbot I think".

"A nice girl". Charlotte smiled knowingly.

They found Katie riding with the advanced group, a huge smile on her face.

"I think your Gran will have to wait until they stop for lunch. Wild horses wouldn't drag her out of that group"

"No I can see that....I think I'd better head her off, see you later". He waved to Katie and set off to find his Gran.

He found her and got her settled back in the car. "Lunch Gran?" He said as he got the picnic basket from the boot. "We've got smoked salmon or chicken" and offered her a plate.

220

"Smoked salmon" came the sharp reply. "I want that pony Barry" she snapped. "Go and find that child".

"It belongs to a friend of mine Gran. I can take you to see it tomorrow if you like, but not now; she's busy with the group".

"Fiddlesticks!"

"Tomorrow you can meet Sue who owns the pony". Somehow that idea appealed to him. "I'll arrange it for tomorrow afternoon Gran, and then you can have a good look at her".

"Hmm...I suppose that will have to do...fix it then Barry. I mean to have that pony!"

Barry 'fixed it' with Charlotte who suggested he called round to tell Sue what was going on.

"Brilliant idea, better keep the owner informed!" He set off jauntily to find Sue at the racing yard.

She was sitting in her kitchen when Barry got there, she invited him in. "Cup o' tea Barry?"

"Thanks Sue...I just called to tell you that you might have a sale for Cilla!"

"Oh...wasn't expecting that, she hasn't been advertised yet!"

"Actually Sue, it's my old Gran, she's very determined to have her".

"Bit small for an adult!"

He sipped his cup of tea and explained about his elderly Gran.

"She had been a great rider, riding in lots of point to points, but had a terrible fall; the horse landed on top of her and broke her back. They said she would never walk again, she's so stubborn, wouldn't listen to them and decided to prove all the doctors wrong!"

"Poor woman, but why on earth would she want a little Welsh pony?"

"I'll tell you why Sue. She had many painful operations and therapy, to get her on her feet again and with sheer determination she made it. Couldn't ride mind you Sue, but she never lost her love of horses. She wouldn't let the family shoot the horse; she kept him for another twenty years when he died of old age.

"Poor woman" Sue said again.

"Now Gran's living in the old family house in Dorset, a big place with God knows how many acres. My brother lives there with his family and looks after her".

Barry went on about his brother's two children, the reason she is so keen to have Cilla. They are young but good riders, away at school during term time. If Gran could get the pony broken to harness she would have fun driving her when the kids were at school and then they would enjoy her when they got home on holiday.

To Sue it all sounded perfect, but the pony had been *very* expensive originally and was worth a lot of money.

"Don't worry about that Sue...what Gran wants Gran gets, she's not short of a bob or two!"

A price was agreed and money changed hands. Poor Katie wept for a week.

Barry arranged to pick Cilla up when he took his Gran back to Dorset. He arrived at Sue's yard early when Gran, of course, supervised the loading of her new pony, which wasn't a problem, Cilla knew all about trailers and walked calmly straight into it.

"Sensible pony...that's good" said Gran as she shook Sue's hand and hobbled to her car. "Come on Barry, don't take all day we've a long way to go" she snapped.

Barry took his time fastening the ramp. "Sue" he stuttered. "Can I take you out for a meal tomorrow; I should be back in the afternoon? Just to say 'thank you'?"

Sue smiled, why not she thought, he's nice...and handsome. "That would be lovely; I'll look forward to it".

"So will I...bye then, till tomorrow".

The luxurious trailer pulled away. Cilla was on her way to Dorset and a new life.

Sue went to close Cilla's stable door. *'I'm going to miss that pony'* she thought.

Life was moving on for Sue. Pa had decided and Sue agreed, that with all the money Serpent had won at Cheltenham, plus the fortune Briggs had given to Sue, they would build a new block of stables and call it 'Briggs Barn!

222

She stroked Serpents neck, would they ever see Briggs or Lizzie again, who could tell. In her heart of hearts she hopped they were both safe....somewhere.

TWENTYONE

Barry drove the long boring way to Dorchester in Dorset to take his Grandmother back home. On the way they made a slight detour to deliver Cilla to the yard where she was to be broken to harness.

Gran watched the unloading and made sure everything in her stable was satisfactory.

Tony and Shirley, the young couple entrusted with her care were friends of the old lady, and were used to her rather abrupt manner. They understood why she was often short tempered with everyone; it must be dreadful to be in almost constant pain and have to watch other people working with horses, doing what she would so much have loved to do herself. They promised to take great care of the pony and keep her informed of her progress.

Barry helped her back into the car and drove the last few miles to Chilcombe, the old family farm where his brother Tim would be waiting for their Grandmother's return.

Tim and his family lived in the farmhouse with Gran since his parents had died; he ran the farm for her. His two children were away at school during term time, they had their own rooms at the far end of the house, and had learnt at a very early age to keep clear of Gran and to keep the noise down when she was about. 'Children should be seen and not heard' was her belief and they had been told many, many times!

She had her own set of rooms in the 'west wing' of the house. A very big old farm house the family had owned for many generations, so she was rarely disturbed by the youngsters. She often entertained her friends in a very comfortable living room, full of beautiful antique furniture and oil paintings of her dogs and horses she had loved over the years. Her best Crown Derby and Wedgewood china was kept in a glass fronted cabinet, only used if someone 'special' was invited to tea! She lived in the past, refusing to indulge in 'modern' conveniences. No television for her!

Vicky, Tim's patient wife, looked after his Grandmother. She ran the house, kept the antique furniture polished and gleaming and tidied up after her, she was quite incapable of doing much for herself. They got on well together most of the time.

224

Cilla was soon broken to harness, she was an intelligent pony and was quickly trotting round the quiet lanes enjoying the new scenery and the sensation of pulling a little carriage behind her.

Some years earlier Gran had seen the little carriage advertised in one of her horsey magazines. It was a copy of a carriage Queen Victoria had designed when she was plagued with rheumatism; the driver had only a very low step to negotiate instead of having to climb up to reach the driver's seat. She decided to buy the carriage and then keep it carefully stored away until she found the ideal pony to pull it.

Cilla! She had found the ideal pony at last and was impatient to take her out for a drive. She could get into the carriage almost unaided and once there she would be totally independent. She could go wherever she wanted, she hadn't been that independent since that terrible day when she'd fallen off, and her horse had fallen on top of her.

Five weeks after Gran got home from Lambourn Cilla was delivered to her new home, broken to harness and safe in every way for her to drive.

Tim had prepared a stable for her in the old stable yard, built in the good old days when horses were used for farm work and the only means of transport.

The little carriage had been stored in the old carriage house, a building large enough to take a big carriage pulled by two or four horses. It looked somewhat lost in such a large building, but it also housed the old Rolls Royce which Gran had insisted on keeping, although it hadn't been driven for many years. Her husband bought it just before the war; it was his pride and joy.

She was anxious to try Cilla and the carriage out and got very cross and impatient when her son said she must wait until he'd tried Cilla out for himself, to make sure she was as quiet and safe as Tony had promised.

There was an uneasy tension in the house for a day or two until Tim found time to drive Cilla round the farm tracks. He was able to declare her as perfect as any pony could be!

At last the day she had been waiting for came and she hobbled out of the front door, as fast as her crutches would allow. Tim had the pony and trap waiting for her.

Cilla's harness was black and yellow which matched the colour of the trap exactly. It was a really smart turnout, anyone would have been proud to drive it, but for Gran it meant freedom; she could go anywhere without help or supervision, just her and the little black pony.

Tim insisted on following her in his Land Rover on her first outing, and soon discovered a problem that Queen Victoria hadn't had to deal with. Hand signals! Gran was giving the correct signals with her whip, but unless you drove horses yourself, you wouldn't know what on earth the old dear in front of you was doing!!

He thought about it for some time and decided he must invent a system of indicators before she went out again.

A quick trip into Dorchester where he bought a battery that would hide away under Grans seat, a switch of some sort that could be fixed to the arm rest of the trap, some electric wire and two indicator lights for the rear. With the help of Charlie, one of his farm workers, he had the job done in no time.

Gran mumbled a bit about newfangled nonsense and ruining her lovely carriage, but had to admit that Tim and Charlie had done a good job and had not disfigured her trap too much. It was certainly safer to drive on the busy roads. Anyway she intended to stick to the quieter lanes, but even there it was very likely they'd meet a car or two.

Cilla was the perfect pony; she ignored all passing traffic and would listen to Gran's voice, twitching her ears back and forth to catch a 'whoa' or a 'steady' command and obeying instantly.

Gran drove herself to the village shop, her first serious outing driving her trap, her basket and shopping list on the seat beside her. The shop keeper was amazed and delighted to see her sitting so proudly and dignified in her new carriage and insisted she should stay where she was and he would get her shopping for her. Other shoppers seeing her sitting there, came to admired Cilla, and chatted away about nothing in particular until Mr

226

Jenkins came back with her basket and a handful of carrots for the pony.

The trip to the village for shopping soon became a regular thing. Alf the gardener and odd job man would harness the pony and back her into the trap, then wait at the front door.

Cilla would hear the click click of the crutches on the polished oak floor and whinny a greeting. Gran always talked to her as she checked the harness.

Alf would grin to himself, he had been putting big farm horses into carts for over sixty years, man and boy, working for her husband and then son, until he was killed, so he wasn't likely to make a mistake with this fancy pony and trap!

"Alfred" she would say. "You may help me into the carriage".

"Certainly Mam". Alfred would say touching his cap. The old customs that Gran grew up with, she expected, and would tolerate no less!

In no time at all it seemed, the Great-Grandchildren were home for the summer holidays. They knew about Cilla and were waiting impatiently for Gran to invite them to meet her.

They could both ride well, they had a Shetland pony, now too small for them. Sam, the eldest was desperate for a bigger pony, one that could jump, his sister, Serena, younger by a year, was less adventurous, she was quite happy playing with her old Shetland pony. She spent hours brushing the long tangled main, putting it in big fat plats and tying coloured ribbons on each. She was quite content to let her brother ride Great-Grans new pony.

Sam found Cilla to be quite willing to jump, in fact had a talent for it. Gran watched anxiously as the rickety jumps got steadily higher!

She was delighted to see Sam riding so well on her lovely Cilla, clearing the jumps with such ease, but she would be glad when the holiday was over and she could have her back!

Gran saw that Sam needed professional help, she knew very well that all the arm and leg flapping was not helping Cilla one little bit. If the two of them were to get anywhere jumping, Sam needed lessons, and she knew just the person, her friend who ran an Equitation Centre near Dorchester who competed regularly in

227

the show jumping circuit. A quick phone call and lessons were arranged for the very next day!

Tim was sent off to the Equitation Centre with Cilla and Sam, who was delighted at the thought of lessons. Gran insisted on going with them, it was after all her pony and any way she wanted to see her friend at the centre. Tim agreed to take them, but made it very clear that he couldn't take any more time off, it was harvest time and they were working flat out, he should be driving the tractor not dashing off to Dorchester.

Muttering to herself she agreed, but she knew very well that one lesson wouldn't be a lot of good, the boy needed a series of tough sessions; she would cross that bridge when it came up!

They left the farm early, although it took ages to get Gran settled in the Land Rover. She hated the vehicle; it was noisy, smelly, and very uncomfortable. Tim agreed, but pointed out that it was a *farm* vehicle and very good at doing the job it was built for.

Sam, although very excited, was anxious that Great-Gran's friend was a bit easier to get on with than she was, Gran could terrify a saint!

Thirty minutes after leaving Tim's farm they arrived at the Centre. He quickly tacked up Cilla and sent Sam off to find the instructor, then unloaded his Grandmother and helped her onto a bench at the jumping school, sat beside her and waited patiently, only looking at his watch a couple of times.

Sam appeared accompanied by a youngish lady, much younger than he had expected. She told Sam to walk round the school quietly letting his pony look at the jumps and then walked over to greet Gran.

"Lovely pony Maude, I see you haven't lost your eye for a good horse even after all this time!"

"Of course I haven't! I know what I like when I see it.....now then Sally, can you sort these two out we can't stay here all day".

"You'll never change will you Maude? I can work wonders, but miracles take a bit longer,,,,,I'll see what I can do. Just for you!"

If Sam thought he was a good rider he was in for a shock. Sally sent him off to canter round the school, he had only got half way round when she shouted "STOP!....come back here boy".

Gran smiled to herself, now the fun would begin. Her friend was talking sternly to Sam, pulling his feet forward, moving his hands and pulling his shoulders back.

"Try again. Sit still and stop flapping your arms about!" Sam looked desperately at his Dad, but he was looking at his boots, Gran was sitting next to him, arms folded, back ramrod straight.

"Get on with it boy" she hissed as he cantered passed.

He must have got it better the second time, because Sally called "Better Sam...much better!" He began to relax a little and Cilla seemed to be going easily at a nice steady pace.

"Good....come to the centre Sam. Now we'll try a nice easy jump". He had been waiting for this, he knew she could jump his home made rickety jumps, but these were proper ones! A big red wall and a white gate, lots of poles of different colours and little jumps like hedges.

Sam looked at the wall as he rode past; it was higher than they were together. He's heart sank to his boots, surly he wouldn't have to jump that?

"Don't worry Sam that one's not for you today". Sam breathed a sigh of relief.

Tim helped Sally put up sets of small jumps with poles and wings around the edge of the school. They looked about the right size for Cilla Sam thought, his confidence began to return.

"Now Sam...I want you to canter round the school, that nice steady canter I know you can do.....just let her see the jumps but don't go near them. When I tell you to turn in and face the first one, get into your jumping position, feet still, knees in tight and get your bum just out of the saddle....lean forward and hold on. Keep her going right in the middle of the jump. If you make it safely keep going all the way round...OK?" She slapped him on the back. "Good luck Sam..away you go!"

Cilla tossed her head, she sensed the tension in Sam's hands, she was ready. They set off at a steady collected canter. Cilla looked at the jumps as they rode past. He sat very still, rocking gently as they rode round.

229

"OK Sam, when you're ready...straight at the middle of the jump, hold her with your hand and knees".

Sam felt a surge of excitement; he got himself in the right position and turned in for the first jump. Cilla wanted to rush at it, but he steadied her.

"Good lad" Sally shouted "On you go!"

Cilla still wanted to rush at the jumps but Sam sat tight in the saddle and held her at a steady pace. They cleared all the little jumps easily and he pulled up smiling.

"How did it feel?" Sally asked

"Marvellous!" He gasped.

"Good...we'll just do one more round and call it a day....I'll put them up just a bit, that looked too easy!"

"OK" he swallowed hard. Cilla was dancing about all over the place, she had never behaved like this before.

"Just a steady canter Sam, keep her steady and don't let her rush at them".

It took two circuits of the school before he was sure he was in control and ready to try. They were a little higher but it made no difference to Cilla, she cleared them with ease, he turned into the last jump. The little brick wall, it was now twice the original height, now three feet high.

Sally stood beside the wall. "Hold her at the centre and ride her Sam". He was determined not to fail and pushed with his legs and drove Cilla at the wall. She saw that it was higher than the other jumps and adjusted her stride automatically. They sailed over it with inches to spare.

Everyone cheered, even Gran clapped. "Well done Cilla" she said as they rode past.

Cilla tossed her head and put in a quick buck, she had enjoyed all that jumping as much as Sam.

"Walk her around Sam and let her cool down, then put her away, she's done enough for today". Sally turned to Maude. "Time for a cuppa I think Maude...let me help you to a more comfortable seat....we need to talk".

Sam rode Cilla out of the jumping arena, he still couldn't believe they had jumped the red wall! And Cilla wasn't going to settle down if there was a chance to jump some more. He walked her quietly down the drive and she immediately stopped dancing around and walked properly.

Tim left the two ladies to have their chat, he could guess what it was going to be about, he sat in the Land Rover, a frown on his face. What should he do, his Grandmother had bought the pony for herself, to drive around the lanes and visit her friends, now Sam had started riding her and Cilla had this hidden talent that he would surely want to develop!? Would she give up her driving for the duration of the holidays and let Sam compete in jumping competitions, or would she disappoint him not wanting Cilla to become too excitable and be difficult to drive safely?

The jumping lesson had caused Tim a whole load of problems he could well do without.

Maude and her friend Sally sat in her office having a drink, not tea or coffee, something a lot stronger. Maude sipped her drink delicately.

"Well Maude my dear, I think we've opened a can of worms here today!"

"How do you mean?"

"Well...that pony of yours is quite outstanding, a natural jumper. Your Great-Grandson's not bad but needs sorting out as you have seen, it wouldn't take long, he's an intelligent lad!"

"Oh dear..I see what you mean. I would hate to give her up...I really enjoy driving, and she's such a pet".

"Well it's up to you dear. Cilla is good...very good, and she's still young. Tell you what...let me have the boy here for some lessons, without Cilla, he can ride one of my ponies...I'll get him going well and you can still drive Cilla! She's a sensible pony and will adapt quickly. Towards the end of the hols I'll take them both to some shows...see how Cilla likes the bright lights. How does that sound?"

She was silent for a while, looking worried. "I'll think about it Sally, thank you for the lesson and the refreshments, I'll sleep on it and let you know tomorrow. Now, where's my Grandson...never in sight when I need him!"

Tim appeared as if by magic and helped Gran back onto her crutches. He needed to get back to the farm. "Come on then Gran, I must get back, there's work to be done".

"Always in a hurry" she muttered. The crutches going click clack..click clack as she struggled to the Land Rover.

Tim smiled; she was a game old bird really...never giving in no matter how much pain she was in.

"Have you loaded the pony...is she alright?"

"The pony's fine Gran, come on, let me help you into the truck...we must get going.....Sam. Get in and stop dreaming!"

He was indeed dreaming! What a pony Cilla had turned out to be, but she was Grans pony and she wasn't the easiest person to get on with, especially as he desperately wanted Cilla to jump with during the hols.

He was quiet on the journey home, Gran sat erect in the front while Tim concentrated on driving, there was no way he could or would try to persuade her to give Cilla to Sam. Trouble is the pony had so much potential, and his son needed a better pony than the old Shetland he had to ride at the moment.

Tim could probably afford to buy a bigger pony, but very difficult to find anything to compare with Cilla. They all had a lot to think about, it was going to be a long worrying night.

Sam unloaded Cilla and quickly put her back in her stable. He checked there was plenty of water and gave her a small scoop of nuts. He was just about to leave her, when he heard the 'Click clack' of Grans crutches coming across the yard, heading for Cilla's stable. Escape was impossible, no matter how fast he ran she would see him.

"Come here boy...I know you're in there with my pony" with a slight but unmistakable emphases on 'my'. There was nowhere to hide, he had to face his Great-Gran; he bolted the stable door and turned to face her.

"Well...how was the lesson?" she demanded.

"Very good thank you Gran" he stuttered .

"Were you scared boy...did that wall frighten you?"

"No Gran...it was fine, but then I knew Cilla could jump it.....she's so good I wasn't scared at all. I loved it!" he knew he

232

was talking too fast, but he was still excited and reliving the moment.

"Hmmm....well do you think you'll still love it when the jumps get higher and higher, because they will you know? Those jumps today were for babies, they won't be that small again...ever!" She looked at her Great Grandson standing tall and straight in front of her. He wasn't scared of her, she half smiled, maybe the boy took after her, he wasn't a bad rider, and a few concentrated lessons with Sally? Well, anything was possible. "Well, I'll think about Cilla and you, I'll make up my mind by tomorrow.,,,,Help me back to the house Sam, I've done enough hopping about for one day"

Sam put a young arm round his Gran's waist and together they made their way slowly back to the house.

"You're a good boy Sam" she said as she poked a steely hard finger in his ribs. "It was great fun this morning wasn't it" she cackled a half laugh.

Sam was surprised at the change in his Gran and laughed with her, "It was bloody good Gran...bloody good fun!"

"Mind your language young Sam" she cackled again, almost a laugh. "I won't tell your mum I heard that! But I agree..it was *bloody* good fun!"

Vicky met them at the door, concerned for Maud who'd been out for a long time on her crutches, but they were laughing at some joke. "Are you alright Gran, you've been gone for ages, come in and sit down.

"I'm fine, never felt better.....here young Sam, help me to a chair, then bring me a cup of tea....we've had a great time haven't we Sam!"

Vicky could only watch in amazement, she looked younger, and she was actually laughing. What on earth had changed her, she was usually always grumpy...she had even *smiled* at her! Sam would know and Vicky meant to find out.

"Hurry up with the tea young man, and a slice of your mothers fruit cake, if there's any left....I'm hungry!" That sounds more like Maud she thought.

"I'm on to it Gran". But not before you tell me what's been going on thought Vicky, I need to know your secret.

233

Sam found it difficult to sleep that night. He tossed and turned jumping that red wall a million times! He had been a tiny bit scared of the red brick wall, but Cilla was confident enough for both of them, Sam had clung on to her and they had sailed over the wall which got bigger and bigger as he lay in bed reliving the moment. His mind was racing, imagining all sorts of jumping competitions and winning red rosettes every time!

Sleep eventually took over his tired body and his dreams faded away. He slept long and woke suddenly to a bright sunny day, the birds were singing and already the smell of bacon frying wafted up to his little bedroom. He lay quietly, listening to the sounds of the family going about their business. His father slammed the back door and shouted for his dogs, he remembered they would be sheep dipping today, he was supposed to be helping!

Serena was calling her puppy to go and play and Cilla was whinnying to anyone who went into the yard. Cilla he suddenly thought, she needs feeding and mucking out or he would be in trouble with his Gran again.

He rolled out of his warm bed and found some aching muscles. Quickly dressed and rushed down stairs, only to be sent back to wash and clean his teeth.

"But mum Ci.."

"Up stairs now, Cilla can wait ...go!" So started another day for Sam. But it was going to get better....a lot better.

As he came down for the second time, washed brushed and with sparkling teeth, he noticed the door to his Grans part of the house was open. He listened. 'Click clack click clack', yes his Gran was up and about.

"Good morning Gran" he called out as he passed her door.

"Good morning to you Sam" came her cheerfull reply.

Well that was different, he usually only got a grunt. Mother caught him at the kitchen door and pressed Grans breakfast tray into his hands. "You seem to have a charmed life" she said smiling, "Go and feed your Gran...she's waiting for you!"

Sam took the tray and walked over to Grans open door. He knocked politely.

"Breakfast Gran"

"Come in..come in boy before it gets cold". The children very seldom were allowed into her part of the house, too many precious objects and old furniture that they might damage, but this morning he was being invited into Grans sanctuary.

He trod carefully on the lovely Persian carpet and put the tray down on a little drum head table beside her chair. He noticed that on her old refractory table was her Purdey shot gun, that was usually kept locked away in her gun cupboard, only coming out when her son was going on a 'shoot' and wanted to show off with the expensive and much sort after Purdey!

"*You're* not going shooting are you Gran!?" She had been a very good shot before her accident, and could still bring down a pheasant occasionally.

"Yes Sam!.....I'm going to Scotland for the Glorious Twelfth, staying with my sister.....try and get myself some Grouse!!"

Sam looked enviously at the shot gun, maybe one day he might be allowed to use it, his father said the Purdey had an enormous 'kick back' and would either knock him off his feet or break his shoulder. He would have to wait a few years yet. In the near future his Gran was off to shoot at her sister's estate, Grouse or Deer whatever her estate manager decided.

Sam gently ran his fingers along the twin barrels of the gun, silky smooth and gleaming in the sunlight.

Maud refused to sell the gun despite many offers from collectors trying to persuade her. No, she might get burgled and would need the gun for protection.

Sam thought the sight of his Gran waving the double barrelled Purdey would be enough to scare off even the most determined thief! He smiled as he imagined the scene.

"Come and sit boy" his Gran ordered. "Stop gazing at the gun, you can have it when I'm dead and gone. I need to talk to you...so sit down". He sat nervously on the edge of a chair facing his Gran. "Now boy...I'm leaving my little Cilla in your care for the month I'm away. You are both to go for lessons with my friend Sally who you worked with yesterday. Listen to her and watch her ride, you have a lot to learn, but in my heart I know you can do it" she put her hand over her heart. "Look after Cilla, when I get back I'll be expecting to see you jumping, and winning!" She sat back looking intently at her Great-Grandson.

235

"Go now; before I change my mind...go on....scoot. I've a lot to do today.

"Thank you Gran" Sam got to his feet. "Thank you so very much" and planted a kiss on her cheek.

"Go now Sam or you'll make this old lady blush!" He ran from the room his feet slipping on the Persian rug, Cilla was his for a month, and lessons with Sally had been arranged. He wanted to shout for joy....then remembered 'children should be seen and not heard', so he left his Gran sitting in her chair smiling, and quietly closed the door. Then he exploded with excitement, rushed into the kitchen to tell his mother!

The whole of that day seemed to be spent getting Maud ready for her holiday. Alfred was going with her to help during the shoot. She always took him to the estate; to drive her over the wild country and help her up onto the back of an open topped Land Rover ready for any Grouse stupid enough to fly in her direction!

Tim gave the Purdey a good clean and oiled various parts, then packed it away in its case, ready to go.

She was really excited about this quickly arranged holiday and couldn't wait to be on her way. Alf settled her in the front seat of the car and got in the back with his small bag. When Maud was sure she hadn't forgotten anything   Tim drove them to Bournemouth airport where they were to catch a plane to Aberdeen. There her sister would be waiting for them and she would drive the last hundred or so miles up into the highlands, to her Estate.

Once Tim and Gran had gone Sam took Cilla out for a practice in the field, he didn't bother with his rickety jumps, but concentrated on the steady canter, trying to remember everything Sally had taught him. She was coming later in the day to collect them both and take them to her Equestrian Centre for two weeks of individual lessons. He would stay in Sally's house while Cilla had a stable in the yard with the big show jumpers. When he wasn't having lessons Sam would be helping the staff mucking out, cleaning tack and being generally useful.

236

His Gran had arranged all this last night while he was asleep. He was a bit anxious about going, he didn't know any of the staff, they were all grownups and very serious about their riding, but his mother assured him it would be fun, and anyway Sally would take care of him...and Cilla.

He packed his case putting in his new jods and wondered whether he would need his best riding jacket, but put it in the case, you never know, he might get to ride in a show before he came home again!

Now Sam needed to spend time grooming Cilla and cleaning her tack, Gran would never forgive him if they arrived at the Equestrian Centre with a dirty pony.

He brushed and combed her lovely long mane and tail until they looked and felt like silk. Her coat gleamed with good health and shone as if it was polished mahogany, he felt very proud of Cilla. He was determined to work very hard at his riding lessons, and not let his Gran down. He made up his mind he would win his first rosette before Gran came home again.

Sally arrived later that afternoon having been jumping at a show in Devon, Maud's farm at Chilcombe was on the way home, so it seemed sensible to collect Sam and Cilla in her big lorry. Sam had never seen anything like it, it would accommodate six horses with living space for grooms, there were bunk beds, a shower, cooker, in fact everything you would need if you had to stay overnight, there was even a small tele tucked away on a shelf!

Sam was glad he had spent so much time grooming Cilla and putting her new cotton rug on. She looked splendid as she walked up the ramp and into her stall as if she was used to such luxury!

Mother gave him a big hug and promised to come to collect him if he wasn't happy. True he was still a little anxious about this working holiday; he sat quietly beside Sally in the cab as she drove the few miles to her Equestrian Centre just outside Dorchester.

He could hear the horses moving about in their stalls and thought he heard Cilla whinny. In next to no time they arrived at the Centre, Sam was quite sorry to get out of the lorry, it had so many gadgets Sally had shown him, he could have sat up there mush longer, he especially liked the CCTV that allowed the grooms to keep a watch on all the horses. Very modern, Sally said, not many horse transport lorries had it yet.

TWENTYTWO

Several students were there waiting to unload the jumping horses, but as Cilla was the last to be loaded, she came out first.

Sally led her down the ramp. "Now everyone, this is Lady Maud Winthrop's Great Grandson Sam. He's joining us for a few weeks to improve his riding....and this" she turned to the pony she was holding, "is his lovely pony Cilla. Give them both all the help you can".

The head girl knew they were coming and had prepared a stable for Cilla. "Come on Sam, let me show you where to put this lovely pony of yours, Welsh section A is she Sam?"

"Yes she is...I think...I'm not really sure". His Gran hadn't bothered to tell him about her breeding.

"Well, she looks Welsh to me...I expect the boss will know" She was heading for a range of loose boxes and horses heads began to appear over stable doors, they were all very curious about that little pony in the bright blue rug! "I don't have to call you 'My Lord' do I"

Sam was embarrassed."N-n-no...that's my Dad, and people just call him Tim". The girl laughed.

"I'm Erin, here we are Sam...Cilla's box, I've put a sheep hurdle across the door so that she can see out, we'll shut the door at night. I think you're staying with the boss up at the big house, so you run up there and I'll take care of Cilla. See you in the morning Sam....bright and early. Don't oversleep, we start *very* early" He set off in the direction Erin had pointed out to him.

Sally caught up with him and saw that he looked a bit overwhelmed. She ruffled his hair. "Don't worry Sam, you'll soon get used to us all" she smiled down at him. "I hope you're hungry, cook seems to have left us a mountain of food!"

"I'm always hungry, thank you".

"Good....we'll eat in the kitchen then, much more comfortable for just the two of us. I'll show you where you're going to sleep...then we'll eat, I'm famished too!"

Sam rode at least twice a day, not always on Cilla, sometimes he had a group lesson with other students, then he rode one of the school horses, the biggest he had ever sat on, but well behaved and responsive.

Erin usually took the group lessons, she was very difficult to please; Sally had him on his own for at least one lesson every day. She had decided to work on his riding first, he wasn't bad, but having such a talented pony he would have to improve dramatically if he was to show her and win that elusive red rosette.

The first week was tough; he crept into his bed every night a lot earlier than he did at home!

Cilla was developing muscles where she'd never had muscle before and Sam was growing blisters where *he* had never had them before! He had been tempted to phone his mother and say he'd had enough, but he could imagine what his Gran would say, so he dug deep and ignored the bruises and blisters and got on with it!

Then suddenly his feet seemed to be in the right place, his hands more supple and his aching back was straight for the first time, and Cilla was going well. Everyone gasped when Sam encouraged her into her lovely floating trot for the first time, Sally grinned from ear to ear.

"Oh my, just look at that!" Erin was equally impressed.

"You little darli'n...I love you, you little beauty!"

Sam thought for a moment she meant *him*...but soon realized his mistake.

From that moment Cilla's future was decided, she would work towards the show ring first of all and then later try the mini jumping classes.

Working Hunter classes seemed to have been designed for Cilla, they started with a round of jumping, rustic poles, hurdles and any natural looking fence you might meet out hunting, then, if you survived the first round, you came back into the ring to do a showing class, the best pony over the two sections would be declared the winner.

Sam had never ridden at a show before and he found the discipline Sally demanded very difficult. They worked out an individual show he could do on Cilla, walking, then that lovely trot and finally a collected canter.

240

Sally became very frustrated with Sam. He would trot when he should walk and canter in the wrong places most of the time, as for being on the right or wrong leg....well it all seemed 'double dutch' to the young boy.

He was very close to tears when Sally finally lost patience with him one afternoon and stormed out of the schooling area. Erin had been watching, she was more used to coaching children than Sally, she could see Sam was totally confused.

"Sam" she called once Sally had gone. "Come here". Sam rode over to her. "You and me will learn this together, I know what you have to do, we'll get it learnt by tomorrow...don't you worry now". They tied Cilla to a post and sat down side by side on a bench to study the test that Sally had set him.

"Now then Sam.....we'll learn this on our own two feet, then when we know it inside out and back to front, we'll teach it to Cilla!" Sam laughed, he felt better already.

Erin looked at her notes. "It says here, *'walk out and face the judge'* come on then" she grabbed his arm and dragged him forwards. "Walk smartly Sam, don't drag. *'Halt and stand square facing the judge'*".

"What does stand square mean?" he asked timidly.

"Front feet level, back feet level..that's standing square! Now..." Erin looked at her notes. *"'bow to the judge'*. No Sam, a quick bob won't do, take your time, right arm down by your side and nod your head slowly, got it Sam?"

"Yes..I think so".

"Right.....let's see you do it then...go back to the fence and start again...I'll pretend to be the judge. Don't forget to walk smartly!"

Sam ran back to the fence, this was more fun.

"Go". Sam walked smartly out to face his 'judge'; he halted in front of her, shuffled his feet about until he got them level, looked at the 'judge' and bowed gracefully.

"Well now that wasn't so difficult!" Erin laughed. "Let's see what the dragon has got next on her list".

After a couple of hours of coaching he had memorized all the movements and changes of direction for the first two parts of his test. He had walked and trotted on his own feet until he was

241

ready to drop. At last Erin was satisfied; he knew what he was doing, so she let him try it on Cilla.

All went well, pony and boy understanding each other for the first time.

"Right now my darli'n, tomorrow we'll learn the next bit....just as long as you've remembered all we've just done!"

"Thanks Erin...I've learnt to 'stand square' anyway. Tomorrow maybe I can learn what's a right leg or a wrong leg".

"Don't you worry boyo; we'll surprise the old girl yet. Put Cilla away now Sam and run in for your tea, I'll feed Cilla for you".

Sam didn't feel he could run any more that day, but he was a much happier boy when he sat down for his tea that evening.

The next day, once all the usual stable duties had been done and the students had gone up to the house for a lecture on feeding, Erin grabbed Sam.

"Come on my boy, we've got some more learning to do before you're lesson this afternoon"

"OK" he laughed, "Let's do it". Fortunately he remembered all the previous day's work and she was quite pleased, although he still had to do it all on his own feet. They both had a fit of giggles when Erin tried to demonstrate a canter hopping round the yard. Sam managed to do a satisfactory collected canter, more giggles, so they then progressed to the 'right and wrong' leg problem.

Once again Erin dragged him round in an imaginary canter. "Now young Sam, when we circle to the left" and she turned in a circle to the left, "You must have your left leg leading". So they 'cantered' to the left, with the left leading, "Correct, that's the right leg".

Sam stopped. "But it's my *left* leg".

"No..It's the correct leg, the *right* leg, to be leading with....now, if your circling to the *right* you must lead with your *right* leg" and she hopped round in a circle with her right leg in front. If you canter round to the right with your left leg leading you'll be on the wrong leg". Sam was still mystified.

"I don't quite understand".

242

"OK...now listen". Erin began to explain again! "If you're cantering round the ring, the pony must lead with which ever leg is on the *inside* of the ring, the *inside*, not the leg nearest the people watching. If you change direction and go round the other way, you're pony must change leg and lead with the other one! So.....whichever leg is on the inside of the ring we call the Right Leg..the correct leg....If the pony has the other leg leading it's the wrong leg". She drew a circle on the gravel and an arrow pointing clockwise. "The inside leg is this one" and she tapped her right leg. "The wrong leg will be this one", she tapped her left leg..."

"Because it's on the outside of the circle" interrupted Sam. "I've got it now Erin....it's got nothing to do with left or right, it's correct or it's wrong!"

"Good boy" Erin sighed. "Now, let's teach Cilla right from wrong!"

Cilla was a very quick learner; she had after all done most of this at her previous home. She quickly got the canter nice and steady and progressed to cantering a figure of eight, the last part of the test Sam had been set.

"You'll have to change leg in the middle of the figure of eight Sam...bring her back to a trot for three paces just as you change direction then set her off on the other leg". Sam smiled to himself remembering Erin's demonstration 'cantering' round the yard. "You're listening boy....stop daydreaming, we haven't got long before the boss is after you".

"Ok Erin....I'll do the whole show from the beginning shall I?"

"Yes...good idea. I'll be the judge, let me get to the centre".

Sam walked Cilla round quietly; he hardly moved a muscle, just a little twitch of the reins to get Cilla's head in and a little leg pressure to make her walk smartly.

"Good boy....that's nice Sam!"

He walked up to the 'judge', stood Cilla square and bowed gracefully, then set off to ride the test.

Cilla was going like a dream; she knew the test almost as well as Sam, now just the last part to do he thought. He hadn't practised this on Cilla, only on his own feet! However she was

243

going so well as they started the figure of eight, they circled to the left, left leg leading, he looked down at her front legs to make sure.

"Sit still!!" Erin shouted.

Now the difficult change over, from left leg to right. He tried to ease Cilla back to a trot for three paces. Cilla wasn't having any of that baby nonsense and performed a perfect change of leg...a flying change...without breaking the rhythm of her canter and proceeded to make a perfect figure of eight! He finished the test, walked to stand square in front of the 'judge', a slow bow to finish properly.

Erin was speechless. "Where on this earth did you manage to learn that flying change Cilla!?" She asked patting the pony's neck. "Don't you know that's quite advanced dressage my girl?"

Sam laughed "She just did it...I tried to bring her back to a trot...but she wouldn't".

A loud clapping startled them. The students had come back from their lecture and had been watching Sam ride his test....so had Sally, the boss!

"Well done all three of you" She said coming over to Pat Cilla. "Not bad for a driving pony is she! I must ask Lady Maud what she knows about her that she's not telling us". They all laughed. "Sam....just canter that figure of eight once more....I wasn't dreaming was I?"

Sam turned Cilla towards the centre of the ring and cantered the test again. It proved it wasn't an accident or just good luck, she performed a perfect flying change again and again as many times as Sally asked.

"Do you know Sam; I think you're about ready for a show. We must just tidy up the jumping a bit and then next week we'll find a show for you!"

A hectic series of jumping lessons started that very afternoon. Cilla seemed to love jumping; she cleared everything that Erin and Sally erected. The only problem was that she got over excited and wanted to dash at them.

Sam was a lot stronger now and managed to control her enthusiasm but found it very difficult to calm her down enough

244

to ride a good test after a round of jumping. He would have to do both in a working pony class.

Sally made him practice time and time again until Cilla got the message and calmed down enough before they had to ride the test.

It was asking an awful lot of such a novice pony, Erin explained he would have to be very conscious of this and help her by not getting over excited himself. Sam nodded, he would do his best. Fortunately there would be a good gap between the jumping and riding test, it would give him time to settle Cilla down again before the second test.

They practised and practised over and over again until Sam's fingers and his bottom were sore!

Sally nagged on at him about riding tall in the saddle, keeping still approaching the jumps and a hundred other things. He could feel his riding improving and he was beginning to enjoy getting Cilla to do a perfect test.

Tim called in later in the week, on his way back from the market, to see how things were progressing. He was amazed at the difference in Sam's riding; he seemed to be inches taller and even elegant as he circled round on Cilla. What a transformation, he must hurry home to tell Vicky and phone Grandma, she would be delighted. He would make time to get to the show on Saturday and encourage his son.

Sam had seen his Dad watching and waved, he hoped he hadn't come to take them home.

The last week flew past. Sam was kept very busy. Erin had made him ride without stirrups to improve his balance, and even jump without them, to be certain he was using his knees to keep him on Cilla's slippery back!

The day before the show Sally declared a rest day for the pony and her enthusiastic rider, although there was tack to be cleaned and the trailer needed a good wash inside and out.

He set to work on the trailer with great gusto and soon had it looking quite respectable. He wasn't so enthusiastic about cleaning his tack, Erin had to reprimand him about one or two things, especially buckles. Buckles had to be polished until they shone and sparkled in the sunshine.

"You're not taking that lovely pony out of my yard with a dirty bridle". And sent him back to do it all again.

Sam decided he still had a lot to learn, not least about Erin, who ruled the yard with a rod of iron, nothing passed her critical inspection.

He climbed into bed that night exhausted, he had no idea how much work went into preparing for a show, but he was learning fast

Sally woke him a bit earlier than usual, Cilla had to be fed and groomed thoroughly, not hurriedly and given plenty of time to digest her food before travelling to the show.

Sally had entered them in the Mountain and Moorland Working Pony class which meant Cilla didn't have to have her lovely long mane plaited. Erin said a quiet 'thank God'! She hadn't fancied trying to get that lovely hair into neat tidy plaits, today she could have it all flowing and Sam could grab a handful, if he felt unsafe.

Finally they were ready to go, Cilla was easy and happy to load into the trailer, while a nervous Sam sat in the Land Rover.

Erin gave him a big kiss for good luck, which made him squirm and Sally laugh!

"Look after the place" Sally called as they drove off. "Wish us luck!"

"You're very quiet this morning Sam. Are you OK?" Sally asked.

"Yes I'm fine"

"This your first show?"

"Yeh...my old pony wasn't much good at anything, except eating!"

"Oh you'll be fine...you.ve got a really lovely pony, *she'll* see you're safe. After today everyone will want her!"

"Is she really that good?"

"Sam, your Gran has always been able to pick a good horse, this time she got herself a cracker....you'll see my lad, you'll see". He sat back in his seat trying to relax. He hoped Sally was right, he really did.

"Here we are Sam...Lytchett Minster Horse Show.....We'll park the trailer then go to collect your numbers from the secretaries tent".

Everyone seemed to know Sally and wanted to chat. She introduced Sam, 'This is Lady Maud's Great Grandson' or just, 'Hi, this is my young protégée Sam'. Sam would shake hands politely and walk on.

"Do they *all* know my Gran?" He asked when he got the chance.

"Most people remember her Sam, she was quite a character and a wonderful rider...she was as bold as brass and quite fearless riding cross country events, then one day her horse fell and rolled on her".

"Yes Dad told me about that, he said she screamed and swore something awful when they tried to move her".

"She screamed even more when someone suggested the horse should be shot. 'It's not his fault, leave him alone'. She was still shouting when they took her off in the ambulance. I brought him home until Maude was back with us again".

"It must have been terrible to be unable to ride again".

"Best not to think about it Sam". Sally smiled down at him and put an arm round his shoulder. Your Gran has bought you a lovely pony and she'll expect you to ride as she would have done...let's make the old lady proud of you, eh Sam?"

The time had come...he had walked round the jumps with Sally who'd explained the best route to take. There was nothing that Cilla couldn't jump easily, just a narrow style that he wasn't too sure about, there hardly seemed room to jump the poles set between two high hedges. 'Don't worry, Cilla can jump that, just keep her straight at the middle and give her time to see it' Sally said as they stood looking at the jump. 'Turn her in here. Don't hurry. Push on the last three strides.'

Sam was concentrating on everything she had told him as he walked round the collecting ring on Cilla, waiting for his turn to jump.

Several competitors had jumped the course and so far nobody had gone clear. That style was causing the most problems, he must do as Sally had instructed, give Cilla time to see it properly and not to let her rush in her usual manner.

"You're next young man". The ring steward startled him. "Are you ready?"

"Oh...ummm..yes" Stuttered Sam

"You're Lady Maud's Grandson aren't you!... Make her proud of you. Good luck lad".

Sally was right, everyone knew his Gran, he simply had to ride his very best for her sake.

Cilla was on her toes and danced into the ring. "Steady girl...let's get this right first time" Walk smartly up to the judge, stand square and bow, he could hear Erin as clearly as if she was there beside him.

"Thank you" he said. Most of the competitors had set off over the jumps without acknowledging him. *A bad mistake* he heard Erin whisper in his ear!

He walked a few paces away from the judge, trotted and then cantered, on the *right* leg towards the first jump.

Cilla tossed her head and pulled hard, but Sam had a firm hold on her. "Steady girl" he said and sat tight in the saddle, gently rocking in time with Cilla's stride.

He sat relaxed and quiet, *'hands loose on the reins'*, he smiled to himself, Erin was still with him.

The style jump was next; he looked for the mark he had mentally made when he walked the course with Sally. He had to change, and that meant Cilla would have to change leg. *'Wait till you turn the corner'*. A change of direction, a slight change of position with the inside leg, and Cilla performed her flying change. Wow!....*'Now set her up for the jump, hold her with hands and legs, straight at the centre of the jump'*. Cilla looked at it....swished her tail and cleared it with inches to spare! "Good girl...now....let's win this for Gran!"

The last few jumps were easy and as Sam cantered out of the ring the crowd clapped and shouted enthusiastically.

"That is the first clear round..well done Sam Winthrop". The loud speaker boomed.

"Well done indeed!" Sally was waiting for them in the collecting ring. "Well done both of you" she slapped Sam on the back as he dismounted. "That flying change was just perfect" she was quite excited.

"Just got to ride the test now...I'd better calm her down. She really enjoyed that Sally....she was pulling like a train!"

"I could see that, but you managed to keep up a steady rhythm. Good boy, well done".

249

He walked Cilla round talking quietly to her; she relaxed after a few minutes and settled down. They waited patiently for the showing section of their class to be called by the steward.

When at last all the ponies had jumped, all the ponies were called into the ring again. They walked, trotted and cantered round the ring until the steward told them to line up in the centre of the ring to begin their individual show.

One at a time they rode out, Sam's confidence was growing by the minute, so many were making elementary mistakes, he knew he had a good chance so long as he concentrated and didn't forget anything.

"Your turn now lad...show 'em how to do it. Good luck son!"

"Thank you sir" he mumbled trying to keep calm as he rode towards the judge. *'Stand square and bow'*. Erin was still there!

Sam acknowledged the judge with his best bow. The judge smiled, "Thank you...show me what you can do please".

'Walk away from the judge, turn and trot'. Cilla knew the test almost as well as Sam, they had practiced it so many times. She broke into her beautiful floating trot, Sam thought he heard gasps from the crowd and smiled to himself, Cilla was going like a dream.

They cantered the figure of eight, Sam's favourite part and Cilla did her fabulous flying change. More gasps from the crowd. He slowed and walked back to the judge, a slow bow to finish and another smile from the judge.

"Thank you..and well ridden". He walked Cilla back to his place in the line and waited while the other riders performed their tests. He felt he had done his best, Cilla was marvellous, and he could do no more. All the riders stood in line waiting for the steward to pronounce the winner; Cilla stood perfectly still, her head tucked in, just the occasional swish of her tail to keep the midges away.

Finally the last pony and rider did their show and returned to stand in the line waiting for the judge to have a close look at each pony. He walked along the line studying each one; he took a long time looking at Cilla. Sam didn't dare move a muscle; he just sat tall in the saddle and stared straight ahead. *Don't fidget.* Erin again! So he did as he had been told.

250

The steward asked them to walk round again. 'This is it' he thought, did I do enough, did he like Cilla? He looked straight ahead, walking round the ring.

There was a sudden burst of cheering and clapping. The steward was pointing at him! "Black pony....black pony come in please".

Sam was stunned. He turned Cilla towards the steward.

"Stand here lad...well done, well deserved".

He searched the ringside for a sight of Sally. She was there and gave him thumbs up and a huge smile! He relaxed a little and patted Cilla. "Thanks Cill, I love you".

The steward handed the judge the rosettes to be given to the first six placed ponies and was heading for Sam. *'If you win take your hat off when you receive the rosette'.* Erin was still there. He struggled to take his hard hat off in time and tucked it under his arm.

"You have a really lovely pony young man...I wish she were mine!" he smiled up at Sam. "And you have very nice manners....well done".

He cantered the lap of honour in a complete daze. Cilla had won; she had jumped a perfect round and he had ridden the test without any mistakes. He would ring his Gran tonight, she would be so pleased, he hoped she wasn't planning on coming home too soon as he still had two weeks of holiday, and maybe Sally could find them another show.

Suddenly he noticed his parents "Well done Sam" his mother shouted as they ran towards him. His Dad was laughing and slapped him on the back.

"I'm proud of you my boy, really proud"

"Can I have a ride?" Serena whined.

"Certainly not" her mother said . "This is Sam's day, he's done so well and worked hard, and any way Cilla needs a rest!"

"Yes...I must put her back in the trailer now". He was quite embarrassed, so much fuss in front of everyone. He really wanted to stand up in his stirrups and shout 'Yahooo', but instead he quietly followed Sally back to the horse box and jumped off.

He found his legs were shaking like jelly; he had to hold on to Cilla for a moment to recover. Sally put an arm round his shoulder and said nothing, she knew that feeling, all that

251

excitement and stress suddenly over, it always used to make her feel a bit queezy.

"Good boy Sam, you've made me so proud; your Gran's fighting spirit has certainly passed down to you! Well done you....and you Cilla. I think I love you both!" She was almost in tears when she went into the trailer to fetch Cilla's rug.

After a lot of hand shaking and congratulatory remarks from people Sam didn't know, Sally took him to the secretary's tent to collect his prize, a large silver cup. "You must sign for it" She said "And write your address, they will want it back next year....then you will have to win it again".

Sam went back to the Equitation Centre with the biggest ice cream he had ever seen, bought by Sally, in one hand and a big silver cup in the other, a small boy's perfect day.

Sam phoned his Gran in Scotland; it wasn't his Gran that answered however, that put him off slightly. "Oh..er..can I speak to my Gran please?"

"Who's speaking....and who is your Gran?"

"Er..my name's Sam".

"And you're Gran?"

"Her name's Maud....Lady Maud". He managed to say at last. Sally giggled. "I've never called her that before" he whispered.

"Och....that's better ladddie, I'll away and find her" He sat down on the floor with a bump. Sally was still giggling at him.

"Well she's always just been Gran to me, not this 'Lady Maude' stuff". He looked at Sally and they both burst out laughing.

"Hello...**Hello,** is that you Sam...**Sam!**" The stern voice loud in his ear.

"Yes Gran...it's me".

Well...How did it go boy. Can I be proud of you and my Cilla?"

"Yes....I think so. We won the working pony and got a *whopping* cup! Cilla was absolutely marvellous". He felt relaxed now and started chatting away.

"Stop boy!" that's enough she commanded. "I'll be back in time to see for myself before you go back to school...well done,

252

now let me speak to Sally, I can hear her giggling!" He handed the phone to Sally.

His Gran was coming home soon, his heart sank, he had been so involved with Cilla he had forgotten she was Gran's driving pony, he knew how much she enjoyed driving. He desperately wanted to win again before the end of the holidays when Gran would take Cilla back.

TWENTYFOUR

Sally found them one more show at Wimbourne. This time a jumping class over proper painted poles!

Sam's spirits rose, although he could see another week of hard training with Erin, but he was his Grans Great-Grandson, and she was renowned as a fearless rider, he would make her proud of him.

He would be entered in a class for 12.2 hand ponies, the smallest of the recognised jumping classes run by the British Show Jumping Association. A much bigger show, and the competion was sure to be of a much higher standard.

Sally said she was going to enter two of her horses in the hope of getting one or both qualified for London. She knew the pressure of qualifying; it was nothing new to her, but Sam!

Cilla had to learn to face any manner of jumps. Coloured poles, gates, jumps with a tray of water under them and a big red brick wall.

Training started the following day.

Erin put the jumps up at about the height Sam was used to, Cilla took it all in her stride, until she saw the water jump.

His first effort ended in disaster! Cilla stopped dead, Sam didn't, he cleared the poles landing seat first in the water.

Erin ran to help but couldn't stop laughing. "You'll have to do better than that my Lord!" She teased "You're supposed to stay on the pony not play about in the water!"

Sam was cross, wet and very embarrassed, some of the students had been watching. "I'm soaking"

"I can see that". Erin was still laughing. "Go and change quickly now...I'll introduce Cilla to the water....although there's not much left, you've practically empted it!" Sam stalked off, water dripping.

"Hurry Sam". Called Sally. "I've got to school my two yet".

He could hear them all laughing as he made his way back to the house; his determination to prove to his Gran he could ride well had taken a nasty knock. Perhaps he should give up and go home? How could he face Gran...or mum and Dad?

254

There were clean clothes in his bedroom. He was pulling on the dry jeans and a polar neck jumper, when he suddenly laughed. *'I suppose it was funny, and any way I bet Sally and Erin have fallen off!'*. So with a big sigh, he squared his shoulders and went back to the jumping lesson. He was Lady Maud's Great Grandson and he would *not* let her down!

During his absence Erin had taught Cilla to jump the water, it wasn't so difficult and within a very short time pony and boy were clearing jump after jump. If Sam had to stop and listen to Sally's instructions Cilla would stomp around wanting to get on with it, she just loved jumping.

Each day the jumps got higher and higher, until Sally was happy that Cilla could challenge any opposition. Sam was becoming a bold and determined rider now and quite up to jumping the pony class in which Sally had entered them.

He sat and watched Sally schooling her two jumpers for hours; if a pole was knocked down he was the first to rush out and replace it, although it was usually above his head.

Sally was a very experienced rider and made it all look very easy, but Sam knew by now how much hard work went into getting these horses up to this standard, he marvelled at her stamina. He was exhausted after just a short lesson, but she seemed to be endlessly jumping huge jumps.

One day, he thought, I'll have a big jumping horse and clear that five bar gate and red wall.

Saturday, the day of the Wimbourne show.

He was used to the routine now and polished the buckles on Cilla's bridle with enthusiasm.

Cilla was having a bath early in the morning followed by the two jumping horses. It would mean a lot of walking for Sam and the two students until their horses had dried off enough to have a quick brush over and their show rugs put on.

Sam enjoyed bathing Cilla and spent far too long in the washing area. The students had to chase him out with the hose pipe so they could get on with Sally's horses.

Cilla resplendent in her blue rug and matching leg protectors rushed up the ramp seemingly wanting to be off, the other two plodded up to their usual places in the lorry.

Sam sat in front with Sally who was driving, while three of her students, who were acting as grooms, sat behind in the living area.

He was very excited and Sally had to tell him several times to calm down, but when they arrived at the Wimbourne show ground his heart nearly stopped!

It was an enormous show ground, much bigger than Sam had imagined. Four separate rings, one exclusively for jumping, the red and white poles already up. The rest for various showing classes, one of them for Scurry Driving.

Sally explained! "We must keep your Gran away from that Sam" she laughed "Although I can well imagine her driving round the course flat out, like Boadicea!"

Sam wasn't sure who Boadicea was, he remembered seeing pictures of a wild looking woman thrashing two steaming horses at full gallop in a chariot with long knives sticking out from the wheels. They must definitely keep Gran away from Scurry driving!

The day was hot and the student grooms were soon complaining, but Sally insisted they wore their uniforms with 'Dorchester Equestrian Centre' printed on the back of their shirts. Sam however, was allowed to run around in his shirt sleeves until it was time for his class, then it was on with the tweed jacket, hot and itchy it may be, but rules are rules, and Sally would never hear of him riding at such a big show minus his jacket.

She relented when they walked the course together which looked fairly straight forward for the small ponies, nothing he hadn't practised at home.

The style was there, but this time it was near the entrance to the collecting ring. A trap, Sally explained, to catch out riders who weren't concentrating, the horses knew that was the way out of the ring and they'd think they had finished. The jump it's self wasn't difficult, it was set deliberately close to the exit to catch the unwary!

256

When Sally was sure he had learnt the course and Sam was happy, they went to find the groom holding Cilla. He was some way down the order to jump so he had plenty of time to watch the other riders, Sally was right, a lot of ponies tried to dash out of the ring as they approached the style and some riders had to fight hard to make their ponies face the jump.

Only one rider had gone clear before it was his turn.

"Don't start before the bell Sam!" Sally warned. "Just trot quietly down the side of the ring, get her to canter at the bottom corner, that'll give you plenty of time to settle her down and get into a nice steady rhythm before you go through the start...Good luck Sam, imagine Gran is watching!"

He swallowed hard, checked his crash hat was on tight, and set off.

Cilla trotted gracefully, on her toes, down the side of the ring when she suddenly leaped sideways. He calmed her with a pat on her neck as he had a quick look to see what had upset her. It was an old lady sheltering under an umbrella from the sun wearing a large straw hat pulled well down. Cilla had a 'thing' about umbrellas.

Concentrate, he told himself, *'just remember the umbrella as you come past it!'* The bell sounded and Sam rode towards the start.

Cilla pulled and tossed her head, Sam sat still, hands steady on the reins. *'Drive her at the centre of the jumps'* Erin was there! She didn't need driving being only too willing to jump.

They were sailing over the jumps with inches to spare, so he was able to concentrate on keeping Cilla steady and well balanced.

The stile was next. Cilla saw the exit and tried to take control. *'oh no you don't young lady'*. And turned her in a bit too early for it and gave her very little time to see the jump.

'Oh Lord' he thought. *'I've done it now. 'Push hard'*. Erin shouted in his head. So he kicked and drove poor Cilla at the stile. She only had two strides to make up her mind....but with a huge effort she cleared it!

Now the Red Wall..the last jump.

Sam had lost his stirrups due to Cilla's ungainly effort to jump the stile, he didn't dare pull up to get his feet sorted out, but he

257

remembered Erin making him jump without a saddle. He gripped hard with his knees and drove Cilla hard at the centre of the last jump, a look of determination on his face.

Cilla was back on her usual steady pace and they cleared the wall with ease. Sam had a handful of her mane and clung on desperately as they cantered passed the finish.

"Clear round". Boomed the loud speaker. **"Now we'll have a jump off!"**

One more pony went clear so the three of them would have to jump against the clock. Sally was worried about this, they had never pushed Cilla jumping, always at a steady pace.

"What do you think Sam...pull out now and take third place? I won't mind, you've done really well".

Sam's spirit was up now, *What would his Gran do?* "No...we'll go again Sally" His voice full of confidence. "Just tell me what to do!"

"Well...you can go steady and hope to have a clear round, and the others don't, or go like hell and hope you go clear faster than the other two! It's just how you feel Sam. Cilla's a mountain pony, very quick on her feet; she'll look after you...Good luck ...and hang on Sam!!"

Just the three to jump off; two boys and a girl, they walked anxiously round the collecting ring while the jumps were checked and the timing clock started.

The first to go was a boy, his pony was very excited pulling and tugging at the reins. Sam started to feel nervous, he had butterflies in his stomach, but he knew he could do it and glad he hadn't decided to withdraw.

His turn now! He rode into the ring knowing he had to beat the first pony that had had a clear round.

"It's up to us now Cilla, let's go!" He whispered. They flew through the start, he had decided to throw caution to the wind and drove his pony at the jumps.

Cilla seemed to understand, she cut corners and jumped at impossible angles, she was as quick on her feet as any breed of pony and obeyed Sam without hesitation.

"Clear round again" The loud speaker boomed. **"In a very fast time, can that be beaten?"**

258

Now the last to go, could she go clear and faster than Cilla and win? But the excitement got to her and the first pole crashed down.

Sally rushed up to Sam, huge smile lighting up her face. "Well done Sammy my boy...**you've won**!!" He hadn't realised they were the fastest, he had been so exhilarated at Cilla's speed and agility, he hadn't bothered to check his time!

"So we were the fastest?"

"By a long way...you made my heart stop once or twice" She grinned up at him. "But **really** well done Sam. Fantastic!" Cilla seemed to want to do it all again, tossing her head and dancing about.

The three finalists walked sedately into the ring for the prize giving. Sam rode as tall as he could and remembered Erin's instructions to take his hat off when being presented with the rosette.

"Well done young man" The judge said and shook his hand.

"Thank you sir".

"Let's see you all canter round the ring"

"Take it steady this time!" The ring steward said as he passed him.

Sam smiled. "Come on Cilla, let's go". A touch with his heels and they were away, cantering up the side of the ring, followed by the other two, but he nearly came to grief when Cilla suddenly stopped.....the old lady with the umbrella, waving the straw hat...and clutching a crutch!"

"Gran!!?" The two behind him shot past.

"Good boy". She shouted.

Sam cantered on, a quick glance over his shoulder. It was his Gran, he was sure.

"Who was that old biddy?"Asked the boy who was originally behind him.

"I think it was my Gran...Lady Winthrop". He said as he dismounted to find her, a very happy and proud boy.

"I had no idea you were back Gran".

She smiled. "I thought you might be getting too attached to my Cilla, so I came home, just in time to see you thrash the

259

opposition! Well done my boy that was some ride, and the wall without stirrups! I'm really proud of you Sam, a chip off the old block eh?"

They watched Sally compete later in the day; she managed to come second in a class of about fifteen, and qualified well for London later in the year.

Tim took Maud home while Sally and the grooms loaded up and set off back to Dorchester.

"You look a bit glum Sam, I'd thought you'd be excited, you scared me half to death" Sally looked closely at him.

"Yeh, I am really...but I'll have to go home tomorrow, and then back to school....It's been terrific these last few weeks. I'll miss you all".

Sally drove on silently for a while. "I'll miss you too Sam...It's been fun. You've achieved much more than anyone expected Sam...you know that?"

He couldn't remember when he'd had such fun, and he'd learnt so much. But Gran was back and tomorrow she would have Cilla back. No more shows this summer.

"Next time you're home it will be Christmas wont it, how would you like a day's hunting?" She was desperate to cheer her young friend up. "We could go down to Devon for the Stag Hunt, that would be really exciting"

"That would be great, thanks...but I doubt Gran would let me have Cilla again....she loves her driving".

"I'll talk to her, one days hunting won't spoil her".

"I don't know, after today she won't think much of trotting down the lanes again". They both laughed.

"You did set her alight". Sally chuckled. "My word that was some round against the clock!"

"Yep...she can go alright can't she". He laughed, at last he had cheered up, it was a day to remember.

Sam was still asleep when his father arrived to take him and the pony home. He told Sally that Maud had already ordered Alfred to clean and polish her carriage. She was looking forward to driving again.

260

"I think Tim, you had better go with her the first time....that pony is now extremely fit, all the hard work Sam put in has made her much stronger you know".

"Yes, I can see that and I'm sure you're right. But you know Maud, she likes a challenge!"

"Well just be careful, I would hate her to have an accident". She was concerned for her old friend, she had never been cautious, even when she was fit and well.

"I'll look after her. I'll take Cilla out myself before she has a go driving. I guess she'll be OK".

Sam said his goodbyes to the students in the yard.

"Good bye Sir Sam" they all giggled. He was always embarrassed, it made him blush especially now when Erin hugged him.

"You're the best pupil I've ever had...look after the lovely Cilla. He rubbed the back of his hand over his eyes, he mustn't cry.

Sally shook his hand; she had noticed he was embarrassed with all the fuss "If I had a son I hope he'd be as brave as you! Good luck at school, it'll soon be Christmas and we'll go hunting".

He reluctantly climbed up into the Land Rover. "Bye" he shouted and waved as his Dad drove slowly out of the yard.

Sally and Erin stood and waved until they were out of sight. It was strange that such a young boy and his pony had made such an impact on them all. Even the students would remember him with affection and respect; he had enough courage for someone twice his age.

Sam slept badly that night, all the excitement of yesterday gone, tomorrow was school.

After looking after Cilla, her breakfast and mucking out the stable, he carefully folded her bright blue rug and travelling boots, then put them in a trunk in the tack room; she wouldn't need them again this year.

The afternoon dragged on, helping his mum pack his trunk, then preparing Cilla's evening meal. He spent a lot of time talking to her, stroking her lovely long mane....he didn't want to leave her and go into the house.

261

Then he heard Gran coming. Click clack as she crossed the yard.

"You in there Sam?" He sniffed and rubbed his eyes, it was silly to feel like this, he was ten years old...not a baby!

"Yes Gran...I'm just saying good bye to Cill".

"Is she alright?"

"Yes, I think she misses all Sally's horses", he mumbled, he missed them too.

"Come into the house now boy, it's getting dark". She put out her hand. "Give her this apple for me please Sam, I'll wait outside". She remembered being his age and having to go away to school, it was hard to say good bye to your pony, even if it was only for a few weeks. "Come on lad, it's getting chilly, I want you to have supper with me tonight and tell me about your holiday. I might even let you have a little wine to celebrate.....don't you tell your mother!"

Sam put his arm round her and helped her back into the house. He had been invited into his Gran's rooms, to have supper, he smiled, she wasn't such a dragon after all.

The crutches went click clack click clack on the polished floor and a happy Sam went with them.

Monday morning and school was only a few hours away, just a few bits and pieces to go into his trunk. He looked at his new jodhpurs and jacket, he wouldn't be having riding lessons this term, saving quite a bit off the fees, which pleased his father!

Sam was starting his last year at the prep' school and would be a prefect, giving him more responsibility. He felt he could handle the position now, the time spent with Sally had changed him a lot in ways he couldn't understand.

His Mum and Dad had notice the difference in him straight away, Gran said he'd just grownup...a good job too she said!

Tim took his son to school, a few miles from Salisbury, and as soon as he got back asked Alfred to harness Cilla and put her back in the shafts. He wanted to be sure all the jumping hadn't got the pony too excited for his Grandma to manage.

Maude was ready and waiting! "Don't think you're driving", she announced in her usual authoritative manner. "I shall drive, and you can sit beside me...*if* you insist".

"Are you sure Grandma?"

"Of course...stop fussing....help me in".

Cilla pawed the ground and tossed her head. "Steady girl", she snapped at the pony. "For goodness sake get in Tim if you're coming"

She settled herself in the carriage and picked up the reins. Tim was not a small man; he was all of six feet tall and built like an oak tree, so it was a tight squeeze for him to get in.

He was hardly seated when Gran flicked the whip at Cilla. "Let's go Cilla" she shouted. Cilla twitched her ears, tossed her head, and went!

She set off so suddenly Tim was nearly thrown out and Maud's hat flew off! The last time the pony had heard 'Let's Go' was at the show and she went down the drive at about the same speed.

Gran clutched the reins laughing. "Go Cilla...go!" she called out encouraging the pony to go faster.

The little carriage wasn't built for speed and it bounced dangerously over the pot holes.

"For God's sake woman, pull up, you'll kill us both".

Maud laughed and flicked the whip again. "What's the matter Tim, this is fun.....you frightened, no guts?"

"Stop for heaven's sake", he shouted and grabbed the reins. "Whoa Cilla...steady now".

Gradually the frantic speed gave way to a dashing trot and finally a steady walk.

"Spoil sport!" She spat as she turned to her Grandson.

"I'll drive today Gran...have you been watching Scurry racing by any chance".

"Maybe", she said coyly. "But I'd need a pair of Cillas for that!"

Tim sighed, would she never grow up, she might be eighty but sometimes acts like an eight rear old!

Cilla plodded on round the quiet lanes and when Tim was satisfied she was calm again, he handed the reins back to Maud.

"*Promise* me Gran you won't try that again", he said looking as cross as he could.

"Oh I can't promise that" laughed the eighty year old driver. "Trot on now Cilla my love".

Sam soon settled back into the school routine, he had six new boys to supervise and he looked them all over critically before they went into the assembly hall. Some looked scared and one was in tears, probably home sick. He sat the tearful one next to him and shared his hymn book as they sang the first familiar hymn.

'Lord receive us with thy blessing,
Once again assembled here'

They all sang this hymn at the beginning of every term. At the end of term an alternative version was sung

'Lord dismiss us with thy blessing,
Once again assembled here'

At the *end* of term it was sung with great gusto as it signalled the end of term, and the boys would be off to their parents as soon as the hymn was finished.

By then Sam's new boys would have become accustomed to school life and would join in the singing with more enthusiasm than they showed today.

TWENTYFIVE

Autumn came on quickly, the leaves on the big oaks beside the drive changed colour, some red, some gold before fluttering to the ground.

Cilla grew a long shaggy coat and stood miserably under a hedge in her paddock until Alfie brought her into the stable for the winter.

Lady Winthrop still drove to the village if the weather was fine. Vicky always made sure she was well wrapped up against the cold

The shop keeper's wife always popped out with a glass of sherry while her husband put the shopping in her shopping basket, plus sweeties and the regular bottle of Famous Grouse, bringing it out and putting it in the carriage beside her.

By Christmas it was too cold for driving and the frosty roads too hazardous for Cilla. The little carriage was   covered with a dust sheet and p arked forlornly beside the old Rolls Royce waiting for spring and the first snow drops to appear on the drive.

Sam came home for the holidays, and true to her word Sally took him hunting in Devon with the Stag Hounds.

Cilla seemed to enjoy hunting as much as her rider, he rode with his usual abandonment and Sally had a hard job keeping him from overtaking the hounds. That would have caused instant banishment; he would have been sent home with a stern warning ringing in his ears.

It was all great fun and very exciting until the big Red Stag was chased into a farm yard and cornered. Sam, in his youthful innocence, thought they would let the animal go, after all he had given them all a good run, he deserved a rest and a drink; what followed sickened Sam literally, and put him off the 'sport' forever.

Sally, slightly embarrassed, took him away from the scene. "We'll go home Sammy...Cilla's had enough for one day...come on, let's go home". They walked slowly away from the horses and riders to make their way back across the moors to the trailer.

"How could they do that Sally, that lovely Stag?"

265

"Well, that's hunting Sam. It's been going on for hundreds of years, in those far off days deer would have been an important food for country folk".

"It's just brutal, just awful".

"I'm inclined to agree, when you see it close up..... It would be kinder to shoot them".

No matter what he would never go hunting again...never. His Gran scoffed at his decision, when she was in her twenties she told him, she had often gone hunting with local hunts, but never again for Sam.

They had a real family Christmas, the sort Lady Winthrop had always enjoyed since she married her husband sixty eight years ago and moved into his ancestral home.

Tim and Alfie took a chain saw into the forestry and felled the tree they had marked for the festive season. The tractor couldn't get in amongst the trees, so Cilla, with a bit of ingenuity, was persuaded to pull the fir tree back to the house.

Everyone stood on the front steps, even Gran with her crutches, to watch Cilla bring the tree home.

Alfie limped along beside the pony, arthritis slowing him down a bit, although he would always deny it was painful. 'Just a wee bit stiff', he would answer if he was asked about his health.

It took a lot of pushing and pulling to get the tree into the centre of the hall. Sam dashed in and out with boundless enthusiasm, getting in the way and being told to clear off more than once.

At last, the Christmas Tree stood in its customary place, tall and proud, if not quite straight; all the family stood back and admired it, the best, and biggest, for many years Gran said.

After a hasty lunch Serena and Sam went up to the attic to find the decorations, and by supper time the tree was adorned with flashing lights, tinsel, and masses of pretty glass baubles, which would remain there until twelfth night, when it would all be whisked away and the entrance hall returned to its grand state.

Barry, Tim's brother, was coming for Christmas, just for three days not able to leave his farm and horses for longer. He was bringing his girl friend.

"A girl friend!!?" Maud shouted into the phone. "High time you had a girl friend Barry, there can't be many girls who would want to share you with all those horses!"

"This one doesn't seem to mind....she has more than me!"

That set Gran thinking, *who could have more horses than young Barry, he could ride a different one every day of the week and still have some to spare.* "Good...I'd like to meet this girl with so many horses, she must be brave, or mad to take you on". She set off across the polished oak floor and passed the shimmering Christmas tree, the crutches click clacking as she went to tell the family!

Barry had a girl friend at last. Well well, we all thought he was a confirmed bachelor. She smiled to herself, a girl friend with lots of horses...well, good for you Barry.

Christmas eve and the arrival of Barry and girl friend was awaited with as much anticipation as the festival day itself.

Maude kept a steady watch from her drawing room window. The sherry bottle and glasses stood on the little 'drum head table. The famous Grouse she hid in the bureau, *'she might not like the girl'*.

The grand piano had been tuned ready for Barry, he was a lovely pianist and Gran was looking forward to a Chopin recital. He could possibly have had a career as a pianist, but like so many youngsters he didn't have the dedication to go on studying after school. Farming was his choice and so he put his music aside, and closed the piano lid.

As a twenty first birthday present his Grandma bought him the farm at Ewe Hill, close to Lambourne, where he indulged his passion for horses and breeding top quality sheep on the chalk hills.

By late afternoon, just as a wintery sun was disappearing behind the tall oak trees, Barry's Discovery came bouncing down the drive towards his child hood home. Sam saw him first.

"He's here!" he shouted. "Uncle Barry's here", and he dashed to open the big front door, his Gran close behind...clickaty clack clickaty clack.

"Open the door Sam,,before the others get here...let's see this girl friend".

He heaved on the heavy door and with Serena's help, it opened as Barry was getting out of the Disco.

"Hello uncle Barry" they shouted.

Barry waved enthusiastically as he helped his passenger out. "Come and meet the family, I know you've met my Gran before!"

"**Barry**..why didn't you tell me!?" Maude had found her voice

"Hello Lady Winthrop, thank you for inviting me to your lovely home".

"And here's Sam and Serena my nephew and niece; I know Sam will want to show you his lovely pony".

"Grans pony". Sam corrected him.

"I'd love to see her" Sue really *did* want to see his pony. "I hear you've won some big classes with her, even got your names in the 'Horse and Hound!" Now he was blushing.

"Why do you call her Silly, that's an odd name isn't it?" Sue said, always ready for a joke.

"She's called Cilla...... "Sibertswold Cilla, as you very well know, Susan O'Rouke!" Maud almost shouted, killing her 'joke'.

"It's so nice to see you again Sue....come along in, it's cold standing here. Please call me Maude, by the way, sounds friendlier". She led them into her living room to meet Tim and Vicky. Sam and his sister couldn't follow without an invitation.

"I'll come and see Silly Cilla as soon as I can" Sue whispered, "I'd better not come just yet". Sam grinned, he liked Barry's friend. She would be good fun over Christmas.

It wasn't until after supper Sue nodded at Sam and they silently left the family gathering.

"We have to cross the yard, do you want a coat?"

"No, we mustn't be long, I really must see your wonderful Cilla though" They ran across the yard into the old stables. "I

268

love these old Victorian stables, don't you Sam, can you imagine all the lovely horses that have lived here, farm horses, hunters?"

"Yes...and the one that nearly killed my Gran, his name was Legend". Sam pointed to the stable they were walking past.

She looked in at a spotless stable, a polished head collar and rope hanging next to the feed trough and a bucket full of clean water. Sue looked enquiringly down at Sam.

"Old Alfie the gardener keeps it all clean and tidy; he won't let me in there! He was Legends groom; it's as if he's waiting for the old horse to come back".

"That's so sad", she said as they continued along the passage way.

Suddenly a pony made a loud long shriek! It was Cilla, head over her door, looking at Sue.

"Hello my love" she said and patted her neck.

Sam stood still, amazed. Cilla was licking Sue's hand...she obviously knew her.

"I never thought I'd see you again" She stroked the long mane and tided her forelock. "You look well, a bit fat perhaps"

"You *know* her!?"

"I certainly do".

"She recognised you're voice!"

"Yes". She looked at Cilla. "We're old friends, aren't we girl? I went to Wales to buy her for a friend and broke her in for his daughter, a little tot of a girl. She had to be sold eventually, that's when your Gran twisted my arm and bought her. She looks great, I'm so glad she's come to such a lovely home, you must tell me about the jumping".

"Yeah...she jumps alright. Oh, I *seeeee*! Barry brought Cilla here for Gran didn't he....so that's where you met him?"

"Yep, that's it Sam..I think we'd better go back in now, someone will miss us".

"You'll see her in harness tomorrow; we always walk to the Christmas service, but I expect Gran will go in her little carriage".

"Barry told me she was driving Cilla. Well well!.... Good night Cilla...see you in the morning".

269

Alfred had spent Christmas Eve searching in the tack room for a set of harness bells; the harness was far too big for Cilla, so he carefully took them off and fastened them to Maud's carriage.

Serena was allowed to sit with Gran on the way to church; the bells jangling all the way, the rest of the family, walked behind, laughing and joking enjoying the sound the bells made as Grans carriage bumped along the road.

Sam walked with Sue, chatting all the way. "It's a good job you're not older young Sam", Barry teased. "Or I might get jealous".

The service over his mother took his hand. "You walk with me Sam, let Barry and Sue walk together, two's company, three's a crowd". She winked at Sam, he understood and laughed.

Gran loved the effort Alfe had made putting the bells on her carriage, and gave him a big kiss along with his present. They made her smile all the way to the church and home again.

Alf was happy; he hadn't seen the old lady smile like that for a long time. Such a little gift, but it made her smile, and that made *his* Christmas a happy one. He had been working for the Winthrop family since he was a very young man, before Sir Albert, Lady Winthrop's husband died, so it seemed natural that he always came to the house for Christmas dinner.

He'd seen Tim and Barry grow up; he held their hands and wiped away their tears when their parents were killed in London in a freak accident on an underground train. He was probably in his eighties, although no one was quite sure, and lived on his own in one of the estate cottages.

He came in his best suit, white shirt and tie, looking anything but the handyman that kept everything working round the estate! He was much loved and had earned his place with the family he'd cared for for so long.

Vicky had prepared a sumptuous meal, turkey and a big ham took pride of place, one at each end of the long table, and between them vegetables of every kind. The wine flowed constantly, everyone over indulged in what ever there was to offer!

Later, when the children had been sent off to bed and Alfred had said his thanks to everyone, they all gathered in Maud's drawing room in front of a huge log fire to listen to Barry playing the piano.

He flexed his fingers, opened the piano lid and played some Chopin Nocturnes for his Gran.

Sam listened intently, he was sitting on the stairs in his pyjamas, he had never heard his uncle play the piano before, and he was entranced. Tim found him, fast asleep, still sitting there when they all retired for the night!

Boxing Day dawned bright and crisp; a hard frost had covered everything, the grass stiff and glistening in the early sunshine, a lovely morning for a walk.

They all wrapped up against the cold, squeezed into the Land Rover and Tim drove them a few miles to the coastal foot-path.

The wind whipped the sea into a frenzy of white topped waves, Sue who hardly ever went to the coast stood and stared. "It's magnificent" she shouted, "I've never seen anything like this, just look at the power of those waves crashing on the shore!"

Barry grabbed her in his arms. "Don't go too near the edge sweet heart", he grinned "I don't want to loose you now that I've just found you!"

"Come on you two", Tim shouted against the roaring of the wind. "The Smugglers is only a mile, and I'm thirsty!"

"And I'm freezing!" Sam added.

"Ok Ok we're coming, can't a fellow get romantic without everyone wanting to hurry". Barry took Sue's hand and they raced down the path.

"Be careful young lovers" Vicky shouted, but they ran shrieking down the hill.

Sam giggled, his Gran would have laughed if she'd been with them, but it was no place for an old lady on crutches.

271

The pub was open, a sigh of relief from Tim. A huge fire was roaring away in the inglenook, Sue wondered if her Dad would restore theirs back at Lambourne? The ceiling was low with massive black beams running from side to side, old tarred fishing nets hung on a wall, beside lobster pots and ships lanterns.

Sam was enthralled, he was too young to be allowed in a pub usually, this place was like an Aladdin's Cave! Tim pushed the two children into a corner and sat beside them.

The publican smiled, if it wasn't Boxing Day he would have them sent outside, the law was the law and publicans have to be very careful, but they were only small children, and the bar was very crowded, they could sit quietly in the corner just this once! He caught Sam's eye and pointed to a sign over the bar.

'*NO PERSON UNDER 18 ALLOWED AT THE BAR*'

Sam smiled and gave him a 'thumbs up'. He understood and tried to make himself even smaller!

There were ships in bottles on the window sills, tiny sailing ships with three or four masts and some in full sail, how on earth did they get them into the bottles? He desperately wanted to have a closer look, but he was imprisoned tight in the corner.

Barry ordered hot pasties, they munched away greedily, they would have to get back to the Land Rover before it got dark. The path was now, of course *up* hill, and Sam began to wish he hadn't eaten so fast. The wind had moved round a degree or so and was blowing straight into their faces, a cold sharp wind that burnt checks bright red and made their eyes stream.

They were tired and buffeted by the wind long before the car came into sight.

"What would I give for a hot cup'a" Tim said as he stopped to catch his breath.

"Give me a kiss then and I'll give you a cup of tea" Vicky teased."I put a flask in the car before we set out".

"Woman the kiss will have to wait until tonight...the tea I need *now*!" They raced each other to the car with the others chasing after them. They all arrived together laughing and trying to get into the car first!

The children were tired and the warmth of the car made them drowsy, they both slept the short journey home, Sam snoring gently, much to the grownups amusement.

After supper Barry played again, this time Sam was allowed to sit on a foot stool at his Gran's feet and listen quietly. Barry needed no music and sat at the piano in the shadows playing. Some Beethoven, more Chopin for Gran, and a lullaby by Brahms, especially for the children before they went up to bed.

Sam wished he could play like that. He'd ask his Dad if he could have piano lessons at school instead of riding lessons next term.

He was mesmerised, Barry's long fingers just flowed over the keys and the most gorgeous sounds filled the room. Before he went to bed he asked Barry if he thought he would ever be able to play as beautifully.

"You might....I seem to have inherited my ability from my mother, or so Gran tells me. I can't remember her, but I know once I start playing something inside me takes over. 'Praps you have the same talent, it might run in the family!....but you won't find it easy to start with Sam.....If you *really* want to try I'll pay for the lessons, but you'll have to promise me you'll practise every day".

Sam was thoughtful. "I'll talk to Dad tomorrow, I really will". He said as he walked up stairs to bed.

Barry closed the lid of the piano and stroked the gleaming wood. "This was my mother's instrument Sue, and when I play it here for Gran I feel close to her....funny that, but I can almost feel her standing next to me".

"It was so lovely" Sue was visibly moved as was Gran.

"Thank you Barry, your mother would have enjoyed that recital" she said.

Sue and Barry left early for Lambourn. Sue had left a good impression, everyone liked her, and she seemed to fit into the family so easily.

"Is this the one Barry" Tim asked his young brother as they were walking to his car. "Do I hear wedding bells in the near future?"

"Don't rush me", he laughed "But if she say's yes you'll be the first to know!"

"Good luck Barry, she's a lovely girl". The brothers hugged each other; it had been a wonderful three days.

Sam was sorry to see them go, he liked Sue, and Barry's music had thrilled him. He had been humming the Brahms, it was going round and round in his head all the time.

His Gran laughed when he told her he wanted to learn the piano. "It's not easy, don't think because you're uncle can play so wonderfully you'll be able to play like that straight away, Barry worked at it for years when he was your age. He practised for three hours every day. It's not an easy instrument to master".

"So he told me" he sighed. "I really do want to try Gran".

When he was back at school, still full of enthusiasm, the music teacher said he would try to fit him in for lessons. First there would be some aural tests to see if he had any undiscovered musical talent, or whether it was just a passing fancy.

Sam was eager to do the tests and waited anxiously for the summons to Mr Nightingales music room.

When it came he rushed across the forecourt to the music wing and arrived breathless at the music masters door.

"Come in Sam"

"Please sir, I've come sir!"

"So I see "said Mr Nightingale. "Come in then and sit down. I see you've been here for three years. Tell me Sam, why do you suddenly want to take up the piano?"

Sam, sitting on the edge of the chair told him how his uncle had played for them at Christmas, how lovely it had sounded, and how he would like to be able to play as beautifully when he was older.

"Can you remember what he played?"

"Oh yes...well....some of it was." He thought for a moment. "He played some Beethoven and some Chopin, for my Gran, oh yes, and a lullaby by....I can't remember the name!"

"Did it sound like this?" Mr Nightingale started playing the Brahms.

"Yes yes that's it sir" Sam was delighted.

"Can you sing it with me?" Sam burst into song, la-laing it since Brahms hadn't written any words to the lullaby. He got to the end and beamed at the teacher.

274

"That's been going round and round in my head since Christmas sir, it's so lovely".

"Yes Johannes Brahms could write beautiful music. Now Sam, let me hear you sing something else, a carol perhaps, something you sang at the carol concert. Sam was still in Mr Nightingale's study when the bell sounded for supper.

"I have to go now sir...I'm a prefect and have some new boys to look after. I'm sorry sir".

"That's alright Sam" he said as he twirled around on the piano chair. "We'll start your piano lessons next week...I'll let you know when exactly....well done Mr Winthrop...a pity you waited so long before coming to see me. Hurry now, prefects must never be late!"

He hopped and skipped back to the dining hall, he was going to have piano lessons, maybe, just maybe he might one day be able to play like Barry.

TWENTYSIX

The winter closed in on the Winthrop farm. Maude had to give up driving Cilla, snow covered the lanes. She fumed and fretted and got in everyone's way, her crutches click clackating on the polished floors; Vicky ran for cover when she heard her coming.

"When will this bloody snow melt?" She moaned. "I get so bored, if only I could get out!"

Vicky suggested she wrote a letter to Sam, ask him how the piano lessons are going.

Gran snorted, would he have the patience to practise enough she wondered ...he wouldn't get anywhere if he didn't. Perhaps she *would* write to him and remind him Barry practised all the time...and then again...perhaps she wouldn't! If the boy had enough talent he wouldn't need his old Gran nagging him...No....Yes she would write about Cilla, he would surely like to hear about the little pony...and Sally who was trying to get a horse qualified for a big show somewhere. The letter got longer and longer, her spidery writing covered several pages before her glasses fell off and she lost her temper!

She sat back in her armchair and smiled to herself. It had been nice writing to young Sam, she'd enjoyed that, and it had passed a dull and dreary afternoon.

When she looked out at the garden the bushes were dripping and puddles were appearing on the paths. The snow was melting at last, it had lain about longer than she could remember, now it was thawing. May be she could drive Cilla tomorrow, she was running short of whisky, they usually had a good stock of Famous Grouse so she could replenish her drink cupboard!

Sam read the letter several times and laughed at his Gran's description of Cilla enjoying the snow in her paddock, he missed the little pony and life at home, but school was important. His Dad was always telling him, you had to have a good education if you were to get on in life.

He sighed; he enjoyed school, especially now he was having piano lessons, but truth to tell he would rather be at home and go to the local school. Unfortunately all the boys in his family,

276

going back several generations, went to his public school. A tradition Sam could do without. He folded Grans letter carefully and put it in his locker, his music tumbled onto the floor at his feet, a reminder he hadn't practised yet. He picked it all up and went to find an empty practice room.

Mr Nightingale was very pleased with his latest pupil, he sensed the boy had talent, it was early days, but there was something about the way he played. Even the simplest pieces he was given were played with feeling.

He remembered his uncle, Barry Winthrop, a very promising pianist who had achieved the Associated Board grade eight exam with distinction when he was barely fifteen, he could have gone on to make a career as a soloist, but had opted out, choosing farming instead.

Barry had inspired his young nephew, so he would start Sam on the long journey, and help him while he was here. How far he would travel along that road would be up to him.

Snow drops were flowering in great white drifts along the country lanes and Maud was out and about again driving Cilla.

Everything seemed to be growing suddenly with green shoots appearing everywhere. Alf was back at work in the gardens he loved so much, talking to the plants encouraging them to grow.

The long cold winter had made his arthritis worse, but he was sure the warm spring sunshine would put that right, he whistled softly as he went about his work.

Sam was counting the days to the end of term, when all the boys would sing the traditional hymn

'Lord dismiss us with thy blessing Once again assembled here'

He was as anxious as any of the boys to get home, even though it was only for three weeks. If his Gran allowed he would ride Cilla again.

Barry had promised to take him 'team chasing' if there was a meeting anywhere near the farm over the Easter holidays.

Sally had written to him sending a schedule for Hunter Trials at Tarrant Gunville near Dorchester. He could enter the pony

277

class if his Gran didn't object. The jumps would be hedges and ditches, just natural jumps that you might meet out hunting. The fastest clear round would win.

Sam read it over and over again; he would ask if he could enter Cilla, it sounded so much fun. Sally promised to twist his Grans arm a little and persuade her Cilla would come to no harm.

Maud thought about it over the next few days, perhaps they had all forgotten that it was during a hunter trial that she was nearly killed and left with withered legs, legs that were a constant reminder.

She was worried; Sam certainly would enjoy the challenge, and Cilla would go hell for leather if he pushed her, and he *would* push that's for sure. She wanted to say 'no' to Sally and her young Great-Grandson.

Her fall had been an accident, soft mud on the landing side of an easy jump, the horse stumbled and she was thrown over his head, then darkness and endless pain. The old lady shivered at the memory.

Could it happen again, to Sam?....No, it was too awful to contemplate, she would try to explain to the boy, he would be upset no doubt, but she couldn't face the possibility it *might* happen again.

Sally tried to persuade her old friend that Cilla could cope well, it was only a pony class after all, with no jump over two foot six inches, but the answer was a definite no, N.O!!

Sam came home for the Easter holiday in a bad mood. He had been looking forward to the Hunter Trials for weeks. Cilla was so fast and clever he was sure they would have had a good chance of winning. He knew he would not get Gran to change her mind.

Almost as soon as he arrived home the phone rang. It was Sally asking him if he would like to come to the Equitation Centre for a few days...he could come to the hunter trials with her!

He didn't need asking twice, the thought of spending three weeks with his smirking little sister didn't appeal to him.

278

Sally came to collect him the very next day as his Dad was busy with lambing and couldn't spare the time.

"I've got a new horse for you to ride" she told him as they dodged around caravans on the coast road, "He's quite small for a horse, only a pony really, 14.2 hands exactly, but quite lively, you'll like him I think"

Sam was immediately interested, he was wondering what he could ride this time since Cilla was out of the equation! "Does he jump?"

"I'm not sure" she said concentrating on the holiday traffic. "He only came to me because his previous owner couldn't keep him in the field...kept jumping the gate!" She took a quick glance at Sam and grinned. "I thought that might interest you".

He couldn't get out of the car fast enough. "Which stable is he in Sally" he shouted as he headed for the yard.

"He's not in yet!" Erin exclaimed as he almost bumped into her. "Steady on Sam...We'll go and get him". She picked up a bucket with a handful of pony nuts. "He's not that easy to catch yet".

They walked out to the field. Empty!! "*Now* where's the blighter gone?" The gates were all shut. "Any of you seen Fred?" Erin called out to the students.

"Not since this morning". One of them replied.

"Come on Sam, we'd better have a look". Erin opened the gate. "Freddie ...where are you. Freddie come on then". She rattled the bucket.

"He's not here".

"Quiet.....listen!"

"Your daft........the field's empty".

"Don't be cheeky young man. Listen!......**Freddieeee...I want you. Freddie come on**". She shouted.

Sam turned away thinking Erin was wasting her breath, then suddenly a shrill whinny from further away, the next field possibly, then a drumming of hooves.

"See...he's coming" laughed Erin. "Wait Sam, he's coming". He saw a flash of gold behind the hedge and with a mighty leap Freddie cleared the five bar gate and raced up to Erin, his nose

279

went straight into the bucket. He looked at Sam as if to say *'Who's a clever boy then'*

"You knew he'd do that" he accused Erin and looked at the laughing students. "You all knew didn't you?!"

"It's his party piece" said Sally" who had joined the group. "The question is will he do it with you on board, that's what we want to find out!"

Sam looked from Erin to Sally and back again. He was speechless. "You want me to ride *him*?!"

"Well think about it while I put the car away" Sally said as she walked back to the car.

Erin led Freddie into the yard dancing along beside her, a big sturdy horse, a bright golden colour with a white mane and tail. Certainly a very pretty boy and he seemed to know it. He looked cocky and self assured, very different from the quiet, well mannered Cilla. It could be fun, certainly a challenge; he loved a challenge....like Gran.

"After tea" He said looking at Erin. "But in the indoor school".

"OK 'my lord' after tea it shall be".

He wondered if he'd been a touch hasty, but he couldn't back out now, and in any case nothing could go wrong in the indoor school...could it?

Erin and some students erected a few jumps, not very high for the pony, 'that was almost a horse', bur high enough to see if he could, or would, jump with a rider on his back.

Two of the more experienced students had ridden him in the indoor school and said he was very 'green' and needed a lot of schooling but seemed to learn quickly. He hadn't been jumped.

Sam swallowed his meal quickly and went to find Fred, who was already waiting for him with his saddle and bridle on, ready for some fun!

Sally was slightly anxious, the pony had a certain look about him, was it just youthful high spirits, or something sinister!

Erin gave Sam a leg up, the pony, or horse, was quite tall compared to Cilla. He stood patiently while the stirrups went up a few holes and then swaggered off around the arena.

280

"Just walk and trot" shouted Sally. "Get the feel of him....don't try jumping yet!"

Sam knew immediately that this was no donkey; he sensed the power under him. He shortened his reins and Fred responded by dancing and pulling at his hands.

"Steady Freddie" He said, he felt very small, the ground was a long way down. A slow trot might settle him down he thought. Freddie didn't have a slow trot; he shot forward and nearly left Sam behind. He could trot fast...very fast, but slow collected trot, never!

Now it was Sally becoming concerned. "You OK Sam?" She called out as Fred shot past.

"Just getting to know him" he shouted over his shoulder. "Won't be long". She gritted her teeth and held her breath. Erin was now much more relaxed and began to laugh as she closed the big doors at the end of the arena, at least they were in an enclosed space!

Sam, getting over the initial shock of so much power beneath him, quickly got Fred under control. He heaved on the reins and sat tight, he was *so* much stronger than Cilla.

A canter seemed a good idea and surprisingly Fred agreed, he produced a nice steady canter. Sam's confidence began to return. "You're just a big bully aren't you" he told Fred, "You don't scare me!" Fred shook his head and pricked his ears.

"OK Erin" he shouted, "I'll try a jump".

"Not too ambitious Sam...try the small one first OK?"

Sam looked for a small jump, couldn't see it. *'Oh hell they all look the same'* He thought, and turned into the nearest, offering up a prayer.

Freddie saw the jump. *'Whoopee'* He seemed to say, and took control again. Sam held on as best he could and let Fred set the pace. The pony was in his element, they flew over jump after jump Fed snorting and tossing his head. *'Let me go'* he seemed to say. *'I can do this. Don't stop me!'*

Sam sensed the pony didn't need any help and gave him more rein, all he needed to do was steer him in the right direction. They did two circuits leaving all the jumps standing. He pulled up to a walk with a lot of effort and walked up to Erin.

281

"Put them up a peg or two" he panted out of breath. "You 'aint seen nothing yet!"

Erin looked at Sally who nodded. Students appeared as if by magic and the jumps went up and up.

Sam lent forward in the saddle and spoke to Fred, quietly in his left ear. "This time we'll go at *my* speed Fred...got it?" He sat up, took a good hold on the reins, short and firm.

Fred set off again, this time *Sam* was in control, sitting firmly in the saddle, knees in tight. "Steady now Fred". They circled round the arena.

"That's better". Sally called out suddenly more interested again. "Hold him at that speed until the last three strides, and then give him his head".

Freddie was pulling, but Sam was ready for him "Steady now". *'Three strides from the centre of the jump'.* "Steady Fred...steady. Go!" Fred had all the rein he needed, his head was free and he lept. Sam felt the power and thrust of his quarters as he rose at the jump. He lent forward sliding his hands up on the white mane, getting his weight off the ponies back.

"Phew!" gasped Sally.

"Holy Mother of God!" whispered Erin.

"Good boy" said Sam as he slapped Freddie's neck. When the jump was measured it stood over four feet.

Erin opened the doors and let Freddie and his rider out. Sam was grinning from ear to ear. Freddie was blowing quite hard!

He slid from Fred's back, it was a long way down for a small boy, and led him to his stable. He had never jumped that high before and Fred had made it seem easy!

He started to take the saddle off, Fred nuzzled his shoulder. "You're a lovely boy; I bet you can jump even higher".

Fred looked at Sam and nuzzled him again. *'You know I can with you'* He seemed to say.

"I wish" Sam sighed.

Sally and Erin followed them across the yard deep in conversation and stood by the door while Sam took Fred's bridle off.

"Well...what do you think of my new horse then Sam?"

282

"Oh Sally...he's just great. He's a bit strong, but he listens. He can't half jump cant he!"

"Yes he certainly can...and he's only half fit yet. Perhaps when he's really fit he'll be too strong for you"

"Oh I don't think so" he replied anxiously. "With a stronger bit, or a martingale, and more scho....." He suddenly heard Erin giggling, he looked up, Sally was smiling.

"You look very small standing there...he's built like an oak tree, just look at his quarters".

"Fat as the cook's back side" Erin added still laughing.

"Yeah,,,but I love him" He said fingering Freds white forelock. "What's the matter? Why are you laughing at me....I rode him alright. Didn't I?"

"Oh Sam" Sally was wiping a tear from her eye. "You're Gran asked me to find you a pony because you're almost too big for Cilla..... Well Sam...Fred is a pony, just, and if you think you can control him? Well....he's yours..... but be sure before you say yes!"

Sam just stood there, speechless. His Gran was going to buy him this wonderful pony...he must be dreaming. "He's for me" he gasped at last. "Really,,,just for me?!"

"Yes Sam....just for you" she laughed. "We've a lot of work to do on him mind you, before we see his real potential".

So he had his own pony, or small horse, he had a fantastic jump and with a lot of schooling he should do very well.

He spent a week with Sally riding Fred every day under supervision and spent hours grooming and polishing his lovely golden coat.

Pony and boy were well suited, they would make a tough pair to beat in a year or so, but he was patient, he could wait and dream. He could ride Cilla this summer; she wasn't such a handful as Fred.

Fred! He *must* find a better name than Fred for his new pony; you couldn't call such an aristocratic horse Fred! No....he must talk to Erin about it.

They went out for a ride together after schooling the following day. "I thought you liked his name, it's all I hear when you're

283

riding round the arena, *'steady Freddie'* all the time! It has a nice ring to it don't you think?"

"It's no name for a horse like this" he scoffed; he had started thinking of Fred as a horse now. He would like to call him Legend, but Gran wouldn't like that...no, he must think of something really nice.

Tim came to collect him after the week with Sally at the Equestrian Centre. Lady Winthrop came with him to see the horse she had bought for young Sam.

After a week of TLC and a lot of schooling, the pony looked quite respectable, not the ruffian he was when Sam first saw him flying over the gate! He behaved impeccably when he rode him in the schooling paddock. Sam didn't jump him, Sally had suggested they left that until the summer holidays, they didn't want to scare his Gran, but they did show her the gate Fred had jumped.

Maude was very impressed with the 'golden' pony. "Where did you find him Sally?" she asked when they were alone.

"Pulling a cart in Dorchester" she replied with a grin. "Actually I bought him for my Equestrian Centre, he looked a useful sort, and it wasn't 'till I saw him jump out of this field, over *that* gate that I thought of Sam".

"I'm glad you did" Maude laughed. "I don't think we'd better mention the cart, he's up in the clouds now, and we don't want to spoil that!"

Sam went home leaving Fred in Erin's capable hands, it made sense to leave him there where he would continue his schooling, while he could start getting Cilla ready for the summer shows.

Vicky was waiting for them when they returned and as soon as they were indoors she announce the great news. Barry had phoned to say Sue had said yes, they were to be married!

"About time" said Gran. "Here Sam, help me to my room, *now there'll be some action around here. More expense"* she went on muttering as Sam helped her across the entrance, hall her crutches going click clack on the polished oak floor.

284

Tim was very happy for his brother. "I'll phone him when I've had a cuppa".

"I might be a bridesmaid!" Serena said excitedly. "When will it be mum...the wedding?" She had always wanted to be a bridesmaid.

"Not for sometime dear, Sue helps her Dad train race horses and they have a lot running all through the summer. It'll be an autumn wedding I expect".

Sam went up to the old nursery at the top of the house. The talk of uncle Barry had reminded him he hadn't practised for nearly a week. His old piano had been neglected for years until it was tuned for Sam.

His fingers were stiff and sore after riding Fred and at first the music was hard, but gradually he relaxed and the notes began to flow and he became immersed in the piece he was working on. 'A Fantasy' the composition was called, it was something he would have to play for the exam at the end of next term.

*'Fantasy......What a lovely name for Fred, **instead** of Fred.'* He thought. *"I must phone Sally when I've finished here and tell her to stop calling Fred Fred. Fantasy is much much nicer.*

He went back to practising his exam music, and as soon as he started playing his fingers seemed to take over, he didn't need to look at the music in front of him, it was there in his head, already memorised. Sam played on and on.

Down stairs his Gran stopped to listen, she smiled, young Sam seemed to have inherited the gift, it was like listening to Barry's first fumbling efforts all over again. How far along that difficult path could he travel, only time would tell?

He went back to school at the end of the week, his last term at the Prep School. After the summer holidays he would be going to the Public School a mile away at Lavington, a family tradition, both his Dad and uncle were educated there.

He played 'A Fantasy' to Mr Nightingale at the first lesson; he played it without the music in front of him, all by memory. It reminded the teacher of another young Winthrop, years ago, sitting at the same piano, his blond head bowed as he played

285

Handel's Largo, tears running down his cheeks. 'It's so sad' he had said.

Mr Nightingale filled his pipe and wondered how young Sam Winthrop would progress in the senior school; he felt he had a very promising pupil to guide over the next few years.

Serena stayed at home when Sam went off to school, she had also gone to a boarding school in Bournemouth She hated it and was allowed to leave, now she was much happier at the local village school.

Although the little girl showed no interest in riding, she nevertheless loved Cilla; she would brush and comb her for hours talking to her.

She also had a little brown hairy dog she adored, he was her constant companion. She was playing with him in front of the house when Alfred brought the pony and carriage to the front door to wait for her ladyship.

"You been in the stable brushing Cilla?" She blushed and turned away, she thought it was her secret. "Next time put the brushes back in the box; don't leave them on the floor". He smiled at her holding her dog in her arms. "Don't you worry missy, I won't let on, it's our secret".

Before Serena could manage a reply they heard the click clack of Gran's crutches as she appeared, ready for her drive to the village shop.

Serena stood at Cilla's head while Alfred helped her Ladyship down the steps and into the carriage. She glanced briefly at her Great-Granddaughter, such a pretty child she was growing into, she thought, long blond curly hair and such a lovely blue dress.

"Would you like to accompany me Serena, you can squeeze in beside me?"

"Oh yes please, can Little Dog come as well...he's very, very small, he won't take up much room. pleeease?" Now Gran had a problem, in a way she'd wished she hadn't spoken to the child, but she looked so lonely with only the wretched dog to play with.

"Come along then, both of you" Gran sighed. "Don't let that dog fall out!". She needn't have worried, Little Dog squirmed between them and sat watching the scenery go by.

286

He loved it, and Gran found she enjoyed having him next to her; that trip to the village shop turned out to be the first of many.

Whenever Alfred brought the pony and trap to the front door, he was waiting, tail wagging furiously, and waiting anxiously while Maud was helped into the carriage, his brown eyes watching for the slightest sign of recognition.

"I suppose you want to come?" she would say, and like a flash he was up on the seat beside her.

Serena went with them whenever she could, sometimes she would take the reins and drive them all home.

Little Dog became Lady Winthrop's loyal friend during the days when Serena was at school. He would sneak into her rooms if the door was left open a crack and curl up beside her on the sofa.

Although she would never admit it, she enjoyed his company, he was a good listener, and never argued with her!

By the time Sam finished school for the summer, Alfie had taught Serena how to put Cilla's harness on and back her into the little carriage. He could sense trouble, but said nothing, then, when Sam discovered Serina harnessing Cilla one morning he was furious.

He had several shows lined up for Cilla, and he needed to practise with her.

The argument could be heard across the yard and in the house. Little Dog ran for cover in the kitchen. And Alfie suddenly found the grass needed cutting!

Tim came storming out and separated the children. "Let me remind you who Cilla belongs to!...it's neither of you.....Cilla belongs to Gran. Has she asked you to harness the pony Serena?...No, I thought not....you're just making trouble, and you Sam. Have you asked Gran if you can ride Cilla today?...No.....So neither of you are to take her out...ever without Gran or Alfie being with you.....now go indoors and apologise to Gran and your mother before I knock your heads together!"

Serena burst into tears. "It's not fair...I got her ready first".

Sam kicked the door "Bloody sister, what does she want to drive for".

"Indoors both of you before I tan your backsides!" shouted their father.

Sam stalked across the yard very, very cross. He hadn't ridden Cilla for ages and he must do some schooling before the first show. "I bet she's forgotten everything I taught her" he shouted".

"An apology or there won't be any shows". Tim shouted after him.

"Oh hell!" he shouted slamming the door and rushing up to the nursery. The piano took some punishment, but gradually his temper abated as the music took over.

He practised for an hour until his temper had gone, he closed the piano lid and went to look for Gran to apologise. His Dad was right, the pony wasn't his, Gran had let him ride Cilla and arranged for his lessons because he had nothing to ride, and she could see he needed something to do, a challenge of some sort.

It had been more successful than anyone had imagined, and now he had Fantasy as well, yet another challenge to overcome. He was a lucky boy really; he would go downstairs and apologise.

Serena had found Gran first. "I just wanted to take you for a drive Gran" she sobbed "That's all, Sam has Cilla all the time...it's not fair!"

"Stop snivelling...and stop lying to me Serena. You were showing off, you knew Sam would be cross.....you shan't drive with me again if you're going to behave like this. Just remember Sam is away at school most of the time, when he is, then you can drive with me...but when he's home he rides Cilla. Is that clear young lady?"

"Yes Gran...I'm sorry, I won't do it again".

The next day peace reigned and Cilla was taken to Dorchester to prepare for the shows.

It would be Sam's last season with Cilla, next year he would be too old for the 'mini jumping', and soon he would be too big for her.

He was determined to do well this summer. He watched and listened to everything Sally told him. His riding improved

288

dramatically, people even began asking Sally if he could show ponies for them

"Sorry" Sally would say, "He's got his own two ponies to show, he really hasn't got time for more".

Cilla had forgotten a lot since last summer, but after a few days at the Equestrian School she was back, perfect flying changes, collected canters and so on.

They worked on showing classes, a lot easier it seemed this time, while Sally concentrated on their jumping.

In next to no time the first show was upon them. He spent hours grooming Cilla, he scrubbed her white socks and when they were dry again he rubbed chalk into the hair, the white socks became *brilliant* white socks!

She looked terrific; Erin gave him a slap on the back. "Couldn't have done better myself! Now shove over and I'll do her plats....here, thread the needle for me, nice long bit of thread please".

Her strong fingers twisted and turned the long silky mane and gradually a long line of neat little plats appeared.

"There...don't she look Grand Sam?" she wheezed, her mouth still holding the needle and thread. "I'll do her tail to match and then we can wrap her up for the night".

Rugged and bandaged Cilla had a restless night. The neat little plats were so tight nothing was going to disturb them, and as for the platted tail, well, if it hadn't got a big thick bandage round it, Cilla would have rubbed her back side on the wall and rubbed and rubbed until all the hair was free again.

She ate her tea time feed and sulked, she had never had to have plats before, it was a first and Sam could see she hated it.

Early, before it was really light, Erin came with a feed and checked the pony. Her white socks could do with some more chalk, otherwise she looked pretty good.

There were four horses going to the show, Sally's two jumpers, a Novice Working Hunter that a more advance student would be riding and Cilla.

There was plenty for Erin to do, supervising the students, and making sure everything went without a hitch. By ten o'clock

289

everyone and everything was ready, the big lorry backed into the yard and the horses were loaded.

All the horses wore distinctive blue rugs with 'Dorchester Equestrian Centre' embroidered in the corner. Cilla had a similar rug but without the logo. Students had the same colour shirts with the logo on the back. Several students were coming as grooms so there was a lot of chattering as they climbed into the lorry.

"Sam...you sit in front with me...I don't trust you with all these lovely girls!". The girls giggled, Sam blushed bright red!!....Leave room for Erin, she's coming as well".

As if on cue she arrived, puffing and blowing, having made sure the senior student left in charge had all Erin's instructions written down and knew what to do until they came home.

"Jump up Erin", Sam called opening the door.

"It's a long time since I jumped anywhere!" she said as she heaved herself into the seat beside Sam.

"OK gang...let's go". Sally let out the clutch and the lorry lurched forward. A horse in the back whinnied and stamped it's feet, they were on their way at last.

The Shepton Mallet show was a big annual show with several rings all being used continuously.

The main ring was used for all the jumping classes. Sam looked with horror at the jumps, Cilla could walk under most of them quite easily. Erin told him not to worry, in the smallest pony class the jumps never exceeded 2ft 6 inches. Cilla could jump much higher than that. He relaxed and began to look forward to the 12.2hh jumping. But first of all they had the working pony class to deal with.

There was no class for the smallest ponies today, so Sally had entered them in the next group. Ponies not exceeding 13.2 hands, a big step up for both Sam and Cilla. The jumps would be higher and most of the ponies bigger.

Sam was a little nervous, but Sally was confident Cilla would cope with the new class, the showing section was up to Sam and his riding had improved so much since last summer shows. He was taller and much stronger. Yeah...they would be alright.

When the class started Sam was walking round the collecting ring with Cilla, waiting for their turn to jump. He could see why Sally had insisted Erin platted her mane and tail, all the ponies, except one or two scruffy ones, were platted.

These were real show ponies, not hairy Mountain and Moorland types. He looked critically at his lovely Cilla, she had more muscle than most of the others, due to all the driving and road work, but she carried herself well and had a lovely arched neck....and that beautiful floating trot.

His turn came. He shortened his reins and they walked into the ring.

"Good luck boyo!" called Erin.

The jumps were quite a bit higher, just hedges and rustic poles mostly, also a narrow gate that had to be opened and shut without dismounting, and that was new!

Sam had watched Sally teaching the most advanced students how to do a 'half pass'. It was simply getting the horse to walk sideways.

He had tried it on one of the school horses once when he was having a group lesson. Then the horse performed it beautifully, could Cilla do it...that was the question!

It would make opening and closing the gate so much easier, and it would save precious seconds, although the class wasn't timed as such, the ponies only had a limited amount of time to complete the course, and then penalty points were added.

He waited for the starting bell to ring. Cilla was on her toes waiting for Sam to say the magic words, 'Let's go Cilla', and she would be off like a mini rocket.

The bell rang and they were off. She flew over the first three jumps, they were a little higher than usual but well within her capability, the fourth nearly caught her out.

Sam was pushing, urging her on, so she lengthened her stride obediently, the jump looked insignificant, just a little brush jump, but just as she was about to hop over, she saw a stretch of sparkling water.

291

Cilla wasn't expecting that, with a massive effort she stretched her front legs out as far as she could and tucked up her back legs, luckily landing safely on the other side of the water!

Now it was really tricky, no sooner had they galloped to clear the water than the gate appeared in front of them. Sam had to pull up and stop to open the gate and walk through.

He had a fleeting vision of Fantasy on this course, he would never stop at the gate, he liked gates, he would simply jump it and get disqualified!

Cilla was better behaved and stopped easily. He lifted the catch and pulled the gate open, they scampered through and Sam grabbed the gate again to close it.

A bit of neck reining, a touch of his heel on the inside, and Cilla managed a pretty good attempt at a 'half pass'. The gate clicked shut and they were off again, hardly losing any time at the gate.

They went clear and well within the allotted time.

Now for the showing class, would Cilla calm down enough to do a good show?

He walked her quietly round and round the collecting ring; there were still a lot of ponies to jump and with Erin's calm hands and voice, Cilla soon relaxed.

"Did you see her jump the water? I thought she was going to stop and dump me in it!"

"I seem to remember you had a ducking once before". She laughed.

"Yeah..I did didn't I....but what about the gate? That was fun....Cilla was so good there, I tried one of your 'half passes', I think it worked....more or less!" Sam rattled on and Erin listened patiently.

They had certainly done an excellent round and must have got high marks, but she wouldn't tell Sam, he needed to calm down as much as Cilla.

Gradually Sam quietened down beginning to think about the next part of the competition, the showing section.

Not all the ponies that entered would get through having had faults, especially at the water and gate.

292

Cilla had done well and they were on the short list for the second round.

He looked at the remaining ponies, they were all taller than his pony, but she looked fitter, not that it mattered, she would have to do a very good show to compete with these ponies.

He was going to stick to the show he did last year with Cilla but with a longer trotting section to show her beautiful floating action, and a better collected canter.

At the end of his individual show he would push Cilla into a gallop and race up the side of the ring before coming back to a collected canter, a walk and then a flamboyant salute to the judge.

When It was Sam's turn to enter the ring he was 'calm and collected'!

The individual show went well, the flying change came off beautifully and the gallop raised a cheer from the spectator's .As the results were read out over the loud speaker, he was amazed to learn he had won. Cilla was the smallest of the winning ponies.

The judge said to Sam as he gave him the big red rosette, "I enjoyed your show immensely young man; it was that mad gallop that clinched the class, well done".

"Thank you sir, she loves to gallop!"

The 12.2 jumping class was much latter, so Erin suggested he could wander round the show ground, so long as he was back at the lorry in plenty of time for his class.

Like all small boys he forgot to keep a check on the time, he was having so much fun in the fair ground. It wasn't until he heard the loud speaker announcing that the competitors in the 12.2 jumping could walk the course, that he realized he was in trouble!

He ran as fast as he could, it was a long way and everyone seemed to be in his way. It took an age before he got back.

Sally was waiting, anxiety showing on her face. "Where on earth have you been Sam? You're almost too late to walk the course,..come on, we'll have to run".

He jogged along beside her "I'm sorry" he gasped. "I'm really sorry".

293

"Stop talking....look at these jumps....you'll have to remember the course we haven't time to go into details".

"Clear the course please" the ring steward was shouting as the first pony was waiting to enter the ring.

"You'll just have to watch and learn the course as they go round....you really are naughty Sam!"

He knew he had been stupid. Now he didn't know the course, he hadn't got Cilla out of the lorry and he hadn't got the right clothes on...could anything possibly get worse.

Thankfully Erin and the students had Cilla tacked up and a small girl was riding her round to get her warmed up.

"Change quickly Sam" Erin was just as cross. "You might just make it in time; your number is at the end of the list. Hurry or you'll miss the class altogether".

He whipped off his blue shirt and fumbled into the white one, he knotted his tie somehow, he was all fingers and thumbs.

The students giggled "Ooo la la" one of them teased

"Shut up" Erin shouted. "Where's your jacket.. *and* your number, really Sam...You'll give me a heart attack".

Finally he was more or less ready, jacket undone, shirt hanging out and number upside down, but he leapt on his pony and dashed for the collecting ring. Sally, Erin and the students ran along behind him.

There were only four ponies still to go when he arrived in a dreadful state. He stood up in his stirrups to watch, he had to remember the order to jump, he had to learn quickly, particularly the last part of the course that he hadn't walked with Sally.

"Tuck your shirt in boy and do up your jacket" Erin ordered. "And now your number is upside down. Really Sam, you are a disgrace".

He felt like crying, Erin had a vicious tongue when she let fly, and today he was the target.

His turn came all too soon. He rode into the ring feeling anything but confident. Cilla was upset by all the rushing about and shouting.

She shied away from the big arrangement of flowers at the side of the ring.

"Steady girl" he said trying to calm her.

294

The jumps were a lot smaller than those they had cleared in his previous class and Sam's confidence came crawling back.

They were going well, clearing everything as far as jump six...where was seven??? He'd lost his way! He just couldn't find jump seven.

People were shouting and pointing vigorously. He circled round, there it was, they were off again, but he heard a groan from the ring side. He had circled in front of jump seven. That counted as a refusal. There would be no clear round for him today!

He finished the course and left the ring embarrassed and hurting. Cilla had jumped brilliantly, he had let her down, and he was ashamed. He had learnt a bitter lesson today, one he would never forget.

Sally had done well with both her horses in the open jumping, a second and a fourth, and the student had had a pole down in the working hunter class. It was a rather quiet journey home this time.

Sam was relieved to see his father waiting as they drove into the yard at Sally's Equestrian Centre. He had received a letter from the senior school secretary asking him to bring Sam for an interview in two days time and to bring his piano music with him.

Mr Nightingale had suggested to the head master, that young Winthrop might well be suitable for a music scholarship, so they were anxious to hear him play.

"But I haven't had time to practise Dad, my fingers are so stiff".

"Well we had better get you home, then you can practise all night and day. Get in the car 'genius'".

"Soak your hands in hot water Sam, you'll be fine, I'm sure". Sally suggested as he was about to do as his father had said.

"I'm sorry about today, it won't happen again I promise".

"Go home and practise that ol' piano boy" laughed Erin. "Get that scholarship an' I'll forgive you anything!"

Sam did as they said and worked and worked at the pieces he might be asked to perform for Mr Nightingale and the head

295

master; Vicky sat on the stairs listening intently, she was no musician, but she found the music most moving. *He had passed an exam at the end of term with distinction. 145 marks out of 150! Barry had said that was an amazing mark, perhaps he would be awarded a scholarship for Dauntsey,* his mother dreamed as she listened.

Tim and a nervous Sam set of for Lavington, a fairly long drive that he knew well from the many years ago, when he was educated there.

They stopped in Salisbury for lunch, but Sam couldn't eat much, then off again across Salisbury Plain to the little village.

Dautsey's public school was the biggest building amongst lovely thatched cottages; it couldn't be missed, with its long tree lined drive and sport fields.

Sam knew where he was, he always came to the senior school for his piano lessons, but had never entered by the rather Grand front door.

A prefect was waiting for them, and having ticked his name off on a list, he led Sam through a maze of corridors to the music wing.

Tim was left remembering when he had been a new boy, dressed in the brown shirt and shorts that was still the school uniform.

He was then very nervous as his father left him with his luggage and walked away out of Tim's life. He never saw his father again. *'Time to forget the past'* he thought, but being here sitting in the same entrance......!

"Would you like a cup of tea" a polite voice asked. "Your son will be about half an hour with the head master".

"Oh yes...thanks. I was miles away.....I stood in this same place thirty five years ago as a new boy!"

"You must have enjoyed it, bringing your son here?"

"I did after the initial shock".

"It's always difficult at first, but it's a good school".

Sam stood nervously in Mr Nightingale's music room where he normally had his lessons. Mr Nightingale was there with the headmaster and two other people.

"Come in Sam and sit down, we just want a chat.

"Good afternoon sir" Sam said very quietly.

"Well now....*I* know a lot about you Sam, but we need to know a little more about you, your hobbies, that sort of thing."

They asked him all sorts of questions, what were his interests, why did he want to play the piano and so on. He told them about his uncle Barry.

Mr Nightingale immediately interrupted to tell them that both Sam's father and uncle were old Dauntsiens and that Barry had excelled while here. "A very talented boy" he added with a touch of pride in his voice.

"What will you play for us Sam?" asked the head master.

Sam gave Mr Nightingale his music and sat at the grand piano and flexed his fingers, as Barry always did, and began to play.

He was nervous, and his hands shook, but as his uncle said, the fingers would take over and the music would flow.

Some Bach first, a minuet from a book of easy pieces he wrote for his wife Anna Magdalina, and then a little Mozart Sonata.

There was not a sound from his audience who were listening so intently to his performance; he was in a world of his own. He finished with the famous Largo by Handel; Mr Nightingale had found an arrangement of the piece which he could manage well enough.

Slowly he played the finale chords and sat motionless, his hands poised over the key board.

"Bravo" exclaimed the bursar, breaking the spell Sam had created.

"Thank you Sam" said Mr Nightingale. "That was very beautiful".

He could relax at last, he had done his best. He stood up to leave. "May I go sir?"

"Yes yes...but wait with your father, we will need to speak to him".

He closed the door quietly, the three men hardly noticed he had gone they were so busy discussing his audition.

297

"Well...how did it go lad?"

"I don't know Dad...I don't know". And he rushed out into the fresh air. Sam sat on the steps and cried, he had no idea why he was crying.

Tim and the prefect were about to go out to him when the phone sounded. The prefect rushed to answer it. "The head master would like to speak to you sir, will you follow me please".

Sam rubbed his eyes with his shirt sleeve and walked back to the car.

He thought he had played quite well, he couldn't quite remember, perhaps he shouldn't have started with the Bach, not an easy piece to play with stiff fingers, to many quick notes and it had to be played accurately, otherwise it just sounded a jumble of notes. *'Too late now!'* he thought, *'I could play it better now my fingers are working'*

He sat in the car and waited for his father. *'Gosh I'm hungry, I hope we can stop in Salisbury again,'* he remembered some lovely cream cakes in the cafe they had stopped at.

Mr Nightingale had come to meet Tim. "Hello Sir Timothy, it's so good to see you, I knew your brother well of course.....Please come and meet the head master, he has good news for you!"

Sam had been awarded a scholarship; Tim gave a big sigh of relief. They believed he had talent and would benefit from tuition at Dauntsey's, and it would save Tim a lot of money.

In a way it was funny, he had never shown the slightest interest in music until he heard Barry playing. What's more if he hadn't found Sam on the stairs and decided to let him sit up late the following evening to listen to him playing, he may never have discovered his talent!

They did stop in Salisbury, where Sam enjoyed a large cream cake, he felt over-whelmed with relief that he had won a scholarship, and the ordeal of the audition was over.

Tim had always assumed his son would follow him in farming. Where had his hidden talent come from?

He wondered which course Sam's life would take? Music, farming or horses, he would support and encourage him which ever path he took.

Sam went back to the Equestrian School and worked on Fantasy. His mother insisted he wore gloves whenever he was riding, it was important he looked after his hands if he was to be a musician

Sally approved and bought him two pairs of soft leather gloves, one for showing and one for everyday riding.

Fantasy was still proving to be almost too strong for Sam. They worked slowly in the indoor school with Erin, and day after day Sam felt both of them were improving and next summer they would be ready for the jumping classes.

Sally surprised Sam when she led him into her drawing room to show him *her* grand piano.

"I can't play anymore Sam....too much arthritis in me joints! You can practise on it every day if you like, while I'm busy with the students".

It was a full sized grand standing in the bay window. "Can I really Sally, gosh it's a big instrument!"

"And it can make a 'big' noise if you want it to" Sally laughed. "You just play it whenever you want...it needs to be used".

What with piano practise, schooling Fantasy *and* riding Cilla the summer holidays flew past; it was time to go home and prepare for the new term at the senior school.

He took home quite an array trophies that Cilla had won, and stood them proudly on Gran's sideboard.

He left for Dauntsey's realizing life would never be quite the same. He was going to have to work very hard to keep up with the other boys and wouldn't be home again until Christmas, by which time he would probably be too tall for Cilla.

It was with a heavy heart that he said good bye to her, they had enjoyed a wonderful summer showing together.

Sam knew there were more important things ahead for him.

TWENTYSEVEN

At the O'Rourke racing yard preparations for Pat's daughter's wedding on the fifth of October were frenetic. The wedding invitations had been sent and most replied to.

The service would be in the village church at Lambourn, with a formal reception in the afternoon, followed by a giant party for all the locals and stable staff in the evening. An Ox-Roast and licensed bar would keep everyone fed and happy!

An enormous marquee was being hired, along with tables and chairs for 120 guests, at Barry's farm on Ewe Bank Hill, where Tim's family would be staying for a few days.

Sue had been rushed off her feet, what with helping Pa with the race horses and getting herself and the bridesmaids organised. Serena and Charlotte's daughter Katie were both to be bridesmaids.

They had a lovely day shopping in Newbury, looking at dresses and trying on several. In the end the two excited little girls agreed on very pale blue dresses with masses of underskirts, silver silk slippers and head bands of mixed flowers, mostly blue cornflowers.

Sue was keeping her dress a secret until the great day, while the men were going the whole hog, wearing grey morning suits and top hats! Tim thought that was a bit extravagant, but agreed to go to Salisbury and hire one.

Vicky, not to be out done, went with her husband to buy a new outfit. Gran who didn't mind being 'out done', thought she had something in her wardrobe that would be suitable, and anyway she would wear her mink coat as it was sure to be chilly in October.

Sam was quite happy to miss all the dressing up, especially when his father had offered to hire him a mini morning suit. He gratefully declined and sent his apologies to his uncle

As the great day grew closer and all the arrangements were completed Tim relaxed. He suddenly thought the next time his family would be involved with a wedding could well be Sams......or Serena's!!

The very thought was laughable. Where would they all be by then? Would Sam be running the farm or off round the world playing the piano in concert halls? Tim favoured the farming option.

October burst upon them; the weather turned warm making everyone think it was an 'Indian summer'.

Tim was driving his family to Barry's farm on Friday morning; Alfie would follow with Cilla in the trailer.

Sue had asked Gran if she could borrow Cilla and the carriage, to transport the little bridesmaids, to and from the church. She felt the pony had played such an important part in her life with Barry, that she should be there on the day.

Gran loved the idea, but Alfie grumbled, he insisted on being there to lead Cilla and keep an eye on the carriage. He polished it with loving care muttering to himself all the time.

So on Friday morning Tim and Alfie put Cilla in the front of the trailer, and by removing the shafts the carriage fitted snugly in the back.

The family were dashing in and out of the house until they were finally ready to go, while Alfie waited, sitting in the Land Rover, for Maud to appear at the front door.

'Click clack, click clack'. Alfie walked over to the front steps as Maud appeared, wrapped in her lovely Mink coat, looking almost regal and smiling at them, all patiently waiting.

He helped her into the car, what would Lambourn make of his old mistress, she would turn a few heads tomorrow.

"You may help me into the automobile Alfred...so glad you are coming as well".

"Yes me'lady" he replied touching his hat. "It looks like being a fine day".

At last they were on their way. Tim drove slowly, partly because he wasn't too happy with Alfie's driving, and partly because his Gran kept a sharp eye on the speedometer. Anything

301

approaching 40mph and he would get a sharp reminder, not to speed!

It would be a long slow journey, they had hardly passed Dorchester before Serina was saying 'are we nearly there..I'm bored'.

Yes it was going to be a long slow journey.

Sue sat in her kitchen looking at all the presents people had sent, she would have to write personally to each and every one, she toyed with the idea of printing a standard 'Thank You' card, just adding an appropriate name on each one.

That didn't feel quite right, so hand written letters it would have to be; perhaps Barry could be persuaded to help out?,,,that seemed unlikely.

She had just made herself a cup of coffee when there was a knock on the front door,

"Half a mo'....just coming". But when she opened the door there was no one there.

A little gift wrapped parcel lay on the step with an envelope attached. She picked it up and ran to the gate. The lane was empty except for a black Range Rover disappearing round the corner. *'Who could have left this'* It was addressed to her, typed, not hand written and no stamp! She walked slowly back to the house, puzzled.

The parcel was beautifully wrapped, tied up with a blue ribbon and a red rose tucked under the bow.

She could put it off no longer and reached for the scissors.....the box contained a necklace, no ordinary necklace but one made of gold and attached to the chain little gold horses galloped as the sunlight caught them....were their eyes little diamonds? She couldn't tell.

Who could have sent her such a necklace, there was no makers name on the box, it had been carefully removed. She was so astonished she almost forgot the envelope that had fallen to the floor.

Quickly she tore it open, and pulled a letter out.

Dear Suzie

So you thought you could get married and not tell us, shame on you.
Fortunately my boys keep an eye on you and your Pa, otherwise we wouldn't
have heard the good news. We hope this young man is worthy of you. I picked
the present for you. She nearly chose a puppy. Wear it for us on your big day
please. We can't be there ourselves as you know but we will be thinking of you. I
sends her love.

A&L.B

PS One of my boys will deliver this, please don't try to talk to him.

Sue sat at the table and shed a few tears, poor old Briggs, still
in hiding, she wished he could have been invited to her wedding.
Lizzie would have enjoyed being a bridesmaid. *'What on earth
did he do to get into so much trouble?'* she thought, no one knew
where he had gone...he just vanished.

Pa came in expecting the coffee pot to be boiling ready for
elevens. There were now sixty horses in training that kept them
busy, so he was surprised to see Sue still sitting at the table
clutching a letter.

He took it from her hand. "Well damn me.....damn me" he
said again looking at the necklace sparkling in the sunshine.
"Phew, you'd better put that in the safe my love....that must have
cost him a pretty penny......poor old Briggs, I miss him you
know".

He put the necklace back in the box and closed the lid.
"You'll have to get that insured love, it's not made of plastic, and
they're *real* diamond....blimey!!"

Sue poured the coffee and cut two slices of cake, still in a
dream. "I'll wear it on Saturday Pa".

"And I'll ride 'shot gun' he laughed. "You'll need a body
guard every time you wear that!.....Hey, you've eaten my slice of
cake".

"Sorry Pa".

The bridesmaids arrived bright and early at Sue's house, to
have their hair done by the professional hairdresser, before the
Bride's hair was washed and set, so that the veil would hang
nicely over her face.

303

Alfie was giving the 'Queen Victoria's' carriage a final polish while bunches of flowerers were being attached by Vicky who had raided Charlotte's garden before breakfast!

The carriage looked splendid in the early morning sunshine; it was going to be a lovely day.

Sue had persuaded Alfie to travel in a car for the service; it was a good mile and a half to the church, too far for him to walk with Cilla.

She was going in a horse drawn carriage that would be followed by the two giggling bridesmaids in the little carriage drawn by Cilla and led by Pete.

He was now a qualified apprentice jockey with several wins to his credit. He had helped her so much with Cilla when they were breaking her in, that it was only right, he should have the honour of taking care of her at the wedding. Serena had insisted that she should drive, but no one listened to her.

Eventually everyone was ready. Charlotte helped the eager bridesmaids into the carriage and gave them their posies.

"Sit still and *don't* fall out. Stay in the carriage until I come to help you out".

"Yes yes we know" replied Serena. "I'll drive...give me the reins boy, whatever your name is".

"He's my friend Pete! And if you're driving I'm getting out". Katie said angrily.

Pete took no notice and took hold of the lead rein. "Walk on girl, let's go Cilla".

He shouldn't have said that. The little pony knew what 'let's go' meant. She shot forwards taking everyone by surprise! Fortunately Pete had a firm hold on the lead rein and no harm was done, apart from nearly dislodging the two little girls, who now stopped arguing and were trying to look dignified as Pete walked behind the big carriage carrying the bride and her father to the church in Lambourn.

Cilla walked alongside her old friend Pete, he'd grown a bit since he'd ridden her around the little paddock.

He had come back from the Jockeys racing school with his apprentice licence, He had done very well and the instructors had predicted a great future for him, providing he didn't grow too big!

Pete had ridden several winners for Mr O'Rouke and other trainers, so his bank account was growing nicely.

He was wearing his new suite, a very dark green tweed made to measure and a dark yellow waistcoat, and soft leather boots.

Jim still chided him about buying his cloths from 'Mother care', but he was used to his teasing and took no notice.

Pat O'Rouke had suggested he bought a suit after his first winner. *'got to look smart boy when you mix with the owners, nothing too flashy...just smart'* Well he knew he looked smart today, even Jim was struck dumb when he paraded round the yard!

He walked beside Cilla thinking back over the time he had been working for Sue and her Dad. A lot had happened since he had arrived in Lambourn and had ridden his first winner, as he had promised his mother he would, in fact he had had several winners since then.

He walked on enjoying the warm sunshine while the little girls were chatting away like a pair of magpies, they were beginning to enjoy themselves, waving to the villagers who had come to watch the procession go past.

Sue was popular with the local people, she's been born here, baptised in the church and educated at the village school, and now she was getting married at the same church. A big wedding, lots of friends and relatives had been invited.

There was a large crowd waiting outside the church, jostling one another trying to get photos of the bride arriving and the little bridesmaids, so pretty sitting in their own little carriage.

Cilla wasn't too happy with the crowds and the flashes of the cameras popping off all around her.

"Steady little one" Pete said stroking her neck "steady now". His quiet calm voice settled her down, she listened to him, twitching her ears back and forth, trusting him.

The two little girls took up their positions behind Sue and her father, then, as they moved into the church the organist blasted out the Wagner Wedding March. The ceremony was beginning!

305

Pete sat on the church wall resting his feet, The mile and a half walk, leading Cilla, wasn't such a good idea, and he was going to have to walk all the way back!

A little girl walked up to Cilla and was talking to her, she seemed to know the pony, patting her neck.

Well, he thought, a lot of people knew her and took no notice, more interested in the smell of frying coming from the chippie just across the square.

He would have loved to pop in there and get some chips, but he was sure Sue wouldn't have been happy to see him munching chips sitting on the church wall. No, he must wait for the reception, but his mouth was watering, he could almost taste the hot greasy chips.

"Ows me lovely 'orse then?" the child was looking at Pete, but people were spilling out of the church and he had to prepare for the return journey, so took no notice, and any way the little girl was whisked away by a giant of a man and they disappeared in the crowd.

Sue and Barry appeared on the church steps and the photographer got busy arranging the brides dress and positioning all the relatives in order of seniority.

The little girl was shouting for Sue. She searched the crowd for a familiar face and then she gasped. A little girl waving furiously, red faced and a halo of golden hair...was it.....could it be Lizzie? Sue felt the little gold necklace, could she see it she wondered?

"Face the camera please" called the photographer.

Sue put on her best smile, the camera clicked, but when Sue looked again the child was gone. A black Range Rover, pulling away, along the road to Upper Lambourn and the M4.

She was sure it had been Lizzie. The hair was different, but the smile was the same. She was glad Lizzie was there, even though she wasn't a bridesmaid.

Barry and Sue jostled their way through the happy crowd and climbed into the horse drawn carriage covered in confetti.

Pete led Cilla up and collected the two little bridesmaids, He thought about the long walk back to the yard on his sore feet.

306

"Shove over girls, there's room for me if you squeeze up a bit"

Serena objected. "You're supposed to walk" she said haughtily, "and you'll crease my dress"

"Would you rather sit on my knee then?" Pete asked her seriously" Katie was having hysterics, tears running down her cheeks, laughing at Serena's disgusted face!

"I'll sit on your knee Pete, any time!"

Serena moved over reluctantly and Pete squirmed in beside the two girls. "Walk on Cilla" he called and flicked the reins.

"You shouldn't *do* that" Serena said "She doesn't like that".

"Well I'm so sorry Lady Serena...Cilla knows what I mean, we are old friends... Cilla and me".

Serena pulled a face and poked out her tongue, but she didn't say another word for the rest of the trip home.

Charlotte was waiting for the girls when they drove into the yard, she was taking them on to the reception in the car.

"Do you want a lift Pete?" she asked.

"No he does not" said a bad tempered Serena.

"You speak when you're spoken to young lady" retorted Charlotte, she had had enough of Serena's bad behaviour for one day.

"No. It's OK,...thanks for the offer, but I have to help Steve with the horses or we won't get to the party tonight".

"Well don't you go mucking out in that lovely suit, you look so smart. And that waist coat..WOW!"

Pete laughed. "Yeah, it took all my savings, but I think it was worth it".

"You look fabulous Pete; we'll see you later then"

She set off for the reception at Barry's home, two little bride maids on the back seat, one smiling having a lovely day, the other looking sour and humiliated.

'Oh well' sighed Charlotte, she wasn't going to let one spoilt brat upset the proceedings, it was Sue's special day, a day she would always remember, damn that miserable little girl.

The reception went well; nearly a hundred guests sat round tables in the giant marquee and enjoyed a sumptuous meal.

The Ox turned relentlessly over the huge fire, it had been cooking since before daylight, a series of chefs keeping it well basted ready for the party later.

Serena soon forgot that she had been so cross and was dashing around with Katie having a lovely time.

The 'Live Band' arrived in a brightly coloured mini bus and set to work setting up their equipment.

Gran took one look at the long haired scruffy musicians and decided to retire! "In my young days the musicians all wore dinner jackets and bow ties" she complained to the ever faithful Vicky.

"Yes I know".

"What's more they played *real* music, not this loud raucous stuff". Gran went on muttering as Vicky helped her into the house. Whatever would the old lady think when they started to play!!

Fortunately Barry had prepared a room for her at the back of the house so she wouldn't be disturbed. It was a quiet retreat for the old lady, with a bell-pull beside the fireplace, which rang a bell in the kitchen if she needed anything.

Vicky lit the fire and waited until it was crackling away merrily; she helped Gran onto the sofa near the fire and lifted her withered legs up onto a stool, covering them with a rug making sure she was comfortable.

The cook looked in a little later, but Gran was fast asleep. She turned on two table lamps so it wouldn't be dark when she woke, then she went back to her kitchen to make a light supper for her guest.

There were quite a few bleary eyed lads working in Pa's yard the following morning! Steve picked the least 'hung-over' to ride out leading the string himself.

Pa was a bit groggy, but not so bad that he couldn't keep a watchful eye on those lads left behind.

It had been a wonderful party, the best there had been in Lambourn for many a year.

Sue and Barry had slipped away, no one notice them leaving and only cook knew when they would be coming back.

Tim rounded up his family on Sunday morning and got them organised. Alfie collected the little carriage from Pa's yard and waited patiently for Tim to help him load Cilla and the carriage onto the horse box.

Finally they were all ready to leave, Gran sitting regally in the front seat. They were going a little out of their way to drop a tuck box off at Sam's school which his mother had filled with as many goodies as she could find, including a large slice of weding cake. Sue didn't want Sam to feel left out. She had written him a letter saying how well Cilla looked and how beautifully she had behaved.

Lady Winthrop soon got back to driving Cilla. She drove to the village, accompanied by the little dog, at least twice a week. The villagers were used to seeing them waiting outside the shop for the shop keepers wife to bring her a glass of sherry and a lump of sugar for Cilla, and now a biscuit for her passenger!

Alfie complained about the crumbs he left on the cushioned seat, but Gran turned a deaf ear. She enjoyed the little dogs company; he was a good listener and never answered back. A few crumbs were a small price to pay for his trips to the village with her!

As the days got shorter and colder Vicky insisted on wrapping Maud up in rugs and a warm coat when she went driving, but even so she managed to get a chill, which quickly turned to a flue like infection and kept Gran in bed for some time.

The old family doctor called in every day and fussed over his patient. He had been her doctor for many many years; Tim thought that he was probably as old as his Gran!

Gradually the old lady began to recover and dismissed the doctor with a curt 'thank you' deciding she would look after herself. Even so he left a long prescription list of medicines which Tim collected and made sure she followed the instructions.

She did get better slowly and impatiently, so by Christmas she was back to her usual busy self. However the infection had left her with a weak heart which she scoffed at. "Fiddle sticks, the old ticker is as good as ever" she insisted irritably.

Sam came home for the Christmas holidays and was shocked to see the difference in his Gran. Her tongue and brain were just as sharp as ever, but she seemed to have shrunk.

"Play me some music" she said one afternoon. "I haven't heard you play since you went away to that big school".

Sam hesitated. "Do you mean on your piano?"

"Well of course boy, where else can you play?"

Gran certainly couldn't get up stairs to the piano in the old nursery. He was going to be allowed to play on the gleaming monster in her lounge!

He stroked the keys and sat down at the instrument only Barry played. There was nothing to compare with Grans piano at school; he was thrilled to be allowed this chance to play it.

"What shall I play Gran, Chopin's a bit beyond me yet".

"Play some early Bach, or Handel...maybe your exam music, your Dad says you're romping through the Associated Board exams!"

"I did grade six this term, got a distinction!"

"Well then Sam...play your exam music".

He sat looking at the keyboard for a moment and then started playing, piece after piece, playing everything from memory as if in a trance.

Gran was quiet for a few minutes when Sam eventually stopped playing after an hour or so.

"Play Handel's Largo again for me Sam, I love that piece".

When the last chord died away and was lost in the silence of the room, Sam turned to look at his Gran. She was weeping silently.

"Thank you Sam, thank you so much, that was so beautiful".

"I'll get you some tea Gran, and a toasted crumpet if you like?"

"Yes go Sam, go now before I make a fool of myself!" she said searching for her handkerchief. "I did enjoy that...perhaps you could play for me again, next time you come home?"

But he never did play for her again. Tragedy was not far away, waiting to change all their lives.

It came on a day early in spring.

Maud decided to drive to the village shop to collect her Famous Grouse and a bottle of Glenfiddich for Alfie who was suffering from his rheumatism and was in quite a lot of pain. She would hide his 'tonic' under the cushion in the carriage where she knew he would find it when he put the carriage away.

Tim suggested that since it was her first outing since her illness he should go with her. To no avail, she was adamant; she would drive herself with Little Dog as company.

She was on her way back looking forward to a cup of tea when she noticed the Primroses were coming into bloom, where the hedges gave them cover from inclement weather.

"Look Little Dog, Spring is coming". The hedges were just showing green shoots and the birds were flying everywhere busy building nests.

The sun was warm on her back and her companion was fast asleep beside her, She suddenly felt very tired, perhaps Tim was right, she shouldn't have come out today for a drive.

Cilla trotted on, the reins suddenly slack and the little axle bells ringing merrily as they slowly turned into the drive.

Alfie was cutting the grass in front of the house and listening for the carriage coming back, he was a little worried; the old lady had been gone some time.

Vicky came to the front door when he knocked. "Excuse me Mam, but her ladyship has been gone rather a long time", he twisted his cap in his hand nervously. "Should I get on me bike and look for 'er?"

Vicky hadn't realised how long Maud had been gone, she began to worry. She walked down the step peering down the drive.

"May be you should Alf" she started to say. "No...wait a moment, I can hear those little bells...yes here they come!" She said with relief as she turned to go back indoors

"Summit's wrong ma'am" Alf said hurrying to meet Cilla. "Something's wrong...get Tim back here,,,,'urry"

"Where is he working?" Vicky felt useless.

"Ring the big bell, he'll come then". The big bell hung in the stable yard clock tower, it was only used in an emergency, if Tim heard it he would drop everything and race back to the house.

Fortunately he wasn't far away and dashed back to the house. The old lady lay slumped across the seat, the reins still in her hands a smile on her face.

"She's gone me Lord" Alf said "She's gone".

He tried to lift her but Little Dog snarled and snapped viscously.

"Get that damn dog out!" Tim shouted.

"He's only protecting her" Alf muttered, but he threw his jacket over the dog and scooped him up, He wriggled and squirmed in Alf's arms, and finallyAlfie let him go. He rushed into the house, tail between his legs and hid in Grans living room.

Tim carried his Grandmother into the house and Vicky phoned for the doctor, although they all knew she was dead.

Alf led Cilla away and into the yard. "You brought her home safely didn't you" he said to the pony. He took her harness off and hung it in the tack room, would she ever wear it again he wondered. He would come back later on to polish it and clean the carriage.

He felt under the cushions and found his 'tonic', maybe he'd have a sip of it now before he went home. Fortunately he had only one sip before he fed Cilla and brushed her down.

"You're a good pony; you brought her back to me...good girl, good girl".

Tim found him later still brushing the pony. "Come up to the house Alf, the police want to see you. Just routine, nothing to worry about".

Alf put the brushes back in his grooming box. "What will become of Cilla sir?"

"Oh....I don't know Alf".

"She brought Lady Winthrop home safely....that was good of her wasn't it sir?"

"Yes yes...you take care of her as usual....until things settle down. I fear we will have to make some changes Alf".

312

The funeral took place a week later.

Gran had always said to Tim. "Don't bury me in that church yard, surrounded by strangers; just throw my ashes on the rose bed, where they can do some good". So they did just that.

People came from far and wide, from the highlands of Scotland and the depths of Wales. Tim didn't realise how many relatives he had until they all arrived. The village church was full to overflowing.

All Tim's farm workers and most of the villagers stood silently outside, all wanting to say goodbye to her Ladyship who had lived amongst them for so many years.

The family stood silently in the first pew; even Serena and Sam stopped arguing for the day and stood silent and respectful as the coffin was brought in.

Sam tried very hard not to cry, while Serena wept continually and had to borrow Sam's clean hankie. It was a dreadful day for everyone.

Barry and Sue had to return to Lambourn immediately, so they took Sam back with them and returned him to school. Most of the guests also melted away after the service, but close relatives came back to the house for refreshments and the reading of Maud's will.

There were no surprises, only two bequests added quite recently. Alf was to have the Gardeners Cottage for the rest of his days and a small income from the estate, a small reward for over sixty years of loyal service, and Sam was to have the piano, in the hope he would make good use of it.

A few weeks later Tim had a meeting with his farm manager, they were going to have to make some drastic changes. Death duties on the estate were huge, there was no way they could be paid without selling off some of the land.

Tim had tried to find an alternative way to raise the money but had failed.

The outlying farms were to be sold reducing the estate by about half. The tenants were all going to be offered a chance to

313

buy their farms at a very modest price. A date was set when they must say yes, or no, to Tim's offer.

Two farmers were able to accept Tim's generous offer, but the other farms would be put up for auction.

Tim and his accountant worked for hours over the estates finances. It was decided that if the farms sold well, he would be solvent, owing nothing to anyone.

Although the estate would be very much smaller it would still be possible to run it at a profit.

Several of his farm workers would have to find employment elsewhere, but Tim wouldn't turn them out of their tied cottages until they found another job.

It took the best part of a year before things had settled down to a new routine, and Tim could plan ahead with some confidence

He decided to buy a small flock of pedigree sheep. He still had a large flock of commercial sheep, but hankered after something better than the Rag Tail and Bobtail flock he saw every day.

Builth Wells, that's where he would go, and see what he could afford at one of the biggest sheep sales in the country.

He thought about some Dorset Horn sheep, they could be persuaded to lamb twice a year, that would be nice, but he also fancied a French breed, Cherolais, funny looking sheep with very short curly wool and pink faces!

The sale in Wales was held in October and Tim asked the auctioneers for a catalogue to be sent, and in due course it was delivered.

He took the catalogue to his office and studied it carefully. There were a few Cherolais entered, Tim would have liked a chance to look at them before the sale, but they belonged to a farmer in Kent, there was no way he would drive all that way just to look at ten ewes and a ram!

Vicky thought he was mad anyway, they had well over a hundred ewes grazing out in the fields, why on earth did he want more.

314

He gave up trying to explain his reason for wanting something special and soon she gave up asking!

September came and went. Tim was busy preparing for the special flock he was hoping to buy; he'd made up his mind which fields he would keep for them, well away from the commercial flock and close to the farm buildings so that if the weather turned bad he could drive them into the barn,

Robert, the farm manager, was a good, patient man, but even he thought Tim was going slightly mad. If the commercial sheep could live out all the year round, why couldn't these fancy French sheep do the same!

Tim was adamant. The Cherolais flock would live close to the farm.

So he went to the sale, cheque book in hand to buy his special sheep.

He was surprised at the size of the sale, there must have been a thousand or more sheep for sale, all sizes and colours. After a lot of searching he found the sheep he was looking for. Two pens with five ewes in each and a large impressive ram which was getting a lot of attention from would be buyers.

Tim stood to one side listening to the comments people were making about these Cherolais.

The general opinion was that they would be expensive, especially the ram that had won at many shows that summer. However everyone seemed to think they were a lovely lot of sheep, perhaps too expensive for the average farmer.

That made Tim even more determined to have these sheep. He went into the pen to have a closer look.

"You interested in them?"

Tim turned round to see a man looking at him with a plastic cup of coffee in his hand.

"Well yes....I like the look of the ewes....yours?" he said casually trying not to sound too keen. He could see that they were all good sturdy animals. Perhaps a bit ugly with their pink faces. The cheque book was burning a hole in his pocket.

315

"They're all young sheep, hardier than they look...they've been running out all year on top of the white cliffs near Dover...Barry's my name" the owner held out his hand.

"Tim". Tim replied as he shook Barry's hand. He was glad to hear that, if they could survive there they would certainly be fine on his farm. "What about the ram?"

"Ah..now that's a different matter. He's pretty exceptional. He won at all the county shows in our neck of the woods...only a two year old...he's some ram Tim".

Tim looked longingly at the ram but felt sure it would be too costly, best try and buy the ewes.

The ewes cost him well over two thousand pounds. What would Vicky say when he got home, he dared not think! Barry offered to deliver them since he had an empty lorry, and it was almost on his way home. So Tim gave him directions from Dorchester to his farm.

He discovered that Barry Skinner was a well known judge of sheep, travelling all over the country, he had in fact, just returned from South Africa where he had been judging!

Tim went on ahead to make sure everything in the barn was ready to receive his little flock. He hoped they would arrive before it got dark.

Alf was talking to Vicky at the front door as he got out of the car.

"Did you buy any?" She shouted

"Yes... they're beauty's...Alf, would you mind hanging around for a bit, we might need some help getting them in the barn? Come in for a cup of tea".

"Thank you sir but I've got a bit of fire wood to chop up for Vi..I mean Her Ladyship".

Vicky was just about to make a cup of tea when Barry arrived and reversed his lorry into the stable yard. Tim asked him in to join them before they unloaded his new flock of pink faced ewes.

The sheep were no trouble and trotted obligingly into their barn and immediately started eating hay, none the worse for their long journey.

316

Cilla was watching over her stable door and whinnied as Barry closed the tail gate of his lorry. She was impatient; it was well past her feed time.

Barry looked and smiled. "What have you got here Tim?" He said walking over to scratch her neck looking critically at her. A lovely head and neck...good shoulders .....nice round quarters. He liked what he saw.

"Oh yes....she's a beauty. She was my Grandmother's, who died recently...we don't know what to do with her really. My son rode her a lot, winning masses of prizes, but he's grown too big for her and anyway, he's got a bigger pony now that keeps him busy!"

Barry was silent for a few minutes. "Would you sell her?...My daughter is back home now, she's been in Holland as a working pupil on a stud farm, she would love this pony of yours".

Tim was taken aback for a moment or two. "Oh...I don't know really.....I wasn't expecting that Barry...she goes in harness as well by the way....I've got the carriage in the coach house. Come and have a look". He led the way across the yard.

In the lorry the ram was complaining making quite a noise. "I hear you didn't get rid of the ram!"

"No, it was too expensive and I wasn't going to give it away..sorry about the racket!"

When Tim opened the doors to the coach house and switched on the lights, Barry immediately spotted the old Rolls polished and gleaming like new. "That must be worth a fortune!"

Tim smiled. "Yep...I guess it is. Still goes well, my gardener runs the engine once a week and polishes it for hours! That reminds me. I must let Alf know before he goes home...he looked after Cilla for my Gran. Alf" He called, and beckoned him to come over.

"Whatever are you going to do with it Tim?"

"It's being entered in a special sale for classic cars the auctioneer thinks it will probably go to America for a lot of money".

"What a car....what a beauty". Barry couldn't tear his eyes away from the Rolls Royce as he was steered away.

"Here's the carriage Barry, and her harness....and here's Alf who has does such a good job with Cilla and this carriage!"

317

"Hallo Alf, the carriage looks a treat........well Tim....what's your price for the whole lot...pony, carriage and harness?"

Tim knew Barry was anxious to be on his way, so didn't want to drag the situation out. "I hadn't thought of selling her just yet Barry.....but I tell you what...I'd swop her and the carriage for the ram you didn't sell!"

Now it was Barry's turn to stop and think. His ram was an outstanding animal. But he had two more at home. He walked back to Cilla. He really liked her and he knew his wife would love driving her.

"OK Tim....it's a deal".

Alf looked taken aback. "So she's going sir?"

"Yes I'm sorry Alf, but it's best for Cilla really, she is going to a young lady in Kent".

"Well I s'pose it's for the best then". Alf limped back to his cottage. "They're all gone" He muttered, *'All gone...Lady Winthrop and now Cilla....all gone and left me alone'* He thought.

"But I've got you Little Dog, haven't I'. Little Dog wagged his tail as he trotted beside Alf, he too would miss her Ladyship and his rides to the village shop.

So a little later, after the men had sorted out the paper work, the two of them pushed the carriage into the back of the lorry where Barry secured it, then Cilla walked quietly up and Tim shut the ramp.

They shook hands and Barry wished Tim the best of luck with his little flock and set off for Kent, and Cilla's new home.

TWENTYEIGHT

Barry knew his way back from Dorchester to Dover. It was a bad road, too many small towns to negotiate and if he kept to the coast road there were all the seaside towns to get through, but he drove on regardless. It would be midnight before he got home.

It would be too late to mess about finding a stable for the little pony, so he would untie her and leave her in the lorry for the night with an arm full of hay and a bucket of water.

He remembered a neighbour who'd done much the same thing, but leaving a bull in his lorry. It was a vicious animal and had an appointment with the slaughter house the next day. It had taken so long to catch the beast and get it in the lorry, no one wanted to take it out just for the night.

During the night the lorry was stolen, bull and all! The thieves must have got a shock when they discovered they had a ton of furious bull in the back. It was a good story and always caused a laugh.

However, he would remember to take the keys in with him and lock the gate into the yard when he got home!

He stopped for some fish and chips in Southampton and drove on, it was a long way, a very long way back to Dover.

The next morning his daughter was up early, she opened her bedroom curtains and saw the lorry parked in the yard. Angie and her mother had waited up for Barry but had given up and gone to bed. They both thought it was crazy to drive all the way to Wales just to sell eleven sheep, but father was convinced they'd get a good price, so they had helped to load them into the lorry, the ram went up first and was partitioned off, then the ten ewes followed him up without any trouble.

Angie was anxious to see if her Dad had sold the sheep, she could hear something stomping about in the lorry and hoped it wasn't the sheep! Then she heard a whinny. That was no Sheep!!

She was dressed in seconds, down stairs...on with her boots and out into the yard without noticing her mother at the Aga getting breakfast ready.

319

A *horse* was in the lorry, Dad had left it there all night. She let the ramp down and came face to face with a beautiful black *pony*, and a little carriage behind it!

"Bloody hell!"She exclaimed... "Where did *you* come from....Wales of course?... Yes you're a Welsh pony aren't you! Come on..I'll find you a nice stable and some grub". She led the pony across the yard and into an empty stable.

Then she stopped and had a good look. *'Definitely Welsh'* she thought. *'Section A...black as a crow and those white socks'* "Oh she's lovely" She said to herself.

The pony was sniffing at the food bin and licking at a few crumbs she found there.

"OK...I'll get you some grub, I can take a hint!" She left her and walked away to the feed shed.

By now the heavy horses had heard her voice, they started calling and stamping their big feet. "All right..all right...I'm coming , just wait your turn".

'But Dad went to a sheep sale' she thought. *'So where on earth did this pony come from'* "He's got some explaining to do" she said to all the animals in the barn.

She found pony cubes and a hand full of oats for the pony and went on to feed the big horses. Two Suffolk Punch mares heavy in foal and a stallion called Parham Rupert, also a Suffolk Punch.

The stallion was a bit special as there were very few Suffolk stallions registered; they were on the verge of being declared a rare breed.

Rupert was a kind horse in spite his size, he was truly a gentle giant. He waited patiently for his bucket of food, sniffing the cold air blowing in from the sea.

Barry's daughter fed the horses and was on to the calves, ten of them that her father had bought at the market, why no one knew! They all had to be fed separately with a bucket of warm milk.

She could smell bacon frying; her father must be up at last, *now* she would find out about the black pony.

When the last calf finished its milk she hurried back to the house. Her Dad looked up from his plate of bacon, eggs and fried potatoes, he liked a big breakfast, said it kept him going all day.

"You found the pony then?" he said smiling at Angie "If you give me a hand in a minute we'll get the carriage off".

She sat down at the table and her own plate of bacon and eggs arrived sizzling hot.

"Eat that first" her mother ordered.

"I put her in the loose box and gave her some grub", Angie mumbled through a mouth full of breakfast. "She was starving...how long has she been in the lorry?"

Barry sat back in his chair and pushed the empty plate away. "Well... thank you all for asking if I sold the sheep...which I did and they made good money".

"So what about the ram, you didn't bring him home!?" Mother asked.

"No I didn't bring him home, and I didn't sell him".

"You shot the bugger!!" said Angie.

"Don't swear dear". Mother scolded.

Noo..I didn't shoot him either. I swopped him for the pony and trap, *and* the harness etcetera. The pony's a registered Section A Welsh mountain pony. She's won heaps in the show ring and jumping. I thought you'd like her, and mother can drive her. Cilla's her name by the way; I've got her papers in the lorry.

He got up and stretched. "My word that was a long drive last night". He muttered. "I'll go and get the papers, and then you can help me with the trap Angie". He pulled on his boots and a coat before stomping out unto the yard.

Angie finished her breakfast and was about to follow him when the phone rang. "I'll get it" said her mother and went into the hallway to answer it.

"Can I speak to Barry Skinner?" said an educated voice.

"I'm afraid my husband has just gone out, can I help?"

"Well yes, my name is Tim Winthrop, I sold him a pony yesterday, but I forgot to mention she may be in foal, she's been running with a neighbours stallion all the summer. I forgot all about it what with all the paper work for the sheep....I hope it doesn't matter. The stallion is called Coed Coch something. I'll find out its proper name and let you know".

"Don't worry Mr Winthrop, It'll be alright I'm sure. Thanks for phoning..good bye".

321

"What was that all about?" Angie asked as she was heading for the door.

"Well it appears you're Dad got a bonus with that pony, she's probably in foal to a Coed Coch stallion".

"Yipee! Good old Dad". She rushed out of the house to have a better look at the pony. A registered Section A mare and almost certainly in foal. What a start for her own stud of Welsh Ponies!

Cilla was walking round and round her big stable, the door was far too high for her to see over. Chickens kept flying over the door and pecking at the straw. There were chickens, ducks and geese everywhere.

Angie came back with a sheep hurdle which she tied across the doorway and fixed the big door back. "That's better...now I can see you and *you* can see me!"

She looked carefully at the little black pony. Sometimes, if her father had been well entertained and had drunk too much wine, he could be persuaded to buy anything, but this time he had bought a cracker, an absolute cracker!

"Do you like her then?" Barry put an arm round her shoulders. "She caught my eye straight away, I just had to have her".

Angie smiled. "She's lovely Dad...did you know she's probably in foal?"

"Haa....I thought so..see how her belly has dropped, that's not just fat, that's a foal, or my name's not Skinner!"

"Can I put her in the small orchard Dad....she doesn't like all these chickens flying around in here".

"Sure . I expect she's easy to catch".

They led Cilla to the orchard beside the house and let her go. She tossed her head and snorted, she'd been shut in for a long time and needed to stretch her legs. She stuck her tail straight up in the air and trotted off alongside the fence.

Angie stood and watched. "Blimey Dad, look at that movement, No wonder she's won a lot in Dorset".

"Let's hope she goes on winning for *you* my love". He said as he turned away. "Come on now, help me get the trap out of the lorry. We'll have to put it in the barn for now".

The Suffolk mares in the adjoining field came trundling over to watch this new little black pony dancing about, but they were soon bored and ambled off.

322

Angie turned and watched Cilla dancing between the apple trees, what a picture she made, what a lovely pony.

"Thanks Dad", she said quietly. "Thanks a lot, she's beautifull.

Cilla soon had company in the orchard. Patches, Angie's old pony was turned out with her and after the initial squeals and kicks, they were soon the best of Pals! Neither had had much company in years. Patches was always turned out with the young Suffolks and he didn't enjoy their rough games! So Cilla seemed to be a perfect companion.

When the days got shorter and the cold winds stronger they came into the big barn at night. They had their own little pens away from the Suffolks who had very big pens with very high gates!

Once Angie closed the sliding doors at night and the chickens had settled on their perches, it soon became very quiet and quite warm. They had plenty of hay in a big rack and self filling water bowls. Cilla seemed happy and content at her new home.

Soon after Cilla had arrived at Geddinge Farm there was a horrific storm. Barry and his family had settled down after supper watching television, when the weather forecast came on.

Michel Fish, the weatherman that evening, announced that the rumour of very strong hurricane winds was not true, it would be windy, but not to worry.

The family were awakened to screaming winds rattling the tiles and rain battering the windows. It *was* a hurricane! The big barn's doors were blown in and hay and straw blown all over the place.

By daybreak when the multi coloured cockerel announced the start of another day, the storm had passed leaving a lot of damage. Trees uprooted falling across roads and fencing. Many people in the south of England had damaged properties, and some had lost their lives.

The road to Geddinge Farm was blocked in two places and chain saws were busy everywhere, there would be no shortage of logs for the fire this winter!

Christmas soon came and went and on New Year's Eve there was a party at the farm, Angie's two brothers came with their young families. Cilla was much admired and had to carry the smaller children round the farm. She was very well behaved, walking slowly and carefully with her tiny passengers.

The foal she was carrying was getting big, Angie thought she would foal about Easter time, the same time her Suffolks were due. It would mean a few sleepless nights, watching and waiting in case something went wrong at the last minute.

The Suffolk mares foaled a few days apart, both were big, chunky foals, and had the benefit of the early spring grass, they seemed to grow a bit more every day.

Cilla just plodded around the orchard watching the new born foals playing in the adjoining field. Her foal refused to be born.

Angie was getting worried and impatience in turn!

"It'll come when it's ready", laughed her Dad. "First foals are usually slow".

"I bet it's a big lazy colt", she said. "You'll see....a big bloody colt!"

When eventually she thought Cilla was about to foal she brought her into one of the big stables and waited and waited looking over the stable door every few minutes. Cilla just looked back at her or went on eating the hay.

Midnight came and in frustration Angie went indoors to make a cup of tea and have a bite to eat. She was back ten minutes later to find a big fat lazy colt foal, bright chestnut with a white blaze!

She watched the foal stagger to its feet; it was a strong foal and soon found the teat and the drink of mother's milk he needed.

Cilla was a bit touchy to start with and the foal was greedy, he wasn't easily put off by a few squeals and gentle kicks!

Angie watched until he was feeding well and Cilla had accepted him, then she felt able to leave and go wearily to bed.

The foal grew rapidly in the warm sunshine and the grass in the orchard made Cillas milk rich. Angie forgot she wanted a filly; this little chap was really lovely, and soon learnt to

324

recognise Angie, always trotting up to her for a scratch behind his ears!

The thought of showing Cilla and her foal didn't occur to her until a friend suggested it. The foal was so pretty and moved like a dream he would surely catch the judge's eye. But Cilla, although she was used to the show ring, had never been shown as a brood mare.

Angie had always concentrated on the heavy horse classes at the shows. Rupert was always in the ribbons looking magnificent when he was dressed for the ring. His mane was platted with raffia and ribbons as was his tail.

If he was entered in the working heavy horse class he wore all the gear and a string of brasses which meant hours of polishing the day before, but when he wore them all he looked tremendous.

Cilla and her foal had new bridles for their first show as a brood mare with foal at foot. Ann, Angie's mum, was going to show the foal, so she made sure he led properly and trotted when asked.

"Have you thought of a name for the foal Angie?" her mother asked one morning as they were about to practise with him in the paddock. "I thought Epic".

"Oh yea...I like that mum, taken from his father's name...Yep, I like it!"

Ann practised every day with Epic until she was satisfied he understood what he was supposed to do. Then they waited for The Kent County Show.

Everyone was sure Cilla would do well considering her past record; she was a lovely Section A mare and had proved she could hold her own in any company.

Epic was another matter. If he behaved in the ring he stood a fair chance of being placed, but it was his first outing and with all the other ponies and people around him anything could happen.

The day of the show started early for Ann and her daughter. Rupert, the big stallion was entered in the heavy horse class so Angie took charge, her mother never could get his mane plated

325

with the raffia tight enough to stay in place, although she didn't mind threading the green and yellow ribbons into the plat at the last moment.

Cilla on the other hand didn't have to be platted, being a Welsh Mountain Pony, so that was a relief.

By nine o'clock they were all ready to go. Epic was very excited and skipped up into the lorry at his mother's heels. The big stallion behind his partition looked down at the foal and snorted. Cilla laid her ears back, ready to protect her baby, but Rupert lost interest in the little one and turned his attention to his hay net.

Ann had been up half the night making pies and cakes to take with them. "There's only three of us mum!" Angie said. "You've made enough for an army!"

"Well you're sure to get hungry, you always do, and Dad never stops eating", Mother replied putting a box full of sandwiches in the cab of the lorry. "Let's go", said Angie. "Where's Dad disappeared to? He was here just a few moments ago!"

"He's coming....he went back for his stick", Ann said as she was climbing up into the lorry. "I'd better leave room for him if you're driving". The lorry rumbled into life a slight crash of gears, and they were finally on their way.

The sun was shining in a clear blue sky, it promised to be a fine day as they joined the road to Detling and the show ground, everyone seemed to be going to the same place; the road was full of lorries and trailers all trundling along at a sedate pace.

Angie was getting impatient and kept looking at her watch.

"You've got plenty of time luv", her father said."They always run late".

"I know....but I'll have to collect my numbers and they always put the secretaries tent miles away from the horse boxes".

"I'll get the numbers, save you a bit of time". Barry said as they neared the show ground.

"Mind you come straight back then", Ann warned him. "Don't keep to chatting to all your friends".

"And keep away from the beer tent!" Angie added.

"Do stop nagging the pair of you....I'll be straight there and straight back. I promise". He had only gone s few yards before he met an old friend he hadn't seen for years.

"Hi George...howya keeping, haven't seen you for ages!"

Before George could answer Angies voice rang out loud and clear. "Dad...the numbers!!"

"Aw. These women!...I'll be back in a few minutes George, we'll talk then". He went off in search of the secretary's tent. "Bloody women...never stop nagging" He mumbled.

He collected the numbers and handed them to Angie, then promptly disappeared for the rest of the day!

Rupert's heavy horse class was first. Angie had plenty of time really to get him ready for the ring, Ann only had to thread the coloured ribbons into the plat Angie had done before they left Geddinge.

She stood on the grooming box so she could reach the top of the plat just behind Rupert's ears. He was an old hand at showing, he'd been doing it for most of his life and stood silently while Ann pulled and poked the green and yellow ribbons into the plat. Then bridle on and he was ready to go.

Angie pulled her best showing jacket on and tied the number card on her back.

Two lovely black Shire horses ambled passed leaving a trail of chalk powder from their sparkling white socks!

"They look nice", Ann said.

"Yeah..too nice", Angie answered. "Come on Rupert old chap, let's give them a run for their money".

Off they went following the two Shires. *'I hope were going in the right direction'* Thought Angie. Fortunately they were and they arrived at the collecting ring huffing and puffing, Rupert was so strong and walked so fast Angie had to run beside him! He snorted and squealed at the other stallions in the ring although he was the smallest one there.

As Angie had guessed, a Shire won the class, but was delighted to be pulled in second. He had almost won, the judge liked him, but it was just his age that had been the deciding factor he said.

327

She was quite happy to be second, but worried that Rupert was showing his age, there were so few Suffolk Punch stallions standing at stud, and Rupert, bless him, kept siring fillies. Perhaps next year he would sire a colt!

The Welsh pony classes were scheduled to start after a lunch break, so they had plenty of time to enjoy Ann's picnic.

The public address loud speaker suddenly boomed out a ten minute warning for the Section A ponies. The stallion class was first to go into the ring followed by the mares and foals.

Angie and her mother gave the ponies a final brush over, oiled their hooves to make them shine and rubbed baby oil on their noses and round their eyes to make them look really black.

Cilla was used to all the fuss and stood patiently waiting for Angie to finish. Epic was having none of it, he stood up on his hind legs protesting at the treatment he was getting.

"Stand still you little bugger!" Angie cursed him. "It doesn't hurt". But he was sure she was trying to kill him. "That'll have to do....he looks pretty good to me. Come on mum, let's get going".

It was a tidy step to the collecting ring and all of mothers training seemed to be forgotten. The foal leapt about and shied at everything that caught his eye. He stood up and squealed, bucked and dashed forward to the end of the lead rein nearly dragging Ann off her feet!

"Here....let me have him mum, you take Cilla, she knows how to behave".

"Thanks dear", she gasped. "I don't know what's got into him, he's usually so good".

Angie took Epic and had a few words with him! "Stand still". *Slap.* "Behave yourself". *Slap.* "What do you think you're doing". *Slap.*

Epic stood still looking at Angie with his big round brown eyes....he knew when to give in. "Now......walk properly". Angie shook his head. "Walk properly". He dropped his head and did as he was told, much to mother's relief. A lesson learnt? "You've got to learn whose boss" Angie whispered as they arrived at the collecting ring.

328

She had a quick look at the opposition. Some lovely ponies and smart looking foals. *Her* boy was behaving well now and Angie thought he stood a good chance...unless he flipped his lid again!

They were called into the ring and the judging of mare and foals began.

Cilla romped away with the mare's class, she only had to demonstrate her spectacular trot and the prize was hers. Now the foals turn to be judged.

The colt stood proudly in front of Cilla, his chestnut coat gleaming in the sunshine. The judge walked along the line of ten foals, and then asked them to trot, one at a time past him.

Some would trot others didn't know what trotting meant! Ann offered up a silent prayer as she led Epic out in front of the judge.

He walked as if he had springs under his feet. Ann took a tighter grip on his lead rein. The judge had a good look at Epic who was standing still for a change.

"Will he trot?" asked the judge.

'I hope so' Ann said to herself. "Oh yes...he'll trot", she said confidently. She took a firm hold on his lead rein. "Trot on Epic". The foal did exactly that, a lovely long trot around the ring, never breaking the trot or slowing down. He flicked his toes out just like his mother. The crowd at the ring side all clapped.

They pulled up in front of the judge, Ann panting and out of breath, but Epic stood perfectly still as if he had done this forever!

The judge was smiling. "Thank you and well done".

Five more foals were led out, some trotted and others dug their toes in and refused to move unless their mothers trotted in front of them.

Angie was getting excited no foal had trotted as well or as far as her boy. The judge kept looking at him. She was sure Epic would get a rosette of some colour, *make it a red one please*, she thought. And it was a red one.

The judge called them forward and handed Angie the prized red rosette.

"Congratulations...a lovely mare and a superb foal. Well done, especially to mother!" He said winking at Ann.

The steward caught Angie's arm. "Don't forget the championship!" He reminded her as he wrote her number on his clip board.

They found a quiet spot in the collecting ring and Angie let off a big sigh. "Oh mum...that was fun wasn't it?"

Mother had got her breath back by now. "Oh God, I hope I don't have to run again....he set off so fast I could hardly keep up. I didn't dare take a pull at him, he was going so well!" She rubbed the foal's ears. "Could you trot a bit slower next time Epic?!"

They had to wait ages for the championship; there were so many Welsh classes to get through. The little foal got tired and lay down, it was a hot day.

"Oh get up Epic", Ann said. "You'll get dirty".

Another competitor nearby saw the foal lying down, stretched out in the sun. She laughed. "They always choose the wrong place and time don't they?" She said smiling at Angie. "Here...I've got all my brushes with me, you can use them if you like".

"Oh thanks.....at least he's on the grass; they usually pick a nice dusty spot don't they!"

The collecting ring gradually emptied until there were only the eight ponies left, all the handlers with a red rosette tucked in their belts, one of them would be champion...but which one?

The ring steward called out the numbers of the competitors who were eligible and sent them in one at a time so that the judge could have a good look at each one individually as they trotted passed him

The stallion went in first followed by Cilla and her foal, then a lovely yearling and a two year old colt and three more stood in front of the judge, all lovely ponies.

"What do you think mum?" Angie Whispered. "Have we got any chance against his lot?"

"I don't know...they're all so lovely".

The judge had a final look at them. He sent the stallion out again to trot, but he was naughty and refused to move, then suddenly he set off at a spanking pace and flew round the ring.

"He's got it" murmured Angie. "He's lovely".

"Can we have the mare again...without the foal". The steward said walking towards Angie

"Crumbs" Said Angie.

"Let me see her trot again please" said the judge.

Cilla floated away, a lovely steady trot, no bucking or shaking her head. She had done all this nonsense all her life!"

Angie pulled up facing the judge and delivered a quick bow.

"Thank you", he said and walked down the line to look at another pony.

Angie could hardly breathe she was so excited.

The judge walked back and stood looking at Cilla and the stallion. He shook his head; he couldn't make up his mind. Finally he gave the Champion rosette to the stallion and the Reserve to Cilla.

"It was very difficult to choose, but the stallion was in superb condition....two lovely ponies....well done to you both".

The stallion gave one final show and trotted out of the ring. Angie went to follow, but the steward called her back.

"We need the foal for the Junior Championship don't forget!"

"Will he be OK without Cilla mum?" Angie asked

"Don't know...but we'll give it a try!"

There were only three of them before the judge this time, Epic, a yearling and a two year old.

Thankfully Epic was the first to trot, he was looking for his mum, but trotted like a dream. His head tucked in and pointing his toes. Ann was well pleased with him. "Good boy" she whispered. "Good boy".

This time the judge had no problem, he went straight to the foal. "What a beautiful foal", he said to Ann as he handed her the Championship rosette. "He'll make a fine stallion one day!"

Ann and her daughter walked back to the lorry, both surprised and delighted to have done so well.

"Didn't Epic do well mum..... fancy, Junior Champion at his first show....phew!"

Barry came rushing up to meet them. "I heard them give the result on the speakers..Champion and Reserve....well done well done...a good start to your stud my girl!"

"Yeah..you bought a good one this time Dad".

"She never cost me a penny, remember I swapped her for that Cherolais ram".

"That makes it even better", Angie laughed.

They went to a few more shows that summer and the results were much the same, Epic remained unbeaten and Cilla won most of the brood mare classes

At the end of the summer showing season Angie was faced with a problem, should she sell Epic or keep him? There had been a lot of interest in the foal since his first show and several people were interested in buying him.

Barry said the sensible thing would be to sell him and buy another mare, but she had grown so fond of Epic and was sorely tempted to keep him for another year to see if he grew into a useful stallion.

It was a tough decision, but in the end she took her Dad's advice and sold him.

In the spring Cilla was sent to the lovely stallion that had beaten her at the Kent Show in the hope she would produce another quality foal, hopefully a filly!

She kept on winning throughout the summer in the mare classes enhancing her reputation further.

Angie bought a promising yearling to add to her embryonic stud and was toying with the idea of getting another mare.

A friend, who also had Welsh ponies, wanted a potential lead rein pony for her daughter. The child was only a few months old, but her mother argued that if she bought a young pony now by the time it was old enough to break in her baby daughter would be old enough to start riding.

Angie thought it was a daft idea......but the offer of a trip to the sales in Wales was too good to turn down.

She counted up Cilla's winnings and was surprised how much it came to. With a trip to see the bank manager she might have enough to buy another pony.

332

Temptation got the better of her and she sent away for a catalogue from the auctioneers and waited impatiently for it to arrive.

Angie sat quietly one evening with the catalogue on her lap. She couldn't decide what to buy at the sale.

Cilla would have another foal in the spring and the sweet little yearling she had already bought would move up to the two year old classes next year.

Common sense dictated she should buy an older mare, but that might prove to be too expensive.

She studied the catalogue from end to end, but still couldn't make up her mind. There were some Sibertswold ponies entered, the same stud that Cilla had come from originally, they would be worth looking at. She would wait and see if anything caught her eye on the day.

Her friend Jane came to collect her at three o'clock in the morning with her Range Rover and trailer! A very early start, but the sale would start at eleven so potential buyers were advised to get there early to have a good look at the ponies on offer.

It was a long way to Builth Wells, right across England and half of Wales. Jane drove carefully towing her trailer on the M25 and M4 until they got to the Severn Bridge where they stopped for coffee and breakfast.

Angie was disgusted at the price she had to pay for bacon and eggs, and vowed never to eat at motorway cafes again, she would rather die of hunger! Jane just laughed; she had brought her own food, once bitten twice shy!

Over the Severn Bridge the roads were ordinary 'A' roads, narrower and twisty, but at least they were now in Wales and they had made good time.

As they got close to Builth they encountered more and more horse boxes and trailers all presumably going to the sale, the biggest sale of the year for Welsh ponies. Section 'A's today and 'B's tomorrow. Cobs had their own sale in a week or so.

"It's exciting isn't it Ange'. We've got heaps of time to look around and find a really nice pony!"

333

Angie already knew which ponies *she* wanted to look at, Sibertswold ponies, while Jane was hoping to find a nice colt foal, they were usually cheaper than fillies. She wanted something pretty with a pleasant disposition.

Angie teased her. "If it's only got three legs but smiles at you, will that be OK!?"

"Better with four legs!"

When they arrived and parked the trailer they split up arranging to meet in an hour by the refreshment van.

Angie was in heaven, so many lovely ponies and foals screaming for their mums. Some foals looked too young to be weaned, she felt sorry for the little things and hoped they'd find good homes today.

Where were the ponies she had come to see? There were ponies everywhere, people looking and people running ponies up and down the aisle shouting *'mind yrbacks'* or *'Coming through'*. You had to watch your step and be ready to jump out of the way pretty quickly!

At last she found the ponies she had come to see, all beautifully groomed and standing quietly on deep straw.

Most were foals, but there were three older mares. A dapple grey caught her eye immediately. According to the catalogue she was four years old and had the same dam as Cilla!.... the more she looked the more she liked the pony.

A tall well dressed man got up from a chair and wandered up to her. "Would you like to see her outside?....she moves very well".

"That would be nice, thank you".

He slipped a lead rein on the ponies head collar and led her out of the enormous covered area onto a grassy paddock where other ponies were being shown off to interested people.

The little mare moved just like Cilla. *'I've got to have her'* thought Angie *'but will I be able to afford her?'*

The man led her back into the pen.

"Thanks, she's a lovely pony!"

"No problem at all..my name's Rhys", he replied holding out his hand,

334

Angie shook his outstretched hand. "Are you expecting a high price for her?" She asked casually.

"We always live in hope".

"I've got her half sister at home...I'd love another like her!"

"Oh...that's interesting. Who've you got?"

"Sibertswold Cilla, I've had her a few years now. We're expecting her second foal next year".

"You've got Cilla!!"

"I have... and she's won lots at the shows!"

"You've got Cilla". He said again. "I can't believe it.....wait here...don't go away, I must find my mother!"

He thrust the lead rein into Angie's hand and dashed off. She was taken aback and didn't know what to think.

She took the opportunity to have a really good look at the pony; she had a lovely dished head and big black eyes, friendly eyes. A strong neck and shoulders, nice round quarters and masses of well brushed hair.

Rhys was back with a tall oldish lady with white hair. "This young lady has got Cilla", he said excitedly. "Fancy mother...after all these years!"

His mother held out her hand. "It's so good to meet you.... how is she?..oh I'm sorry I don't know your name!"

"Angie...Angie Skinner".

"How is she Angie?..I'm Anwyn by the way".

"She's absolutely fine, in foal I hope".

The questions went on and on. Eventually she managed to change the subject.

"I'm really interested in this little mare". She managed to get in-between questions.

"Her name's Merrylegs" Rhys raised his voice over his mother's excited chatter.

"Oh I'm so glad you've got Cilla...she was my pet you know...I loved that little pony. She was the top price pony here, made well over a thousand!"

Angie was shocked, but she didn't dare tell Anwyn her Dad had swapped a ram for a pony that was sold for such a lot of money, some things are better left unsaid!

"Well...I'm afraid I can't afford anything like that. I'd better leave you in peace".

335

"Wait Angie...I'd really like you to have Merrylegs" Anwyn looked at her son. "What can we do Rhys?"

They were silent for a moment. "I can't sell her out of the ring", Anwyn explained. "She'll have to go through the ring".

"How much can you afford Angie, if you don't mind me asking?" Rhys inquired.

"£350...I know that won't be nearly enough!"

Rhys looked at his mother. "We are selling her much too cheaply mother...why don't you see the auctioneer and increase the reserve....she *must* be worth at least £1000 surely!"

Anwyn looked startled....then suddenly she understood what her son was thinking. If Merrylegs wasn't sold Angie could have her!

"I think you're right...I'll go straight away. What a brilliant idea, what it is to have a lawyer in the family! Why don't you take Angie for a cup of coffee?"

"That's very kind, but I promised to meet my friend before she does something stupid. She's searching for a foal, but I'll be back, you're being very kind and generous".

"Well I'm off to see the auctioneer...how about £2000. Do you think anyone can afford that?!"

"The Dutch buyers might" Rhys said.

"Well if they can I'll have to let her go...can't refuse that kind of money! You understand Angie?"

"Absolutely..you can't turn away from that sort of money".

"Maybe I'll make it £2500. That should stop 'em!"

Angie hurried off and was soon lost in the crowd, she wasn't sure if she'd bought Merrylegs or not. However now she must find Jane and help her look for a pretty foal with a friendly face.

What a job...there were hundreds of foals, all with pretty faces and kind eyes.

They spent ages walking up and down the ranks of pens. Jane eventually decided on a little palomino, very pretty and friendly.

She was keen to get back to Kent but agreed to wait for Merrylegs to come into the ring. They both hoped it wouldn't be too long as Angie was a bundle of nerves.

336

She had to have Merrylegs even though it would take all her savings.

Time was getting on and the crowds started drifting away. Would the Sibertwold ponies ever come into the ring?

Angie rushed back to their pens, but they had all gone from there. Back she ran just in time to hear the auctioneer announce a consignment of ponies from the well known Sibertswold Stud.

A few empty seats round the ring were quickly filled as the first of the foals was led in, a pretty filly with a lovely head, typical of Sibertswold ponies.

She made a good price for a foal. Then three colts that only made the average price of the day.

A three year old mare believed to be in foal made £300, not a bad price, two for the price of one!

Then came Merrylegs. The auctioneer started explaining to the crowd what a lovely mare was in front of them, then suddenly stopped, he had just seen the reserve price for the pony.

He coughed and called Rhys, who was leading Merrylegs, over to his rostrum. A look of amazement on his face, he checked the reserve price with Rhys who nodded and continued walking round the ring.

The auctioneer coughed again.

"Well ladies and gentlemen; it appears the owner wants a high price for this exceptional mare. Who has £1000 to start?" Nobody moved

"£750 then,,,surely, such a beautiful well bred pony"...Still nothing.

"£700!"

"£500.....to start!

One arm went up. "Thank you sir".

"£700 ?"

Another bidder raised his arm.

££1000?

Nobody wanted to go higher, even the Dutch buyer turned his back

"Come on gentlemen. I will take another £100........no further interest?...Not sold"......The gavel went down.

Rhys looked relieved and led Merrylegs out.

337

Angie ran all the way back to the pen arriving as Rhys was leading Merrylegs in, laughing fit to bust! "Did you see the look on the auctioneer's face when he saw the reserve price mother?. I didn't dare look at him again".

"Well I did put a whopping high reserve on her...now I'd better go to the office and get a pass to take her out...won't be long".

"Shall I give you the money now?" Angie asked as she was stroking her new pony's nose.

"No....not here or we'll be in trouble. Better wait till we've got her in your trailer, then it's only an ordinary sale and no one can object!"

"Anwyn said you were a lawyer, you look too young!".

"Well thanks! Actually I have a little longer to do at university, and then I'll grow a beard. They both laughed.

Anwyn was back with the exit pass and the pony's registration papers. "We named her Merrylegs after her mother who died when this one was only a few months old; she was grey as well to start with, but gradually turned white as she got older.

"Merry was my lead rein pony, my God that seems such a long time ago!...It's been so nice to meet you Angie. I'm glad you've got her. Keep in touch". Rhys said as he shook her hand. "I must go and sort out the other ponies that are leaving us".

Angie and Anwyn led Merrylegs out, handed over the pass and looked for Jane's trailer.

She handed Anwyn £350. Thank you so much, she is a lovely po...."

"Wait a moment Angie, the original reserve was only £300. I won't take all this...here". Anwyn said passing £50 back.

"Well, if you're sure that's enough".

Anwyn smiled. "I know she's going to a good home and that's worth more than anything to me. Give my love to Cilla. Tell her Anwyn still misses her". She turned away and went to find Rhys and the other ponies that had been sold.

Angie gave Merrylegs a drink and tied hay nets up next to the pretty pony Jane had bought. The poor little pony looked tired

338

and frightened, but seemed to relax when Merry came in to the trailer.

"Let's get going Ange, it's been a long old day for us and the ponies".

"Yes it has Jane,,,,,but a *very* successful one". Angie added.

It was unfortunately a slow journey back to Dover; the traffic had built up and was very slow moving due to an accident on the M4. They both sighed with relief when they were passed Detling and on the A2.

Angies mother guessed they would come home with a pony of some sort and had prepared a stable with water and a big hay net, now all she could do was wait, impatiently.

At last she heard Jane's Range Rover , and the lights came on in the yard.

"Is that you Angie?"

"Were back mum...stick the kettle on".

"I've made the first stable ready".

"Thanks we won't be a minute".

Ann slid the kettle onto the Aga hot plate; it was always ready to boil for a quick 'cuppa'. People were always in a hurry and she could have a cup of tea ready in a few minutes.

Angie led Merrylegs into her stable and gave her a quick check over in case she had had a bump on the long journey home, but she was fine.

Jane wanted to get home so refused the offer of tea. She waved goodbye and got ready for the last few miles of driving.

"Thanks for coming with me Angle...I think we've both bought lovely ponies....see you soon!" She backed out of the yard and was gone.

Angie had a lot to tell her mother who was surprised how generous the owner was, particularly raising the reserve to such an extent that no one was likely to buy the pony.

"They sound nice people" said her Dad when he heard the story. "Anwyn Griffith did you say Angie?"

"Yes...they own the Sibertswold Stud, that's near Brecon".

"The name rings a bell with me!.... I had a quick look at her on my way in...lovely head. I think you did alright my

339

love....now where's my supper mother, I've been counting sheep all day and I'm starving!"

Supper was soon on the table and they chatted and laughed all evening.

Before Angie went to bed she creped quietly across the yard and had a peep at her new pony. She was stretched out on the straw fast asleep. "Tomorrow we'll go and find your sister....good night Merry". She whispered.

Early the next morning she took Merrylegs out to the orchard next to the house.

Cilla and her foal were grazing quietly, but as soon as Merry appeared her head shot up, ears pricked. She trotted over to examine her new companion, gave a loud squeal and put her ears back. 'Don't you touch my baby' she seemed to warn her!

Did they know they were related Angie wondered?

The little grey pony soon got tired of being squealed at and trotted to the fence to have a look at the Suffolks who were attracted by all the noise Cilla was making.

Merrylegs was a bit put off by the sheer size of them, she'd never seen a horse that size before and backed off quickly, trotting round the orchard, snatching the occasional mouth full of grass!

Cilla followed her for a while trying to be friendly, Angie was amazed, Merrylegs trotted exactly the same way as Cilla, just seemed to float over the ground.

"They make a good pair" Barry said joining her at the gate. I like your new ponies head....and those black eyes!"

"Yeah I think these two mares are a bit special Dad".

"I'm off to the market love, you coming?"

"No Dad...I'll just watch my little stud for a while".

"OK...... Oh by the way. Griffiths. I met him at the Royal Welsh soon after the restrictions on cattle were lifted after the foot and mouth, I was judging him, he had a cracking ram, I remember!..Don't stay too long admiring them, there's the mucking out to be done". He said slapping her on the back.

"Thanks for reminding me Dad!"

Eventually she had to tear herself away from her embryonic stud. They had all settled down and were busy looking for apples fallen during the night.

Cilla's foal was curious about the new comer and kept trying to get close to her, but Cilla was always there stopping her, the little foal just trotted away and waited for another chance. Angie was delighted to see she had inherited the same lovely action as Cilla, she would keep this foal to add to the three other fillies Cilla had produced over the years. When she was weaned she would join them on the cliff top pastures.

The grass growing on the chalk land was wonderful for building young bones and the sea air was good for everyone.

Angie walked along the cliff usually every week to check her youngsters, and to make sure the fencing along the foot path hadn't been tampered with by summer walkers.

One evening when the family were sitting round the big inglenook with logs crackling in the hearth, her Dad, puffing away on his pipe, he asked Angie about her new pony.

"You'll have to get a stallion soon my girl, can't go on paying stud fees to someone else." Angie sensed a lecture coming. "There's Cilla's youngsters on the cliff fields growing older but doing nothing bar the odd show......Then there's Cilla and Merrylegs, both mares. Cilla will have another foal 'bout Easter, probably another filly....there's a lot of mares out there. You really need your own stallion my love. Have you thought about that?"

She had thought about it many times, but where could she find a stallion good enough for her lovely mares that she could afford? All her savings had gone on Merry.

"I can't afford a good one Dad, and there's no point in buying a rubbishy thing, the mares are too good for any old stallion".

Barry puffed away on his pipe sending smoke rings drifting across the room. The logs crackled in the inglenook and apart from that there was silence in the room..........

"OK" he put his pipe to one side. "Here's what we do!.....you find the best colt or stallion you can find, the very best mind you, and I'll buy it for your birthday".

341

Angie looked at her Dad, speechless. "You'd do that Dad...oh I love you Dad....thanks so much. Wow....I can't believe you said that!"

"You want it in writing!?" He teased.

"Wow my own stallion, now I can really call it Geddinge Stud".

"Well before you get *too* excited go and pour me a good measure of that whiskey I bought the other day...I think I might need it".

She poured the drink, then decided to take the bottle in as well. She put them on a little table beside her father. "I'm off to bed" she said and planted a kiss on her Dads curly hair. See you in the morning. Good night Mum good night Dad". She climbed the creaking stairs deep in thought.

Her own stallion would make the stud complete, but where would she find one good enough for her mares. She must start asking around, there must be a good stallion closer than Wales, but maybe she should phone the Sibertswold Stud, may be they had a colt not related to her mares.

There was still plenty of time, after all she didn't need one urgently....next week would do!

Her night was very disturbed at first, she couldn't sleep. She heard her father go out to check the animals and come back in again. Kick off his boots before climbing the stairs. He coughed a bit, a troublesome cough he couldn't seem to shake off, and then all was quiet.

She dreamed of stallions, lots of them, all galloping round the orchard. Which one would she choose.....unfortunately she woke before she'd made up her mind.

Angie decided she would be patient and wait for the shows to start in the spring.

Last summer she had noticed a nice looking two year old colt winning young stock classes time and again. He looked like growing into a lovely pony when he matured.

Barry had an old friend who judged horses and knew a thing or two about Welsh ponies. He was always saying *'If a horse fills your eye when you first see it, buy the bugger or you forever will regret it!'*

342

Well the young colt had certainly 'filled' Angie's eye when she first saw him. He would be a three year old this year, old enough to hold a stallion licence, providing he passed the vetinary examination that the Welsh Pony and Cob Society demanded, and still be young enough for the young stock classes.

She must be patient. He was certain to turn up in the first spring shows and then Angie would pounce! Now however she must asses her own youngsters and select one or two she thought would be good fun to show.

Last summer one of Cilla's two year fillies had done very well, but had always lost in the championship to this beautiful colt! Dad said a young colt would always beat a young filly no matter how lovely she was. That extra something, you couldn't quantify, but they would always beat a filly!.

Angie would love to prove her Dad wrong, so she set about selecting her show team with renewed energy.

Christmas was approaching fast so Ann was beginning to worry about it. All the family would assemble, Angie's brothers Tim and Steve both farming locally, would arrive with their assorted children and all would expect a huge Christmas dinner.

Out in the barn a fat turkey strutted around little knowing his days were numbered, Ann had been feeding him up for ages but still wasn't sure if he was fat enough! Barry laughed and reminded her there was a fat pig ready to be slaughtered before Christmas, which would mean plenty of pork and ham to add to the already bulging pantry.

Barry had a special surprise for his wife this Christmas which needed Angies co-operation.

The carriage that came with Cilla had stood abandoned in the barn for ages. Ann had driven it once or twice and had described it as a horse drawn wheel chair, and she wasn't ready for a wheel chair yet! So it was covered with a dust sheet and forgotten about.

Barry had a very good friend, known as Uncle Dick by the family, who had a profitable side line buying and selling horses.

343

When they met at the Ashford market he was asked to look out for a Governess Trap or something similar that Ann could drive; they had after all the pony to pull it.

"Funny you should ask me that Barry. I've got just the thing back home". *I thought you might have* Barry thought. "Been in my barn for ages...I'll pull it out so's you can have a look"

Barry and Angie went to have a look. Angie didn't need any persuading. He had obviously had the hose pipe out for the little trap was running with water. Yellow and black, it gleamed in the sunshine.

Uncle Dicks yard had always been one of Angies favourite places, all manner of treasures could be found if you had the time and patience to have a rummage.

He also always seemed to have a selection of horses for sale at reasonable prices, *'All sound and genuine 'orses'*. He would tell you with a twinkle in his eye.

"It's a Spindle Back Gig", Dick informed them. "Just right for your little Welsh ponies...well sprung and just look at those wheels. Rides lovely...really comfortable". Dick rattled on about the virtues of the Gig while Angie was looking closely at the wood work and fittings. She lifted the shafts and checked the balance, it all seemed genuine enough.

"Now then young lady, I've never sold your Dad a wrong'un, have I?" He joked.

She smiled. Not too her Dad, true enough, but some hadn't been so lucky. Still, Dick would always buy anything back if you weren't happy with your purchase.

"It looks fine Dad...could we take it out for a spin.....have you got a pony that goes in harness uncle?" She knew he would have.

"Sure enough my dear, I've just the fellow in the shed....let me tack him up, then you'll see. He's a grand little chap". He disappeared into the depths of his shed.

Angie looked at her Dad trying to suppress a laugh. "I hope the 'grand little chap' is broken to harness", she whispered, you never know what to expect with Uncle Dick!"

After a few minutes he reappeared with a nice looking pony that backed into the shafts like an expert and stood patiently while the harness was adjusted.

344

"There you are Barry. As good a turnout as you'll find anywhere in Kent!" He was doing a great job of selling the gig, and, he hoped, the pony!

"We'll just go down the lane a bit...see how well it's sprung. Climb up Dad, I'll give you the thrill of your life!!" He hoped it was a joke.

The Gig was really comfortable, the seat cushion was black with yellow trimmings and they found a leg rug to match, rolled up under the seat.

"What do you think Angie, do you think she'd like it? She's always wanted a pony and trap". Barry sounded anxious.

"It's good Dad, nicely balanced and well sprung and it will fit Cilla when she's had her foal".

"Oh thank goodness...I like the pony don't you?...he's quite jolly".

"We.ve got lots of ponies Dad, lots and lots".

They drove back to Dicks yard and Angie took the pony back into the shed while her father did the business with uncle Dick. She could hear then laughing and guessed they had come to an agreement on the price.

She hung the harness up and turned to go when the pony whinnied and nudged her arm. "You're a lovely pony...I hope you find a good home". She whispered .

"Come on Angie ...time to go". Her father called.

She walked back into the sunshine, both men were smiling. "Thanks uncle Dick...I hope you find a good home for that little pony..he's cute". She hugged Dick and climbed into the car.

"Don't you worry about that my dear. He'll go to a lovely home. Take care now.....good to see you again". Dick was waving and still smiling as they left his yard.

Barry was humming to himself as they drove along the quiet country lanes and tapping his fingers on the steering wheel.

"Did you get it for a good price Dad?" She asked eventually, curiosity getting the better of her.

"Oh yes....you know old Dick, always out to make an extra quid. Nooo...it wasn't expensive...I bought the whole turnout". He was still smiling.

Angie was silent. Then after a while. "Dad, tell me I'm wrong, but did you say the *whole* turnout...as in trap *and* pony?"

345

"Yeah......well he was such a jolly little chap and obviously easy to put in the shafts, your mother will be able to cope with him by herself. I liked him straight away. I'm not usually wrong".

Angie sat back in her seat, her Dad was right of course; he could tell a genuine horse a mile off.

"Father Christmas will have a hell of a job getting that lot down the chimney!"

"Oh dear...I never thought of that".

Christmas day arrived and so did all the family, plus Barry's young shepherd Dave who had been had invited to join them. He had only an aged father, in an old people's home, who didn't recognise his son any more.

Steve, one of two sons, had also asked if he could bring a friend who was staying with him, Chris. He was an expert mechanic, a wizard with motor cycle engines. So fifteen sat down to dinner that Christmas day at Geddinge.

After lunch Barry took his wife for a drive in the trap, while Steve took his friend Chris to have a look at an old generator his father had bought at a farm sale in the summer.

The machine had refused to start in spite of the efforts of both Steve and his Dad. Chris could find his way round most mechanical problems and it wasn't long before the generator spluttered, coughed, and settled down to a rhythmic chug chug chug.

Steve cheered and shook Chris's hand! Angie heard the generator burst into life and came running across the yard.

"You're a genius Chris...a bloody genius....Dad will be so glad to see that pile of junk working!" She grabbed him lifting him clean off his feet, Angie had consumed a lot of wine with her dinner, and Chris was only just over five feet tall!

"I think that deserves a drink" Steve said to Chris who was trying to recover from the assault on his person! "Lets see what Dad has got locked away in the cellar, that's where he keeps the best stuff".

"I'll get on with the horses", said Angie. "I reckon I've had enough to drink already". She was still laughing.

"I'll help you", Chris offered. Angie looked at the diminutive size of the volunteer and thought of the ton or more of Suffolk horse waiting to be fed!

"OK Chris...you feed Rupert. Here's his bucket, and that's his stable". He set off in the direction pointed out.

Steve looked at his sister. "You shouldn't have done that sis, Rupert will eat him and spit out the bones!" They both watched anxiously as Chris strode purposefully out across the yard.

Angie was chuckling quietly and Steve was about to rush after hs friend when with a roar Rupert's head appeared over the stable door. He was hungry! He didn't mind who brought him his food as long as it arrived quickly.

Chris froze in his tracks staring at the horse. It was the closest he had ever come to a horse, let alone this enormous stallion looking down at the man holding his bucket of food.

Rupert roared again!

Chris jumped, turned and was ready to run. "Haven't you got something a bit smaller I can feed!" he asked quaiking in his boots.

"Here...I'll feed him Chris", said Steve taking the bucket. "He's a real softy really".

Rupert seeing his food coming at last stood patiently while Steve tipped it into his feed bin. He slapped the big horse on his quarters. "You're a noisy beast aren't you". He turned to say something to his friend....but Chris had gone!

Across the yard the generator chugged on, chug chug chug.

TWENTYNINE

The little pony Ann had called Casper, because he arrived on Christmas day, soon settled in with the other ponies. Cilla was his favourite and he followed her everywhere.

Unfortunately she lost her last foal long before it was due, Angie felt sorry for the little mare. She had given them eleven lovely foals while she had been at Geddinge. She was the foundation mare of Angie's stud.

Perhaps it was a sign that she had done enough and deserved a rest, anyway she decided to retire Cilla and let her act as nanny to the youngsters running on the cliff tops at Dover.

The young colt that she had set her heart on last summer came out again at the early shows. He was now a three year old and still full of promise. He was gorgeous!

Angie wasted no time in getting her Dad to try and buy the colt.

The owner was reluctant; the pony was already entered in most of the County Shows within reach and was going to the Bath and West Show next week.

Angie was very disappointed and asked Barry to have another go at persuading the owner to sell. Her Dad could talk most people into anything.....he could charm the fuzz off a peach...or sell ice cream to the Eskimos'!

Anyway, he went back again, cheque book in hand and this time 'sort' of won. Angie could have the colt at the end of the summer when all the shows had finished.

She whooped with joy, he was well worth waiting for.

"Did he cost a lot Dad?" She asked when mother wasn't in ear shot.

"Phew...you don't want to know my love...you don't want to know!"

Angie never did know.

During the summer two events changed all their lives.

Barry's cough got worse and he had to have an X-ray to discover the problem, and Chris arrived at Geddinge more frequently.

348

He could usually find an engine that needed his attention or tweak up a bit. Certainly both cars were running better than ever.

However it wasn't only the engines that had his attention. Angie fell in love.

It took a while, it certainly wasn't love at first sight, but gradually she began to enjoy Chris's company, although he kept well away from the ponies, especially Rupert!

Ann was pleased for her daughter but her father wasn't so sure. "He's a townie my love, never will be a farmer, and farming is all you know. It's bred in you; we've all been farmers for years and years. Think Angie, think carefully that's all I ask".

Well whether she thought or not a wedding was arranged. It was to be in late autumn because Barry had been invited to judge at the big agricultural show in South Africa, he couldn't refuse an offer like that.

Dave would run the farm while he was away, Barry had complete trust in his young manager, and if anything went badly wrong Tim was only a mile or so away.

Ann took to driving like a duck to water and joined the Canterbury Driving Club. Casper was an ideal driving pony much admired by everyone. What breed he was could be anyone's guess but the majority opinion was that there was a lot of New Forest in him. Ann didn't care what he was, he was a great driving pony, and she loved him!

Ann went to several driving rallies with Angie as the groom, it was at one of these when Angie was joking about the 'horse drawn wheel chair' that another driver showed interest in it.

"I'd love to have a look at it Angie, could be just the thing for the disabled drivers I help with!"

"Of course Rita...it's just standing in the shed, it's the chickens favourite perch!"

"I'll try not to disturb them!"

Angie forgot all about their conversation, until later in the week Rita phoned and arranged to call in to see the 'horse drawn wheel chair'. Angie was busy with wedding plans which were a

349

bit strained, but she welcomed the visit, it would enable her to forget the wedding plans for a while!

"Come on Rita, let's chase the chickens out and have a look at mother's wheel chair". She laughed.

Rita was a bit more serious, she had an idea of what she was about to see, a copy of Queen Victoria's carriage, she'd seen pictures of it...but was this the real thing?

Angela shooed the chickens out and whipped off the dust sheet.

"Oh wow!" Was all Rita could say. The little carriage, dusty and grubby, stood there amongst the straw as lovely as ever. She walked round it grinning. It was dirty, true enough, but this was what she had hoped to see, just what she had been looking for, for years!

"Do you know what you've got here Angie?"

"Yeah, a horse drawn wheel chair".

Rita sighed and took a deep breath. "Where did you get it?"

"It came with my little section 'A', I only wanted the pony, you know, my Cilla. Mother tried it out a couple of times with Cilla, but she didn't like it...too uncomfortable, those little front wheels made it very bumpy". Rita listened and was silent for a few minutes.

"This carriage Angie, is an exact copy of one made for Queen Victoria when she was elderly. I actually met the man that made it; he showed me several photos of it during its construction. Apparently he made it for a titled lady who was confined to a wheel chair. The pony and trap were sold after her death and he lost track of it".

Angie was for once speechless. "Are you sure it's the same one?"

"Yep", she rummaged in her hand bag. "Have a look at this photo, taken soon after it had been finished". Sure enough it was the same carriage.

"Well I'll be dammed!" Angie exclaimed as she started to replace the dust sheet.

"Will you sell it to me?"

Angie was more than just surprised. She wondered if her Dad had realised what he had bought that night in Dorset. He never

350

mentioned the trap as being anything special. He'd probably congratulated himself on having got such a lovely pony!

"I can't Rita. Not until I speak to Dad, and he's in South Africa for another month".

"That's a pity...we've got a driving gala in two weeks with a display of interesting vehicles, this would be a marvellous addition to the exhibition....could we borrow it do you think?"

"I tell you what....I'll bring Cilla back from Dover to pull it and we will come.....maybe Mum would like to come and drive Casper in her Spindle Back Gig?"

"That would be lovely, but you won't forget....I really want to buy that carriage for our disabled drivers will you!?"

"Don't get your hopes up Rita, Dad collects all sorts of things. There's an ancient threshing machine out the back there, it must be sixty or seventy years old. My fiancé reckons he can get it to work, but it needs a steam engine to drive it!"

"Well please ask your Dad Angie. I'll send you the details of our driving display. Look forward to seeing you and Ann on the day".

Angie went straight down to the cliff pastures at Dover and brought Cilla back from retirement! The little pony seemed to be glad to be back at Geddinge with all the farm animals and the familiar noises.

Angie knew she would have a lot of hard work ahead of her if she was ever going to get Cilla back in show condition. She had put on so much weight there was a chance she wouldn't fit between the shafts of the trap anymore and then there was the carriage.

The chickens hadn't done real damage and a good wash with the power hose would remove mast of the grime, but it was all extra work she didn't really need.

Dave noticed Cilla was back at the farm and when Angie told him about Rita's carriage display he told her he would clean both traps so not to worry!

He not only cleaned them and polished the brass work, but polished all the harnesses for both ponies as well. Angie swore he

351

must have sat up all night working on them after spending all day out in the fields getting the harvest in.

No wonder her Dad thought a lot of his farm manager!

The driving rally went well. Cilla and Queen Victoria's Trap caused a lot of interest, especially amongst the disabled drivers, and more than just Rita wanted to buy it!

Ann won an award for the best novice driver, she learnt that the driver of horse drawn carriages was called a 'whip', she was thrilled."I can't remember when I last won an award for anything...except my jam at the church fete!" She laughed

A week or so later Steve had to go up to Heathrow to meet his father arriving back from South Africa. The British Airways flight was over an hour late touching down.

Steve caught sight of his father and was shocked to see how pale and exhausted he looked. He was being supported by a stewardess who explained to Steve that Barry had been taken ill and they had given him oxygen to assist his breathing.

"Nothing but this damned cough Steve....the air in Africa didn't suit me..too dry, much too dry".

His father chatted for a bit on the way home but then fell asleep; it had been a very long day for him.

Ann wanted him to have a check up at the hospital, he looked so tired.

"I can't do that....Angela's wedding is next week....can't miss that, I.ve got to give her away!...Maybe after that I'll see the Doc'".

Angie and Chris were married at a registry office in Canterbury, a quiet wedding with family and a few friends. Ann thought, with Barry being unwell, it was better to keep things simple.

Mr and Mrs Bloyce, Chris and Angie, had renovated one of the farm cottages and they moved in there after a short honeymoon in France, which strangely coincided with a big motor cycle race meeting.

When they got home Angie went to collect the young stallion. He was very well mannered and easy to handle, she was thrilled with him and for a while was very happy.

She soon became pregnant and cursed herself for being so carless; the baby was due right in the middle of the showing season. How stupid could that be! Now the young stallion wouldn't get shown this summer.

In early March Barry was taken ill and rushed to hospital, the latest X-ray showed an advanced case of Extrinsic Allergic Alvelitis, or Farmers Lung, as it was more generally known. The prognosis was not good.

The family were devastated, how could it happen? He was strong, always out in the fields with his sheep. Fate had no favourites, and to Angie there seemed to be no justice in life. Chris could do nothing to console her and turned away.

The baby was born in June, a big bouncing boy who slept all day and cried all night! They named him Sam.

The constant bad nights got his parents down and tempers became short. Ann didn't want to interfere and tried to cheer Angie up, but for a while it wasn't a happy home.

Barry could hear raised voices in the cottage across the lane and the occasional door slamming. He watched his daughter creep into Cilla's stable one day, he knew she was in tears, but he could only shake his head knowingly. *'I told her to be sure'*, he muttered to himself.

Angie was soon pregnant again and yet another year flew past, but this time she had got her timing right and Kitty arrived in October, just after the showing season had finished!

The young stallion won a lot with Angie showing him in all the local shows until her mother told her to stop or the baby would arrive in the middle of the show ground! Rita came to the rescue and finished the season for her.

He was proving to be a valuable addition to Geddinge Stud, his stock were winning time and time again

A friend, who produced and showed ponies as a profession, admired her ponies. Over the years he had bought several of her young ones to break in and show for clients, always waiting with cash in hand for anything Angie had to offer!

Cilla came back from retirement once again for young Sam, though only two, he was strapped into a basket saddle and taken for walks around the farm.

Cilla hated the basket saddle; she had a sour expression, ears back and just plodded round the fields every time Angie took them out.

Sam was much the same. He hated Cilla and loathed being strapped into the basket saddle as much as Cilla loathed it on her back!

Sam cried and screamed, his little legs beating a tattoo on Cilla's neck until reluctantly Angie could see he was never going to enjoy riding, so he was left to roar around the yard on his tricycle.

Cilla was left in peace again and returned to the youngsters on the cliff top pasture and the view of the English Channel, while Angie waited patiently for Kitty to grow old enough to use the basket saddle.

By now Barry could only breathe with the help of oxygen from a cylinder which he carried around with him in a satchel. Never the less he was determined to work as much as possible, and drove himself to local shows judging sheep as if he was the action man of old!

However there was no way back for Barry and one night he drifted away in his sleep.

Fate had not finished with the Skinner family yet. No sooner had they laid Barry to rest than ugly rumours started to circulate in the village.

Back from an early morning ride Angie picked up the post as she opened the door to her cottage. Mostly bills and adverts which were thrown in the waste bin, but one large envelope demanded attention!

'Proposed dual carriage way connecting the Chanel Tunnel with North East Kent'

It was a thick document which included a map of the village and the surrounding country side. There was a black line showing the proposed road, which went straight through Geddinge farm land!

Angie couldn't believe her eyes; she sat at the kitchen table going over and over the document from Kent County Council.

She eventually jumped up and rushed across the lane to the farm.

"Mum...have you seen this?" she shouted.

The same document had been sent to all properties along the proposed route.

"I have! Come and have a cuppa and we'll talk about it".

"Look where the bloody road goes Mum! Close to the house and cutting our land in half...how the hell are we supposed to get the sheep in or the cattle to market..It's just bloody ridiculous.....can you see me driving a flock of sheep across a dual carriage way. Christ almighty!" Angie was really worked up.

"Calm down love", her mother said quietly. "We'll have a cuppa tea and think about this!"

Angie was in tears. This new road was the last straw, in the past few years she had lost her Dad, got married too quickly, and that was going wrong, and now this damn road which would make it impossible for the farm to flourish.

That morning they drank copious cups of tea and tried to think of a solution.

The village was only a mile away, but they would be cut off from their friends and shop! An access road was promised, but no one believed it.

A campaign was started and there were meetings with the council in the village hall to persuade them to divert the road away from the village.

Some of the villagers marked out the route with pegs so that everyone was aware of the proximity of the road in relation to the village. They marked badger sets and got the RSPCA involved. There were Nightingales, a protected species, in the woods that were to be felled!

355

The planners did change the route, moving it about a hundred yards north away from the village!

It became very obvious the council would win.

Ann and her daughter decided they would have to move, after a lot of discussion with the rest of the family. Tim pointed out that land in Wales was very much cheaper than here in the south of England.

After searching through Farmers Weekly and other publications it was decided they would move lock stock and barrel to Wales.

A local farmer who would loose a lot of his land to compulsory purchase offered to buy all Geddinge land that lay on his side of the new carriage way.

The house was no problem, it had stood there for over three hundred years, so was protected from demolition, it was mentioned in the Doomsday Book.

Ann called in the services of an estate agent to value what would be left of the property. The agent had known Barry for years so was glad he might be of help. It turned out he had on his books a pop singer who he thought might be interested.

He set a very high price for the house and barn, partly because of its historical aspect. The barn had stood there probably as long as the house. It was built like a cathedral with massive oak beams. And in any case he wanted to do his best for his old friend.

The pop star duly arrived with his entourage and several children. They loved the old house with all its nooks and crannies and were speechless when they saw the inglenook fireplace.

The barn took their breath away....it would make a fantastic recording studio for the group. Angie pitied the owls and bats that lived in the roof!

They spent over an hour looking over Geddinge with the agent and discussing options with Ann's estate agent......He decided to buy it!

Angie found him to be a well educated young man, he apparently had a degree in history...she changed her mind about pop stars, although she didn't like their music.

356

THIRTY

After several fruitless trips to look at farms they settled on buying a ninety acre property near Abergwesyn. To move 'lock stock and barrel' was going to take some planning. They all sat down to work out how to do it.

Their plan worked, and within weeks it was all settled. Ann and the children would move in as soon as the legal papers had been exchanged leaving Angie and her brothers to sort out the animals.

All went pretty much according to plan and finally, at last, Angie loaded Cilla and the five youngsters. They were the last of the Geddinge stock to run up the ramp.

She slammed the ramp up behind them, thanked her brothers for all their help and turned to look at her old home, the home she had known all her life.

'Good bye...I've loved living here' she whispered as she reluctantly drove away, tears in her eyes.

The new farm was high up in the mountains, so very different from Geddinge where the land had been practically flat.

Chris lived there for only a month and then decided to go back to Dover. It was an amicable parting, in fact Angie wasn't the least bit sorry, it had been a big mistake all along.

Ann loved her new farm on the hill side with its magnificent views for miles around. They were busy every day, fencing! It seemed all of it needed to be replaced or repaired.

"Angela I think we're going to have to get some help with this fencing, it's too much for you on your own". Ann suggested at breakfast one day.

"I was thinking the same" Angie replied. "I expect we can find a young lad around here to help, I'll ask when I go for more posts".

The hens' geese and ducks had to be shut in stables until a safe house could be built for them. There were foxes always prowling looking for an easy meal!

357

Cilla and the young ponies she looked after, were living in a paddock close to the house until a larger field could be fenced for them. The Suffolk mares had the run of the rest of the land for the time being.

Rupert had died during the winter; he had been at Geddinge for thirty years and was greatly missed. He had never been ill in all that time; Angie swore it was the shock of fathering a colt that finished him off. It was a nice foal but not as good as its sire. They called him Teddy.

Ann was out in the yard one morning feeding the hens when a Land Rover drove in. It was Dave!

Ann rushed to meet him scattering the hens in all directions "Dave what on earth are you doing here?" she cried in delight.

He smiled as he stiffly climbed out of the old Land Rover. "Well I met Tim in the pub a couple of days ago and he mentioned you were struggling a bit, so as I'm unemployed just at the moment I thought that maybe I could be of help up here".

"Oh Dave you couldn't have come at a better time ...there's so much to do it's getting us both down. Come in...I'll fix you something to eat. Angie will be back soon, she's just gone to get some more fence posts.....what a welcome sight you'll be when she see's you!"

Dave let his young dog out of the Land Rover and followed Ann into the house. He could see there was plenty for him to do.

It was good to be back with the family he'd worked for at Geddinge, ever since he'd left school. He stretched his long legs under the kitchen table, the same table he'd sat at so many times.

The dog slipped under the table and settled down quietly as if he'd lived here all his life. They both felt at home.

"Bloody hell Dave!" The peace and quiet in the warm kitchen was suddenly shattered. "Where the hell did you come from....can you stay for a bit, we can't half do with a bit of help!!"

So Dave and his dog stayed...no one mentioned going back to Kent.

Spring turned to summer and the fencing was nearly done. Dave always started as soon as it was light in all sorts of weather

358

while Ann and her daughter looked after the animals and the children.

With the farm came grazing rights on the hills. Angie was a bit dubious about turning her ponies out where they could wander off for miles, but all the neighbouring farmers said they'd be fine, they were after all Welsh Mountain Ponies! Cilla was the only one of them that had ever seen a mountain.

Dave had finished the fencing so all the paddocks were secure, but Angie decided to let her little group of mares out onto the hill and let them go. It would allow the grass to grow for hay. *'Please don't get lost and come back safely'* she prayed as she let them go.

When she went to bring them in there were no ponies in sight! She remembered her neighbour had told her to ring the bell that was hanging beside the gate, the ponies would soon learn the bell meant food and come trotting home.

She rang the bell doubting the theory and feeling slightly foolish, but suddenly Cilla came galloping over the hill followed by her young friends. Angie counted them, all present and correct. Cilla didn't follow them into the barn; she just stood looking up the hill. Angie thought that maybe one of the group had been left. She put her arm round Cilla's neck. "Come on old girl, they'll eat all the food if you're not careful!"

Dave not only replaced and repaired all the fencing round the ninety acre holding and hung new gates where necessary, but was now tackling one of the old buildings.

Since he had arrived Ann was able to spend more time with the children and looking after the hens and ducks, not to mention cooking!

The geese were not the friendliest of creatures and looked after themselves.

THIRTYONE

Autumn crept in and thoughts began to turn to winter, the first for them up in the hills of Wales.

Angie wondered if she dare leave the ponies out on the hill all winter. Dave had been talking to some farmers at the market; nearly everyone turned their ponies or cobs out for the winter, there was plenty of grazing and gorse bushes for shelter. Dave thought they would be fine.

She hoped they were right.

Dave took charge of the hundred ewes Angie had brought from Geddinge, they were a mixed bunch with a few of the Cherolais Barry had bought years ago.

He carefully sorted the Cherolais out and penned them up separately. With their short curly coats he wasn't sure they'd survive out in the winter, and anyway Mr Skinner had been very proud of these special sheep and Dave would give them great care and try to get them back in prime condition. Something they could all be proud of.

Reluctantly Angie turned her ponies out. They wandered further away than usual and she had to use the quad bike to go and find them to make sure all was well.

Winter, when it came, was quite severe. It snowed all night covering everything with a good eighteen inches of crisp white snow. Then it snowed again and again!

Angie fretted about the ponies; they weren't used to this amount of snow and would have been brought into stables back at Geddinge.

It was impossible to drive the quad bike and Dave's old Land Rover hardly made it out of the yard before it stuttered to a halt steam pouring out of the radiator.

They were cut off by the blizzard, a new experience for all of them.

Luckily Arwyn Evans, their neighbour, came in his tractor with milk and an offer to help in any way he could. Ann gave him a loaf of home baked bread to take back with him.

360

Eventually the snow eased a little and Angie was anxious to find the ponies and bring them in.

The quad bike would be no good in the thick snow so she decided to take the cob she had bought.

She wrapped up in a sheep skin coat and a couple of pairs of trousers, but even that didn't keep out the cold, the wind was strong and found any exposed skin very quickly. She turned up the collar of her coat, pulled her hat down over her ears and plodded on up the hill.

For miles all she could see was crisp white snow, only the 'foot' prints of birds and they just perched in the bushes watching her go by. *'It's no use...I'll never find them up here'* she said to herself.

Then she heard a tractor, it appeared slowly over the hill pulling a big trailer, it was her neighbour Arwyn. He saw Angie and waved vigorously.

"Over here" he shouted "They're over here". Her heart gave a big leap, could he be right, there were several herds of ponies running on the hill.

She kicked her cob on towards Arwyn, the horse was making hard work of the deep snow but kept going.

"Over there Angie...I dropped them off a bale of hay in case you couldn't get out".

"Thanks Arwyn....I was worried about them they're not used to this sort of weather".

He laughed. "Their mountain ponies Angie, tough as old boots, pretty ones I agree. They look quite happy to me, nothing to worry about!"

"Where about did you see them?"

"Over there by those fir trees".

"I'll go and find them".

"Good luck Angie, mind how you go!"

The wind was getting stronger blowing snow into drifts. Commonsense told her to turn for home, but she had come this far so it was silly to give up now.

Buster plodded on sinking up to his knees, it was hard work for him. Suddenly she saw them crowded together sheltering under the fir trees all eating the hay Arwyn had put out for them....quite unconcerned about the weather. *'Well damn me'* she

361

thought, '*I've come out in this weather and they're not bothered at all*'

But where was Cilla? May be she was behind those rocks. **"Cilla"** she called...no answering whinny. **"Cilla where are you"**. Still nothing.

She was old now, the matriarch of her little herd, four of them were her daughters kept because they were too nice to sell. Merry Legs was there almost invisible in the snow, and so were *her* daughters, all five of them, and the orphan Angie had picked up in the market for just a few pounds. Cilla had adopted her straight away. But there was no sign of her!

What should she do? It was snowing hard again and the sky was leaden promising still more snow. Buster was fidgeting about, he was wet and cold, just wanting to go home!

There was nothing else she could do but get home before it got dark. She would come back tomorrow with Dave and drive them home, Cilla was sure to be back with them by then.

"OK Buster...let's get home". She could find this group of trees easily; there were so few trees up here on the hill. "We'll find them tomorrow", and Cilla would stay in for the rest of the winter.

Next day Angie woke to blue sky and brilliant sunshine and was anxious to set off to collect the ponies. Dave was worried about the quad bike in the deep snow, the wind had driven the snow into great drifts, some a good six foot high, and where the snow lay 'deep crisp and even' there were hidden ditches and potholes.

He wasn't happy about going out there and yet he mustn't let Angie go by herself. "I'll see if I can borrow a tractor...just wait a bit Angie".

Arwyn was about to set off with more hay when Dave phoned him, "I'll pick you up on the way. When I've dropped the hay off I'll help drive the buggers back!"

'*Thank goodness*' thought Angie, the three of them should surely be able to drive the ponies home.

Buster wasn't at all keen and needed a lot of persuasion, trying to turn back several times, but Angie was ready for him. "Get on with you" she shouted and landed him a good hard kick!

It took her a good hour to go just a short distance. *'I'll never get through this'* she thought. but once she got out onto the bare hill side the snow wasn't nearly as deep, the snow had been swept into great drifts against the gorse bushes and left only a few inches covering the ground. Buster lifted his head and began to walk faster, and Angie's spirits began to rise.

Arwyn and Dave, safe and warm in the tractor, soon caught up with her. Dave was pointing towards the trees, would they still be there she wondered or had they moved on during the night?

She pushed the cob into a canter, a bit risky, but she was worried about Cilla...would she be with them?

They were still there picking at the remaining bits of hay and whinnied as she got close.

A quick check confirmed Angie's worst fears, there were only eleven ponies waiting for more hay.

Alwyn drove round looking for any sign of Cilla and Angie rode up onto the high ridge, bur the snow covered everything, nothing was moving on the white landscape. She rode back to her little herd under the fir trees. Cilla was gone.

Dave sat on the back of the tractor with a bag of pony nuts between his knees, every few yards he dropped a handful while Alwyn drove leading the ponies home. It didn't take the ponies long to realize where the nuts were coming from and were soon following the tractor in an orderly bunch.

Angie and Buster walked behind ready to move on any stragglers, but the ponies were happy, they seemed to know they were on their way home.

There must have been a bit of Welsh Mountain Pony blood in all of them, but a very small amount, these ponies preferred a warm stable and a bite of hay. The wild mountain life was not for them!

They followed the tractor back and allowed themselves to be driven into the barn where there was food and hay waiting for them.

363

Ann had made a big pan of soup and homemade bread for the rescuers and they soon thawed out in the warm kitchen.

It was a shame about Cilla, but Angie wasn't giving up on her, and would keep looking up on the hill. Alwyn said he would ask around the local farms and when he went to the market. Someone would surely find her, she couldn't just disappear.

Angela started joining the hunt twice a week, not that she enjoyed hunting so much, but because someone might have seen Cilla. She made sure all the locals knew a little black pony with white socks had got lost on the mountain and that she was quite old and not accustomed to living rough.

She didn't mention that this little pony had won more championships than you could count, or that she was a regular winner at the Royal Welsh Show. That piece of evidence she kept to herself.

She asked everyone she met out riding, she put posters up in the corn merchants, the vets, the saddlers and everywhere horsey people might visit. But to no avail, no one had seen the little black pony.

THIRTYTWO

When the snow had started Angies twelve ponies were sheltering in a stand of fir trees, their tails facing the bitterly cold wind. It had been snowing most of the day and it was now heavy.

Cilla was restless; she had an uncontrollable urge to cross over the mountain. The terrain seemed strangely familiar, like a distant dream, so she started to walk up the steep track to the top of the hill. She thought she heard a tractor in the distance, but took no notice.

The snow was hard and made her eyes run but she carried on, head down, as the heavy snow covered her tracks. All night she trudged on always heading in the same direction. As it got light she found shelter amongst a clump of gorse bushes and stopped to rest

The sun rose in a clear blue sky, she had travelled quite a long way during the night. In the distance a busy road was baring the way she wanted to go, a snow plough was clearing the road followed by a line of cars. Cilla watched as a lorry skidded causing a lot of cars too crash into it. There was no way for her to get across the road; she would have to wait for darkness and try then.

When darkness fell she could see the lights of a town, she mustn't go that way, so she walked quietly along the side of the road looking for a gap in the stone wall.

The traffic had stopped, just two cars abandoned by their drivers were half buried by snow on the side of the road.... and *there* was the gap in the wall she was looking for, she scrambled over and through what appeared to be a gap on the other side of the road. It was a tunnel with sheep munching away on hay, she thought of stopping and sharing the shelter with the sheep, but instead she helped herself to some mouthfuls of hay and then moved on.

The moon suddenly came out from behind a cloud and she could see her way clearly. In the darkness she had come under the railway line and empty hills were waiting for her to cross.

She plodded on relentlessly, the ground under her feet was hard and where ponies had churned it up it was like walking on

365

stones. It was difficult but she was out on the hill side, now clear open hill side!

Cilla saw ponies moving in the distant moonlight. She whinnied and hurried to join them, but they weren't ponies.

She stopped, puzzled.

The ponies were men, lots of me. She turned and galloped away, but there were men everywhere and in her panic she trod on something sharp which stuck in her foot.

The pain was awful, but she dared not stop, there were loud bangs going off behind her. She galloped over the hill side looking for an escape. Ahead of her she caught a glimpse of a wire fence shining in the moonlight; she galloped at it and jumped.

The pain in her foot made her stumble, but she was over and galloped on as fast as her three legs would allow.

Frightened and exhausted she found a stand of fir trees to rest in for a while.

That distant memory that had been worrying her since she had come to these mountains from her last home, the vague sounds that had just frightened her, and suddenly she could remember clearly galloping with a herd of ponies once before....but it was a long long time ago.

Her foot was very painful and she lay down to rest it. She was soon asleep and for a few hours the little pony was free of pain.

Something warm was blowing on her face. She woke with a start and found she was surrounded by curious ponies. As she lurched to her feet the pain in her foot returned so she had to stand on three legs.

They were a mixed bunch of wild ponies that roamed the mountains at will, no one seemed to own them, so they lived up here on their own, a tough hardy group of nondescript ponies.

Cilla was glad of their company and when they began to move further up the mountain she followed. When they splashed across a stream she stood for a while in the ice cold water soothing her foot, but as soon as she climbed out, the pain was back, there was something buried in her foot.

The pain got worse and worse over the next few days, she could no longer put it to the ground.

366

The wild ponies went on their way going higher up the mountain; she would follow later if the foot allowed it. Now she just stood quietly in the warm sunshine looking around.....she felt sure she had been here before, was this why she had come all this way?

Someone was coming, she could hear the noise of a quad bike, and then it came into view bouncing over the rutted track. She wanted to go after the wild ponies but could now hardly move.

The man on the quad bike stopped, he was looking for Red Kites he knew were here. He got his binoculars out and started to scan the hill side and had a shock when he found a pony instead!

For a while pony and man stared at each other. *'Why was this pony on its own, where were all the rest?'* This was too good an opportunity to miss.

He quickly got his sketch book and pencil out and within a few strokes he had 'captured' a wild hill pony to paint later, on canvas.

There was something wrong with this pony, it hadn't moved at all while he was sketching and it was standing awkwardly. *'I think I'd better have a look'* he thought.

The little pony watched him getting closer and whinnied. "Well now my beauty, what have we got here" he said stroking its neck.

He gently lifted the injured foot. It was hot and very messy. "Hold on now little one" he murmured as he took a pen knife from his pocket that he used for sharpening his pencils.

Gently he felt round the foot and found a piece of metal, he cleaned the mud and grit out of the hoof exposing the injury. It looked like shrapnel buried deep in the foot.

"You've been on the army ranges haven't you my girl?" He said half to himself and half to the mare. "Steady now...I must dig it out....it's going to hurt!"

Cilla didn't flinch as he gently removed the shrapnel. He went to his bike and came back with a thermos flask full of hot water for his coffee. He felt around in his bag and found an apple.

He washed the injury and plugged the hole he had made with cotton wool. "There you are, that should see you alright for a day

367

or two" he said as he gave her the apple. "I'll try to find your owner when I get home".

The quad bike coughed into life and the artist went on up the hill looking for Red Kites.

Cilla tentatively put her foot on the ground; it was still sore but much better. She walked slowly down the hill....it seemed the right way to go.

The next day her foot was much more comfortable and she made good progress to somewhere she had to go.

That afternoon she came across another group of ponies. They all rushed over to her exchanging a few squeals and 'friendly' kicks, but they all were happy to let her join them and spent the rest of the day grazing together.

Most of the group were mares heavily in foal, and the rest were babies. They were all nice looking ponies with a lot of quality about them.

Cilla fitted in well and apart from the slight limp she looked like one of the herd. She stayed with them for several weeks her foot getting better all the time.

The early morning spring sun was warm and most of the group were lying down when a lady, riding a beautiful stallion, trotted up to them.

They all scrambled to their feet, not at all frightened. Cilla tried to keep in the middle of the bunch as the lady looked closely at them, calling out names, talking to them.

Finally she shook her head, turned her horse and cantered away.

When Averill got back to the farm she had forgotten all about the ponies on the mountain. The girls would be home from school at any moment and their tea wasn't ready.

Her husband was upstairs in his office working on a case for another farmer.

"Rhys!" she called. "Teas ready".

"OK...be down in a minute". He had an office in Brecon but did a lot of work at home. He was a tall young man with a neat

368

little beard; he'd lived on this farm all his life apart from the years at university.

He stood in front of the fire warming his hands looking at a painting his brother had done many years ago. The painting was of their mother, running her favourite pony at the Royal Welsh Show, a black pony with white socks.

The painting was full of action, they used to laugh and say you could almost hear mother puffing! She had hung the painting there after the pony had been sold.

Visitors had offered to buy it several times but mother would never part with it. It was a pity in a way, because Tomos's paintings were fetching good money these days, especially his paintings of birds.

"I think I might take the horse hunting tomorrow", Rhys said. "It's the last meet, over at Beulah. You don't mind do you?"

"No no.....you take him. He nearly pulled my arms out today! Oh, by the way.... how many ponies have we got on the hill this year?"

"Eleven....why?"

"I was up there this morning, there were twelve".

"No eleven".

"That's what I thought, but there were defiantly twelve, I'm sure!"

Rhys was puzzled, "I know we took eleven up there September time. I expect it's a stray. I'll get them in this week, foals are due fairly soon".

The two girls crashed into the kitchen back from school.

"Daddy Daddy there's a pony standing at our gate when we got off the bus. It tried to come in with us but we shooed it away....it's very dirty, Sue thought it was a bit lame".

"I'll go and have a look. You have your tea....and then home work!"

"Oh Daddy let's come with you pleeeease!"

"Tea and home work!"

"Oh you're mean. We saw it first. It's not fair".

"Life never is fair my darlings". He put on his hat and went to look for this dirty pony, but there was no sign of it.

369

THIRTYTHREE

It was several months now since Cilla had disappeared, but Angie had never given up looking for her. She must have ridden over most of their corner of Wales!

With so much riding up and down hills her Buster was well and extremely fit. She decided to take him hunting.

The meet was at Beulah on Friday and they were going to hunt over a very wild part of the country. She was looking forward to it immensely. Her horse was fighting fit and would keep going all day!

She filled her pockets with sandwiches, said good bye to Ann and the children and led her horse into the trailer. Dave wished her luck and went to work on an old tractor they had recently bought that needed a new head gasket.

It wasn't far to the meet but she would probably be glad of the trailer it if she stayed out all day.

There were a lot of people saddling up as Angie brought Buster from the trailer. "Found your pony yet?" someone asked.

"No...still looking!"

"She'll turn up one day".

"I hope so" she said as the hunt moved off out onto the hill side.

Almost immediately the hounds were on to a fox. This bit of country was really wild so no wonder they didn't hunt this way very often.

Buster loved hunting, he ploughed his way through everything, gorse was nothing to him, rocky places he would skip over and rivers he'd swim if he had to. He was a big powerful cob and he was in his element out here!

The hounds lost the scent and everyone pulled up, riders out of breath and the horses blowing after a mad gallop, they were happy to stand still for a few minutes while the hounds scattered amongst the rocks trying to pick up a scent.

"Excuse me". Angie turned in her saddle, there was a man riding an excitable horse moving up beside her. He had his collar turned up and his hat pulled well down. He touched his hat, nice manners she thought. "They tell me you've lost a pony this winter, a black pony?"

"Well yes...she's quite old...I can't be sure she would have made it out on the mountain".

"Stand still you stupid beast" his horse was twisting and dancing about. "He belongs to my wife; I don't know why she likes him so much!"

"He's very pretty", she couldn't think of anything else to say.

"Well....as I was about to say. I seem to have acquired an extra pony. A black mare, I think she's got white socks.... She's so dirty it's hard to be sure!"

A black mare with white socks. It has to be Cilla! Angie felt warm tears running down her cheeks.

"Oh are you alright?" He was shocked at her reaction.

"Yes...more or less....I think you might have got my pony!" She couldn't keep her voice under control. "Can I come and have a look.....tomorrow...it's too late now".

"Of course you can. I'll get her in".

"Where do I find you?"

"Oh of course, you don't know. Sibertswold Farm, about five miles west of Brecon, Any one will direct you".

"Did you say *Sibertswold* ?" Angie's heart missed several beats.

"Yes do you know us?"

"Oh..my..God.....My ponies name is Cilla.....Sibertswold Cilla!"

Now it was the man's turn to look shocked. "Cilla..It can't be. Not after all these years...how on earth did she get here......how did she find her way home?"

Neither of them knew what to say.

"I'm going home now, I'm sorry,I don't know your name... I can't believe it's my Cilla, I really can't...and yet it must be!"

"Rhys...Rhys Griffiths"

"I'm Angie"

She led Buster into the trailer and set off for home deep in thought. Cilla had survived the winter walking miles across the mountains and found her way back to where she was born more than twenty years ago.

371

Dave was driving some sheep across a field and waved at Angie but got no reply. *'that's odd'* he thought but concentrated on the sheep which were running in all directions.

He was training a young collie today which was no use to him at all. "Daft dog...come back here. You're useless". The dog dropped his tail between his legs and followed him. He knew Dave didn't mean it, but it was fun making the sheep run.

Angie put Buster in his stable and rugged him up. She wanted to rush indoors and shout 'I've found her, I know where Cilla is', but he had been brilliant today and had done everything she asked of him, she must see to him first.

"Hello pet, have a good day? Mother asked. I've got the kettle on and scones just fresh out of the oven". No reply from Angie. Ann turned to look at her daughter. "You alright dear, you look a bit flushed".

"I've found her Mum...I've found Cilla....she's gone home". Then all the emotion she'd kept to herself all afternoon got too much. She sat at the kitchen table and cried until there were no tears left.

Her mother poured the tea, buttered the scones and waited. She would tell her about it when she was ready.

Dave came in still cursing the dog that ran under the table and hid. He sensed something was upsetting Angie, so he poured himself a mug of tea, grabbed some scones and went out again without saying a word.

Later that evening Angie told her mother and Dave about the young man and his frisky horse, how he had discovered an extra pony that was running with his mares. It seemed to be fairly old, black with white socks, "It must be Cilla!"

Ann was cautioned. "How can you be so sure".

"Because she's gone home mum...they're Sibertwold ponies she's running with".

"Well damn me" Dave exclaimed. The dog wagged his tail; perhaps he could creep out now.

"What are you going to do?" Mother asked.

I've arranged to get her tomorrow...bring her back!"

She spent a restless night tossing and turning until the early hours. It would be lovely to have the old pony back, she had missed her and was sure she had died somewhere in a lonely place in the mountains. But she was alive and well!

Why had she gone all that way that was what worried Angie, and would she go again, after all she knew the way now?

Finally the answer was clear and happy with her decision she slept peacefully.

FINALE

When Sue and Ann got off the school bus the next day the same pony was standing at the gate again. This time they opened the gate and let her through.

They ran after her laughing as she trotted down into the yard and straight into the barn. Daddy was in for a surprise when he got home.

They put the pony in a sheep pen and went in for their tea saying nothing to their mother about the pony.

Rhys heard the pony in the barn as he walked through the yard. *'What have those girls been up to'* he thought, all though he had a pretty good idea. One quick look confirmed it!

Cilla whinnied. She remembered him from all those years ago. "Welcome home old lady" he said scratching her neck, "Welcome home". He found some corn and filled her hay net. He was pleased to see the two conspirators had given her a bucket of water and clean straw to lie on. There was hope for them yet!

He had arranged for Angie to come in the morning but wanted his mother to see the pony she loved so much before she went.

Rhys went into supper thinking of a plan, he would need the help of his daughters to make it work!

They were being particularly giggly tonight; he went along with their game pretending he hadn't seen Cilla in the barn.

"Have you had a good day girls?" he asked.

"Oh yes Daddy" they said in unison.

"Did anything exciting happen at school?"

"Noooo, not at school" more giggles.

"How about..err..how about on the way home?" Now he'd got them...they couldn't lie to him!

They looked at each other guilt written all over their faces.

Well.....what have you got to say to me?"

"Oh Daddy...don't be cross. We found the black pony again and we let her in....she trotted all the way down the track and into the barn. We put her in a sheep pen. She's ever so sweet...can we keep her Daddy......we'll look after her!"

"That's enough girls. The pony belongs to a lady and she's coming to collect her tomorrow".

374

Their faces dropped, it had never occurred to them that someone owned the pony; she looked so dirty and neglected.

"I'm sorry girls ...but let me tell you about that pony. You've seen her every day of your lives!"

They sat looking at Rhys with a puzzled expression; they had seen the pony for the first time yesterday. Their father pointed to the painting over the fire place.

"That, my girls, is the pony you've hidden in the barn!" The girls sat speechless, no more giggling now. "Today out hunting I met a lady who'd lost a black pony, and when she described it to me I realized it was the pony running with our lot on the mountain. The very same pony you found standing at our gate. The lady had brought some Section 'A' ponies with her when she moved from Kent...that's a long way away in England...the one she lost is called Siberstwold Cilla, Grandma's lovely pony. Well she must have made her way back here, to where she was born. She would have crossed busy roads, a railway and those army ranges where they fire the guns and things. No wonder she is so dirty!"

"Poor pony" Ann said softly.

The kitchen was silent; no one knew what to say. Finally Rhys broke the silence.

"Now....the lady is coming tomorrow, but...I want to get Grandma over here before that happens. So here's what we must do. First we'll clean Cilla up and get her looking as near to that painting as we can. Then mother will think of a way to get Grandma over here early tomorrow, when you two can pretend you've just found a pony and show it to her. We'll see if she recognises her old pony!"

Rhys and the girls spent the rest of the day cleaning Cilla. Rhys combed her mane and tail hair by hair, until he had every twig and piece of bracken lying at his feet. The girls brushed and combed until their arms were ready to drop off!

Then from the scruffy dirty pony emerged something pretty close to the painting they all knew so well.

"That's enough girls...well done. I think it's time for bed". The girls looked exhausted, "Good night Cilla...sleep well". They murmured.

375

Rhys and Avril were waiting for Angie while the girls were waiting for their Gran.

"Come in and have a cup of coffee", said Avril when Angie arrived, "The girls will get Cilla for you".

Angie was anxious to see Cilla but another few minutes wouldn't hurt. They ushered her into the kitchen and she immediately spotted the painting of Cilla. "What a lovely painting", she exclaimed. "You can almost hear her hooves pounding the ground, it's so full of life and movement, it's really lovely".

"Yes...my brother Tomos painted it when we were still at school...you could see he had talent even then. He's quite famous now!"

The door burst open. "Grandma's here!" shouted the girls. "Shall we get the pony out Daddy?"

"Just let her go".

"OK...were onto it!" They slammed the door and were gone.

"Just give us a moment Angie". Rhys said quietly. "Come and watch".

Grandma had just got out of her car when she was pulled away from the house.

"Oh Gran come and see the new pony we've got to show you. Wait here and we'll get her".

Grandma waited patiently as the girls rushed to the barn very excited.

There was silence for a few minutes and then a little black pony appeared. She lifted her head and the wind blew her silky mane away from her face.

Gran looke and looked again. "Cilla?" she called. "Cilla is that you?" Cilla whinnied and trotted across the yard and nuzzle Gran. "Oh Cilla...you've come back to me at last". She could say no more as the tears ran freely down her cheeks.

Angie was nearly crying herself. "I must go Rhys. Please keep Cilla, this is where she belongs and it'd where she wants to be. I won't take her away from you mother again.... good bye Cilla". She whispered as she drove away from Sibertswold.

376

Cilla lived on for several more years, happy to be back on the mountain she was drawn back to and well love by everyone.

She died peacefully in her stable one night aged forty. She was buried in a quiet corner close to the mountains she loved.

SLEEP WELL LITTLE CILLA

Pauline Braddock

Pauline started riding at about ten years of age, paying for her lessons from an Irish Dealer by riding whatever came into his yard. He was a master horseman from whom she learnt a great deal.

She was also studying the Cello at the Royal College of Music and later continued at the Guildhall School of Music with William Pleath.

She married a fellow student and so began her career in music, first in Manchester and eventually moving to the cello section of the Bournemouth Symphony Orchestra. Pauline and her husband lived on the edge of the New Forest where her love of horses was rekindled.

All of their three children, a girl and twin boys. could ride at a very early age, also learning to play a variety of instruments.

Pauline retired from the Orchestra when the twins were born and taught the cello in Hampshire schools for many years allowing her time to dedicate to her horses.

The passion for horses is still as strong as ever, and noe retired, Pauline and her flute playing husband run a stud of Shetland Ponies.

She has written several pony books, mostly for children.